The Heart's Harbor by Cynthia Ruchti
Amanda Brooks retreats to picturesque Egg Harbor in Door County,
Wisconsin, to escape an empty holiday season in her Chicago apartment. Peace on earth is what she needs but instead finds herself
in charge of the legendary Christmas Tea at the Heart's Harbor
Victorian Inn. Dealing with its quirky guests, bare-bones budget,
antisocial puppy, matchmaking owner, and her match-resistant son,
Jordan, deepens her doubts that Christmas and love have anything
in common.

Ride with Me into Christmas by Rachael Phillips
An offbeat innkeeper offers Joanna Flick a Christmas cactus, promising the flowerless plant—and hope—will bloom. A recent widow,
Joanna can't believe it. But new neighbor Paul Sorensen, a fifty-
something flannel-shirt fanatic with a bad haircut, shares Joanna's
passion for bicycling through gorgeous landscapes and faith in the
One who created them. Will love flower this bleak winter, or will
their Grinch-y grown children nip romance in the bud?

My Heart Still Beats by Eileen Key
Hired by two octogenarians to escort them on their last visit to their
bayside cottage in Ephraim, Wisconsin, Madison Tanner literally
"runs into" Realtor Grant Sterling. Grant is intent on selling the
cottage before Christmas, but every prospective buyer finds a new
problem with the property, prompting Grant to suspect Madison is
guilty of sabotage. Each new setback pushes Grant further from his
goal and closer to the hazel-eyed chauffeur.

Christmas Crazy by Becky Melby
Jillian Galloway sacrifices her fall colors vacation in Sister Bay to
help Uncle Buster, owner of Doorbuster's Comedy Theater, salvage
his business in time for the Christmas crowd. With a hole in the roof,
no chef, and only two oddball actors, Jillian's eternal optimism is put
to the test. Enter Ricky Jimmy, a mysteriously handsome Brazilian
with an offer to help. Should she listen to the rumors of Ricky's suspicious clandestine behavior or trust those dark Latin eyes?

A DOOR COUNTY CHRISTMAS

FOUR-IN-ONE COLLECTION

FOUR ROMANCES WARM HEARTS IN
WISCONSIN'S VERSION OF CAPE COD

EILEEN KEY
BECKY MELBY
RACHAEL PHILLIPS
CYNTHIA RUCHTI

BARBOUR
PUBLISHING

©2010 *The Heart's Harbor* by Cynthia Ruchti
©2010 *Ride with Me into Christmas* by Rachael Phillips
©2010 *My Heart Still Beats* by Eileen Key
©2010 *Christmas Crazy* by Becky Melby

ISBN 978-1-60260-968-6

Cover design: Kirk DouPonce, DogEared Design

Cover design: Lighthouse photo courtesy of Jon Jarosh, Director of Communications & Public Relations, Door County Visitor Bureau.

Published by Barbour Publishing, Inc., P.O. Box 719, Uhrichsville, OH 44683, www.barbourbooks.com

Our mission is to publish and distribute inspirational products offering exceptional value and biblical encouragement to the masses.

Member of the
Evangelical Christian
Publishers Association

3 1984 00290 0510

THE HEART'S HARBOR

by Cynthia Ruchti

Dedication

"Trust in Him at all times, you people; pour out your heart before Him; God is a refuge for us."

PSALM 62:8 NKJV

Door County, Wisconsin, holds many sweet memories for me—looking across a candlelit table into the eyes of my first-and-forever love at the White Gull Inn; rounding a corner on a hiking path in Newport State Park and discovering a heart-stopping lake view; singing three-part harmony with my sisters in the best acoustics ever while sitting in the pool at the Landmark; standing in the middle of a wonder-moment as the breeze tickled the deep-voiced wind chimes in the gazebo at the Blue Dolphin House; riding bikes through Peninsula State Park and on an uphill climb hearing our youngest call from his seat on the back of my husband's bike, "Dad, we ran out of fast!"; riding the ferry to Washington Island and renting mopeds on which to explore the back roads with a friend who knew Who to thank for the scenery; unplugging from the "hurry" the night the lights went out on a research trip and we four authors settled into the comforts of a prayer-hemmed friendship; skipping rocks at the tip of the peninsula and missing the water but not my daughter (okay, not my best memory); finding a heart-shaped rock on the shore and celebrating a daughter-shaped spot in my heart on yearly "just us" trips. . .

This story—The Heart's Harbor—is dedicated to those who share the same memories—friends, sisters, children, my husband, and to those who have found or are looking for a safe Harbor for their heart.

Thank you, Barbour Publishing and Rebecca Germany, for letting us tell our stories. I'm deeply grateful to agent Wendy Lawton for representing me and feeding my hope. My friends and colleagues in ACFW. Thank you Eileen, Rachael, and Becky for making this collaboration a joy and for indulging me with gluten-free pizza.

Thank you to those who've inspired me with your romances, your comedies, and the times when romance is funny and laughter is romantic.

Chapter 1

On any other person, swim goggles would have seemed out of place in the foyer of an elegant Victorian inn. But on innkeeper Lola Peterson, the effect was. . .

Amanda searched for the right word.

"Amanda Brooks! Welcome back." Lola tilted her chin as if the bottom of the goggles offered a better view. She wiped her hands on her flour-dusted chef's apron and approached the spot where Amanda stood, letting snow from her boots drip onto the entry rug.

Amanda felt the fine grit of sugar and flour in Lola's two-handed grip and the irrepressible warmth of her smile. "It's good to be here. Door County at Christmas—nothing more beautiful, except Door County any other season of the year."

"It's been too long, my dear." Half-turning, Lola called, "Harland, get on out here. Amanda's back."

"Who?"

Lola's husband didn't remember her. The man whose voice answered from somewhere in the back of the inn coped with two disadvantages—early hearing loss and way early short-term memory problems. The combo offered no hope Harland Peterson would recall someone like Amanda, someone he hadn't seen for almost three years.

"It's Amanda!" Lola shouted back. "You know, the one whose fiancé—"

Lola's head whipped around to face the younger woman. Her dove-gray eyes widened, an effect heightened by the goggles and stemless eyeglasses duct-taped inside. "Sorry, dear. No need to bring that up. Pre-holiday getaway?"

Choices, Amanda. You can choose not to react. "Can't beat the off-season prices, Mrs. Peterson."

A door creaked open and out flap-flopped a bib-overalled Harland Peterson wearing swim fins. Purple swim fins.

"Good afternoon, Mr. Peterson." Amanda felt her smile muscles awakening from a too-long nap. "Going snorkeling, you two?"

"In this weather?" Harland held his stomach out of the way and gazed down at his footwear. "Oh, the flippers. Just wearing them so the wife doesn't feel so odd."

Amanda rolled her lips in and pressed them together to stifle a snicker.

"He means the goggles," Lola offered. "They were his idea. Broke the stem on my glasses. Had to truck down to Sturgeon Bay to the eye center, but they haven't got the same frames anymore, wouldn't you know? Ordered new ones, but what am I going to do until they come?"

She adjusted the goggles to sit straighter. "So Harland suggests we slap my old ones into the swim goggles like we did for our twenty-fifth anniversary when we took that trip to the Cayman Islands, which always seemed like a waste of time to me since we live in paradise already with plenty of water around. But you know Harland. Always an adventure brewing."

Despite their speed, the rush of words comforted like a mocha with whipped cream.

"So," Lola said, tilting her head back again, "can I have Harland get your bags from the car?"

Amanda pictured the disturbing footprints a man in swim fins would leave on the snowy path where her car was parked. "I only brought one bag." With the side of her foot, she nudged it.

"Hard to travel light in a Midwest winter."

She was right. Sweatshirts and wool sweaters take up a lot more room than the attire needed for a tropical holiday vacation.

Amanda wondered if her parents had struggled to stay within the weight restrictions on their way to Maui for the winter. Who spends an entire winter in Maui? Those whose daughters are independent, or make them think so.

Lola pressed her warm palms against Amanda's cheeks. "I can't tell you what it did to my heart when I heard you were coming back."

"You know Chicago this time of year." Amanda unwrapped the neck scarf that suddenly felt like a loose noose. "Hoopla. Holiday hoopla."

Tilting her head to the side this time, Lola took Amanda's scarf and jacket. "The lights along Michigan Avenue. Concerts. Theater. The store window displays. Walking hand in hand up the steps of the Art Institute. I always loved Chicago at Christmas."

The view loses its luster when seen through the window of a cold, hollow apartment, Amanda wanted to tell her. Instead she said, "The quiet here has strong appeal."

"Appeal. Yes." Lola draped Amanda's jacket over her forearm and nodded toward her husband, as if dismissing him to whatever had occupied him before Amanda's arrival.

The smell of pumpkin something hung in the air. Pumpkin and cinnamon and comfort. "I'm glad you had room for me in the inn. I've needed this."

Lola blinked. "You have no idea how much."

How could Lola—intuitive as she'd always been—know how desperately Amanda needed the comfort? "Pumpkin pie?"

"Bread," Lola answered, slipping the neck of Amanda's jacket over the porcelain knob on a branch of the antique hall tree. "Mini loaves. I'm baking ahead for the Christmas Tea."

Amanda pictured a thick slice of warm pumpkin bread with a pat of butter melting into puddles on its surface. Real Wisconsin butter, not that heart-healthy pseudo-butter she'd thought a wise purchase.

"Hungry? You must have been on the road for five hours or more."

Amanda followed as Lola headed toward the kitchen. "More than six. Construction."

"This time of year?" Lola pointed toward a short hall. "I suppose they're in a rush to finish roadwork before— Harland, what are you doing?"

He lay on the floor, arms spread, fins flopping, a classclown grin on his face. "The backstroke."

"Harland Troy Peterson, you get up and go make yourself useful. Don't you have a project waiting on you? Now scoot!" Lola clapped her hands as if to shoo a puppy out of her flower beds.

He scrambled to his feet faster than Amanda imagined he could. "Where's your sense of humor, Mama?"

"I have things on my mind," she retorted, then glanced at Amanda. "And one of those things is getting some nourishment into this starving child." She wrapped an arm around Amanda and the two squeezed past Harland while he decided whether he was coming or going.

If Amanda ever had a daughter, she'd "get some nourishment" in her rather than remind her how many calories were in a crouton.

Harland's hall opened into the light-splashed sunroom. The view of Egg Harbor—its winter-crisped water sparkling like glitter on a Christmas card—stole her breath as it always did. "Oh!"

Lola directed Amanda toward a wing chair near the stone fireplace. "The harbor put on her fancy clothes for you. Fresh snow along the shore and on the shoulders of the trees always makes a postcard scene, doesn't it? I imagine the watercolorists and photographers are out in full force today. You sit here, dear. I'll get some tea and a little something to tide you over until supper."

Amanda felt for the upholstered arms and lowered herself into the chair without taking her gaze from the harbor.

The waters of Lake Michigan—the same Lake Michigan that lapped against Chicago's shore—ducked around the corner of the tip of Door County and formed the pool that now captured her attention. Technically, the waters of Green Bay.

From the direction of the kitchen came the sound of Lola singing a Christmas carol lullaby and fussing with something that clinked and clattered.

Amanda traced the wide, embrace-like curve of the shore that wrapped itself two-thirds of the way around the waters of Egg Harbor.

White-barked birch stood thin and stark against the dark folds of corduroy pines and cedars. Why did this view soothe in a way the city's couldn't?

Was it because here someone cared about her?

❄

The furnace kicked in. Amanda noticed. No other sounds competed for attention.

What was the quietest moment she'd known in her apartment in The Loop? Chicago could boast many things—arts, entertainment, architecture, business—but the word *quiet* hadn't made it into any of the PR materials for the city.

In this inn, tucked around the corner from a village that had settled from its busy season like a grateful snow globe scene, sounds respected the difference. With its normal complement of tourists now back home fighting traffic and work schedules, Door County nestled into quiet like an overworked mom sighs when the last of the Thanksgiving dinner dishes slide into their spots on the shelf.

Ah. Quiet had returned home from the war.

Only locals in a tourist spot could fully appreciate the benefits of both. The summer flood-stage of bumper-to-bumper and elbow-to-elbow vacationers paid the mortgage and the electric bill so the locals—the privileged few—could live year around in the place where cedars, birches, water, orchards, limestone cliffs, and protected harbors linked arms.

Amanda leaned against one wing of the brocade chair to which she'd been directed and took a deep breath of quiet, which at the moment smelled like apple blossom soap. Oh, to be a local.

She shook off the thought as Lola returned with a tea tray. Amanda rose, took the tray from her hands, and positioned it on the coffee table with the teapot closest to Lola and the blue-white milk glass plate of muffins pointing her own direction.

"What kind of tea?" Not that it mattered. Lola had yet to steer her wrong, on almost any life issue, including tea choices.

"Lemon drop."

Amanda met the tea spout with the lip of her Blue Willow cup. "Smells divine."

"Half the joy of a good tea is its aroma." Lola served her guest, then herself. She added a twist of lemon peel and a generous dribble of honey, then drew the cup to her chest as if she intended to wear it as a pendant.

The sunroom was different than Amanda remembered it from previous visits. The white wicker furniture had been replaced by a scattering of small tables and Windsor chairs except for the sitting area on this, the south end of the room. Starched white tablecloths with doll bed–sized antique quilt overlays were topped with protective glass.

In the center of each table reigned a candlestick made from stacked teacups and saucers. Charming.

"Do you serve breakfast in here now, rather than the dining room?" Amanda imagined winter guests shivering at the tables near the endless stretch of windows as snowflakes skittered across the icy bay.

"Depends on my mood. And my guests."

Lola sipped her tea then replaced the cup on its saucer tucked close to her breastbone. "My book club meets here for lunch on Wednesdays. High tea every Thursday afternoon at four. Bible study in the evening. Bridal showers. Baby showers. Neither the room nor I are idle for long."

Amanda smiled. Who worked harder than Lola Peterson? And with as much grace?

Lola toed the heel of one shoe—something Scandinavian-looking—and slipped her foot out, then did the same with the other.

Grunting with the effort, she plopped her feet onto a free spot on the coffee table and crossed her ankles at the pumpkins. Autumn-themed socks. Pumpkins and apples and maple leaves splashed against a black background. Socks with an individual pocket for each toe.

Wiggling the piggies that went to market and those that stayed home, Lola sighed so deep the tea in her cup sloshed like a wind-whipped wave in Egg Harbor. "I'll miss the Christmas Tea this year."

"What? No, you can't!"

Lola worked kinks out of her ankles. "It's become quite the production."

"It already was three years ago when you had me help with the prep work."

Lola's expression shifted, a small course correction. "I could have used you every year since then."

Amanda's throat tightened. Serving others had been outdistanced by survival instinct after Todd interrupted the minister's sermonette to say he couldn't go through with the wedding.

She'd failed at every task but self-pity for a while. Even now, a memory would slap at her and remind her she didn't fully have her land legs back yet.

She made her own course correction and rewound a few sentences of their conversation. "What do you mean, you'll miss the Christmas Tea? You *are* the Christmas Tea, Lola."

"No one's indestructible."

"Pardon?"

"Indisputable."

Amanda lifted her teacup to cover the giggle forming behind her teeth. The warm, lemony liquid calmed her enough to offer, "Indispensable?"

"That, too." Lola swung her feet to the floor and leaned forward. She planted her teacup on the tray, wiped her mouth with a napkin, and said, "I'm not indispensable."

"Of course you are!"

"That's not what the State of Wisconsin says. And my own heart. It's my civic duty to serve on that jury. Tea or not."

Wasn't there a selection process during which the attorneys determined a juror's suitability? What would they say about swim goggles and pumpkin socks?

"I report tomorrow morning."

"What about Harland?"

"Oh, honey." Lola looked beyond Amanda's shoulder. "He's. . .he's going with me. He'll stay with his brother while I'm out of commission. That should create a story or two."

Amanda hadn't unpacked. Hadn't even checked in, officially. No need for that now. The Heart's Harbor Victorian Inn would temporarily close its doors in the morning.

Lola's loss of income and the threat of canceling the annual Tea with its legacy of elegance and camaraderie for the invited locals were dwarfed by Amanda's disappointment.

Not only would she miss out on a few days of respite from the thrumming of Chicago's holiday pulse, but she'd be forced to return to an apartment she still resisted calling *home*.

Get a grip, Amanda. This is Lola's livelihood at stake. You? You've known disappointment before. You should be used to it.

Stocking-footed, Lola padded across the painted floorboards to the small, white rolltop desk near the door that connected the sunroom to the inn proper. She picked up an open Bible, glanced at the page, hugged the book to the spot where her teacup had rested moments before, then returned it to the desk surface and retrieved a half-sized three-ring binder from the desk drawer.

Extending the notebook toward Amanda, she returned to her wing chair and said, "Here's what you'll need."

"For what?"

"To run the inn in my abstention."

Amanda gripped the arm of her chair. "Your *absence*?"

"That, too."

❉

Amanda trailed Lola into the inn's massive maple and granite kitchen. "You can't be serious! I don't have any experience running a bed-and-breakfast."

Lola didn't break stride on her way to the commercial-grade stainless steel refrigerator/freezer. "You've been a guest here how many times?"

"Six. Maybe seven. That hardly qualifies me to—"

Lola yanked on the freezer handle, and the door opened to reveal an array of neatly stacked plastic containers so precisely organized they would have made California Closets jealous.

"Peanut butter fudge. Spritz cookies. Bacon-wrapped water chestnuts. They'll need crisping in a hot oven before serving."

Lola pointed to her button-sized date pinwheels and mini-cheesecakes, raspberry tarts, crab-stuffed mushrooms, Door County Cherry Nut breads, and miniature Swedish meatballs. "It's all recorded there in the procedure mandible."

Amanda braced herself against the kitchen's center island. "Lola, stop. I can't do this. You have to be here. I only planned to stay until the weekend when—"

Lola folded her arms across her chest as if waiting for Amanda to come to her senses.

"You have a procedure manual for your Christmas Tea?"

Lola closed the freezer door with a nudge from her hip. "Jordan wants me to get it computerized. That boy of mine should have considered becoming an efficiency expert instead of a landscape designator. Not that he isn't good with shrubs."

"Designer. If we could get back to the issue. . ." Something tightened in her stomach. "I can't run an inn."

With a *tsk* in a voice a notch softer, the older woman reached across the island, gripped Amanda's hands in hers, and said, "You know how to serve and how to love people whether they love you back or not. That's all there is to it."

Amanda searched Lola's eyes for a hint she was ready to admit it was a spoof, a "gotcha" ruse, a hidden camera practical joke. Nothing but sincerity returned her stare. "All there is to it? That, and a two-inch-thick notebook of instructions."

"Mostly helpful hints. Menu list. Traffic flow for the buffet items. Phone numbers. Information for ordering more invitations if necessary."

"Invitations!" Amanda leaned back on her heels.

"Already delivered. Harland took them up to Fish Creek to mail them. He likes their postmark."

"How could you even think about relinquishing something as legendary as the Heart's Harbor Christmas Tea to someone like me?"

Lola's smirk crinkled her mouth, cheeks, and eyes. "Since when did the Lord ever use someone supremely qualified for any task He assigned? If I read my Bible right, He used shepherd boys and tax men and a woman who ran a fabric store that only sold purple cloth, if you can imagine. Talk about specializing."

"I have a job. Had a job." Her argument screeched like a train derailing.

Lola stepped back and twirled once with one hand raised heavenward. "Layoff couldn't have come at a better time."

"I have a—" Amanda stopped short of finishing with the word *life*.

"Jordan will help you, although. . ." Lola's eyes widened behind the goggles. "Bless him, sometimes he can cozy up to an Autumn Glory sedum easier than he can an inn full of guests."

"Jordan's here?" Amanda's mind raced to the foyer of the inn where an almost life-sized portrait of the Peterson family told passersby that Harland and Lola were proud of their only child.

And no wonder. God must have been very pleased with Himself when He finished sculpting that face.

"Drove up yesterday." Lola beamed. "He's staying at the Landmark since you'll be innkeeping for the next three weeks and it wouldn't be proportionate for him to be here at night."

Which part of that statement should she refute first? "Not *appropriate*?"

Lola snatched a Honey Crisp apple from the pottery bowl on the island. She buffed it on her sweater sleeve and took a noisy, crispy bite while motioning for Amanda to grab an apple, too.

She turned down the suggestion. "You assumed I'd say yes?"

"Dear girl, we're both in a desperate place. Seems ideal, doesn't it? Now, if you'll excuse me, I have packing to do while you're unpacking. I was told the jury might be equestrian."

What? A twelve-person jury of horse-lovers? Equestrian?

A cold, clear realization hit. *Oh, no!* Amanda swallowed hard. *Sequestered!*

❊

Like a surgical patient trying to shake off the remnants of anesthesia, she allowed herself to be led upstairs to a room

Lola had yet to admit would be Amanda's for only a few days.

When Lola retreated to her quarters off the kitchen, Amanda opened her small wheeled case and unpacked her toiletries, as if it mattered, as if she could seriously consider accepting the unthinkable assignment Lola proposed.

The assignment Lola had *plotted*.

Her son, Jordan, bunked at the Landmark instead of here, his home? Because Amanda—in Lola's words and goggled way of thinking—would be "innkeeping for the next three weeks."

Amanda lay facedown on the bed's richly textured matelasse coverlet. It smelled faintly of bleach. Clean, not overpowering. She'd be responsible for the inn's sparkle factor, if she took the job.

Her forehead propped on her crossed hands, she mumbled into the woven cloth, "Ridiculous. It's a ridiculous idea. But. . ."

But?

Somewhere deep within her stirred a longing to wake in the morning with a reason to fuss over something, a challenge to propel her forward, an opportunity to tackle a project more productive than rehearsing the scene of her almost-wedding and her remorse over ignoring what Todd said were obvious signs of his not just cold but frostbitten feet.

Three years ago. Time to write a new chapter worth rehearsing. It could start with an impossible assignment from a friend and mentor who'd plotted a challenge for her.

She turned her head so her cheek rested on her hands. A low rocker sat in the corner with an ironwork reading lamp arched over its back.

Amanda slid off the bed, grabbed the three-ring binder

from where she'd left it on the oak dresser, and settled into the rocker and the idea. She'd crammed for tests before. Too bad this one wasn't multiple choice.

❄

The manual accompanied Amanda to the Log Den south of Egg Harbor for a soup, salad, and page-turning supper. The restaurant was new to her but beckoned first with its chunky, hand-scribed log structure, then with its tantalizing aromas of seared meat and broiled seafood.

An hour later, she made the short trek north on Highway 42, wound through the twisting downtown, took a left at the Chocolate Chicken coffee shop and a right past the municipal beach.

The lower fairways of the Alpine Golf Course hugged the limestone cliffs, couched in the darkness that descended so early in late November and early December in the north. By daylight, their snowy expanses would create as captivating a scene as the verdant greens of summer.

She turned right again. The shoreline road took her even nearer the water's edge. Cottages gave way to elegant summer homes, with an occasional historic structure tucked between, alternating houses lit for the upcoming holiday, or dark and abandoned until the season of lilacs and trillium.

The Heart's Harbor Victorian Inn spread its arms wide to welcome her home.

How easily that word slipped into her thinking in this setting—*home*.

A single electric candle in every window glowed with halos and ribbons of light that skittered across the floorboards of the wraparound porch. Lampposts on either side of the driveway lit the way in and out of the property.

She was a few minutes early yet for her tutorial. Lola

promised her an evening of Innkeeping 101 after she and Harland returned from a quick trip to an orchard-owner friend for a case of cherry salsa for Jordan to take back to Arizona. Amanda had tasted the orchard's cherry salsa. It was worth his driving that far for it.

The sunroom glowed in the dark. *They must be back.*

She took the side entrance stairs as fast as the winter slick and her soup-and-salad would allow. No time to waste.

As she reached for the doorknob, she caught sight of Harland in the well-lit sunroom. He wasn't doing the backstroke this time. It looked more like crop-dusting, swooping low then pulling up fast to avoid field-hemming trees and upholstered wing chairs.

Lola appeared in front of him, stopping his latest pass over the "field." Amanda watched, blessed, as Lola took her husband's face in her hands and kissed his forehead.

Chapter 2

As flawless in person as he appeared in the family portrait in the foyer, Jordan pulled a knit cap off his Patrick Dempsey too-casual-not-to-have-been-styled waves as he burst into the inn's kitchen through the back door. No one could accuse the photographer of having been heavy-handed with the airbrush. Jordan Peterson's face needed no touch-ups. That little scar high on his cheekbone? Hardly an imperfection.

He tucked the hat in his pocket, then slid out of the jacket and tossed it onto the brass hook on the wall five feet away. A practiced move.

Amanda watched the show from her perch on the window seat. She unpretzeled her legs and closed the Christmas Tea how-to book. Lola Peterson's son didn't need to know she was married to the *Mission Impossible* procedure manual.

She stood and brushed imaginary crumbs from her lap. "You must be Jordan. I'm Amanda Brooks."

Jordan squinted. Was that his way of asking, "What are you doing in my mother's kitchen?"

"Nice to meet you." He smiled small, as if he'd been given a can of creamed corn for a Christmas bonus. "Where's Mom?"

Aww. He called her Mom. Not Ma or Mother or Mama. It said something about him. As soon as she figured out what, she'd—

"Is she here?" He angled from the waist as if peering down the hall. . .through the closed kitchen door.

"You just missed her. Fifteen minutes ago. She and your dad intended to stop at the Landmark to see you on their way to Sturgeon Bay. She texted you about it." Amanda nodded toward the cell phone he'd pulled from a clip on his belt.

His lips parted when he smiled this time. He thumbed a couple of buttons on the phone. "Baby steps. She's texting. I should have checked my messages. Every time I try to take Mom's advice and unplug, it backfires. Wonder what she wanted."

Lola probably wanted to explain to her son—who would one day inherit the inn—that she was temporarily turning over its care to a joyless woman named Amanda with no measurable experience and less confidence than a wad of dryer lint at a fashion show. "Me, I think. She wanted to explain me."

He looked up from his cell phone screen. "*You're* the one."

She'd heard those words before, but with the emphasis on *one*. Look how that turned out. "Your mom's stand-in? Yes. If that's okay with you."

Oh, the power of a moment's hesitation. The face Amanda knew so well from the portrait but so little in person broke eye contact, making words unnecessary. What did he find attention-grabbing in the heart pine floorboards?

She waited. He sighed.

A pause *and* a sigh. Double-barreled doubt.

"Ms. Brooks, I'm sure you—"

His cell phone and the inn's landline clashed a discordant duet.

Pointing toward the phone base on the counter, she said, "I'll just get the—"

"I'll just get the—" His words tumbled over hers as he pointed with equal apology toward his phone. "Hey, Mom. What's up? Yes. She sure is. I'm here with her now."

Amanda lifted the handheld from its cradle and clicked TALK. "Hearts Harbor Victorian Inn. Amanda speaking." Could she carry on this conversation while eavesdropping on the other? Jordan rubbed his right hand across his forehead while he talked, as if ironing furrows with his fingertips, and disappeared deeper into the house.

She attended to the voice coming through the earpiece. A request for a gift certificate—one more thing she hadn't been trained to handle in her warp-speed B&B boot camp the night before. She took the number and promised to call back within the hour.

The form she needed for the gift certificate processing was on the computer in the entry, no doubt within earshot of Jordan, the Unconvinced.

Leaning her backside against the lower cabinets, she picked at a snag in a fingernail and her schedule. *Join the crowd, buddy. I'm not convinced this is wise, either.*

A jet of cold air goose pimpled her arms, despite the long-sleeved *Door County Rocks* sweatshirt she wore. The back door stood ajar a quarter inch. She bumped it shut. *Boys. They can be—*

Jordan burst into the room as if on a mission. He rested

his forearms on the island and bent toward her. "Okay, Amanda. What do you need from me? I'm here to help."

Adorable. They can be adorable.

Chapter 3

D o you have the trees yet?" Jordan held his pen above a scrap of paper and waited.

Christmas trees. Multiple. Lola usually had one in each of the public rooms. The procedure manual said the decorations were stored in the attic. Maybe she could get Jordan to—

"I know a place," Jordan said. "Won't cost us a thing except a little gas. You'll need boots. I'll get the saw."

And just like that it was decided they'd cut their own trees despite the time it would take and a stack of projects thicker than pine needles on the forest floor. Amanda grabbed her coat and gloves and the manual. She could cram on the way to the "place."

She followed Jordan down the back steps, expecting him to veer toward the coppery SUV with Arizona plates. His strides took them instead to the double garage.

He punched a code into the keypad, and the automatic garage door opener clicked, growled, and hoisted.

"We can fit more trees in the truck." Jordan's facial

expression lit like a teen handed the keys to the good car.

The heavy curtain of garage door lifted to reveal the object of Jordan's affection.

"That's no truck." Amanda braced herself against the opening's frame. "It's. . .it's an ambulance."

Jordan opened the back as if to slide out an accident or stroke victim. He tucked the D-shaped saw into a compartment along the hull and closed it with a heavy metal *thunk*. "Used to be. It *used* to be an ambulance. Now it's Dad's joyride."

A man who does the backstroke on the hardwood floor drives a recycled ambulance. Good old Harland. What a character.

The box on wheels filled the garage like ground pork fills a bratwurst.

She had an inn to prepare for weekend guests, breakfast menus to create, and a party for a hundred to plan. Instead, she'd been asked to tour the Door County landscape in the passenger seat of an ambulance.

Jordan skinnied himself to slip alongside the monstrosity toward the front of the vehicle. With Harland and Lola's real car gone from the other stall, Amanda had plenty of room on her side.

She opened the passenger door, shoved the Tea manual across the bench seat, and chose footholds like a mountaineer. A grab bar on the dash gave her one handhold, but still, she had to bounce twice to propel herself into the cab.

Jordan waited with his hands on the steering wheel. "Sorry. I should have assisted."

"I'm fine." She tugged the seat belt across her parka and snugged it for the joyride.

He turned the key in the ignition. Something akin to

space shuttle afterburners kicked in. Jordan snatched a square walkie-talkie attached to the dash by a droopy, curled cord ready for its next perm. "Unit Five leaving Base Station. Repeat, Unit Five is leaving the Base Station." He slid the mic back into its holder, turned to Amanda, and spurted a clipped chuckle. "I've wanted to do that since Dad brought her home."

He eased the ambulance out of the garage and backed around to face down the driveway. With a grin that curved at the edges, he reached for a switch labeled SIREN. She slapped her hand over his. "Don't do it."

"Just the lights?"

Amanda cringed.

"Thanks to my dad, they're red and *green*," he said, as if that changed everything. "Christmasy."

He wasn't crazy, just. . .adorable, right? Harland and Lola Peterson's flesh and blood.

❄

Ambulances scream through countrysides. This one puttered. As unobtrusively as possible, Amanda peeked at the speedometer. Thirty-five?

"She shudders a little at higher speeds," Jordan said.

So much for unobtrusive. Amanda stared at the line of Jordan's jaw with its pencil-thin hint of a beard. Nice. Rugged, but not lumberjackish. Not at all like a lumberjack.

He mumbled something about a computer shortcut for processing reservations with a minimum of human contact.

It might have been sleep deprivation—or the line of his jaw—but all Amanda could envision was the stocky robot maid on *The Jetsons* reruns. Rosie. One leg. Caster wheels. A monotone techno-voice reciting, "Welcome-to-The-Heart's-Harbor-Inn, Mr. J."

A Victorian bed-and-breakfast with a minimum of human contact? Amanda focused her attention on the flash of Jordan's eyes when he glanced her way, the narrow side road less of a challenge to navigate than it would have been at a higher rate of speed. Eyes the color of pewter but with a sheen. Definitely Lola's son.

Was he all business—except for the occasional ambulance ride—or did he share Lola's genetic code for serving others? They were on the hunt for free Christmas trees and discussing automated reservations. Enough said.

They passed quaint Scandinavian-looking cottages neighbored by chunky log homes—both ancient and modern—adjacent to simple farms and sprawling magazine-cover estates. The mix of structures mimicked the Door County mix of fancy tourists and simple fishermen, of bejeweled executives on vacation and work-worn farmers tending their orchards and making caramel apples for fancy tourists.

She listened to Jordan's theories about fiscal responsibility—was he talking national budget or innkeeping?—with her gaze on the captivating scenery. Someday she'd visit the barn converted to a hands-on art studio. The wood sign promised the opportunity to work with clay, paints, metal, or glass. Someday.

"—by cutting corners. Don't you agree?" Jordan looked to her for confirmation.

Piggy bank. She'd make him a pottery piggy bank.

❊

Walking across a carpet of potato chips. That's what it sounded like as Jordan's and Amanda's boots broke through the crust of snow.

Jordan parked the ambulance near a weathered, listing, farmhouse-less barn. He blazed a trail through the silent rows of a retired orchard then directed their crunchy steps across an open field toward a line of scrubby-looking pines at the crest of a rise.

She matched her stride to his, or was he matching his to her pace? Jordan glanced over his shoulder frequently and seemed to slow his steps when she lagged behind. Todd wouldn't have glanced.

She should have read the truth in Todd's you-can-come-along-if-you-want attitude about everything in life.

Jordan wore the bow saw over his shoulder like a back-pack strap. She kept her distance from the saw's toothy edge despite its school bus yellow plastic guard.

Her leg muscles burned from the effort of trudging through almost a foot of snow. Lifting her knees high, she broke her own trail beside rather than behind Jordan. "What did your mother say to you?"

"What do you mean?"

"I don't think it's a huge secret you were uncomfortable with the idea of my running the inn in your mother's absence." The puffs of their conversation formed short-lived clouds.

He shifted the saw to his other shoulder. "It seemed so. . . sudden. Did Mom know you well enough to trust you with the inn and her famous Tea?"

Good question. Amanda's imagination started another checklist of reasons why almost anyone else would have been a smarter choice.

> A. A ten-room inn was a far cry from her hand-width apartment above a Chicago deli.
> B. Lola had spent how many years perfecting the art of hostessing? Amanda had—what?—two hours of training plus that weekend three years ago?

C. Jordan didn't know her from the guy who ran the drawbridge over the channel in Sturgeon Bay.

❋

One-horse open sleighs dash through snow. The two of them slogged, a task made all the harder by the unanswered question between them. Who in their right mind hands the keys to an inn and a project like the Heart's Harbor Christmas Tea to a woman little more than an appreciative guest?

Amanda relived the sight of Lola reaching up to plant a kiss on Harland's forehead in the soft glow of the sunroom the night before. Was Jordan's brain overheating, too? She wasn't about to use a kiss to find out.

She zipped her parka a couple of zipper-teeth higher. "Your mother is an incredible woman, but not always predictable. What did she say to change your mind?"

"Other than 'Because I said so'?" Jordan turned to walk backward and face her directly as he spoke. "She said you—"

Feet flying, he landed on his back in the snow.

And didn't move.

Eyes closed, he lay expressionless, all the life of a moment ago gone.

Amanda fell to her knees. "Jordan!"

She pulled the saw away, noted the guard still intact, and tossed it aside. With fistfuls of his down jacket sleeves, she tugged enough to see he wasn't responding. She whipped off a glove and laid her palm along the side of his face. "Jordan, can you hear me?"

His eyes popped open. She tried to jerk her hand back, but he held it firmly against his cheek.

"She was right," he breathed. "She said you had a caring heart and needed a chance to show it."

❄

The whole Peterson family needed therapy. Especially the one she'd left in a snowbank a few yards behind her.

"Amanda, wait!"

Stomp. Crunch. Stomp. Crunch. She stepped into the oval caverns of her previous footsteps that would take her back to the barn and the. . .the. . .ambulance.

What had she gotten herself into?

"Amanda! It was a compliment."

Jordan's voice grew no closer. Stubborn man.

"Besides," he hollered over the sound of smashed snow-flakes, "if I pick out the trees myself, you never know what you'll get."

She one-eightied and marched in a laser line toward the stand of trees that had been the original goal.

Her pulse still hadn't returned to normal after the moment he fell lifeless. In an instant her mind had raced ahead to how she'd get him help, if she could drag him back to the medically worthless ambulance, if she could manage to drive it, and how she would tell Lola she'd lost her son in a Christmas tree accident.

Caring heart? See if I care.

She stomped a bypass in the snow around where he stood. Up close, the scrubby pines looked even sadder than they had from a distance. An elegant inn decorated with trees Charlie Brown would reject?

Granted, it would cut down on the number of ornaments she'd need. . .

She'd given a mental thumbs-down to a dozen scattered, misshaped spruce by the time Jordan caught up.

Huffing more than she was, he waved the saw in the air, triumphant. "Took me awhile to find it."

"Jordan, your taste in trees is surpassed only by your taste in. . .in. . .tasteless jokes."

"Not these puny trees." He slipped the saw over his shoulder and grabbed her hand. "Through here."

With arm extended, he parted branches hanging heavy with the recent snow. Her resistance compromised by the effort of the last few minutes, she allowed him to pull her through the arch of tree limbs.

In three neat rows stood several dozen full, healthy-looking, precisely shaped trees, any one of them perfect for Christmas. The taller ones in back towered ten or twelve feet high, with the middle row of trees seven or eight feet, and the adolescents in front only four or five. "Beautiful!"

"Balsams. My favorite. Soft needles. And that fragrance. Here. Smell." He rubbed needles between his thumb and pointer finger and lifted his glove to her nose. The fragrance of Christmas.

"Did you plant these, Jordan?"

"Dad and I did. We try to replant as many as we harvest each year, if I can arrange to get back here in the spring."

Amanda drank in the scene and the crisp air's hint of Lake Michigan and Green Bay a few miles to the east and west. "What would keep you from this place?"

Jordan busied himself brushing leaves and snow off a third row tree on the edge of the stand. "Work," he said.

She watched him scuff snow out of the way at the base of the tree, forming a space in which to kneel. He turned to her and nodded toward the tree. She nodded back. It was ideal for the front parlor's bumped-out window.

He set the teeth of the saw against the trunk and drew it back and forth. "Work," he repeated, "and my girlfriend."

❄

The body of an antique ambulance is well short of twelve feet, so the doors hung open on the trip home. But by careful planning and no small amount of coaxing, the two managed to stuff three trees of varying heights into a spot usually reserved for patients, EMTs, and IVs.

It was a relief Jordan had a girlfriend. It cleared the air. He'd grabbed her hand to direct her. He'd winked because guys that cute wink. He pretended to pass out because—

Well, certainly not to get her to lean close to him, or get her to care about what happened to him.

He was his mother's son. His father's son. They were adorable. He was a tad annoying.

She pulled off her gloves and wiggled her fingers in front of the dashboard heater vents. Her torso sweated—probably not good—from the exertion of dragging the smaller of the three trees across the field and through the orchard while Jordan handled the other two. The work gloves he'd brought for her to slip over her doeskin ones bore the brunt of stray needles and pine sap, but the cab reeked of nature like a too-strong evergreen candle or pine air freshener.

"Kick off your boots," Jordan suggested.

"I'm not sure I can. My toes are stiff. I think they're still attached to my feet. Not sure."

He adjusted something on the heater panel and the flow of warm air on her fingers diminished. "Swing a foot up here." He slapped the vinyl seat.

She scooted enough within the confines of the seat belt to get her right foot onto the seat. He hugged her wet boot under his arm so she could slip her foot from its trap. He did the same with her left.

"The floor vent's on the right," he said.

"Aah."

"City boots. Not worth much up here."

She removed the boots from the seat, set them on the floor underneath her, and used her glove to wipe melted snow from the vinyl. "I'll have you know these have made it through three Chicago winters."

Jordan turned his head to look at her. Just as quickly, he refocused his attention on the road ahead. "You're from Chicago?"

Why had his voice sobered? Did he have a thing against the Chicago Bears?

He leaned his elbow against the window and his head into his hand. "*You're* the one."

Chapter 4

She did not need Jordan Peterson—or anyone else for that matter—feeling sorry for her. It's true her almost-husband bailed in the middle of the ceremony. She was so over that. What else had Lola told him? Amanda wondered if the lawyers for the defense knew one of their jurors was a blabbermouth about personal matters.

The tenderness in Jordan's voice unnerved her.

She could handle embarrassment and humiliation. She'd had plenty of practice explaining why she was returning wedding gifts and dealing with debt from a reception that didn't happen and a groom who didn't feel obligated to help foot the bill.

Humiliation, she understood. Tenderness was disconcerting.

"That must have been rough." He unzipped his down jacket.

"We can turn down the heater. My feet are toasty now."

He didn't move, so she did, flipping the heater blower to low and tucking her feet underneath her, cross-legged.

"You. . ." He rubbed a spot on the steering wheel from

36

noon to three. "You didn't have any idea how he felt?"

This was a conversation she wouldn't have with the girls at work, much less her employer's well-meaning but way-out-of-line son.

Tension finger-walked its way up the back of her neck. "New subject. Tree stands. Where are they? Attic?"

One second. Two seconds. Three. . .

He braked the ambulance near the side entrance of the inn. "Amanda. . . ?"

"Basement?"

He shifted into PARK and turned the key. A spot somewhere beyond the windshield held his gaze. "Yes. Basement."

❄

With the trees snugged, tightened, plumbed, and left to let the remaining snow drip onto skirts of plastic garbage bags before ornamentation, Jordan and Amanda turned to technical issues.

His nearness over her shoulder while she sat at the registration desk made her claustrophobic. Wasn't that what claustrophobia felt like? Rapid heartbeat? Difficulty breathing?

He leaned even closer, spilling "adorable" all over the place. She dared a glance at his face.

His eyebrows angled toward the bridge of his nose in a look of concentration. "Did you catch that?"

She turned her vision to the spot he indicated on the computer screen and squinted, as if that would help the spreadsheet make more sense. "I'm not sure I—"

"Let me walk you through this again." His hand lay over hers on the wireless mouse. The cursor on the screen jumped.

"Jordan, I understand the concept. I don't agree with it."

She pressed her lips together. Would her mouth never

learn to behave itself?

He stepped back from the office chair and looked not at the computer, not at her, but somewhere in between. "I've had this discussion with my mother."

Good. She's a smart woman. I hope you listened to her.

Jordan plucked a cherry fudge caramel from the basket on the ledge above the desk, untwisted its waxed paper cover, and popped the caramel into his mouth.

She took advantage of his need to chew and swallow. "I realize a century-old inn needs to step it up when it comes to plumbing and a few other issues."

A faint clunk from the direction of the kitchen told her the automatic ice maker appreciated the nod.

"But this setting dictates the kind of service guests will expect. Hospitality can't be automated, Mr. J."

Amanda punctuated the last statement by tapping the engraved brass dome bell on the ledge beside the basket of caramels. Its high-pitched *ding* lasted far too long.

Jordan cupped one hand over the bell to silence it. With the other, he reached for a second caramel, frowned, and asked, "How much do we charge for these things?"

❄

"Midweek this time of year, not much is open in the evenings." Jordan angled his lean frame against the antique Hoosier cabinet in the kitchen, one ankle crossed over the other.

The nutmeg was in the Hoosier. Amanda decided to wait to make Honey Crisp Apple Coffee Cake until later.

She turned to the sink, squirted waterless hand sanitizer on a paper towel, and polished the faucet. Again. "That's true."

Did he realize how much she was saving the inn by re-purposing hand sanitizer?

"You shouldn't have to cook."

What? Was he staying for dinner?

Amanda heard his footsteps pad across the floorboards. One, two, pause, three.

"I thought we should find something open and discuss things. Business things."

She wadded the damp paper towel in her hands and pinched back what she wanted to say: *The orchards aren't giving out free samples tonight, Jordan.* "Guests arrive day after tomorrow and I have work to do. I shouldn't leave."

"No guests right now."

"Someone might call."

"That's what answering machines are for."

Lola's hand-stenciled Heart's Harbor Inn apron hung on a hook on the wall in Amanda's line of sight. During their Innkeeping 101 discussion, Lola had specified she needed Amanda to fill in both as innkeeper and peacekeeper. Did she mean with her son?

She tossed the paper towel into the wastebasket. "I guess I could afford to be gone for a little while. Give me an hour. I have laundry to fold and pillowcases to iron."

"I can help."

"You iron?"

"I fold." His smile and the slight tilt of his head disarmed her.

He snatched a vintage dish towel from a wooden towel bar on the side of the Hoosier. With flair and maddeningly slow precision, he unfolded it, laid it flat on the island, smoothed, matched corners, smoothed again, and folded the towel into a form that likely had a geometric name.

Dodecahedron, or something like that.

"That's okay. I've got it." She took the towel from his outstretched hands. No self-respecting towel bar would accept it.

"Suit yourself. I'll just— I'll be—" He gestured toward the back door and lifted his jacket from the hook.

"Dinner then. In an hour."

Jordan zipped his jacket and clapped his hands together—one clap. "Good. It's the Christmas Tea. We need to talk budget."

❄

No more free caramels. Automated reservation system. The next thing, he'll want me to water down the tea!

The phone call changed everything.

Halfway through a grilled portabella mushroom panini at the Bistro at Liberty Square, Jordan fielded a phone call. Amanda sincerely tried not to eavesdrop, but the man was sitting right there beside her.

"Blake! Hey, it's been awhile. What have you been up to?"

Jordan looked to Amanda for permission to suspend their number crunching until after the call. She mouthed, "Go ahead."

She sipped cinnamony apple cider and directed her attention to the lettering stenciled on the curved soffit scrolling around the room's joint between the walls and ceiling.

"Seriously, man? That's wonderful. Kudos to you." His words celebrated but he leaned an elbow on the table and rested his forehead on his palm.

She took a dainty bite of her sandwich and discovered dainty and messy are not mutually exclusive. Something divine oozed down her chin. She caught most of it with her napkin. A small drip landed on the front of her sweater.

The scarf she'd worn for warmth with her jacket became camouflage. She looped it around her neck and let the tails lie flat over the spot.

Jordan, still listening to an apparently wordy Blake, whispered to her, "Are you cold?"

"Not anymore," she whispered back.

"Yeah, Blake, I'm here. You would? Yes, of course. I. . . I think." He looked at Amanda as if she had the answer to the question.

It would help if I knew the topic.

"Can you give me. . .us. . .a day or two to—?"

Us, who?

"Wow. I mean, it's an honor to be considered, but. . ."

Okay, that was enough to stir any woman's curiosity.

"Where can you be reached? I'll get back to you within the hour. And Blake? Thanks, man."

Jordan laid his now silent phone on the tabletop. "Amanda, we have a problem."

❄

Jordan's Arizona tan lost a few degrees of depth. He pushed his half-eaten panini to the side and spread both palms on the table. "That was Blake Folsom. Recognize the name?"

Amanda flipped through her mental address book. Folsom, Folsom, Folsom. Nothing but a prison. "Should I?"

"You've probably seen his byline. He's a feature writer for *Inns and Outs* magazine."

She'd seen the high-class magazine on the nightstand of every room in the inn and suspected copies showed up in every inn from Seattle to Key West. "He sounded like a friend."

"He beat me out of valedictorian by a technicality. Won the college scholarship I wanted. Aced Calculus. I took it twice."

She glanced at the budget he'd scratched onto a legal pad. He must have done pretty well the second time around.

Jordan swung his chair to face north/south to her east/west.

"He heard about the Tea. And wants to do a feature."

"This year? I mean, now?" She scrambled for a gracious way to say *You've got to be kidding!* She found none. "You've got to be kidding!"

"If he likes what he sees, it'll be the ultimate free PR, but—"

So much hung on that three-letter word. The missing link to success was Lola. "Oh, Jordan!"

"I know." He rubbed his palms on his thighs. "How could we pass up an opportunity like this?" His eyes widened. "On the other hand. . ."

She was the other hand. No Lola, no lollapalooza of a Christmas Tea.

"I haven't spoken to Blake since he beat me by two strokes at the golf outing at our class reunion."

"You remember the score?"

"Well, yeah. But that's not the point. He's interested in featuring the inn." He shook his head. A frown dropped the corners of his mouth and his eyes. "Delia will have a fit if I'm not in Phoenix for Christmas."

Oh. Her.

"Are you rambling now, Jordan, or is there really anything to decide?"

Their waitress laid the bill on the table and cleared their plates.

Jordan peeked at his watch. "I'm not sure what to do, other than pray."

"Always a good place to start."

"It's just that—"

"Jordan, if you think we should say yes, please know I will do everything I can to make this work. I'm no slouch."

"I didn't think you were."

"It might have to be simpler than in years past, but I have your mom's instructions. Think of how many more people would hear about this place if it were featured in *Inns and Outs*. That's huge."

He bowed his head for a moment. Two moments. When he raised his head, the tension in his face had eased a little. "All right, then." With that, he snatched the piece of paper from the table and ripped the budget into confetti.

Chapter 5

The five-foot tree in the dining room perched in the corner by the sideboard. Decked in mini-lights and hundreds of wooden cherries on rope "twigs" with green satin ribbon bows, the tree shouted "Door County," as did each pair of Montmorency cherries—the word *Door* on one and *County* on the other.

The eight-footer in the second parlor twinkled with white lights and all things musical—miniature musical instruments, scroll-like snatches of sheet music, clef signs, and eighth notes. The tree snuggled into the curve of the grand piano. Its lights doubled in the piano's ebony surface.

The twelve-foot tree lent a sweetly nostalgic air to the front parlor, if Amanda did say so herself. Jordan had used miles of bubble lights to illuminate the branches and the room.

When he was done, Amanda set to work hanging Lola's collection of antique ornaments. The fanciest rotated like pirouetting ballerinas.

While she fussed over ornament placement, Jordan draped

strings of lights and garland on the banister of the stairs to the second floor.

During rare breaks, they took turns offering each other a cup of coffee or tea. Jordan ran out for a pizza, slipping into the pizzeria minutes before closing time.

They ate at the kitchen island, a meal largely devoid of conversation, focused on the flecks of green pepper and black olives. Remarkably, they liked the same kind of pizza. Vegetarian. . .with three meats.

Jordan lifted a slice of pizza from its cardboard box. Warm, gooey cheese linked the slice to the rest of the pie. "We're doing our bit to support the dairy industry," he said.

"Do people from Phoenix say things like that?" She'd forced her voice to remain light.

"I guess my heart will always be in Wisconsin."

"Have you thought about moving back?"

He set his pizza down and brushed dough crumbs from his hands. "New subject," he said, his shoulders tense and his words halting. "I have good news and bad news."

He slid off the high stool and walked toward the mat near the kitchen entrance. "I found the notebook about the Christmas Tea."

"Found the—?" Amanda hadn't thought about it since the trip to get the trees the day before. She'd been focused on. . .

Her mind traced back through the ride home, pulling the trees from the back of the vehicle, wedging them through the doorways, fighting to get the tree stands to hold securely, decorating.

What had she done with the notebook? She couldn't remember seeing it since she flopped it and then herself onto the front seat.

"G—good," she said. "You found it. What's the bad news?"

"It's been run over by an ambulance."

❋

Her pizza threatened to make a second appearance.

She swallowed hard. No longer a three-ring binder, the notebook boasted one pathetic ring and multiple tire tracks. Water spots had wrinkled the handwritten pages and washed out most of the ink.

Jordan cleared his throat but didn't speak.

Like a car with a bad starter, he gave it another try. "We ran over it—okay, *I* ran over it—when we—"

Her brain hurt. "Where did you find it?"

"Out at the farm."

"Yesterday? Why didn't you tell me then?"

"I found it tonight. Stopped there on my way home from the Basil Leaf." He sat but pushed his plate of pizza to the side. "I just had a hunch. Don't get those often. Good thing it didn't snow since we were out there. The headlights shone right on it."

"Yeah. Good thing."

"Can you salvage any of it?"

She pressed her forehead into the granite surface of the island. Its cold welcome did little to ease the throbbing in her head, but quieted the nausea.

"Just this page." She held it aloft without moving her head.

He took the guest list from her hand. "Oh, Amanda. If I knocked it out of the—"

"It wasn't on the driver's side."

"But. . ."

She raised her head and patted his forearm. "As disappointments go, I've had worse."

He covered her hand with his own. How was it he

understood at all? Or was it misplaced guilt that seeped through his grasp rather than warmth? He was, after all, the hit-and-run driver.

She slipped her hand from under his. "It's been a long couple of days. Thanks for your help." She closed the pizza box lid. "You're leaving for Phoenix in the morning?"

"Yes. I'd better get back to the Landmark and pack." He closed his eyes for a long moment. "We can cancel, you know."

The aroma of roasted garlic and remorse lingered in the room. She breathed in both.

"I thought you couldn't miss any more work. It's more than a two-day drive, isn't it?"

"The Tea," he said. "We can cancel the Tea."

Neither blinked.

That was it, then.

She'd invested hours in the fruitless pursuit of worry. Even more in the now pointless study of Lola's guidebook. How much time had she spent in prayer about the Tea?

Had the "project" become an emotional crutch, a way to survive the holidays as opposed to a way to serve Lola and her guests?

She'd repositioned a gold filigree ornament six times to get it just right. How particular had she been about things that mattered?

Jordan's first instinct was accurate. She had no business masquerading as a competent person, much less a fill-in for Lola Peterson.

"You're probably right," she said, watching for a sigh of relief that never came. "Let's call it off."

❋

The inn creaked too loudly for Amanda to get any real sleep.

At six she gave up wrestling with the bedcovers and called it morning. She laid her Bible on the marble vanity while she brushed her teeth. Circling enamel with her toothbrush, she found the place on the page in Galatians where she'd stopped reading days earlier.

Galatians chapter six. She leaned over the sink and turned only her eyes to keep reading. One verse. Two. Three. Uh-huh. Uh-huh. Uh-huh.

Oh.

Bracing herself on the vanity, she reread verses nine and ten. It couldn't mean what she thought it did. Or if so, it couldn't apply to her situation.

Galatians 6:9 began, "Let us not become weary in doing good, for at the proper time we will reap a harvest if we do not give up."

And verse ten—"Therefore, as we have opportunity, let us do good to all people, especially to those who belong to the family of believers."

Jordan had left his cell phone number. She could call him on the road and talk to him about—

That was crazier than Christmas lights on an ambulance.

She threw on yesterday's jeans and sweatshirt, promising herself a shower after she'd had coffee.

Two couples and a single were scheduled to check in mid-afternoon. She needed to dust one last time, run into Egg Harbor for fresh fruit from the market, and make another pass with the vacuum to catch any straggler pine needles.

But first she needed to think.

She grabbed her Bible and headed downstairs. In an hour or so, the natural light from the kitchen windows might put the verses in a less challenging perspective.

She stopped short on the bottom step.

She'd checked all the door locks last night, hadn't she? Living alone was commonplace for her. . .in a refrigerator-box-sized apartment. But the creaks and groans the many-roomed inn expressed in the night had turned to rattles and scratches without an "it's an old building" explanation.

She followed the sounds to the sunroom.

"Jordan!"

"Building a fire." He brandished the cast iron poker to prove his point. Small flames licked a pick-up-sticks stack of kindling.

"I can see that. But why? And why now? Aren't you supposed to pick up Delilah in Kansas City in a few hours?"

"It's Delia and Iowa City. She'll fume, but I'll call later and beg another day. We have to talk."

"If you have to beg your girlfriend for one more day off work, you two do have to talk."

Where had that come from? She pinched her mouth shut, but Jordan hadn't flinched at her words.

He set the poker in its cradle. "Not Delia and I."

He took Amanda's forearms and guided her to the same wing chair his mother had suggested a handful of days ago.

Backing up a step, he pointed first to her then himself. "*You* and I need to talk."

She wasn't ready with her "God told me" argument. Something of this magnitude needed at least a three-point defense.

Jordan sat on a corner of the coffee table. "I read something this morning in God's Word."

"Me, too." Her heart warmed at the connection.

"I don't want to twist the Bible to suit our situation."

"Me, neither."

"But I think the Word *fits* our situation." His eyes shone in the fire's growing light.

Amanda leaned forward. "Have you been reading in Galatians?"

"No." The twitch of his eyebrows questioned what she meant.

Maybe they weren't on the same wavelength, spiritually, after all.

"Second Thessalonians 3:13." He waited while she flipped the pages of the Bible in her hand to locate the verse. " 'And as for you, brothers, never tire of doing what is right,' " he quoted.

Their gazes locked.

The Tea wasn't about advertising the inn. It wasn't about Jordan proving himself to Blake or Amanda proving herself to. . .herself.

It was about serving the guests, about celebrating Christmas in a style worthy of the Christ Child, warming people's hearts, honoring Lola's friends and the people she cared about. It was about "doing good."

Jordan rubbed his palms together. "I secured my room at the Landmark until the end of December."

Why did that thought send a ripple of joy through her?

"I'll call Delia later. It looks like I'm spending Christmas in Door County. You, too?"

She swallowed against the tightness in her throat. "Me, too."

Chapter 6

Weekend guests with reservations seemed an imposition on the flurry of planning and prepping for the Tea. Amanda caught herself before resentment took hold. "This is what we do. We serve."

She found Lola's notes on the Solomons from Dubuque, and the hyphenated couple from Los Angeles.

The Solomons took more coddling. Their trip from Dubuque that day had not prepared them for romance, it appeared. Sweet Jill was silent and reserved. Gary was tart-cherry sour, finding fault with everything from traffic conditions around Madison to the water pressure of the showerhead to the absence of covered parking for his BMW to the choice of scented candles on the mantel.

Amanda fielded his concerns as she assumed Lola would have.

How many times a day did she wish she could contact Lola by phone and find out the "real" way to respond? Her mantra became WWLD—*What Would Lola Do?* The answer was always, "The same thing Jesus would do in that situation."

Good goal. Great goal.

The reminder came in handy when the Fitzgerald-Rileys toured the inn's public rooms. Fitzgerald—or was it Riley?—touched every table, chair, lamp, pine bough, wreath, and every one of the Christmas trees. Welts rose on the backs of the woman's hands. The way she itched her forearms under her sweater sleeves, other welts must have joined the party, too.

Riley—or was it Fitzgerald?—rushed to his companion's side. "Are you okay?"

"I don't understand it." She scratched and rubbed.

"Honey, your face!"

The developing blush on her cheeks sent Amanda running for the Benadryl in the emergency kit.

"I knew I was allergic to pine," the female half of Fitzgerald-Riley explained. "I didn't know that meant Christmas trees, too."

It would be a long weekend.

Gary Solomon switched pillows six times before he found one to his liking. Amanda's. Jill snacked incessantly on potato chips and pretzels, but requested a salt-free breakfast—doctor's orders. Jill patted her tummy, flat but apparently not for long.

A late check-in—a mystery writer as intent on architectural research of the inn as he was on his daily word count—lost his "muse" every time the hall clock chimed.

The guests' quirks would make fun stories to tell Lola and Harland when they returned. And Jordan.

Flopped across the bed in her own room now, between immediate responsibilities, Amanda couldn't help hearing the tense conversation taking place across the hall in the Hearthside Room.

The eating establishment she had suggested to the Solomons had not been to their liking, either. Their anniversary dinner had been hampered by slow service and who knows what other inconveniences.

What a large part prayer would play in her assignment! Sprawled on her bed fully clothed, she spent a good deal of time praying for the Solomons and their relationship.

That is what I'm doing here, isn't it, Lord? I'm on assignment. You didn't want me here to refresh me, but to use me, right? Or will that come, too? No matter. It feels good to serve these people in Your Name, whether they know that's what I'm doing or not. Make me sensitive to true needs, and sensitive to my boundaries, Lord.

Interesting how a challenge presses a person to be more faithful to pray.

Sometimes.

Amanda's sigh pressed her deeper into the embrace of the bed beneath her. That's not the response she'd had to the crisis at the altar.

Lord, forgive me.

Interesting how forgiveness is a sleep aid for the soul.

❄

The morning sun spread bizarre patterns of light and shadow as it bore through the lace curtains on the windows. The patterns inched their way across the floor and climbed the bed to tickle Amanda's chin.

Seven o'clock.

She hadn't set the alarm so she whispered a prayer of gratitude that she hadn't slept longer than seven. Already the day would start with her running behind schedule.

She camp-showered—in and out in five minutes—and dressed in a long-sleeved, butter yellow sweater and jeans.

Not particularly figure flattering, but comfortable. Breathless with the responsibility and uncertainty that lay before her, she tackled her hair with the blow-dryer.

A quick swath of blush on her cheeks, a swipe of translucent lipstick, two flicks of the mascara wand, and she was ready to head downstairs.

The aroma of fresh coffee told her the coffeemaker had responded to the timer instructions. She crossed the dining room, noting with pleasure that the table looked as lovely in sunlight as it had when she set it the night before.

It had been awhile since she had cooked for more than just herself. And it had rarely mattered to her if each item of the menu were ready at the same instant when she ate alone. She would often stand in the kitchen of her apartment eating her eggs while she waited for her English muffin to finish toasting, or eating her banana while her oatmeal perked away in the microwave.

Today, everything had to be coordinated—for Lola's sake, for Jordan's peace of mind, and for the satisfaction-challenged Solomons and the other guests.

❄

Scraps of bark clung to the front of Jordan's pale blue chambray shirt. He'd been hauling wood for the fireplaces. His diligence to dive into whatever task needed his attention warmed her heart and distracted her from the piecrust she was rolling for the next morning's quiche.

"Thanks for doing that," she said, nodding toward his chest.

He followed the track of her eyes. With two quick flicks he brushed the wood onto the floor.

She folded her arms and leveled him her best you're-a-blessing-but-that's-not-acceptable scowl.

"Oh. Yeah."

"The broom's in the laundry room, Jordan. In case you need it."

He smiled as he headed off to retrieve the broom. Heartwarming. Jordan Peterson was doing entirely too much warming her heart lately.

He had Delia Whatshername. Amanda had no business enjoying his company or his attention to her—the inn's— needs. Why couldn't he become irritating again?

He snitched a fresh cookie from the cooling rack when he returned with the broom.

That's better.

She tapped his cookie hand. A cloud of flour puffed a punctuation. "I need those for the guests."

He paused, then took a bite. Through the sweetness he mumbled, "Mom always made chocolate chip."

Oh, that's much better, Jordan. Worm is better than warm. Compare me to your mom.

Leaning the broom against the exposed side of the refrigerator, he snatched another from the rack. "I prefer these. They'd be killer with a cup of tea. Can I make you one?"

Great. Just great. Warm again.

The pie dough called to her. She couldn't let the chunks of butter melt from the heat that radiated from her.

Jordan had set a steaming cup of tea on a coaster near her by the time she'd trimmed the excess from the rim.

With a plastic blade, she scraped dough bits and excess flour into her palm and deposited them in the wastebasket just as Jordan reached to dump the dustpan of wood scraps. Their actions collided, scattering both flour and wood on either side rather than into the basket.

It was too funny not to snicker, even though it did make

more work for one or the other of them. His snicker followed, setting off an escalating series that erupted into full-blown laughter.

The stress of the challenge they faced could have been so much worse if Jordan had been a different kind of person.

Even before the laughter subsided, he sprinted for the broom. It slid out of his reach and dropped, handle first, behind the fridge.

"I've got it. I've got it." He bent at the waist and let out an "Ooph!"

Oh, please, not a mouse.

He stayed bent.

"What is it? And if it's a rodent, make something up." She stepped back.

He grimaced. "Twinge."

"What?"

"My back."

"Come on, Jordan. You have a livelier imagination than that." She forced her breathing to match the nonemergency of a small, relatively harmless rodent that would soon be history.

She rubbed her forearms, then noted that her sweater sleeves now boasted a dusting of white. "Jordan?"

He leaned his forehead against the side of the refrigerator and clamped a hand to the small of his back.

"No mouse?"

"I wish." He eased upright an inch then retreated. "Could you. . . ?"

She moved to his side. "What can I do?" Wrapping one arm around his shoulder, she offered him her other hand. "Lean on me."

He lifted his head to look at her and moaned.

Like turtles with limps, they shuffled through the dining room to the rear parlor and its settee. He clung to her with one hand and eased down onto his left side.

"Nope—nope—NOPE!" He dug his fingers into her biceps and sat up, then lowered onto his right side. The grip on her arms relaxed.

She grabbed two pillows from a nearby chair. She tucked one under his neck, the other behind his back.

"Thanks." He grimaced again. "It'll let up any minute."

She knelt beside him, a too-familiar position, it seemed. "Does this happen often?"

His gray eyes sparkling, he took her hand from where she rested it on his shoulder and pressed her palm to his cheek. "Not often enough. . ."

As she had in the field, she snatched it back, more slowly this time.

His expression sobered. "Not. . .often. . .enough for me to know what to do about it." He adjusted his position.

How many loads of firewood had he cut, stacked, and hauled for the inn's fireplaces? "Don't you get a workout on the job, toting baby palm trees and bougainvillea bushes?"

"I get," he began, punching the pillow behind his back, "a workout at the gym. My boss has me in the office. I like landscape design, but I miss the hands-on."

Feet hanging off the end of the settee, Jordan looked as comfortable as a basketball player on a jockey's cot.

She nudged an ottoman from across the room and butted it against the settee.

"You have a boss? Lola gave me the impression you owned your landscape design company."

Jordan closed his eyes against one pain or another but smiled. "She's my mom. I don't think she wants me to become an owner of the company the way Delia does, though."

"Oh?"

"It's Delia's father's business. She'd like me to marry into it."

He let out a double-intensity groan.

Chapter 7

Quiche prepared and in the fridge, guests directed to several don't-miss-this spots like the Cupola House and the Washington Island Ferry landing, Jordan tucked under a chenille throw with an ice pack, and a roaring fire in the parlor fireplace, Amanda hustled to take care of inn bookwork and sketch out a traffic flow plan for the Christmas Tea hors d'oeuvre buffet.

Jordan's presence in the parlor would make a unique traffic flow obstacle.

What was she saying? Once his back muscles relaxed, he'd be fine. She'd be fine. Her concerns could be redirected toward her assignment and off the twinges she felt every time he winced.

Compassion was one thing, but this soul-deep caring could exit at any time.

The kitchen cleanup had to wait this once. Good thing guests weren't expected in the kitchen. The floor still needed a good sweeping.

She made a mental note to change the lightbulb in the

refrigerator when she had a chance, if she could find that size and wattage bulb among the supplies in the pantry. She'd put Jordan on that case, but at the moment, he was—

Calling for her.

She could see what he wanted before he told her. And smell it.

"Smoke!" She rushed to the parlor fireplace with her nose pressed into her sleeve. Black smoke snuck into the room through the slit above the glass doors, a wide curtain of smoke like a larger version of a snuffed candle. *Many* snuffed candles.

"Try the damper!" Jordan suggested, but she was already on the case, wiggling the curled iron handle until it caught and the smoke reversed direction.

Black-brown soot discolored the glass doors and stole up the fireplace tiles toward the mantel. One added thing to clean before more guests arrived. And before the arrival of Jordan's rival, Blake.

"Won't this make a lovely cover shot for *Inns and Outs*?" she said as she whirled around to face him, palm extended, covered in soot.

He crouched on all fours, head low like an errant puppy. "I tried. I did try."

In that much pain, he attempted to save the day? Her crouching hero.

"No harm done," she consoled, "except the smell. And the soot."

She wiped her blackened palm on the dish towel that seemed always in hand, flung it over her shoulder, and reached to help him back to the settee.

Tinny music signaled a call coming in on Jordan's cell phone. He'd uploaded a ring tone. What do you know? A song she recognized—"Where Have You Been All My Life?"

Still crouching, he answered. "Blake. Hey, man. What's up? Me? I'm doing. . .well, nose to the grindstone, you know."

More like nose to the Oriental carpeting. She held her comment and pondered it in her heart.

Jordan listened and commented with short okays and uh-huhs.

Details about the article, no doubt. Her pulse raced at the thought of presenting the inn in its best possible light to someone accustomed to five stars and valet parking.

Door County could give him a sky full of stars, his fill of artistry and cherry jam, an eclectic mix of rocky shorelines and apple blossoms, and a wide spot next to the inn's garage.

But could she live up to what the inn deserved? How long would a Broadway play hold the interest of the critics if the stand-in for the lead actress missed the high notes?

She slumped onto the settee, waiting for Jordan's conversation to end. Her feet tingled their gratitude for the break.

All the layered muscles in her shoulders ached. Rubbing the back of her neck with both hands, she found two knots the size of grapes. But the sight of Jordan crawling toward the nearest piece of furniture—the one where she sat—silenced her internal whine.

He easily won the "who hurts worse?" contest.

"It dawns on me," he said, phone now quiet, "that tension might be playing some minor role in these muscle spasms."

Gingerly, he hoisted himself onto the settee, refusing Amanda's aid. He sat this time, curled forward but more vertical than horizontal. "That was Blake, as you might have gathered."

Light from the fireplace flickered in his face. How late was it that the fire showed up so well? The oven timer hadn't dinged yet. But daylight had made itself scarce. "Everything okay?"

He rested his forearms on his knees and clasped his hands together. They moved up and down as if he were using a two-handed grip to cast a fishing line. "Blake wants to bring a film crew."

"What?" The muscles around her windpipe stiffened.

"He thinks there's promo potential for the magazine's video spots on their Web site. I—I couldn't tell him no."

"Why not?"

"Because I'm a slug."

Chapter 8

Why did a river run through the kitchen? She should have taken time to sweep the floor the night before. Now bits of bark floated on a congealed, butter-slicked creek that flowed from its headwaters—the refrigerator.

Amanda splashed through the flood on tiptoe and yanked open the fridge door. Still no light. And not cool.

Milk stared at her from the shelf on the door. Leftover turkey gave off an odor faintly resembling the inside of a well-used Dumpster. And the quiche!

She grabbed the handle of the freezer compartment. It gave way too easily. The reassuring fan was mute. And the air that oozed out of the freezer was disturbingly close to room temperature.

The door had been left ajar? How had that happened? And how does a state-of-the-art appliance like that stop working for no good reason?

Though they stayed in their containers, in her mind the preparations for the Christmas Tea formed melted, moldy, inedible globules.

She slammed the door shut. With a jerk, she opened it again. Same outcome. A waxed carton of cherry pecan ice cream collapsed when she picked it up, releasing a tributary of cream and flotsam to join the water on the floor.

The sound of running water overhead told her the guests in Beach Rose were awake and showering. They'd expect breakfast in the sunroom within the hour.

The quiche she'd half-baked the night before puddled in its pie plate. The cream for the coffee was just shy of sour. Fresh ingredients couldn't be trusted. Probably passable for family, but certainly not for company.

She pirate-arghed and stomped her foot. Flotsam splashed up the leg of her jeans. She'd have to change clothes, too.

But first, she'd answer the doorbell.

"Jordan, what are you doing here so early?" And why was he using the front door?

"Thought you could use some help."

She stepped to the side to let him in, judging his pain level by the tilt of his axis. Not bad. Almost good posture. "Are you feeling better?"

"Much. Thanks. I spent some time in the hot tub last night. Between the ice, the hot jets, and your TLC, I think I'm on the mend. Thank you."

She brushed off his words. "You don't have to keep thanking me."

His gaze held hers captive. "May I keep. . .appreciating?"

A tenor version of Barry White—smooth, his voice landed on her ears like a long-awaited burst of heat from a cold vent. Ahh.

He glanced down at the hems of her jeans. "Fall through the ice skiff on the edge of the beach this morning?"

It did look as if she'd been cavorting in spume. "Long

story. I think we're well into the Book of Job."

"What?"

He set a white bakery box on the seat of the hall tree and shrugged out of his jacket. Reaching toward one of the hooks he stopped mid-move.

"Your back?"

"I won't be moving mountains today, but I'm grateful to know Someone who can." He dropped the jacket next to the bakery box.

She didn't feel up to moving any moun—

Oh. He meant the Lord. Yes, she was grateful, too.

Eyeing the mystery object, she asked, "What's in the box?"

"Caramel apple fritters. Couldn't resist."

Fritters and fruit. Practically an entire breakfast. "How . . .how many?"

Back straight, he bent at the knees to pick up the box. "I don't know why, but a dozen jumped out at me."

It may not have been "proportionate," but she stood on tiptoe and kissed his smooth-shaven cheek. His winter-cold, muscled, clean-smelling cheek.

Heart pounding, she swiped the box from him and headed to the kitchen, calling, "Thanks for breakfast!"

"You don't have to keep thanking me," he said, his voice and pace losing ground to her sprint.

She turned to back through the swinging door. "May I keep appreciating?"

She hoped her smile conveyed the depth of her gratitude. Now to wade to the counter and cut open a muskmelon before the guests upstairs made their way downstairs.

❄

"What happened here?" Jordan stepped across the kitchen

floor on the few dry spots as if crossing a creek on mossy rocks.

"A miserable disaster." She stood on a sandbar of dry floor to scoop seeds from the melon. "I don't even know all the damages yet, but the fridge isn't working."

Gathering sugar and—horrors—artificial creamer from the cupboard above the coffee machine, she arranged an antique serving tray of supplies.

"Oh, Amanda."

"I know. Some of the things in the freezer section are gone. I hope I can salvage the items that could afford to thaw overnight."

"A closed freezer will hold cold for more than overnight. We should be okay."

Amanda's shoulders tensed. "Well, see, that's the thing. The door was ajar. I must not have shut it. Don't know how I did that."

She puttered with cups and saucers and grabbed a jar of home-canned sweet cherry juice from the pantry shelf. If she nestled it in the snow outside the kitchen door for a few minutes, it would chill nicely.

"Oh, Amanda," he repeated, his voice tinged with profound weight.

The apple fritters looked and smelled both divine and enormous. Practically—she sighed again—a whole breakfast.

Six of them filled the platter she'd chosen. Without pausing in her efforts, she said, "Look, Jordan, I'm drowning in guilt here. I don't need more. Just so you know."

"No. It was my fault."

"Noble, and all that, but it's pretty obvious I—"

"When I dropped the broom." He pressed one shoulder against the wall by the back of the refrigerator and peered into the blackness. "The cord's unplugged."

She couldn't afford the time to stop and assess whether she were more grateful it was his fault, not hers, or more sad that at least some of Lola's careful preparations would wind up in the garbage.

Taking a deep breath, she decided to be thankful she didn't need to replace the appliance lightbulb after all.

The light had been out. She should have thought to check the plug first. Too much on her mind.

"I guess I know where I stand," Jordan said, his face masked in a pain she'd seen when he'd hobbled to the settee.

"Your back again?"

"No. I asked if you'd forgive me. You didn't answer."

Footsteps and laughter announced hungry breakfast guests.

"Jordan, I have to go play hostess."

He nodded. "Go. I'll clean up." At what must have seemed incredulity in her facial expression, he added, "I can't bend over, but I have feet."

He dropped a wad of paper towels on the floor and scooted them around to sop up the mess. The first batch of towels well soaked, he looked up, sheepish, with no power to get them any farther.

Chuckling, she pushed through the kitchen door muttering, "Jordan, what am I going to do with you?"

It must have been the competing conversation from the Fitzgerald-Rileys and Solomons. She thought she heard him say, "Love me anyway."

❋

Off for another day of sightseeing, dried cherry tasting, gift-shop–hopping, and a festival or two, the inn's guests would enjoy their Saturday while Jordan and Amanda pushed paper towels and filled plastic garbage bags with things well shy of their true expiration dates.

A healthy dose of forgiveness all around, they worked companionably.

She encouraged Jordan to rest often, as much concerned for his back as with the selfish need to keep him in good shape for the challenges of the next two weeks.

She mentally ticked off what she remembered from the pages of Lola's notebook. Invitations and advertising had been printed and delivered before Amanda arrived. She'd pressed tablecloths and cloth napkins already. More than a hundred snowy white napkins with The Heart's Harbor Inn embroidered in gold metallic thread in one corner. After the kitchen cleanup, she'd take inventory of what foodstuffs she'd have to eliminate from the menu.

And how she'd manage to disappear when Blake's film crew arrived.

"How long did it take you to get over it?" Jordan emptied a carton of whipping cream into the sink while he asked.

"I think I'll hang onto my remorse about the freezer door a few more hours, if you don't mind." She wiped something sticky off a glass shelf inside the belly of the fridge.

"I mean about the wedding."

She popped her head out of the cavern.

Tapping the carton on the inside lip of the sink, he said, "You don't have to tell me if you don't want to. But I need. . . I'd like to know."

She dove back into the fridge and scrubbed at a stubborn spot. "You mean, when did I stop crying about it?"

He held the door to prop it open. "I would guess the pain wasn't gone when the tears stopped."

The washrag in her hand needed rinsing. That's why she

backed away. "Is this about me, Jordan, or about you and Delia?"

His eyes clouded like a bad day in November. "Both."

"What do you want to know?"

"Just tell me it's better to speak up if you can't see a future with someone, no matter how much it might hurt that person."

She studied him. A new ache rippled through her. The kiss. He'd assumed it meant she was growing attached to him. She wasn't. She'd have to make that clear.

To herself, too.

The counter sat littered with the salvageables—catsup, salsa, tamari sauce, orange marmalade, lemon curd, blackberry jam. The ice maker hummed again. The last smudge disappeared as she rubbed it away.

"All I can say is what you already know, Jordan." She abandoned invisible spots, filled a glass of water from the faucet, and handed it to him for the ibuprofen he'd dug from his shirt pocket. "It's not even remotely kind to wait until the wedding day to show your true feelings."

He downed the pain reliever and set the glass on the island. "We've been a couple for so long. People expect we'll plan a honeymoon one of these days." He laughed, but not full-bodied. Pinched and strained. "She already is. Mediterranean cruise."

"Is that what you want?"

He twirled the water glass. "I prefer the Northwoods."

"That's not what I meant."

"I know." He scrubbed his face with his palms. "I don't want to hurt her."

Amanda gulped back her history and her discomfort that this conversation meant as much to her as it did. "How long have you known you and she were heading different directions?"

"Six months, maybe."

She exhaled the breath she'd held. It wasn't her fault.

"Delia has a lot of good qualities, but every time she drools over a ring in a jewelry store display or sees a commercial for a bridal shop, a hollow emptiness overwhelms me. I wouldn't feel that way with. . .other people."

The thermostat must have been bumped. The room grew stifling hot.

He shrugged. "I thought it didn't matter that she. . . assumed things about our relationship. . .and that I let her. That wasn't fair. Not to her or to me."

Voices in the front foyer signaled the inn's guests had returned.

Jordan tilted his head as if more intent on that conversation than the one before them. His back rigid, he pushed open the kitchen door like a football player might stiff-arm a defender.

She followed him, breathing deeply to regain an innkeeper's welcoming decorum.

He stopped abruptly, his gaze focused on the woman engaged in conversation with the Solomons.

"Delia! What are you doing here?"

Chapter 9

Delia's fur muff turned out to be a sweatered, ribboned, booted Yorkie named Pendleton. It did not surprise Amanda to learn both had done some modeling, a fact the woman managed to work into the conversation shortly after, "You must be the temp. Arlene, was it?"

"Amanda."

Her smooth-as-polished-marble skin seemed incapable of moving despite the vocal animation of the harried tale of her flight into the Ashwaubenon airport. "Or should I call it a landing strip?" She removed gold lamé gloves from her slim fingers without losing her grip on Pendleton.

The Solomons excused themselves and disappeared up the stairs while Delia batted her squirrel-tail eyelashes at Jordan.

Jordan, the Dumbstruck.

"What are you doing here, Delia?" He looked back and forth from the pencil-thin, wouldn't-be-caught-dead-in-something-from-a-clearance-rack woman to Amanda.

"Silly, I came for you." Delia grabbed him by the front of his shirt and drew him toe-to-toe with her pointed,

71

Titan-missile boots.

Amanda tugged at her sweatshirt where it rode up in the back and noticed the tips of her leather flats were dotted with something unrecognizable that probably originated on a refrigerator shelf.

Delia offered a coat sleeve to Jordan.

He obliged with a look on his face that told Amanda his pain relievers had not yet kicked in.

"Poor Pene"—Delia pronounced it like the pasta—"had a tough time on the flight. Didn't you, sweetest?" She rubbed snouts with the dog. "The attendant was not at all sympathetic. I told her, 'That's what dogs do when they're nervous!' Arlene, would you be a dear and get me a diet soda? I'm parched. Thanks so much."

A muscle near Amanda's left eye spasmed. "I have tea . . .or tea." At the last moment, she remembered to smile a hostess smile.

Delia turned her attention to removing Pendleton's woof-wear. "Just water, then."

Jordan headed for the kitchen. "I'll get it."

Oh no, you don't. You're not leaving me here with— "I need to set out cookies for the guests. I'll take care of it." She caught up with Jordan and pushed him Delia's direction. "You two probably have a lot to talk about."

With the cupboard door open and an array of choices of glassware before her, she contemplated something in a fine plastic. *Lord, I apologize. Jealousy is as ugly on me as on anyone else.* She sighed and selected a cut-glass, stemmed water goblet. Serving had nothing to do with whether or not the person deserved it.

Delia accepted the glass of water with a quick "Thanks," sipped, then lowered it for the dog still tucked under her arm.

"Don't drink too fast, Mr. Pendleton. You'll get a cold pain."

With cookies rattling on the plate in her hand like loose shutters in a windstorm, Amanda asked the Lord to supersize her request for grace, left the two, and climbed the stairs to deposit the cookies on the small table in the up-stairs hall.

By the time she returned to the foyer, it was empty except for Delia's luggage and Pendleton's carrier.

Her luggage.

She planned to stay.

Amanda located Delia and Jordan in the front parlor, standing with their backs to the Christmas tree.

"It's charming in a primitive sort of way." Delia slipped one arm around Jordan's waist. He reacted as if stung by mid-winter static electricity.

The supersized grace disappeared like a small order of fries.

Delia tweaked the fabric of his shirt with her thumb and forefinger, sighing melodramatically. "Oh, you are such a prude! Leftovers from your mother's iron hand, I guess. I'll wear you down one of these days."

Amanda picked at a hangnail and avoided eye contact with Jordan. She should show Delia to her room. *How does the garage sound to you? It has a lovely view of the workbench and an* en suite *ambulance for your convenience.*

In the ensuing wordlessness, Amanda heard two distinct sounds—the thrumming of her pulse in her neck and the *tick-tick-tick* of canine nails on hardwood.

She turned to see the Yorkie trot across the foyer with a glittered harp in his mouth, proud as a hound dog who remembered where he buried a bone.

How many ornaments were missing from the lower

branches of the music tree?

"Baby, give that to Mommy! Glitter's not healthy for you." Delia trotted after him, her boots mimicking the dog's *tick-tick-tick*. He disappeared around the corner, in the direction of the second parlor.

Amanda signaled to Jordan in SWAT team sign language to circle around through the pocket-door archway that connected the two parlors. She followed Delia.

The three humans reconnoitered as the nonhuman took off running with his new chew toy—a string of Christmas lights.

The humans ran for cover as the tree toppled, laid flat by an animal the size of a gallstone.

❄

Amanda left Delia to warm Pendleton's ground sirloin to an estimated 89 degrees—visibly miffed that Amanda couldn't locate the inn's meat thermometer—while she righted the tree and Jordan registered another guest.

He'd volunteered to tackle tree cleanup, but his body language let her know his back was more suited to processing credit cards than ornament retrieval. He acquiesced without a fight, which said a lot.

She finished, vacuumed pine needles and sparkling debris from the Oriental rug, checked the piano for collateral damage—none—then headed to see if the new arrival needed a restaurant recommendation.

"All taken care of," Jordan announced.

"Are you feeling okay?"

He refilled the bowl of caramels from a stash in the desk drawer. "I'm...fine." His line of sight drifted to a spot near the base of the stairway.

Delia's luggage perched where it had landed when she

showed up. She entered from the dining room and handed Amanda a saucer that looked as if it came from the antique Blue Willow set in the china hutch. It smelled like ground meat.

"I don't know how you get anything done in that kitchen, Arlene."

"Her name's Amanda." Jordan moved away from the desk.

Delia startled. "I would insist on two dishwashers. The one you have is full."

Jordan took the saucer from Amanda and extended it toward Delia. "You'll find the dish soap in a dispenser near the sink."

"Oh." She glanced around as if searching for a place to deposit the dish. "Well, first things first. Jordan, my bags?"

"What was I thinking?" he said, but made no move toward the luggage. "What was I thinking?"

Amanda chewed on her bottom lip and waited for one or the other to say something more.

A radio announcer would have called it dead air.

Delia repositioned the perky-eared dog in the crook of her left arm. "Jordan?"

"Amanda?" Jordan said, taking Delia by her right elbow. "Would you excuse us? We'll be in the kitchen."

"This silly plate can wait," Delia said, her voice registering a note of concern.

Jordan glanced at Amanda before addressing the woman who didn't have pinesap and glitter on her hands. "Yes, but our conversation can't."

❄

The items lining the aisles of the Main Street Market in downtown Egg Harbor swam before her as Amanda trudged through the task of restocking the now operational fridge and freezer. Breakfast ideas for her guests. Staples. And what would she do about replacing the supply of hors d'oeuvres and desserts for the Christmas Tea?

She picked up a package of Medjool dates. Bacon-wrapped dates stuffed with an herbed goat cheese. Not the everyday menu in her Chicago apartment but worthy of the Tea.

The price on the sticker made her think of Jordan.

Everything made her think of Jordan.

Elements of the meals they'd shared together. Ingredients for meals she wanted to have a chance to share with him. The way his jaw moved when he bit into an apple. Molasses and ginger for cookies he "preferred." Carrots—*does he carrot all?*

Ground sirloin. Actually, that made her think of Delia and the conversation in which she and Jordan were engaged at that moment.

Somewhere between jars of lingonberry jam and lemon curd, she turned a corner. Not in the aisles. In her thinking.

Lord God, preserve their relationship, if that's what You want.

He wouldn't want that, would He?

She caught herself. If her heart obeyed her mind, she'd want what God wanted more than she longed for the opportunity to see if she and Jordan Peterson could build a genuine friendship. . .or more.

Delia may have assumed too much between them. Amanda couldn't afford to be guilty of the same thing. Again.

At the checkout, she realized letting Jordan go would take a lot more praycr. She'd loaded the conveyor belt with artichoke *hearts, hearts* of Romaine, *heart*-healthy granola, *heart*-shaped Cheddar, and *hearts* of palm.

❄

Delia's rental car had disappeared from the driveway. That either meant she and Jordan had left for a candlelit "Baby, come back" reconciliation dinner or—

Jordan's car was gone, too.

She trucked the groceries into the kitchen, then left the bags on the island and stared through the unfettered windows into the deepening night.

Where the weak light of a slivered moon reached, the bay glistened—snow and ice. Ice covered much of the harbor. Before long, it would be dotted with ice fishing shanties and crisscrossed with footprints of hearty locals braced by winter's invigoration.

Tonight, it looked blue-cold, stark, frozen.

She'd be okay. The Lord would see to that. But why couldn't things ever work out the way she wanted?

Somewhere beyond the kitchen door, the inn settled for the night, guests returning like sons and daughters from their adventures, finding their rooms, whispering secrets, and cozying up.

She left the grocery items untended and made her way to the laundry room. Towels could agitate while she found room in the inn for ridiculous things like artichoke hearts.

Jordan must have moved his mother's Christmas cactus. It sat on the table near the window, boasting tiny pink buds on the tips of several jagged branches, buds the size of swollen grains of rice.

Lola's notebook had specified the Christmas cactus serve a prominent position of welcome and hope in the Heart's Harbor foyer during the Christmas Tea. A few days ago, it had sat abandoned and forlorn on a high ledge. Its lifeless branches held no visible promise. Now. . .

As she slid the last of the refrigerated items into spots on the blissfully cool fridge shelves, the inn's phone rang. She eyed the bowl of apples on the island, contemplating apple slices with caramel cream cheese spread for her late supper, and reached for the phone.

"Amanda?"

"Jordan. Where are you?" Not that she had any right to ask.

"At the airport."

"Oh?" Her pulse quickened. "Delia's leaving?"

A crisp intake of breath told her Jordan wasn't ready to spill the whole story. "She is. I'll be on the same flight."

Her back pressed into the cupboard and knees bent, she slid to the floor. "You're not staying?" Her voice sounded like audible fog. She must be coming down with something.

Disappointment.

"I have every confidence in you, Amanda."

That makes one of us.

"You'll do a great job with the Tea. It's as if you were born to innkeeping."

She had her answer about how the couple's conversation ended. Jordan was on his way back to—

"What are you doing about your SUV?"

"I have a buddy who lives here in Green Bay. He'll let me park it at his house for now."

"You'll come back for it." She cringed at the pathetic hope threaded through her statement.

Had they lost the phone connection? No, she heard people noises in the background.

"Amanda. . ."

Over the sound of his sigh, she heard the distinct bark of a gallstone-sized dog.

❄

Dateless weekends consumed with Food Network reruns weren't for nothing. Amanda was flush with ideas for charming tablescapes and clever ways to make chicken salad look fancy by scooping it into endive nests. She knew how to dip dried apricots in melted chocolate chips and how to make a curlicue on a piece of homemade fudge.

She was grateful Lola had the foresight to block off the ten days prior to the Tea. No guest rooms to ready. No conversation to carry. No award-winning breakfasts to prepare or clean up after.

And no Jordan.

The inn suffered from his absence. It missed him.

The week passed with no communication from him other than a couple of e-mails bent on business. Was the debit card working out okay for inn expenses? Had she had time to fill out the preliminary information for Blake's production team? What was the long-range weather forecast for the night of the Tea? No mention of Delia or how deliriously happy he was with his choice.

She answered his questions, hit SEND, and then ate a piece of chocolate.

Every time he e-mailed.

Lola's Bible study women showed up the Thursday before the Tea, mops, dust rags, and Pledge in hand. "Tradition," they said.

Tears burned behind Amanda's eyes. She'd worked so hard, but it never seemed enough. Always another surface to dust, another floor to mop, another load of firewood to bring in or clean up after.

Like everything these days, firewood made her think of Jordan.

Innkeeping was a job for two people. How did Lola do it alone now that Harland was swimming in hallways, flying biplanes, and directing invisible concerts?

While Amanda tended the oven timer and stayed out of their way, the Bible study women sparkled up the place to background music of Josh Groban's latest Christmas CD. They took great care with the inn's furnishings and decorations, as if they, too, respected the role the inn played in people's relationships, not just their vacations.

"What do you want me to do with this?" Kari Anne Johannsen peeked out from behind an armload of Lola's Christmas cactus. Buds covered the plant. Tight-lipped yet, they gave only a hint of what was to come. Was there any hope it would be in full flower in less than forty-eight hours?

Amanda fingered a bud. It broke off into her hand.

"Well, don't mess with it!" Kari Anne said, her plump arms turning the plant from Amanda's reach. "Lola always says love and plants bloom best if you don't mess with them." She winked at Amanda.

What was that for? Amanda felt a rush of heat creep up her neck.

"This usually sits on a plant stand in the foyer. Is that where you want it?" Kari Anne headed toward the foyer as if the answer were already yes.

"I do," she said.

Unfortunate choice of words.

Amanda, get that thought out of your head. Jordan spoke his mind when he purchased a plane ticket back to Phoenix. So much for budding hope.

❄

Kari Anne and the rest of the crew of women left—smelling of furniture polish, bleach, and failed antiperspirant—promising to arrive early enough on Saturday to help Amanda with last-minute preparations. They surrounded her in a stifling but heartwarming group hug and prayed for her and for the Tea's success.

She was certain they didn't measure success by numbers. Or by the volume of *oohs* and *aahs*. She bit back an impossible longing to join their circle every Thursday night and keep her lifelong focus where it should be.

Though glistening and polished, the inn felt especially empty when the women returned to their homes and families. Amanda switched the CD player to soft instrumental carols and turned her attention to the misbehaving lights on the tree in the front parlor.

Which bubble light had gone on strike and taken the rest of the string with it?

Problem solved, she checked the inn's e-mail inbox. No messages from Arizona. Half a dozen messages requesting information about future reservations. An ad from an animal talent agency that somehow slipped through the spam filter. Nothing from jpeterson@.

Blake and his *Inns and Outs* crew would arrive late afternoon the next day. Amanda forced her breathing to slow. The inn told its own story. Lola's legacy of caring—and showing it—lingered in every corner, even without her physical presence. Amanda needed only to get out of the way and let it speak.

Still. . .

They'd requested three of the guest rooms for Friday night but planned to head south as soon as the Tea concluded. They had planes to catch for Myrtle Beach early Sunday morning and would stay near the airport Saturday night.

Amanda had only to survive entertaining a crew used

to high-end accommodations and five-star breakfasts for a little more than twenty-four hours. . .in the middle of pulling together the final details for the inn's biggest event of the year and the feature article that could ensure its fiscal health.

No sweat.

She started to sweat.

❄

The road-weary crew arrived seven hours later than expected. Friday was almost Saturday before they put away their cameras and video equipment for the night. Amanda lost her train of thought several times in the glare of the lights and lenses, but Blake served as a skilled and charming interviewer.

Amanda apologized for Jordan's absence. Blake acted as if he knew the story and didn't press the issue.

She gathered bowls and mugs from the crew's popcorn and hot cider. "Tomorrow's a big day. I think I'd better turn in."

Blake pointed toward Kyle, the cameraman, stretched out on the rug in front of the fire, a purring snore coming from his open mouth. "Looks like one of us already did." He gave Kyle a nudge with his foot. "Come on, man. Let's clear out and let this lovely lady get her beauty sleep." He said the word *beauty* as if leaning on the *ooo* syllable.

A little too charming.

❄

The cattle are lowing, the poor baby wakes.

What?

Why would cattle be lowing outside her window?

She bolted upright in bed, threw back the covers, and raced to the window. A livestock truck sat idling in the driveway.

On the snow-covered lawn stood a Holstein, a donkey, three sheep, and a camel.

A camel!

Bales of hay formed a semicircle corral. A man in an ear-flap hat and barn boots held a bevy of reins in one hand and a travel mug in the other.

She turned the brass lock on the window and urged it open. A blast of cold air shivered her timbers.

"What are you doing? Can I. . .help you?"

She caught the attention of Mr. Barn Boots but didn't have to worry about disturbing the sleeping film crew. They'd already joined the zoo in the yard.

"Lady, you in charge?" He gestured toward her with his travel mug.

She watched Kyle film a close-up of the cow ripping a snack off a hay bale. "Not as much as one would think."

"Where you want we should set up the stable?"

"What stable?" A pinprick of a headache stung her temple.

"For the live nativity." He held his arms out, which yanked the reins of heretofore docile sheep.

Kyle zoomed in for a close-up of her.

She threw on her clothes and shot down the stairs, grabbing a breath mint on the way to substitute for brushing her teeth. This was not how she envisioned the "Big Day" starting.

Frost on the porch steps made her take them more gingerly than her pounding heart would have wanted. She slid to a halt beside Mr. Barn Boots as he handed a crumpled brochure to a grinning Blake.

"Animals Got Talent. That's us. Birthdays. Bar mitzvahs. But not much call for a camel in them scenarios, you know?

Ernine don't get out much." He patted the camel's muzzle.

The morning air froze the lining of her lungs. Or was that because she was gasping?

"Mr. . . ?"

Blake held the brochure to her. "Franson."

"Mr. Franson, you must have the wrong place." Amanda gritted her teeth as the cow made a yellow canyon in what was once an unbroken stretch of snow. Hoofprints—large and small—punctured the snow like a quilter with no sense of direction.

Kyle captured it all.

"The wrong place."

"No, ma'am," Franson said, taking a slug of something from his thermal mug. "Look, you don't want the stable? Okay. You're still paying for it. I already cut you a deal by agreeing to play Joseph. And the wife's no spring chicken, but she's pulled off Mary before, the year our niece got the rabies, which by the way, was not Stinkster's fault."

Did high blood pressure run in the Brooks family? Stroke? Her pulse throbbed near her tonsils. "We can't have— We don't need— I don't know how—"

Blake stepped over a pile of something and thumbed a message on his BlackBerry, chuckling as he did.

Amanda's right knee buckled, nudged by a sheep who needed to blow his nose.

She stabilized her footing, chose to ignore the smear on her pant leg, and addressed the animal talent agent/Joseph look-alike. "I'm sorry if there's been a misunderstanding. I did not order a live nativity."

From behind her came the words, "I did."

She swung around sharply. "Jordan!"

❄

After handshakes and back slaps and a miniature version of catching up, Blake took his crew to the Bistro for breakfast. Under the circumstances—and the threat of a sheep revolt over Ernine upstaging them—it seemed the best plan.

Amanda's Cherry Drizzle Puff Pancakes wouldn't make it into the magazine spread. By the chortles and snorts coming from Blake, she wasn't sure the Heart's Harbor would make it.

Mr. Franson and his truck-driving nephew staked the animals and set about erecting the birch bark stable.

Birch.

Somehow she doubted the woods around Bethlehem held stands of birch, but the dark notches of black were pretty against the snow scene.

While they worked, Amanda and Jordan retreated to the kitchen.

"I forwarded you the message about the nativity," he said, pouring a cup of coffee for her and one for himself.

Her thoughts raced back through the incoming e-mails. "Animals Got Talent."

"Right." He leaned against the sink.

His back must be feeling better.

"When you didn't respond, I thought. . .I thought you'd be fine with it." He stared into his cup. "I didn't think about the mess. It seemed like a good idea, a way to keep the focus of the Tea on the reason there's a Christmas."

"There's a camel in our yard."

He caught her gaze and held it. "The elephant was too expensive."

Tension's dam released in a flood of laughter. It swept through them, washing away barriers and softening hard edges.

They guffawed like the audience at Doorbuster's Comedy Theater. The laughter settled, only to erupt a moment later when they tried to keep a lid on it.

Amanda choked down another outburst but saw a look on Jordan's face that undid her. Joy. The look was one of joy. And she was privileged to share it.

His joy sobered her.

"Jordan, why did you come back?"

He turned his head toward the windows through which the sunlit harbor beckoned despite the snow and ice. "I didn't come back."

She exhaled a shuddery breath.

With movements as slow as a melting glacier, he turned his attention to her and reached for her hand. His thumb drew half moons of warmth. "I didn't come back. I came home."

❄

"You quit your job?" Amanda snatched her hand away—an action in which she was far too practiced. "What were you thinking?"

"Exactly. What was I thinking building a future there with someone like Delia, rather than here with someone like. . ."

How long can a person hold her breath before passing out?

"Someone like you, Amanda."

"You went back with her."

"With her. Not *to* her. I had a long talk with her father. He gave me grief for a day and a half, then started wooing my replacement. So did Delia."

"Oh, Jordan."

"This isn't heartbreaking. It's liberating." He stretched his arms to the side. "I'm finally obeying what the Lord's been telling me for a long time. And a short time."

She kept her eyes on his and felt him encircle her hand again. "A. . .a short time?"

"Since I met you." He swallowed. "I waited too long to tell someone I didn't love her. I don't want to wait too long to tell someone I do."

Love?

He swallowed again. "I know we haven't had much time together, and every minute has been filled with one crisis or another."

Love?

"But I'd like an opportunity to pursue this and see where the Lord leads our. . .our relationship."

Did he say love?

The ceiling was caving in. Either that or someone was knocking at the door.

Mr. Barn Boots. "Yeah, uh, where could I get me some water to keep them animals happy? Ernine may be a camel, but she drinks like a fish."

Chapter 10

Working together, Jordan and Amanda prepped the inn for the influx of Lola and Harland's friends and local businesspeople. Blake's team took shots and video footage of three-tiered dessert plates and sheep tugging on Baby Jesus' blanket, of chicken salad in endive cups and gurgling bubble lights, of the orchid sunset over the harbor and the orchid-like flowers blooming in profusion on the Christmas cactus in the foyer.

"Blake, buddy," Jordan said, "believe me, I value this chance to have Heart's Harbor featured in your magazine. But this Tea is for our guests. And to honor Christ. Can your crew make as little disruption as possible?"

Blake's raised eyebrows communicated he wasn't used to being asked to step aside and had probably never been asked to step aside for a King.

"If that's how you want it. We have plenty of footage. I'd like to have Kyle get a few candid shots and maybe a couple of quotes from the guests. Then we'll take off."

Jordan slipped his arm around Amanda's shoulders.

"Thanks. We appreciate it."

We. Our. Us. She liked the sound of that.

BlackBerry in hand, Blake asked, "Can I print our boarding passes?"

Amanda looked down at her thrown-together outfit from her early morning visit to the stable. "I need to change."

Jordan invited Blake to use the registration desk printer. Joshing again as college roommates should, the two men angled for the desk and Amanda headed for the stairs. She heard Blake ask, "When do you expect your first guests?"

A rush of air from the front door accompanied a sweet voice saying, "The first one's already here."

Flush-cheeked and sparkle-eyed, goggles gone, stood the infamous Lola Peterson.

❄

If Lola were a candy, she'd be called Hugs-a-Plenty. With no time for talk but a quick round of hugs for all, including Blake, Lola tried to shoo Amanda upstairs to change.

"Pretend I'm not here," Lola said, with a wink toward her son. "I'm invincible."

Invisible. "But the Tea is your passion," Amanda protested, her pulse thumping like timpani sticks in the hands of a hyperactive teen. Her assignment was over.

It was—

An ache started at her toenails and worked its way toward her heart. "And now you're home, just in time."

Hands on her hips, Lola faked a frown. "I will have my hands full keeping Harland away from my mini-cheesecakes."

Amanda shot a "how do we break this to her?" look Jordan's way. "About your cheesecakes. . ."

Jordan joined the conversation. "Where's Dad?"

"He took Joseph and Mary for a ride in his ambulance. They won't go far. There's a shepherd with pierced eyebrows and motorcycle boots watching the animals."

Lola wagged her hand at Blake. "You might want to get some pictures when Harland parks the ambulance outside the stable and Mary climbs out."

Blake chuckled. "Kyle! Come here. Bring your camera."

❄

With the Bible study ladies checking coats and manning the beverage station, pushing the specially created Heart's Harbor Cheery Cherry Christmas Tea, Jordan and his parents mingled with the guests. Amanda did her best to stay in the shadows, slipping in and out of the kitchen with trays of desserts and platters of hot hors d'oeuvres.

The inn rang with laughter and Hugs-a-Plenty. Amanda smiled with satisfaction, happy to have played a role in such a special evening. She ran a fresh sinkful of sudsy hot water to wash a stack of serving dishes.

The door to the kitchen swung open.

"There you are." Jordan's voice landed softly on her heart, like a boat gliding into harbor. He drew close and pressed a kiss to her cheek. "Everything turned out beautifully, Amanda. Thank you for all you did. Thanks for. . .for being here when we. . .when I needed you."

With her hands still in the suds, she turned her head toward him to say, "You're welcome," but was stopped by his tender kiss on her lips and his hands cupping the back of her head. One glorious moment. Two.

"Just as I perspective. Suspected."

"Lola!"

"Mom!"

"Oh, don't let me stop you two. This is frosting on the

cherry turnover. I love it when a plan comes together." She closed her eyes and lifted her hands in a "Thank You, Jesus" pose.

Amanda took the towel Jordan offered. "A plan?" Her supercharged brain synapses snapped and sizzled. "Lola, a plan? You *were* on jury duty, weren't you?"

"Well, of course, dear. I judged you two perfect for each other."

Jordan folded his arms across his chest. "No trial?"

Lola pursed her lips. They broke into a coy smile. "I'm sure you've had plenty."

"Mom, you lied to us?" Jordan growled.

The older woman clutched her hands to her chest. "I *was* called for jury duty, but I flunked. Those lawyers. I think they differentiate against scuba gear."

"Discriminate, Mom. And I'm not sure I blame them. Why didn't you come home, then?"

"So my jury only had one person on it. Two. Your father and me. We ruled in favor of the plaintive."

Plaintiff? Amanda couldn't suppress a giggle.

"And in favor of this inn. It's time for Harland and me to retire. He needs. . ." She leaned closer. "He needs a little more help than I've been able to give him."

Jordan and Amanda stepped toward Lola in unison and offered their shoulders and embrace.

"Lola, what can we do for you?"

She looked from one to the other, her eyes glistening. "You could kiss again. We need to kick this romance into high gear if you two are going to run the Heart's Harbor together."

Lola tipped her head back as if expecting them to comply while she waited.

And they might have. But the lights went out.

❄

Jordan used the blue glow of his cell phone to light the path from the darkened kitchen to the main rooms of the inn. They were semi-dark with small circles of cell phone illumination and the radiance from Amanda's—Lola's—well, *their*—well-placed candles.

"It's not just us." Harland pointed to the off-duty ceiling light. "Power's out in the whole village."

Artificial lights were snuffed until all that remained were the flames. Conversation in the room quieted. Faces caught in the glow of firelight registered hush, not panic.

Amanda leaned toward Jordan's ear and whispered, "Is that the end of the party?"

"Everyone, could I have your attention?" His voice rose above the subdued undercurrent. He sank onto an upholstered ottoman and pulled her to sit beside him. A long moment passed as he seemed to study her hand in his.

His gaze circled the room. Then he began, " 'And there were in the same country shepherds abiding in their fields, keeping watch over their flocks by night.' "

He recited the Christmas story, the night the Light of the world was born, in a voice thick with emotion.

Amanda warmed to the familiar words and the man through whom they poured, a man beside whom she'd served. Here, in this inn, she'd learned the joy of serving in the same direction.

Power outage. One last disaster-turned-opportunity. Perfect ending.

Jordan's final words—" 'Glory to God in the highest, and on earth, peace to men on whom His favor dwells' " —swept through the room and harbored in her heart.

Whether for radio, novels, or her grand-children, Cynthia Ruchti is a storyteller at heart. She writes and produces the drama/devotional radio broadcast, *The Heartbeat of the Home* and serves as editor of the ministry's *Backyard Friends* magazine. Her debut novel—*They Almost Always Come Home*—released in May of 2010. She is the current president of American Christian Fiction Writers and speaks for women's events and writers' conferences. She and her husband of 38 years live in the heart of Wisconsin. Readers can connect with her through www.cynthiaruchti.com or www.hopethatglowsinthedark.com.

RIDE WITH ME INTO CHRISTMAS

by Rachael Phillips

Dedication

To my husband and best friend, Steve: May the Lord grant that we ride together many more wonderful years.

Door County Sundaes to my writing partners: Eileen Key, Becky Melby, and Cynthia Ruchti, not only creators of the finest fiction, but also connoisseurs of chocolate and cherries.

Special thanks to Rebecca Germany of Barbour Publishing, who surprised me at the 2009 American Christian Fiction Writers Conference with this marvelous opportunity.

Blessings on Kim Peterson, my meticulous mentor who helped edit my manuscript.

Thanks to Peninsula State Park and the businesses and people of Fish Creek, Wisconsin, who all kindly answered this Hoosier's questions.

Glory to Jesus Christ, who desires "to comfort all who mourn, and provide for those who grieve in Zion— to bestow on them a crown of beauty instead of ashes, the oil of gladness instead of mourning, and a garment of praise instead of a spirit of despair."

Isaiah 61:2–3

Chapter 1

Joanna Flick had loved teaching with all her heart, soul, and lesson planner. But this week, she wished she had trained as a plumber.

She'd spent fun, relaxing summers in Door County, Wisconsin. But her new retirement home had become a nightmare. Monday, the dishwasher vomited into the sink. Yesterday, the washer spat like a Little Leaguer. The plumber she called wouldn't give her a two-calls-for-one deal. Now this glum April Saturday, the downstairs toilet moaned and groaned.

She almost yelled for Jim, then choked down the shout like a giant dry pill. Joanna strode into her cute fire-engine red bathroom—the only room in her Danish house that wasn't white. She gave the toilet her famous killer glare.

"Stop that right now." Her steely tone had halted many a student in Milwaukee's Burdick Elementary. With those four magic words, Joanna straightened recess lines, cleared hallways, and halted cafeteria food fights.

But the toilet ignored her.

Joanna lifted the tank's lid. If she jiggled the thingama-bobby, the disobedient toilet would shape up. Nose wrinkled with distaste, she reached into tank water and shook the shaft.

Instead of halting the noise, an Old-Faithful–sized geyser shot into the air.

Joanna clunked the lid onto the tank. It split. Water spurted from the crack like blood from a broken heart.

"Jim!" His name slipped out like a swear word. Her husband had died ten months, one week, and three days ago. These bad spells should be getting further apart, shouldn't they?

"Jim, why did you leave me?"

Only nine thirty in the morning, and she'd already blown it. No gold star today. Joanna kicked the groaning toilet. More water flowed. She bounced her favorite tulip soaps against the shower wall like tennis balls. "I'm so *mad* at you!"

As she retrieved the mop, her glance raked the kitchen, looking for something cheap to destroy.

Her eyes fell on Jim's scraggly plants in the bay window. He'd pitch a fit if he knew she'd neglected his pampered pets these past awful months. In their midst drooped a Christmas cactus. Lola, that odd innkeeper she'd met only twice, sent her the bloomless plant last fall, months after the funeral. Joanna appreciated her thoughtfulness, but the cactus demanded special watering schedules and darkness/light periods. Supposedly, this TLC would make it flower during Joanna's first Christmas alone.

Lola's note said, "I'm praying every day hope will bloom for you, too."

She'd ignored the care sheet. And the cactus hadn't

bloomed that first Christmas without Jim.

Now, this nasty spring day, her fingers itched to shred the withered clump. Her eyes swept over near-dead philodendrons and geraniums. Why not toss out the whole shebang?

"They're history," Joanna muttered in an it's-all-your-fault tone. She reached for the cactus's red ceramic pot. "You first!"

Guarding the cactus, an enormous black spider with scary, hairy legs dared her to take one more step.

She could almost hear its slow, squishy breaths as the swollen, ugly body moved toward her. A shudder ran down her like a horror movie organ scale. Jim, her knight in shining armor for thirty-five years, had killed every arachnid that dared invade their house. But Jim was gone.

For months, Joanna had been telling God she wanted to sit in a lump and never move again. But her body displayed a distinct difference of opinion. Her legs burst through the deck's French doors, and she fled outside.

"Something wrong? Can I help?" A man's deep voice. Her neighbor.

His coffee-colored eyes looked so kind, she blurted, "A spider!"

"What?"

"A spider the size of a Volkswagen! In my kitchen!"

He coughed into his arm, but his eyes twinkled.

Was he laughing? She gave him her killer look, but it didn't work any better on him than it did the toilet.

"I'll take care of it." He cleared his throat. "Where is the spider?"

"On the bay windowsill among the plants." She shuddered. "What if there's more than one?"

He almost patted her shoulder, then pulled back. She followed him slowly. His thick iron gray hair looked as if it had been cut by a combine. But his broad shoulders in the red-and-black flannel shirt made her feel safe enough to mount the steps to the deck.

Lord, please get that thing out of my house. Her miniscule prayer startled her. She and God hadn't talked much lately.

Tiny faith words gave way to fearful fantasies. What if the creature held a family reunion in her kitchen?

After what seemed hours, the man emerged, paper towel in hand. "Mission accomplished." He held it almost under her nose. "Want to see?"

Joanna shook her head violently.

He dumped the wad into her trash can. "I searched the cabinets and around appliances, but didn't find any relatives."

"Thank the Lord." She'd never meant it more.

The man grinned. He had a nice smile.

"I turned the water valve off in your bathroom. Top's broken, but I can fix your toilet—temporarily."

"No, I'll call a plumber. I've inconvenienced you enough, Mr.—"

"Sorensen. Paul Sorensen."

"Joanna Flick." She shivered in the chilly April sunshine and realized she still wore her teddy-bear-footed flannel pajamas, the ones Jim had threatened to burn. Her neighbor probably thought she was an escapee from some psycho geriatric slumber party. She backed toward the French doors. "Thank you so, so much."

"You're so, so welcome."

She dove into the room as if into an ocean.

Inside at last! But the woodstove fire burned low. She'd have to head for the woodpile.

First things first. Joanna edged toward the bay window. No spider, thank heaven. She'd mop the bathroom and get that plumber back ASAP, even if he charged her the moon. But her toes had lost sensation in the damp PJ feet. She shivered. More than anything, Joanna wanted a cheerful fire to warm her feet and heart.

"Stay of execution," she told the plants. "At least for today."

Put on a clean outfit to haul firewood? No way. Joanna stuffed her feet into Jim's boots, grabbed a long coat, and headed outside. She glanced toward Paul's house, a slightly shabby Cape Cod. Nothing like her modern Scandinavian cottage. But very homey.

Budding lilac bushes hid Paul's woodpile, near hers. But his presence was unmistakable. Above the rhythmic *thump* and *cr–r–rack* of his chopping, she heard the happy thunder of his laughter.

❄

His neighbor did it again.

As Paul opened his truck door, she slammed her front door shut. Whenever he turned into his driveway, Joanna dropped whatever she was doing—washing windows or sweeping her deck—and popped back into her house like a cuckoo into its clock.

Paul understood. After Suzanne died, he didn't want to talk to anyone, even God—especially God. It had taken him awhile. *And nobody caught me outside in teddy bear PJs.*

His chuckles soon faded to sympathy. Last summer, he heard of his new neighbor's loss and sent her a card. But Joanna had lived like a hermit. Yesterday, he wanted to give her a hug. But those violet eyes spat laser sparks when he laughed at her spider phobia. Her face, so pale and smooth, it might break with a touch. . . .

He dared glance toward her living room windows. Joanna flitted past like a shadowy silver moth.

When April turned cold, he'd stacked wood on her deck. Once he left a loaf of his apple cardamom bread on her welcome mat. So far, no welcome. But that was okay.

He dragged his leather backpack from the truck, inhaling its pleasant old-friend smell. It weighed a ton. Stacks of papers to grade this weekend. Paul loved teaching math at UW of Green Bay, but he almost hoped Saturday would fulfill the Weather Channel's gloomy prophecies. Otherwise, May sunshine would make him truant.

Angie and Doug and the kids were coming tonight. Not exactly a break. His grandsons, ages eighteen months, four, and six, specialized in destroying his house.

He peered at Joanna's empty window, then lugged groceries in. Louie, his elderly basset hound, didn't stir. Paul watered his cherished plants, then chopped onions and garlic at chef speed. He wanted to bake the boys' favorite lasagna—and maybe a small one for Joanna. The woman looked too thin. She needed to eat.

He'd better move. Dinner even five minutes late caused a major mutiny.

❄

"Grandpa, when can we see the Teddy Bear Lady?" Four-year-old Elijah sounded as if he expected Paul to buy tickets to Storybook Land.

"Were you listening to my silly story?" Paul scrubbed tomato sauce from his face.

"I want to see her." Elijah tuned up his familiar fire-engine wail.

Louie whined and took cover under Paul's chair.

"Shut up, 'Lijah." Six-year-old Daniel covered his ears. P.J., a toddler, imitated him.

"Elijah, don't bother Grandpa." Angie frowned. "She's just a neighbor. You boys play in the other room."

Paul wasn't sure about that idea. But Angie needed space. He sighed. Since her mother died, his daughter didn't smile much.

"I'll watch them." He rose and poured coffee for Angie and Doug. "I want you to sit still five minutes straight. Relax."

"Thanks, Dad." Doug gave him a grateful look.

A crash from the living room sent Paul running. Those boys were too much like their grandpa.

❋

What had possessed him to take all three boys overnight? Daniel wanted seven bedtime stories. Elijah had nightmares. Worst of all, P.J. escaped from his Pack 'n' Play during the night. Paul, hearing the fridge door open, found piles of soggy cereal on his kitchen floor—and P.J. "watering" Paul's favorite potted palm with a half gallon of milk.

Thank the Lord, the weatherman goofed. Paul took them outside to protect what remained of his home and sanity.

"Grandpa! Come race!" Elijah, all smiles, slept well after last night's excitement. So did Daniel and P.J.

Sharing his bed with three octopuses was not Paul's idea of a restful night. Especially when two wet on him.

Still, he lined up beside Elijah at the end of the sidewalk. Daniel joined them. "I'm gonna win."

"No, you won't." Elijah's grin faded.

"Yes, I will." Daniel laughed. "You're just a little boy."

"Can you both beat Grandpa?" Paul interrupted Elijah's shriek.

"Yeah!" The two fighters became allies.

They dashed madly to the fence. P.J. joined them, giggling and running the wrong way. Paul congratulated himself on his superior psychology and the fact he could watch all three.

An hour later, he felt less positive. How many races had they run? Now they were playing cops and robbers. Paul let himself be captured, but the boys fussed about who grabbed the bad guy first. In the middle of a knock-down, drag-out fight, Paul's heart dropped to his feet. *P.J.*

"Boys, where's your little brother?" Paul ran to the bushes by the woodpile. No P.J. He sprinted to the screened porch. No sunny, dirty little face greeted him. No one in the side yards.

"P.J.! Where are you?"

The gate hung open. A thousand terrifying nightmares leered at him. He turned to the boys, still scrapping like puppies. "Daniel, Elijah, sit on the front porch where Grandpa can see you. Do not move. Understand?"

They nodded, suddenly quiet. Daniel led his brother to the Adirondack chairs.

Paul sprinted toward the road. No toddler in sight. When did P.J. disappear? Five minutes ago? Ten? He'd been trying to keep the other two from killing each other. Paul gripped his pounding head and prayed aloud. "Lord, have mercy. Watch over P.J. Please help me find him. God, I'm sorry. I was trying to help Angie. . . ."

His daughter was due in forty-five minutes.

Joanna. Maybe she could help. He dashed for her front door, keeping one eye trained on the boys.

"Can we come, too, Grandpa?"

"In a minute. Stay there!"

His stern tone might keep them still a little longer.

104

"Paul?" Joanna waved from her side yard. She held a happy, muddy P.J.

Paul feared he would fall apart like a handful of Pick-up Sticks.

"Is this little guy yours?" Her calm voice resuscitated him.

"My grandson. Thank you." P.J. came to him, a little reluctantly. "I was playing with the boys in the backyard. Somehow, he escaped."

"They're fast." Joanna patted P.J. "Once I lost my grand-daughter, and I only supervised one, not three."

"Grandpa, are we still in time-out?" Daniel yelled.

Paul gave a small chuckle. "They're confused." He called, "You may get up!"

Daniel and Elijah ran to him. He tousled their hair. "You weren't in time-out, okay?"

"You sounded mad." Daniel looked unconvinced.

"Yeah." Elijah's lip trembled.

Paul hurried to head off another crying jag, trying to hug them all. "I was worried about your brother. I wasn't mad."

"Who's she?" Elijah stared at Joanna.

"This is Mrs. Flick. She found P.J."

His eyes widened. "The Teddy Bear Lady?"

Paul's cheeks overheated like a bad radiator.

"But she doesn't have teddy bears on her clothes." Elijah touched her khakis.

"I'm not wearing them today." Joanna smiled. "Are you hungry? Yesterday I baked *pepparkakor*—Swedish cookies. I like them too well to wait till Christmas."

"Cookies!" Elijah and Daniel cheered.

Joanna's laugh began as he expected—sort of shimmery and sweet—but ended with a snort like his Uncle Herman's.

"I owe you for the nice things you've done." Joanna smiled at Paul, and he forgot all about Uncle Herman.

"You don't, but thanks." Then he remembered his kitchen disaster. "We can snack on the porch."

"Fine. But I need these two big, strong guys to help me."

"Sure." Maybe he could clean up P.J.

The boys followed Joanna like lambs. As Paul carried a fussy P.J. to his door, he heard Elijah say, "I saw you smile at Grandpa. Do you like him?"

Chapter 2

Tap-tap-tap. Sleet rattled her bedroom windows. Joanna, wrapped up like a big burrito, stuck her head out of her quilts. Her calendar said May. The weather said Christmas. A great morning to hibernate.

But last night, an idea teased her. This morning it tickled with get-out-of-bed ruthlessness: a Christmas gift for her granddaughter, Michaela. A rag doll. She rose, yawning. An ideal day to start the project. Maybe a way to kick her morning coma habit.

She dressed, then moved boxes in the spare room until she opened one marked "crafts." Tangled strands of ribbon and lace. A rainbow of scraps, but nothing useful. She'd make a trip to the fabric store, but she wouldn't buy a new pattern. Joanna found the yellowed packet her mother used to make her Christmas doll, Sally Ann.

Memories sent Joanna to her bedroom. Sally Ann, wearing a faded red Christmas dress, possessed one eye and one pigtail. Still, Sally grinned from her dresser, ready to play.

Joanna pondered her idea. Dolls today resembled snooty

miniature mannequins with Hollywood wardrobes. Would Michaela find a rag doll outdated as a dinosaur? Joanna cuddled Sally Ann. Her old friend's hugs still felt good.

Hugs would never become obsolete. She decided to create a "sister" for Michaela, an only child with an absent mom.

Joanna would give the doll yellow yarn pigtails and green eyes like Michaela's. She'd create her own doll face, sketching her granddaughter from photos so this sister would display a definite family resemblance. Excited, Joanna skimmed JPEG files on her kitchen computer.

Inquisitive sunbeams startled her. She peered out the bay window. Fickle Wisconsin had changed her mind. Christmas this morning, May this afternoon. All in a day's moods. Not unlike her own. Joanna chuckled.

She touched a tiny green sprout on the Christmas cactus, glad she hadn't followed through on her threats. The plants deserved a break, having survived her neglect.

She wandered out the front door. Andrew, her son, planted hardy pink and red tulips around her front porch that now surrounded it like a forest of lollipops. Chilly day. But sunbeams hugged her, and the Fish Creek Harbor breeze lured her with its liquid spring touch.

Her cranky stomach complained. She'd forgotten breakfast and lunch. But her fridge was down-to-the-condiments empty.

Her hunger led her like a leashed pet down Main Street to Not Licked Yet, a quirky log-walled restaurant that made the best frozen custard in the civilized world. She shivered at the back of a line of goose-fleshed patrons wearing shorts. The teacher in her couldn't suppress a smile. In spring, everyone was in junior high.

"A Door County Sundae," the man in front ordered.

Rich, creamy custard drenched with gooey hot fudge and warm, luscious cherries, lost in clouds of whipped cream. . .

She had to have one. Cold and warmth. Christmas and May. Yum. She'd eaten half the enormous treat when she spotted Paul wheeling a gimpy bicycle across Main Street. As he passed the restaurant's sign, with its hungry-looking guy wearing a blue-striped beanie, Joanna decided it was too cold. She ducked into the dining room and ordered coffee, hoping Paul would remain outside.

As she ate, she ran her eyes over his Raleigh bike's sharp-looking 1980s gold-and-white frame. Paul drove a junkyard pickup. He probably bought his wardrobe at Goodwill. But his bike, complete with friction shifters, rated a classic. Not everybody could handle those gears.

Paul extracted tools from his bike bag, upended the Raleigh on a level spot, and tinkered. Joanna felt a twinge of longing for her bike—still buried amidst moving crates in the garage.

Paul replaced the inner tube and spun the front tire to "true it up." But he glared at the wheel as if it were his enemy.

She took a final sip of coffee. Perhaps it was her turn to be a good neighbor and help Paul. Joanna arranged her face in a casual smile and walked out the door. "Hi."

"Hello." He didn't look pleased to see her. He was sucking fiercely on candy and wearing that awful red-and-black flannel shirt again. Didn't the man ever wash it? She folded her arms. "Got a problem?"

You can't help. She read his face as if a billboard. He answered politely, "The wheel wobbles. Can't figure out why."

"Nice bike." Joanna knelt. "Ever since Team USA rode Raleighs during the 1984 Olympics, I've thought I might like one someday." She strummed the front wheel's spokes like a guitar.

"How. . .what—" He stared.

Joanna placed a finger to her lips. They listened to her play the spokes. Each one sang the same tone. Except one that gave a low *sproing*.

Paul jiggled the off-key spoke, and the head fell out. "Worn out. Should have thought of that. No wonder the wheel wouldn't true up. Maybe Lance Armstrong is your cousin?"

She laughed. "No, I just helped my late husband fix our bikes."

"Lady, I owe you a Door County Sundae." He shook her hand.

"I just finished one. And you don't owe me a thing. I've been eating your delicious sweet-and-sour chicken all week."

His calloused hand still clasped hers. His fingertips lit her cold ones like candles.

Joanna pulled away and stood. "You really don't need to leave food on my doorstep, as if I were a helpless old lady."

"Helpless old ladies don't fix racing bikes." He set the Raleigh back on its wheels. "Door County Sundae, huh? Good choice. When you live alone, it's easy to forget to eat."

"I'm perfectly healthy." She tilted her chin defiantly. "I could beat you in a race any time."

"Oh, really?" He leaned forward, his dark eyes suddenly glowing.

He was her height, so she felt his warm peppermint breath on her cheeks, her mouth. Joanna looked down at her hands, the ground, anywhere but into his eyes. "Yes, really."

"Have you ridden lately?" His voice sounded rich and warm as maple syrup.

"I've been working out."

Right. If you could call running the vacuum twice a month a fitness regimen.

"Then you won't mind putting your miles where your mouth is." He stepped back and pointed at her, then at his own broad chest. "You. Me. A bike race from park's entrance to exit. Two weeks from today."

She ignored the screaming voice of reason within. "Done."

"Does the winner get a prize?"

She shrugged. "Like what?"

"If I win, you accompany me to Community Church."

A churchgoing guy. She struggled to hide her growing interest. "And if you lose?"

He bowed his shaggy head over her hand. "My lady, I concede to your will."

❄

What was I thinking? Paul gripped his head as if pushing sense into his brain. He slapped the Raleigh, as if his ineptness was its fault. He should follow, tell her to forget it. But she'd already walked several blocks. He wanted to ride with Joanna, be her friend. He longed to help her find comfort and healing in the Lord, but beating her in a bike race maybe wasn't the way. A lovely woman. . .he felt as if he viewed a Monet painting he could never afford. Plus, he knew nothing about her spiritual state.

"Sorry, old partner." Paul patted the Raleigh's handlebars. "Anything I learned about women with Suzanne, I seem to have forgotten the past five years—except how to make them mad."

He pushed the bike toward Angie's. He'd load it into Doug's pickup and haul it home. As he pushed, Paul tried to make sense of it all. Joanna obviously knew bikes. She'd been training. Still, could she actually beat him?

What if she did? What prize would she demand?

Probably that he move. To Texas.

He raised his eyes heavenward. "Father, what do I do now?"

❄

Joanna was sketching a portrait of Michaela when the phone rang. Andrew usually phoned right before bedtime, the hardest part of her day.

Probably another telemarketer. She didn't want a timeshare in Armpit, Arkansas. But she grabbed the phone. "Flick residence."

"Mom? You okay?"

She disarmed her tone. "Hi, hon. Great to hear your voice."

Dear Andrew. After the funeral, he'd wanted her to live in Indianapolis. But eventually, she'd returned to Fish Creek, to the house Jim built. "I'm fine. A little tired. I took a walk today."

"Really." His tone brightened.

"Finally enjoying sunshine."

"Great! Michaela and I want to play outside with you. May we visit over Memorial Day weekend? We would probably arrive Friday night."

"I'd love it!" The day's craziness dissipated.

"Only two weeks till then!" Her son enthused.

Uh-oh.

She'd promised to race in two weeks.

Now what?

Chapter 3

His head pounded. His bones cracked, creaked, and rattled. Any band would welcome Paul as the perfect one-man percussion section. No man knocking sixty should leave his nice soft bed at six thirty on a Saturday.

Paul rode past Joanna's garage, then turned onto Main Street, cycling toward the park alone. No sense fraternizing with the enemy.

At least, *she* viewed them as adversaries. He'd hoped Joanna would remember their fun cookie time with his grandsons and "Hi, neighbor" hand waves, keeping this race in friendly competition perspective. But the past two weeks, she'd returned to her cuckoo clock habits.

He could take a hint. Honoring her wishes, he stopped delivering dinner. Instead, he showered a happy Angie with Swedish meatballs.

Arriving at the parking lot, Paul stuck a peppermint in his mouth. He checked the Raleigh's tires, gulped water from his bottle, and re-tucked his shoelaces so they wouldn't catch in the bike chain.

Finally, he walked back to the park entrance. No sign of Joanna. "Lord, this must be Your answer. She doesn't want my friendship. Let somebody else help her—"

Joanna turned out of a nearby side street. Had she taken an alternative route to avoid him?

He sure couldn't avoid Joanna. In a normal race, he'd focus on her bike, a blue LeMond Etape. But the sun lit her blue, purple, and green jersey like stained glass. When she pulled up and removed her black helmet, her glowing silver hair nearly blinded him.

"Helmet hair." She shook her short, feathery waves. "You'd think some scientist would find a cure."

That was one of those woman-statements best left alone. "Sure your company doesn't mind this?"

"Andrew and Michaela never rise early, not even on Christmas."

Her smile dazzled him. Paul wondered how he ever considered beating this bicycle angel in a race. "Want to review the map?"

"Good idea. You don't want to lose on a wrong turn." Her eyes sparkled like twin jewels.

So much for a sweet angelic visitation. He hadn't made a wrong turn in this park since he was ten. Paul flapped the map open. "It's a holiday, but this early, we can take paved roads. Let's go Shore Road, then jog onto Highland."

She nodded. "First one at the Highland bike parking lot wins?"

"Right."

He'd never raced a woman. Shouldn't he offer Joanna a head start? But hey, nobody put a gun to her head. When his conscience still needled him, Paul decided he wouldn't go all out—until close to the end.

114

She straddled her bike.

Paul did the same. "Want to get us started?"

"My pleasure." She leaned over her handlebars.

He hunched over his.

She shouted, "Ready. Set. *Go!*"

Paul felt her blue-flame intensity as she passed him. Joanna wanted to take the wind's friction—and the bugs—in her face? Fine. He'd let her break for him. As they rode the western side of the peninsula, he remained a little behind, inhaling air that smelled as if God just created it, colored with damp forest fragrances. Cedars spread fans of spicy foliage above. He pretended they rode together, savoring God's creation, with a breakfast picnic at Sven's Bluff, where they would laugh and talk.

Occasional Green Bay vistas swept aside the forest, the sun glinting on white-waved water so blue his heart ached. He upped his speed and glanced sideways at Joanna. Did she—could she—ever love Door County as he did?

Poker-faced, she rode as if wearing blinders, ignoring the magnificent land, air, and water, ignoring him. Annoyed, he pulled ahead.

She accelerated, too.

You really think you have a chance? He powered the Raleigh past Eagle Bluff Lighthouse.

So the lady wanted a real race? She was gonna get one.

❄

Joanna panted like Paul's old basset hound. She'd done a few hundred-mile rides. That training kept her from falling apart. But her leg muscles burned—a sure sign of overdoing it. Joanna guzzled Gatorade and rounded a curve, only to face another hill. She stood on the pedals and pumped.

Paul, wearing his red and blue jersey and gleaming gold

helmet, rocketed ahead like Captain America. Even Jim, at his best, would have eaten this guy's dust.

She'd never judge a rider by his flannel shirt again.

❄

Paul glanced over his shoulder. He'd left Joanna and her superiority complex behind after Welcker's Point. Now, as he forged ahead toward Highland Road, concern crept over him. Maybe her bike gave out. Did she hydrate enough? Load up on carbs beforehand?

Who am I, her mommy? He'd finish with plenty of time to gloat before the loser showed. Then he'd shower her with kindness, making her even madder. Paul chuckled. He was good at chopping wood and building fires, but even better at kindling flames in those beautiful, icy eyes.

A bass "Woof!" startled him back to the present.

"Rats!"

Paul's high-powered squirt gun usually discouraged dogs with dinner on their minds. But he assumed he didn't need it because of the park's leash laws. This one probably escaped out a camper door.

Oh, well. Dogs chased him a few blocks, then decided he wasn't worth it. Paul turned for a quick look.

A huge white dog, the kind kids hug in Disney movies, sprinted behind him. The beast resembled a polar bear, teeth bared in a not-so-lovable snarl.

He'd outrun it. But the polar bear would find fresh prey behind him. *Joanna.*

Instead of turning onto Highland, Paul steered the Raleigh straight onto Skyline Road, a less populated loop that would take them near South Nicolet Campground and possibly the dog's owner, yet away from Joanna.

"Go home!" He used the deep voice that worked even with

Sunday school kids. But the dog didn't quit.

Paul upped his speed.

An enormous Winnebago filled the road. He slowed.

"Woof-woof!"

He almost felt the dog's hot saliva on his ankles.

"Go home!" Paul bellowed. He kicked at his pursuer, connecting with its snout.

The polar bear yelped with rage.

"Snowball! You bad girl!"

Tongue hanging out, the animal bounded to a small elderly man standing by the road. "Why did you run away?" he crooned. "Now you're all hot and tired. Poor baby."

Paul pulled over, panting. Yes, poor baby. . .who wanted more than a piece of him. At least, he'd found the owner.

The guy's smile disappeared. "What did you do to Snowball?"

Paul stuffed his water bottle into his mouth. Partly because he was about to die of thirst. Partly to avoid saying what he shouldn't.

"I heard her cry!" The man's face flushed fiery red.

"The poor puppy's hurt!" A little girl's voice called from behind Paul. He turned to see a troop of Brownies running toward him like truant lambs. Two threw tiny arms around the polar bear's neck. Paul dropped his bike, ready to rescue them.

"They're safe. My grandchildren love Snowball." The owner gave Paul the evil eye.

The polar bear now acted like a giant cuddly stuffed animal. She whimpered on cue.

"Snowball would never harm anybody." The owner glowered. "Not like some people who *hurt* dogs."

A dozen hostile little stares pierced him like straight pins.

The Brownies' leader glared at him.

"Is there a problem?" A park ranger stuck her head out of a DNR truck. She frowned. "Sir, did you think you were doing the Daytona? The park is especially crowded this holiday weekend. You could have injured someone."

"That dog wanted to turn me into hamburger!" He tried to hold his temper.

"He hurt Snowball!" The polar bear's owner shook his fist.

They probably wouldn't believe how much he loved Louie. Paul bit his lip. Snowball warranted an Academy Award for this performance. She'd almost convinced Paul she'd been mistreated.

"We'll discuss this in my office." The officer gestured with her head. "Please come with me."

❄

No Paul at the finish line?

Joanna rubbed her eyes as if the empty Highland parking lot were a mirage. Halfway through the race, he'd vanished around a curve ahead of her. She'd never caught up.

She waited ten minutes. Paul didn't show. She reviewed their conversation, rechecked her map. Yes, they'd agreed on this spot.

Had she won? Her imagination threw a little confetti. She pictured a victory lap around the parking lot when he arrived.

Still, she didn't buy it. Had something happened? Concerned, she retraced their route to where he'd disappeared. No sign of him.

Doubt, like a troublesome worm, bored into her mind as she rode back to the parking lot. Lost? Highly unlikely. They'd reviewed the course together. At the speed Paul was riding, he should have beaten her by at least five minutes. Why wasn't he here?

Questions pushed against her like stormy water against a dam. Gradually, worry levels dropped. Anger levels rose.

She'd blown money on a new jersey. Even tried a new body splash. As if this were a date. . . .

Some date. Had Paul proposed this stupid race just to dump her halfway? She bared her teeth. *Grrr.*

If only Paul had worn that flannel shirt. Instead, the scarlet and blue jersey hugged his broad shoulders and chest. The helmet hid his bad haircut. His muscular calves devoured the miles. . . .

She didn't want to go home and dodge Andrew and Michaela's questions about her wonderful ride. But she forced weary muscles to pedal back. Hopefully, her family would sleep awhile longer. The day would look better after a little rest. At least, she wouldn't be alone. Again.

Andrew wanted to take them sailing. She wouldn't see Paul revving up his grill for a family barbecue or smell the fragrance of his secret sauce on chicken and ribs.

Her empty, eager stomach knotted. Her mouth watered. Joanna scowled and ignored them both. If Paul showed up with barbecue or those Swedish meatballs, she would take great pleasure in bouncing them off his bike helmet.

Chapter 4

Y ou're spoiling me." Joanna had devoured every bite of the cream-cheese-stuffed French toast with Door County cherry topping. She absorbed the elegant, yet homey atmosphere of the White Gull Restaurant, with its black tables and chairs, cream-colored walls, and red accents.

"A little spoiling won't hurt, Mom." Andrew gave her Jim's sideways smile. "You've lived in Fish Creek a year. Have you eaten here even once?"

She didn't answer. Both knew she hadn't eaten out anywhere.

"Grandma's spoiled!" Michaela sang out. She looked like a daisy in her yellow sundress.

"We'll just have to take her to church and straighten her out." Her son grinned, wiping maple syrup from his daughter's face.

They drove to the Moravian Church in Ephraim, where they'd attended years ago during summers in Door County. The white-steepled church with its stained-glass windows, built in 1859, reminded her of better times, when Jim was still with them. Her bicycle muscles ached as they climbed the front steps. In the foyer, she inhaled the same Sunday morning fragrance of hymnals and pews, but instead of bringing comfort, gray mists of despair swirled around her. Michaela tugged on her sleeve.

"Jesus is here, isn't He?" Her granddaughter's trusting green eyes shone through the fog like a lighthouse's beam. "Just like at my church at home?"

"Yes, He is." Joanna hugged her.

Andrew slipped his arms around them. "Jesus is with us everywhere—no matter what." He led them to a pew.

Andrew learned his lessons here very well. A gentle yet relentless voice prodded her. *Have you?*

She bowed her head as the organ began the prelude. Andrew's wife had left him soon after Michaela's birth, and his faith had sustained him through a terrible storm. God had made him strong.

Was He unable to help her recover from Jim's death? Maybe the teacher needed teaching.

"I'm sorry, Lord," she whispered into her Kleenex.

Michaela whispered, "Can I sit on your lap?"

Joanna drew her close and inhaled her baby-shampoo fragrance.

Would you like to sit on My lap?

The gnawing pain of her anger didn't seem worth it. She felt a sudden longing, as if someone had opened an oven full of freshly baked cookies. *Yes. Yes, Lord, I would.* She sensed His strong arms closing around her, Michaela, and Andrew. She wished she had a photo of her family at that moment, snuggled together on Jesus' lap.

❄

After church, they went to Fish Creek Beach, waded in the still-chilly water, and lay on warm beach towels. While

Andrew dozed and Michaela played with another little girl, Joanna practiced embroidering on muslin scraps. She hadn't done this in years. Such crooked, bunchy stitches. She'd better practice every day, or the doll wouldn't resemble Michaela. Or any other human being.

Later, they ate frozen custard cones from Not Licked Yet and watched a carp attempt to swim upstream in nearby Fish Creek.

Michaela tried to change the big fish's direction with a stick. "Doesn't he get tired? Why is he so silly?"

"He doesn't know any better," Andrew said.

"Or maybe he's stubborn." Joanna looked sideways at her son.

"We smart humans are never like that." He laughed.

She gave him a playful smack, then a hug. She savored the creamy butter pecan cone and watched Michaela dance along the creek like a woodland fairy.

❄

So hard when her family returned to Indianapolis.

Too much time to think. About the race. About Paul. During Memorial Day weekend, she'd seen him cleaning his grill. But she'd heard nothing. Joanna thumbed her nose at Paul's house and laid out pattern pieces for Michaela's doll. They looked sturdy enough for another go-round. She pinned them to unbleached muslin and began to cut. She'd just finished when she realized, with a start, that she'd almost forgotten her hair appointment. But she still had time to ride. After an endless winter and temperamental spring, Joanna had learned not to waste a lovely day.

She zoomed past Paul's empty driveway and down Main Street. How would she deal with that race fiasco? She had no idea, but she'd decided to forgive him—no matter how lame his explanation. Their paths would probably cross soon.

Pausing at Fish Creek Beach, she felt like a teacher let out of school. Sailboats floated in and out of the marina like brightly colored waterbirds. Mothers with flocks of children crowded the beach. One child reminded her of Michaela. Joanna's eyes stung. But she shook off the sadness like a coat too heavy for the season. She would see Michaela and Andrew in a month, when they visited for Independence Day. In the meantime, she could work on her granddaughter's doll.

Joanna parked her bike in front of the Kut 'n' Kurl Beauty Parlor. Inside, every dryer was occupied. Permanent solution prickled her nose. Beauticians dabbed and combed. A radio sputtered static as it sang golden oldies.

"Hi, Brittany." Joanna slid into the stylist's chair.

"Hi, Mrs. Flick." The pleasant young woman spritzed and trimmed.

Joanna surrendered to her usual beauty shop catnap. . . until a name caught her attention like a fish on a hook.

"Did you hear what happened to Paul Sorensen last weekend?" A red-haired woman giggled like a schoolgirl.

An older woman whose hair twirled into peaks of lavender-gray meringue snorted. "I heard at church. A park ranger threatened to charge him with speeding. On a bicycle!" She rolled her eyes. "Too much time on her hands."

"Wayne said a monster dog was chomping at his heels." A wrinkled woman with snapping dark eyes crossed her arms. "The owner wanted the ranger to arrest Paul for cruelty to animals!"

Her listeners laughed as if they'd never heard anything so funny.

Joanna didn't. *Arrest?*

"They should see Louie!" Redhead wiped her eyes. "Paul scrambles eggs for that dog every morning."

"Claire came home upset from a Brownie campout. 'Mr. Paul hurt a doggie!'" A mother shook her head. "I told her the dog's bite must have been worse than his bark. Paul's a good man. My son loves his Sunday school lessons."

The dark-eyed woman looked relieved. "Anyone who knows my brother-in-law knows how kindhearted he is. Paul was afraid the dog would attack some rider behind him, so he led it away from her."

Joanna's heart slid toward the spotless linoleum. *He did that for me.*

"Always the knight in shining armor." Redhead gave a demure smile.

"Good thing Chuck Johnson was on duty." Lavender Lady *humph*ed. "He set that other ranger straight."

Dark Eyes grinned. "Actually, Chuck almost charged the owner with letting his pet run loose."

The shop reverberated with laughter again, then with stories about other runaway dogs and false arrests.

But Joanna sat hunched like a hair dryer.

What should she do? Her brain sizzled as if set on extra-dry.

And how did that redhead know so much about Paul?

❋

A package for him?

It lay on his doorstep, wrapped in fancy black and gold paper. Not the usual tape-encrusted surprises he received from his grandsons. Taking it inside, he opened the small card. From Joanna?

He felt a thrill of joy. . .and alarm. Should he call the local bomb squad?

Paul brewed a mug of extra-strong coffee. He should have talked to her. But she'd had company all weekend.

Plus, he felt like an idiot. The whole town had razzed him, even the pastor during his sermon. He'd stopped answering the phone. Paul shook his head. Suzanne had always jumped on him about avoiding conflict. No doubt Joanna was mad by now.

He and the package eyed each other. Finally, he opened it.

A gleaming trophy rested in folds of black tissue.

A trophy for second place.

❄

Bam-bam-bam!

Paul rubbed his eyes. He hadn't heard that much racket since a Girl Scout's high-pressure tactics netted him twenty boxes of Do-Si-Dos. Right now, he preferred to avoid Brownies, Girl Scouts, and anything else with double-X chromosomes.

Bam!

Paul slid Louie off his lap. The hound stared with reproachful eyes.

"Sorry, guy." Louie—and he—had adjusted too well to extra time in the recliner, avoiding the rest of humankind. Paul yawned and opened the door, hoping it was only the IRS.

Uh-oh. The dreaded double-X chromosomes had shown up. Paul gulped. Had they ever.

Joanna caught the sun's rays, as always. Slim in her black shorts outfit, her glittering silver hair stood on end in some new hairdo that reminded him of *Star Trek*. His drowsy brain wondered if she had beamed onto his front porch.

"You owe me, mister!"

"What do I owe you?" All systems were wide-awake now.

"Maybe an explanation?" Her eyes, like blue flashlights, blinded him.

"I'm sorry." He felt as if he'd been sent to the principal's office. "Extenuating circumstances—"

"A dog chased you?"

"You've lived here long enough to sign on to the Fish Creek Snoop Loop?"

For the first time, her pink mouth twitched. "Never, ever underestimate the communicative powers of a woman."

"I don't." Underestimate? She held him helpless, as if he were standing in a force field.

"You might try communication sometime." Her tone sharpened. "One of those nice things that prevents misunderstandings. At first, I thought you'd been hurt. I retraced our route." Her lower lip quivered. "When I didn't find you, I thought you'd finished first and left m—given up on me."

"I would never do that." She'd worried about him? He wanted to pull her close. Instead, he gazed into her eyes, unblinking, hoping she would listen. "I'm sorry I didn't talk to you. I felt stupid. Then I figured you'd be mad."

"May I hear your version of what happened?"

Paul gestured toward his Adirondack chairs. She sat, her back straight as a ruler.

"Dogzilla wanted to make a Happy Meal out of me. I was afraid if I shook him, he'd go after you."

Her eyes softened to low beam.

Paul plunged ahead. "I took him on a side route and ran into his equally nasty owner, a clueless ranger, and a mob of Brownies who wanted to stone me because in their eyes, I 'hurt the poor doggie.'"

She giggled with her signature Uncle Herman snort. "Did you?"

"When he threatened to chomp my feet off, I kicked at him. It took way too long to straighten things out. I wasn't surprised to find the parking lot empty when I finally arrived."

He exhaled and fell back into his chair. Now what?

"I'm sorry for thinking the worst, Paul. And thanks for coming to my rescue."

Her apologetic, almost shy smile nearly knocked him out of his socks.

But her mood changed within three seconds. She cocked her head and laid a finger alongside her jaw. "Item two on the agenda."

He hadn't known they had an agenda. "Which is?"

"You still owe me, mister."

"What?"

"Didn't we have an agreement?"

"Yes, but—"

"No buts. I won." Her eyes clicked to high beams again. "You placed second. Right?"

"Oh yeah. Second place." That trophy. She sure knew how to rub it in.

"And I choose my prize?"

"So choose, already."

Her sun-smile slipped out of hiding again. "I'd like you to go on a picnic with me. After we attend church next Sunday."

Chapter 5

Was the picnic for Paul too romantic? Joanna had fought the urge to buy exotic meats, cheeses, and sparkling grape juice, sticking with honey maple ham and Swiss on limpa bread, whole-grain chips, and plain, honest strawberries with no alluring chocolate dips to confuse the relationship.

She had enjoyed worshiping at Paul's church and meeting his friends. His cute grandchildren remembered her. His daughter seemed in a hurry. With three little ones, no wonder.

She and Paul took a leisurely bike ride through arches of cool, whispering trees to Eagle Terrace, eating side-by-side at a picnic table. They laughed about their grandchildren. He gave her plant care tips. A lovely, relaxed day she wanted to last forever.

"Have you been to Eagle Panorama?" He offered her a peppermint and popped one into his mouth.

"Several years ago at Christmas. Beautiful. Lots of big ice chunks in the bay." She began to clear the remains of their meal.

"Oh no, you don't." He grabbed their soiled paper plates. "You won, remember?"

She hadn't specified clearing the table as part of her prize, but she would take it. Joanna dropped back onto the bench and stretched. Ohhh, yes, how she loved to see a man clean up.

They strolled to the nearby Panorama, 150 feet above the water. Joanna didn't look down. She gripped the fence a couple of yards from the lookout's edge. Paul didn't comment. She appreciated his sensitivity to her dislike of heights.

Swirls of gulls celebrated the sunny day, soaring above green Horseshoe Island, dipping toward blue, blue Nicolet Bay. "I love God's exterior decorating."

"He's the best there is."

She didn't realize she'd spoken aloud until Paul answered. They stood in silent communion—the land, the lake, Paul, and her, all praising the Master Artist who had designed them.

"Thanks for taking me to your church today." Her words fit the moment, like the wind's sigh through the trees.

His hushed voice matched hers. "I'd hoped you would enjoy it."

"Enjoy? Too small a word." She felt honesty, fresh as their surroundings, flow into her voice. "I've neglected church. My relationship with God has suffered since. . .since—"

"Since your husband died?"

The usual rip of agony seemed out of place. She'd brought sadness into Eden.

Paul touched her shoulder. "It's hard." While others' sympathetic looks seemed to weigh her pain, Paul's gentle eyes absorbed it, lessening the burden. "My wife, Suzanne, died suddenly of a blood clot after routine surgery five years ago."

"Jim had a heart attack." She looked down. The first anniversary of his death had passed, yet sometimes it still didn't seem real.

"I don't know that an advance warning would have helped either of us. Or even an explanation." Paul took her hand. "After months of whys and where-are-You-Gods, I just decided to believe Jesus loves me. Like the Bible says. Like the Sunday school song says."

He grinned a little. "If Elijah were here, he would sing it good and loud for us. And very off-key."

A small smile prodded her lips.

"For a while after Suzanne died, even this"—he waved his big hands at the magnificence—"didn't communicate that God loved me. But eventually Elijah did. And Daniel. And P.J."

"Michaela convinced me." Thank God for grandchildren. With one question that Sunday at the Moravian church, her sweet little girl had nudged her away from the edge.

"I didn't mean to preach." Paul looked abashed. "I just wanted to tell you I've been praying for you. And that I truly know how you feel."

"Thank you. I'm glad to have a friend."

She and Paul drank in the scene as if taking nourishment. Energy flowed into Joanna. Suddenly, she wanted to *do* something. Something brave. Walk to the edge of the lookout? Not enough.

"Let's climb to the top of the tower!"

"Eagle Tower?" Paul looked at her as if she'd grown antennae. "It's seventy-five feet high. Have you climbed it before?"

"Never. But I want to. Now." Joanna walked swiftly, afraid her new courage would vanish. Jim and Andrew had climbed and waved from the top, kidding her about her fear. Joanna quickened her pace. She refused to stay on the ground today.

Paul followed slowly. "You sure about this? I thought—"

"Yes, I'm afraid of heights. But today, I can do it." She stopped and looked deep into his eyes. "I don't want to be afraid anymore. Will you help me?"

An expression she couldn't interpret passed over his face. "All right. I'll go with you."

"Then let's climb. Quick, before I change my mind." Joanna dragged him to the foot of Eagle Tower. She tilted her head back. The giant stared down at her. Her stomach lurched. "I hope nobody else sees me if I make a fool of myself."

"You're not going to make a fool of yourself." Paul put his hands on her shoulders. "You, Joanna Flick, are going to climb to the top. Today. I'll be right behind you."

She took a deep breath and headed for the steps. How she wished Paul could hold her hand. But he was there. Better yet, God was there. *Underneath are the everlasting arms.* Where in the Bible had she read that?

One step. Two. Three. Four. She felt the next step shiver. Joanna stopped.

"This is easier than navigating ball-game bleachers," Paul said. "You can do it."

True. She'd lived through years of baseball with Andrew.

They climbed the whole first flight, then the second. She slowed, climbing the third. On the fourth, she halted halfway.

"Only a few more until the first platform. 'I can do everything—'" Paul sounded a little hoarse.

" 'Through Him who gives me strength.' " Joanna pushed her feet, one at a time, until she reached the wide wooden platform. If only this platform weren't so, so. . .open. She blurted out the only Bible verse that came to her mind:

"'I lift up my eyes unto the hills—'"

"*Don't* look out. Not yet." Paul gently steered her toward the next flight. "We'll enjoy the view at the top."

"Don't count on it."

He gave her a tiny push. " 'My help comes from the Lord, the Maker of heaven and earth.'"

She tried to recall her earlier rush of courage. But the magical adrenaline level had fallen, along with the brisk wind's temperature.

"You've made it another flight. Let's try for two." Paul spoke in her ear, his warm peppermint breath tickling. She couldn't help giggling. She took a step before she thought about it. Another. She dug her fingernails into the wooden rail like a cat on a bed and climbed.

On the next flight of steps, Joanna's knees began to tremble. Where to look? If she focused on each step, the faraway ground made her feel as if she were in orbit. If she looked up, she felt dizzy. She might faint and land on Paul, hurtling them both to the ground. Taking him down didn't seem fair. Besides, she had to finish Michaela's Christmas doll. So she lifted a foot to the next step. And the next.

At the second platform, she had to rest. Joanna's panting echoed across the platform. All Door County must hear her hyperventilate. The twentysomething couple descending from the top stared. She turned away, closing her eyes.

"Can we help you, sir?"

"We're fine," a weak voice answered.

Joanna turned back and opened one eye. Paul, his face pasty and pale, was breathing hard. He white-knuckled the stair rail and waved them away. They bounded down the stairs, obviously relieved at not having to play nurse.

"You're *not* 'fine.'" Joanna panicked. "Are you having chest pain?"

"No, it's not that." He wouldn't meet her gaze. "It's just—"

"Paul Sorensen! Are you afraid of heights, too?"

Now he did look like a little boy. "I'm sorry. I should have—"

"Yes, you should have. Why did you encourage me to do this?" She glared at him. "Even quoting Bible verses at me."

Paul stared her down. "You dragged me along on this little adventure. As for the Bible verses, I didn't know it was unscriptural to quote them when needed."

For a man short of breath, he made himself heard.

"We should have asked those people for help."

"What were they going to do?" He shrugged. "Call the fire department? Give us piggyback rides down?"

Down. Joanna didn't want to think about it.

Up. Even worse. Three more flights.

"What do you suggest we do?" She wanted to put her hands on her hips, but didn't dare let go of the stair rail.

"Well, when I can't figure out what to do, I pray." The words sounded pious, but Paul didn't. "Unless that's a problem for you, too."

"No, prayer's not a problem." Despite his sarcasm, she felt her irritation cool. "It's a good idea. Why don't we pray?"

"Okay." He unlocked one hand from the rail and reached toward her. She slowly extended a finger his way. He linked his with hers and bowed his head. "Dear Jesus, this wasn't the smartest thing we've ever done. But we really did it with You in mind, trying to grow a little in our faith and courage. Please help us."

We. Our. Us. The words took Joanna's breath away almost as much as the tower's height. But she echoed his prayer. "Please, Lord. Help us know what to do."

Joanna opened her eyes and almost jumped. Paul's face was only inches from hers.

Fresh, terrified joy coursed through her veins. A kiss? No. She wasn't kissing anybody until they'd made it to solid ground alive. She refocused her thoughts. "Paul, I think God wants us to finish what we started."

He nodded, unblinking. The afternoon sun found green glimmers in his wood brown eyes.

Joanna reluctantly unlinked her finger, took a deep breath, and clutched the rail.

"We're right behind you," Paul whispered.

Joanna didn't need to ask who "we" was. She planted one foot, too hard. The step shook. She felt Paul wince. Sweat coursed down her cheek, but she took the next step. She felt lighter, stronger. The next, even better. Inch by inch, they climbed to the top.

"Beautiful." Joanna spoke in a shaky, reverent tone. "Incredible."

They clung to the stairwell rail in the middle of the highest platform and inhaled the magic of the haloed sun, the polished ceramic blue sky and water molded around jade green land. Joanna slowly reached a foot out toward the edge.

"Don't go there, because I'm not going with you." Paul's eyes twinkled. "We'll do that the next time."

Chapter 6

Perched on her front steps, Joanna and Andrew watched Michaela ride her bike, getting the "antsies" out before the trip home to Indianapolis. Joanna slipped a muslin strip from her doll workbag and practiced her embroidery stitches—again.

"Glad you've been getting out, Mom." Andrew rattled the ice in his tea glass.

"We've hit the Tuesday night concerts at Noble Square." Joanna had forgotten how fun Door County could be. "And we saw the Peninsula Players do *The Lady with All the Answers*—a comedy about Ann Landers."

"But I heard that spelling bee at the Cookery didn't go so well." He chuckled.

"You!" Joanna made a face. A retired language arts teacher should have won the restaurant's spelling bee hands down. "Why couldn't I remember *embarrassment* has two r's? Paul's a much better speller than I imagined." He wouldn't let her forget it, either. A second place trophy waited on *her* doorstep the next morning.

"You've been lonely, Mom." Andrew cleared his throat. "I'm glad you're having a good time—"

"But?"

"But aren't you spending a lot of time with Paul?" His face reddened.

Joanna crossed her arms. They'd almost made it through the July Fourth weekend without the Paul Conversation.

"He's a good friend."

"A very good friend." Andrew pressed his lips together.

She poked the cloth with the needle. Since when did she need her son's stamp of approval? Remembering this morning's scripture about soft answers turning away wrath, Joanna paused. "We enjoy common interests."

"Like biking together. Every day."

Three or four times a week, max. "I've found new friends at his church. I might join a Bible study."

Touché. Then, a little ashamed, she reached for his strong, freckled hand. "I really am growing in Christ, dear. I probably wouldn't have connected with a Fish Creek church if Paul hadn't introduced me." No way would she tell her son her initial visit was the result of their race.

"You've been through a lot." He clasped her other hand. "I don't want you to get hurt."

She kissed his hand, smiled, and summoned her best teacher's voice. "I appreciate your concern, but please don't worry about me."

She waved good-bye as they drove away, wishing they could stay for the fireworks. Maybe it was better she and Paul shared the evening with one adult child at a time.

❄

Paul lit up like a Japanese lantern in the twilight. His grandsons dashed from the picnic table, trailing taco chips.

"It's the Teddy Bear Lady!" Elijah hopped around like a windup toy.

P.J. imprisoned her knees. Daniel offered a wilted bouquet of pink clover.

While she pronounced it the loveliest she'd ever received, Paul grabbed Elijah and detached P.J. "Guys, we're happy to see Mrs. Flick. But don't knock her down, okay?"

Joanna hugged the trio. Such darling little boys. But their hair looked as bad as Paul's. Was it genetic? Or did he cut his *and* theirs? Grinning, she helped Paul herd them toward their mother's blanket.

"You remember my daughter, Angie."

She heard the love in his voice. But the glow on Paul's face flickered.

"Sure, at church. One busy Sunday morning." Joanna smiled at the young mother, who resembled her dad. Except her hair. Not a wheat-colored strand strayed from her smooth ponytail.

"Sorry your family couldn't see the fireworks with us." Polite words.

"They had a long drive ahead. But thanks for letting me join you tonight."

Silence. Angie did not smile.

Paul talked fast, as if trying to spread a thin layer of words over a vast, empty space.

"Doug, my son-in-law, is working late. Hopefully, he'll make it before the first boom."

Angie said nothing. Fortunately, P.J. dumped a bag of marshmallows down Joanna's back. The other boys kept them laughing with their antics. But not Angie.

Thank heaven, the fireworks would soon start. Afterward, Joanna could escape this lovely sociable evening.

Doug arrived and quieted the boys with one look, which soothed his wife's stress. But when he discovered Joanna's son lived in Indianapolis, he talked about Colts football until she thought Angie would explode.

Fortunately, the fireworks erupted first.

Daniel cheered. P.J. clapped his hands.

Elijah, however, thought they signaled the end of the world. Only when he snuggled between Paul and Joanna did he enjoy the jeweled fountains of fiery red, gold, and blue shimmering against the velvet night sky.

"Are the angels playing with matches?" he asked.

Paul gave Joanna a helpless look. She laughed and wanted to hear his answer, but another *boom!* nearly shattered her eardrums.

Elijah's chubby arms Velcroed her and Paul together. Her neighbor's eyes, like coals, reflected ruby fire with every explosion.

The sultry night and the scorched, sweet fragrance of smoke made her light-headed. Or was it Paul's nearness?

Finally, the spectacular show melted into onyx water. Joanna helped gather children, blanket, and picnic gear.

"I'll help Doug load up, then walk you home." Paul resembled a peddler from an old reader, loaded with camp chairs and Wiffle bats.

In the dark, she felt, rather than saw Angie's frown.

"No, I'll be fine." She forced a smile.

"Can you come with us?" Elijah tugged on her.

She hugged the boys. "No, I'm going to my house."

Elijah's eyes. Paul's eyes. Angie's. She couldn't handle them all.

"Thanks again. See you." She turned and walked away, each step faster than the last.

❄

"You think we should hide our friendship?" The French-pressed coffee from Paul's thermos suddenly tasted bitter. The morning sunshine that lit their breakfast picnic at Sven's Bluff tiptoed away.

"Of course not." Joanna set her cheese Danish aside.

"Then what do you mean?" Part of him wanted to know the truth. Mostly, he didn't.

"I mean, I've been praying about us. And our kids."

It didn't relax him. But he needed to hear it.

"We could ignore their needs. After all, they're adults—or supposed to be." Lavender lights twinkled in her eyes. "But I don't think that's what God wants."

He had prayed for her to grow in Christ, hadn't he?

"You're right." Paul nodded. "Angie never has accepted Suzanne's passing."

"Andrew doesn't say much, but he misses his dad."

"Surely, you don't mean we should cave in?" He held his breath.

"No. I don't think that's what God wants, either." Joanna's calm words rocketed him into a bright blue sky.

This "friendship" fascinated him more than he'd realized. Paul dropped abruptly back to planet Earth. Lately, he hadn't thought much about what God wanted.

"But we should slow it down. Not only for their sake, but for ours."

"You're still dealing with Jim's death." Though he understood her struggles, he didn't like saying the man's name. Paul shook his head. Jealous of a dead guy? He had more praying to do.

She looked him full in the face. "I want to know how I can serve God in Fish Creek. Maybe I'll help with the library's literacy program. I also need to focus on spiritual growth and connecting with other Christians. Neither of us can do that if we spend all our time together. Jesus first, right?"

"Always." His selfish side yelled in protest, but the godly guy inside rejoiced. What a woman! She'd leveled with him. He should do likewise.

"I've considered doing the Door County Century Ride in September," Paul said.

"A hundred miles?" Her eyes widened. "It's too late for me to train."

"You'd probably get hurt." He couldn't stand the thought. "I didn't want to mention the century because it would mean hours of riding without you."

"It's a great idea. I'll cheer you on."

Oh, that smile. He shuddered with delight and near-terror.

Joanna loosened one hand from his grip and patted the other. "Also, I don't think we should always sit together in church. Angie probably misses you."

"I'll miss you." He grinned. "But we'll have fun freaking out the church matchmakers. Especially if we alternate Sundays."

She giggled, then clicked her tongue against perfect white teeth. "During the Independence Day weekend, I should have gone with Andrew to the Moravian Church, where he was comfortable. But I was so excited about our church."

Our church. He tried to calm his rat-a-tat heart. "Guess we have some things to rethink and re-pray about."

"And discuss." A glint sneaked into her eyes. "We definitely need to spend more time in discussion."

"Maybe over Sunday dinner at the Whistling Swan?" He wanted to celebrate their whatever-it-was. Friendship? Going steady? He'd never celebrated "spiritual space" before with a woman.

"How did you spend Sundays before we met?"

He hesitated. "With Angie's family."

"Andrew called me Sunday afternoons. So let's make it Tuesday."

"Fine." He touched her cheek. "But when will I see you after that? Can we ride together next week?"

"We'll talk about it at the Whistling Swan." She grinned like a pixie and stunned him with a quick, potent kiss.

Chapter 7

J im wouldn't have believed it.

Thanks to Paul's tips, the Christmas cactus now fought the philodendrons for possession of her bay window. Next month Joanna planned to start the cycles of darkness and light needed to make it bloom by Christmas. She tipped her tin watering can, pouring just the right amount of water.

She marveled, too, that the thought of Jim brought mostly the gentle pain of missing him—not the festering agony that had paralyzed her. *Thank You, Lord.*

Loneliness still tried to be her friend. Besides training for the Century, Paul was teaching full-time again. She hadn't seen him all week.

Working on Michaela's doll usually helped. But Joanna's latest facial sketch bombed. She didn't want this "sister" to look as if she'd been stamped with a Michaela cookie cutter.

More attempts. More failures. Maybe she should buy a design by people who knew what they were doing. Joanna doodled, drawing cartoons. Out of habit, her pencil found Michaela's likeness.

Her jaw dropped. And her pencil.

"That's it!" The grinning little face made her smile. Hopefully, the doll would give Michaela smiles, too, during lonely times.

The September day looked eager to help her celebrate. She'd tutor literacy students at the library tomorrow, so she deserved a nice long bike ride.

First, she'd mail Michaela's package, a sparkly sticker book. Her granddaughter had cried at the end of Joanna's Labor Day visit. She wanted this gift to reach Michaela quickly. Joanna zipped the bright-colored mailing envelope into her backpack and rode past Paul's empty driveway.

They needed together time. She thought of the tandem, the red bicycle built for two she and Jim gave each other several Christmases ago. Memories of their fun-filled rides made her wonder if she should bring the tandem out of retirement.

She pedaled down Main Street along the marigold-lined sidewalk past the Cookery. Soon she'd take Paul to enjoy their succulent pork tenderloin with cherry chutney sauce. Then she'd spell him into the ground.

Joanna pulled up beside the Fish Creek Information Center/Library/Post Office and carried Michaela's package inside.

Angie, standing in line with the younger boys, looked as if she'd like to lock Joanna out.

Elijah and P.J. ran to her. "Teddy Bear Lady!"

She hugged them and risked a look at their mother. Paul had downplayed Angie's polite unfriendliness at church outings, but without him or friends as buffers, Joanna wanted to turn and run.

"What's that?" Elijah pointed to her package.

"A present for my granddaughter, Michaela."

"You're a grandma?" Elijah's eyes widened.

"Yes." Joanna smiled, then felt her stomach hit her toes. *Oh no.* He wasn't going to say it—

"Would you be *my* grandma?" Beseeching eyes. "Please?"

"G'andma!" P.J. roared. "G'andma!"

"Boys, we're running late. Let's go." Angie's words pricked, cold and sharp as an icicle.

Joanna stared at the U.S. mail envelopes for sale. But she felt Angie pass like an arctic wind, Elijah and P.J. howling appropriately.

She mailed Michaela's gift, vaulted onto the bike, and rode her fastest stretch in years. Her thoughts carved out a resolution rock-firm as the limestone hills behind Fish Creek. She would invite Paul for a tandem ride.

❋

"She's a beaut." Paul patted the tandem's handlebars.

"Tandems can be tricky." Joanna fiddled with the brakes.

"That's why you should take the front seat." Paul strapped on his helmet. "I've never done this before."

The front seat? Jim, the more experienced rider, had always guided their route and shifted gears. Joanna shrugged off her misgivings. After all, she had ridden all kinds of roads on all kinds of bikes. How hard could this be?

Joanna gave Paul a quick kiss. He gave her another, not so quick. Mmm. Good idea, the tandem.

She straddled the bike, hearing Paul do the same. "Ready?"

"Ready."

She steered into the alley. But turning the tandem felt equivalent to turning a semi. They swerved toward her neighbors' trash cans.

"Look out!" Paul's voice shot up an octave.

Joanna avoided crashing them like bowling pins, but took Paul on a close-up tour of another neighbor's thorny rose-bushes.

"You do know what you're doing, don't you?"

"Main Street will be easier." Now that she had this thing moving, she wasn't going to give up.

Main Street proved busy, but long and straight as a gray ribbon. Paul supplied plenty of pedal power. Still, Joanna struggled to balance a long bike with a weight roughly twice hers on the back. She had ridden with Andrew in a baby seat, but Paul was no baby. Though right now, he whined like one.

"I can't see ahead."

"Enjoy the side views." She took a swig from her water bottle. "You don't need to watch traffic, because I'm steering."

"That makes me feel lots, lots better."

She considered aiming for a deep pothole, but reminded herself this ride was supposed to bring them closer.

As they approached the outskirts, Joanna congratulated herself on a successful, though very wide turn onto a country road. Only an old red pickup chugged a quarter mile away. Her knotted shoulders relaxed. Birds sang, and the sun looked like a huge yellow flower pasted on a child's crayon-blue sky. If she and Paul mellowed a little, they could enjoy this ride. Joanna offered a quick prayer and resolved to do her part.

Without warning, the bike lurched toward the center line.

The red pickup's horn squawked, and the driver threw profanity out the window like litter. Joanna yanked the tandem to the right.

Safe. Sort of.

"Tell me before you lean down so low!" she screamed.

"My water bottle's at the bottom of the frame!" he yelled

back. "How was I to know grabbing it would mess up our balance? Maybe we should go home."

"Fine." Joanna hit the brakes and jumped off.

"Would you mind telling me before you do that?" Paul grimaced. "I don't control brakes or gears, remember? You could have jammed my ankles, and I'm riding the Century next week."

She cringed at the thought of injuring him. "I. . .I'm sorry, Paul."

His little-boy look, the apologetic version. "I haven't been a lot of help."

Together they reversed the tandem. The trip back went a little better. It had to, Joanna thought as they approached Not Licked Yet. It couldn't go worse.

A group of boys on bikes darted across the road like a school of minnows. An oncoming car screeched its brakes and laid rubber. Joanna hit hers hard, then swerved down the restaurant's steep driveway to avoid the kids. Unfortunately, they took a similar direction.

"No-o-o!" She heard Paul yell as bikes, boys, and would-be diners scattered like pigeons. The abrupt change of speed and sharp turn toppled the tandem, and Joanna hit the pavement with a crash.

She lay still a moment, her eyes closed.

Had she gone to heaven? Apparently not. Her body ached from head to toe. Frightened kid voices accused each other. Bikes rattled as they fled. Adults cursed. Worst of all, she heard a low, deep moan behind her.

Paul.

Chapter 8

"Louie, is this what a dog's life is like?"

Paul stretched luxuriously on the sofa, then winced. His bruises and painful knee reminded him to exercise caution until the strain healed.

Louie flopped off the recliner to nose him and whine. What a shock for the old guy. Probably the first time the dog had seen someone lazier than he was. Exhausted by his effort, Louie dropped to the floor to nap.

A tap at the door. Probably Joanna. He limped to answer it.

"Hi, Paul." She looked incredible, as always, bearing a picnic basket and her Christmas doll bag.

Did blue pearls exist? He had no idea. But if they did, surely they glowed like Joanna's eyes. As she tucked a kiss under his jaw, he caught whiffs of lavender. The fragrance of homemade bread wafted from her basket.

"You're adventurous today." Her be-careful voice.

"I need to move more. Classes next week. Doc says it's fine, as long as I don't run any marathons."

Too late, he shut his mouth. But the damage was done. She was reliving that stupid crash.

"Paul, I'm so sorry you missed the Century. Just because I wanted to ride the tandem—"

"Joanna, it wasn't your fault." He lowered himself to the sofa like a piano from a three-story window. He pulled her down beside him. "Kids rode out in front of us. You tried to avoid them. Could have happened to anyone."

"I know." The glow had left her eyes. "But I need to tell you more."

"Like what?" Sure, he'd wanted to ride that Century— hours of training down the tubes. He'd find work piled to the ceiling next week. But on the plus side, he saw Joanna every day. Why relive the crash? *Women.*

"Paul, I saw Angie at the post office."

Huh? Having stopped the prescription painkillers, he'd presumed his head was clear. But the logic of this was. . . ?

Her eyes filled. Paul forgot logic. "What about Angie?"

"I didn't tell you because you were hurt." She grabbed the hankie he offered and snorted into it like Uncle Herman. But no silvery laugh. "I wanted to mail a package to Michaela."

"Michaela?" This eventually would make sense. Maybe. "Is something wrong with Michaela?"

This time, a weepy laugh preceded her Uncle Herman snort. "No, no. I was mailing a 'grandma' package to Michaela at the post office. I ran into Angie and the boys. Of course, the kids asked me about the gift. I told them it was for my granddaughter, which I shouldn't have, because Elijah asked if I could be his grandma. P.J. yelled 'Grandma!' at the top of his lungs."

Paul stifled a laugh, although he, like his grandsons,

loved the idea. Finally, he saw where this was going. "Angie was upset."

Sparks sizzled in her eyes. "Paul, she. . .she can't stand me."

That was a little harsh. "Joanna, she's just a tired young mom. And she's never gotten over Suzanne's death. Give her time to get used to us." He said carefully, "I still don't quite see what this has to do with the crash."

She twisted his hankie. "After Jim died, I planned to sell the tandem. But I couldn't. We had such fun times on it. Still, I never pictured riding that bike with another man. Bringing it out of storage was a big step."

Paul's heart beat faster. He'd hoped as much.

"B–but we shouldn't have tried it. I'd never ridden on the front!" Tears dripped down her cheeks.

He cleared his throat.

"Joanna, dear." He placed his hands on either side of her face and made her look at him. "Believe it or not, I figured that out."

Blue flames shot from her eyes, then drowned in laughter. Joanna snorted and cried in his arms. Finally, she hiccupped and said, "Why did I think I could hide that from you? I guess I wanted to be strong."

"We all play those kinds of games." His mind wandered. How could anyone that wet and snotty be so beautiful? Still, he'd better get one thing straight. "Uh, Joanna? I still can't understand what the tandem has to do with Angie."

Her face fell again. "Paul, I felt her try to shut me out of your life. I wouldn't let her. That's why I invited you to ride the tandem."

O–kay. Paul cautiously readjusted his position and drew her close. "I guess I need to talk to Angie. Because no one. . .no one. . .is going to shut you out of my life."

"Would you, Paul?" Joanna lifted her face, glowing again with hope. "Promise?"

"Sure." He'd never crossed his daughter much—Suzanne had taken care of all that when she was growing up. But he'd talk to Angie this weekend or next. It would work out.

He kissed Joanna's forehead, then her lips, and held her. How could they return to the deliberate avoidance patterns of the summer? Nursing a bum knee was no fun, but he couldn't picture beautiful October living next door to this beautiful woman, trying to push her away.

❄

"I read the Bible this morning!" Electric joy lit Sadie Simmons's faded eyes. "Been wantin' to read the Bible for years. Today, I did it!"

Joanna clapped her hands, forgetting they met in the library. She hugged the elderly woman. "What did you read?"

"The very last verse." Sadie opened the back cover of the tattered King James. "I like to know the end of a story." Pointing at each word, she read, "The grace of our Lord Jesus Christ be with you all. A-*men*."

Sadie's smile lit the room. "I've heard that all my life at church. But today, I read it with my own eyes. I read the Word of God."

"You did!" Joanna wanted to throw confetti. But the teacher inside reminded her to challenge Sadie at the moment of success. "Would you like to read more?"

"Yes, ma'am!"

They searched the scriptures, and Joanna had never felt so rich.

❄

"It was the best moment of my teaching life." She had to call

Paul on her cell to share the joy. The empty library restroom echoed her gladness. "Why didn't I help someone read the Bible before?"

"Don't be hard on yourself. You just gave that woman everything."

Paul's words sent her heart soaring even higher.

"God has plans for you here in Fish Creek." His voice softened. "I hope they include me."

"So do I." Joanna loved talking with this man. His honesty and godly approach meant so much. "He'll show us the way, step-by-step." She checked her watch. "Are you home from class?"

"Getting ready to leave."

"I wish you could have rested another week. You're hurting, aren't you?"

"A little. I'll be fine, with an evening's worth of TLC."

"I'm getting good at this nurse thing." She fluffed her hair in the mirror.

"You are. I can't wait to see you."

"I'll be over in a half hour, bearing mountains of meatballs." Last night, Joanna had cooked his special Swedish recipe.

"I'll be waiting."

As she flipped her phone shut, a stall door opened. Angie, looking odd without a clinging child, faced her. "Well, I'd planned to talk to you today, but this wasn't exactly what I had in mind."

Guess I should have checked for feet. Joanna's all-time high plummeted. "Should we go for coffee?"

"No, what I've got to say won't take long. And you're due at my dad's in a half hour. With meatballs."

"I'm helping your father recover." Joanna fought to keep

her voice even. "He's still hurting from the bike crash. I know you're busy with family—"

"Oh please." How could a person own Paul's big dark eyes with no trace of kindness in them? "You're just using this to take over his life. Not that he's fighting it much." Angie's cheeks turned a hot, angry red. "Dad's recovered just fine. He fixed our car two days ago. He even helped Doug change a tire."

Change a tire?

"His doctor gave him a full release ten days ago. He does not need help. He does not need *you*."

The words bruised Joanna on contact. There must be some mistake. She tried to think, to pray.

"Why did you have to move next door to him? My dad was just fine—happy with us, with his work at the college and church." Angie stared down her nose. "Now all he wants is to be with you. At his house, no less. People are talking—"

"We've done nothing wrong." Joanna gripped her hands, trembling.

Angie *humph*ed.

Joanna turned on her heel and left.

❄

She yanked Paul's door open. His eyes brightened, though he limped slowly across the room. "Where's the Christmas doll bag? You can't come see me without it."

"It's at home." She scowled at him. "Change any tires lately, Paul?"

Concern pooled in his eyes. "Did you have a flat?"

"No." She couldn't bear the gentleness. "But apparently, Angie did. Or Doug. Right?"

He gaped at her. She almost threw a full casserole dish into the refrigerator. "Enjoy. Personally, I will never eat a Swedish meatball again."

"Joanna, what's wrong?"

"What's wrong?" She stuck a finger in his face. "I had a fun session with Angie. In the restroom—"

"Restroom? Joanna, you're making no sense." The first time she'd heard his teacher voice. Maybe the last.

"At the library. After you and I talked on the phone." She gritted her teeth and realized how much she hated his ugly kitchen curtains. "Your darling daughter eavesdropped on our conversation and filled me in on your clean bill of health, since you didn't bother to."

Paul's eyes fell. Silence. Then, "What did Angie say?"

"She said your doctor gave you a full release ten days ago—that you haven't needed my help." She crossed her arms. "Paul, do you walk with a limp when I'm not around?"

Silence. Again. His eyes didn't move from the old brown linoleum she'd mopped yesterday.

"Angie also said I was ruining your life. She. . ." Joanna couldn't repeat the rest.

"What else?" His teacher voice had fled.

"Ask her. Perhaps Angie concealed how she really felt about us during your little talk together, the one you promised me you would have." Joanna's nails dug into her arms. "You did talk to her, didn't you?"

"I—"

"Paul, we were moving toward something good." *Something wonderful, actually*. Vinegar tears burned her eyes. She shook them out. "But you haven't been honest with me. I can't believe what you say, what you do." She turned on her heel and nearly tripped over Louie, sprawled like roadkill before the back door.

"Joanna, don't go! Listen to me! Joanna—"

She climbed over the hound, jerked the door open, and escaped.

Chapter 9

Even if her life had exploded two weeks ago, the house hadn't.

Joanna pulled into her driveway, eyes focused straight ahead. Her gorgeous backyard maples waved scarlet banners in welcome. She didn't mind that she'd missed the peak of the heart-stretching fall colors—she'd been stretched enough.

Indianapolis had proved an oasis. Michaela escorted her to the zoo and the Children's Museum. After her granddaughter's bedtime, she sewed look-alike green satin Christmas dresses for Michaela and her doll. Andrew gave sympathetic hugs and never once said, "I told you so." Still, she felt his self-congratulation more than once.

She decided to go home and face her life near, but not with, Paul.

Hauling her suitcase, Joanna almost tripped over a casserole dish at the back door—empty, except for the envelope visible through its glass lid. She pushed it aside with her foot and entered.

Soon her mother's brass teakettle sang its whistly song. Although the calendar said November first, she brewed spiced tea in her favorite Christmas holly mug, an old friend that would help her through the holidays. Sipping the hot brew, she decided to make herself a "look-alike" dress, too. It would be another difficult Christmas. But she would celebrate Christ's birth.

Her eyes sought the Blue Copenhagen pitcher and plates atop her polished pine cabinets. She could hardly wait to eat food served on her china again. Andrew owned a nice home, but he and Michaela ate off Styrofoam. And no matter how Andrew teased, she liked her canned goods alphabetized.

Joanna opened mail, unpacked, cut out a pants outfit for Michaela's doll, and avoided bringing the casserole dish in. But an evening blast of sleet convinced her nothing, not even a dish, should stay out in this weather.

The sight of Paul's terrible handwriting brought everything back.

Joanna, thank you for the meatballs. Yours taste much better than mine.

If she'd been a casual reader, she would have read the word as "mudballs."

I can't tell you how sorry I am. I didn't intend to trick you into taking care of me. I just loved having you in my life and I got greedy. I talked to Angie. She's sorry, too.

Joanna didn't see one jot, tittle, or P.S. from his daughter.

Please give me another chance. Give us a chance. Paul

She searched for mindless activity. If she finished the doll's pants, she'd probably sew the legs upside down. The plants? The plant sitter had done a good job, but they looked a little thirsty. She watered the philodendrons and geraniums.

Joanna paused before the Christmas cactus. Probably too late to help it bloom. Joanna bit her lip hard. Did she want it to bloom?

Hope. . .love. . .that innkeeper had prayed they would flower in her life. But Angie didn't want that.

Suddenly, Joanna wanted to turn that cactus into compost. Grabbing the pot, she yanked the door open.

The demon wind drove sleet needles into her face. She fought it, clutching the cactus to her chest, then retreated into the warm kitchen. Stanching water, mud, and tears with a towel, she dumped the plant back in the window.

"And I thought I had a higher IQ than you." She dropped into a nearby chair. "You should be a cactus-sicle by now. If it hadn't been for a spider"—she shuddered—"you would have met your Maker last spring. Maybe you have nine lives, like a cat?"

She dropped her forehead on her hand. "Four hours here, and I'm conversing with a cactus." Her eyes fell on Paul's note again, lying by the phone like a bill too high to pay.

"Not tonight. I'm going to bed."

Before she switched off the kitchen light, she caught herself telling the cactus good night. Maybe she should have stayed in Indianapolis.

❄

Joanna was home. She must have seen his note. Coming home after work, he'd spotted the empty stoop.

But no call.

Tomorrow?

He dropped into his recliner. Louie climbed up on his lap. Louie didn't smell like a girl, but at least, Paul wasn't alone. Together they watched lights blink on next door, blink off, blink on.

And stay off.

❄

Should she attend church this morning?

Angie wouldn't be there. Last month, Paul had told her his daughter would visit friends in Minneapolis this weekend. He and Joanna had planned to do something special.

She threw her house keys down. Would she make a fool of herself at church? What if Paul tried to talk to her? She should have called him four days ago, even if she didn't know what to say.

She wanted to go to her church. Not another. She wanted to worship God. Listen to Pastor Morton teach His Word. See her new Bible study friends. Joanna paced. If only an angel would appear and announce an official end to this mess.

Gabriel did not show.

Finally, she gripped her Bible and marched out the door.

❄

Not one more day. Not one more hour. Now.

After church, Paul planted himself in front of Joanna's front door like a tree.

They had to talk. He hoped and prayed Joanna would talk to him.

Her big purple hat turned the corner. He hated that hat. It reminded him of his crabby Aunt Ethelene, married to Uncle Herman of snort fame.

Hat or not, he luxuriated in the sight of her, walking that

long stride in black boots. But only a moment. Her eyes found him.

His heart thudded. Was she looking at him the way he'd looked at her?

But her expression faded to blank.

He tried to summon a smile. "A smart lady once told me never to underestimate the communicative powers of a woman."

She crossed her arms over her Bible. "I thought I made myself clear."

"I certainly understood you." Hurt vibrated in his very bones. "But communication is a two-way street. Joanna, you expressed yourself very well." He took a step toward her. "But did you listen?"

The wicked November wind yanked her hat off. He grabbed it before it dove into a puddle.

"Thanks." She stuck it on her head again. Sideways. "Perhaps you're right. I didn't listen much."

"Want to go someplace to talk? Not Licked Yet has a fireplace, you know." He wasn't playing fair, using her Door County Sundae addiction. But if chocolate and cherries would sweeten the situation, he'd buy the place out.

"No. I'd rather walk."

"All right. How about Sunset Park?" Even on a less-than-perfect day, the bay always lifted his spirits.

She agreed, then left her Bible inside. As they walked, he battled the urge to hold her hand. "Joanna, I took advantage of your kindness. I wasn't straight with you, and the fact I enjoyed your company was no excuse. I'm sorry."

She hesitated. "I accept your apology."

He stuttered his thanks. *I will never deceive you again,* he wanted to say, *ever.* But would there be an "again"?

Joanna sighed. "I was at fault, as well. But you said Angie was sorry." She sped up like an angry robot. "What makes you think so?"

His dad instinct rushed in to defend his little girl. But he remained silent as they passed their church and started down the park's wooded path. Birches waved skeletal arms. Cedars moaned in the wind. Perhaps he should have chosen a more cheerful setting—like a cemetery. "I told her how hurtful her words sounded to you. She apologized." He pulled his gaze away. "But mostly, I think she felt sorry she had upset me."

"I appreciate your honesty. However, the fact remains. . ." A tremor in her cheek spread to her voice. "We cannot have any meaningful relationship with your daughter around."

"Is that in the Bible?" He stopped in his tracks.

"Paul, that's not funny."

"I'm not trying to be funny." They had reached the water, dark, wild, and white-capped. Gulls circled like white buzzards.

"I know I've ignored Angie's problems." Memories, like mist, rose out of the stormy water. Two gulls flew closer. "She and Suzanne were very close—like sisters, actually. Neither Doug nor I have been able to talk her into going to a counselor."

"I'm sorry for her pain and yours." Under the floppy purple hat, Joanna's face looked gentle. "But that doesn't change—"

"No, it doesn't. Nor does it change the fact the few times I met him, your son acted as if I were a kidnapper."

"Yes. Andrew was happy to discover we. . .we—"

"Angie lives here in town, and her attitude will be tough to deal with." He gripped her hands in his. "But, Joanna, to say we can't have a relationship because of her problems—or Andrew's, or anybody else's—does that actually mean you don't want the relationship? At least, not enough to stick with it?"

Her face matched her gray eyes now. The two gulls scolded from a nearby dock.

He ignored their big mouths. "God is able to help us, if we pray and listen and love and forgive. I believe that." Exhausted, he released her. "Joanna, whenever—if ever—you decide to believe it, too, let me know."

He turned to go. But the laughing gulls spoiled his dramatic exit.

Splat.

Chapter 10

"L ola Peterson," Sadie called. "Haven't seen you in weeks."

Joanna winced and smiled. Sometimes Sadie forgot they met in a library.

"Come meet my tutor, Joanna Flick."

"We've met. So glad to see you." Joanna shook hands.

"I hope things are better." Lola's eyes both warmed and penetrated. "How's the Christmas cactus?"

"Fine. Although I can't believe sticking it in the closet helps it bloom at Christmas."

"Dark places are key to blooming. I'll keep praying for you, dear." The woman patted her shoulder.

"You having that Christmas Tea this year?" Nobody ever accused Sadie of being shy.

"You bet." Lola grinned at them. "I hope to see you both there."

"Sounds wonderful." Joanna managed to smile. "But I haven't made holiday plans yet."

"You never know what good things the Lord has in store."

Lola's eyes twinkled as if she and God shared a joke. "See you then."

Later, watering the cactus, Joanna told the Lord she'd like to know the punch line, too. Plus a few other things. Since that weird afternoon at Sunset Park, she didn't know what to think or feel. She saw Paul often, but only in passing or at church. He appeared content, even happy. How dare he.

Paul had said she should pray and listen. As if she never prayed at all. But when Joanna tracked her prayer time as she did exercise, she realized a promising beginning last summer had degenerated into ducking her head with a hasty "thank you" over a Lean Cuisine. She decided to make Thanksgiving a time of true gratitude. She began to read her Bible and pray daily.

Jesus' words burned into her mind: "Pray for your enemies."

She didn't have to look far to find one.

Had she prayed even once for Angie?

Did calling Elijah-fire down on her head count? Probably not.

She found it easy to pray for Michaela, especially as she stitched her Christmas gifts. And for Andrew. For Paul.

At first, she had to force herself to pray for Angie. But gradually, she found herself sincerely praying for the unhappy young woman. Joanna still avoided her at church.

But one morning she pulled into a gas station. Too late, she saw Angie's van at a nearby pump. The boys called to Joanna from their car seats. Thankfully, she saw them every week, now she was teaching Sunday school. Joanna waved. Their mother crossed her arms, a smirk consuming her face.

The old, hot hurt shivered down Joanna. But her prayer habit kicked in. *Lord, help Angie. Help me.* Joanna stepped forward, waved, and smiled.

Angie looked incredulous, then confused. She thumped the nozzle onto the pump and left. Fast.

Joanna fell limp into her front seat, grateful God had given her the courage to take a first step. *Thank You, Lord.*

❄

"Gobble-gobble-gobble."

"Mom, the game's on." Andrew covered his ears with sofa pillows. "Can't you turn that thing down?"

"*Gobble-gobble.*"

"'Fraid not." Joanna pressed the belly of the gaudy rubber turkey she'd purchased for her son's Thanksgiving pleasure.

"It's worse than those stupid singing Christmas elves you bought my senior year in high school." He shuddered. "No wonder I left home young."

"Can we take it home?" Michaela begged.

"*No.*" During a commercial break, he rummaged for Tylenol. Joanna and Michaela, giggling, took turns pressing the turkey's belly.

Joanna felt a little ashamed. But holidays brought out her grade-school taste for bizarre battery-powered noisemakers. She needed extra smiles today.

Andrew forgave her at dinner. "Mom, that's the best turkey you ever cooked." He served himself a second piece of pumpkin pie.

They'd excused wiggly Michaela. Joanna savored her family's love and her hot mug of spiced cider. She tried not to miss Paul's presence at the table.

"You look great, Mom."

My, the boy was full of accolades today. "Thanks, dear."

"More like yourself." His words were muffled by a full mouth. "Much better, now you've stopped acting like some lovesick teenager."

Lovesick? *Teenager?*

She looked away as he chewed. Who was acting like a teenager?

Joanna didn't want to waste this special day fussing with Andrew about some silly remark. But it peeked around the corners of her mind, then hid with na-na-na-boo-boo persistence. At bedtime, she tried to read her Bible. But the past year played through her mind like a dreary movie: months of grief over Jim's death, with no effort to deal with it. Weeks of infatuation with Paul. Her fury when she discovered he wasn't perfect. Her own spiritual smallness. Her attitude toward Angie. . .until recently.

Andrew didn't know the half. *Lord, I'm sorry I've been so immature.* Tears trickled down her face. *Please forgive me.*

God's presence surrounded her, lifted her head and heart. She realized, as she had known deep down for months, that Paul was not a crush, not a teenaged, temporary love. *Thank You, Lord. I see what You want me to do.*

Joanna peered out her window. A light gleamed in Paul's living room. She sneaked downstairs and wrote Andrew a note. Taking her peace offering, she slipped out into the night, where a million shimmering stars danced with her joy. Joanna's footsteps crunched the blue snow to Paul's house. She prayed with every step.

❄

Someone knocking at his door on Thanksgiving night? Had an epidemic hit Angie's family since dinner? No, she would have called if recruiting him for puking-flu duty. Maybe Angie needed another late-night talk.

Nothing prepared him for the sight of Joanna. His knees nearly gave way.

"May. . .may I come in? Just for a minute?"

He nodded. His heart performed somersaults on top of his extra-full stomach.

She handed him a package wrapped in fancy black and gold paper.

"What's this? Another second-place trophy?"

"No trophy. I promise."

He opened it. Louie waddled over and sniffed.

Amidst folds of black tissue, a discolored rubber turkey with squishy blue wattles lay in the box. Truly ugly.

Joanna pressed its stomach. *Gobble-gobble-gobble.*"

Paul jumped. Turkey, box, and wrapping flew through the air. Poor Louie yelped and actually ran for cover. Joanna collapsed to the floor, giggling.

Lord, I'm glad You understand this woman. I sure don't.

"Joanna." She was still yukking like a vaudeville comedian. He pulled her to her feet. "What is this? Some kind of warped show-and-tell?"

Her laughter faded to Herman snorts. She put her hands on his shoulders and fixed him with that blue-pearl gaze. "Actually, it is show-and-tell, Paul. I wanted to *show* you that I know I've been acting like a turkey." She paused. "I want to *tell* you I'm sorry."

What do you say when the woman you love attacks you and your dog with a gobbling rubber turkey? He'd never seen that in eHarmony ads. He kissed her gently, savoring the sweet, soft lips he'd missed so much. No holiday feast ever tasted so good.

"Joanna, in case you don't remember, I blew it, too."

"But you were right." That blue-steel look. "God has shown me I've been acting like a self-centered child."

"We all have our kiddy moments." He chuckled. "Thank God, He loves all us turkeys."

"Amen." She stayed serious. "Paul, I know He wants me to love and forgive Angie." She paused. "I've been praying for her."

"You have?" Now his heart double-somersaulted.

"Yes. And I believe God will work things out for us in His time. Not ours. Not mine."

He buried his nose in her hair. So wonderful to smell lavender again.

She touched his cheek. "I really should be going." Her eyes sparkled playfully. "And I'm sorry, Paul, but I must take the turkey home—at least, for the weekend. Michaela will miss him." She gave an evil little laugh. "Andrew, too."

"I'll bet." He picked the turkey up by one skinny leg.

"I can bring it back—"

"No, thanks." He grinned and dropped it into its box. "Joanna, you are one scary woman."

She gave him a long kiss that left him weak. "Mister, you have no idea."

Chapter 11

Joanna snuggled in her antique rocker near the woodstove, savoring this Christmassy afternoon. Tiny lights sparkled on the blue ornaments and silver snowflakes adorning the seven-foot spruce before her French doors. Joanna hemmed Michaela's lovely green satin dress.

The phone broke the Thomas Kinkade picture-perfect silence. She picked it up.

"Just what are you teachin' my grandsons in Sunday school?"

Joanna almost dropped both phone and dress. Then she laughed. "I'm teaching them about Jesus, mister. You sound like you should come, too."

"I'd love to. But I may be past the age limit." Paul sobered. "Seriously, the kids have been thinking about your Christmas lessons. Especially Elijah."

"I could tell the wheels were turning."

"With Elijah, they never stop." He paused. "Now, he wants to invite the class—and you—to a birthday party for Jesus at his house next Sunday afternoon."

Joanna knew Angie had begun talking to Paul about Suzanne. Was it her imagination, or was his daughter softening a little toward her at church?

"Joanna. Are you there?"

"I was thinking about Angie." Joanna paused. "Is she ready for this?"

"She didn't fight it. I was surprised."

"I'm not sure I'm ready." She tried not to remember Angie at the fireworks. At the post office. In the library restroom.

"She's coming over tonight to talk. If God keeps this little miracle going, will you come to the party?"

"With God's help, I will." She almost whispered. "Tell Angie I'll help with games."

❄

P.J. possessed the reach of a basketball pro. "P.J., leave Jesus' birthday cake alone. Go play with the kids."

The blue cake made Paul think more of Smurfs than Jesus, but Elijah had insisted it was His favorite color.

The doorbell again. He squinted through the window. Joanna.

"I'll get it." His daughter jogged to the door. "Dad, will you do crowd control?"

Paul nodded and squeezed a thousand prayers into ten seconds. When both women he loved more than life entered the room together, he felt as much relief as if they'd emerged from a foxhole.

Neither smiled, but neither glared. An improvement.

Joanna set up the games while Angie kept the kids busy gluing macaroni and beans to cardboard ornaments. While Paul spray-painted their creations gold, Joanna's Christmas Bible game show, complete with buzzers and lights, wowed them. Angie, wearing an angel costume, awarded prizes.

The children took turns hanging their ornaments on Jesus' Christmas tree.

When Angie lit the cake's candles, Paul led in singing "Jesus Loves Me," "Away in a Manger," and "Happy Birthday." But his voice proved traitor. Both Angie and Joanna sang loudly, sweetly, as if they meant it. *Lord, can there be peace on earth? Here and now?*

Cleaning up afterward, both organized women got in each others' way. He sent up prayers like emergency flares. But they finished without major difficulty. He carried Joanna's game gear to her car and returned to find her face-to-face with Angie in the living room. He caught his breath.

Joanna spoke first. "Thank you for the wonderful party. It was so much fun."

"The kids loved your quiz games. Thanks for all your help." Angie sounded sincere. Even pleasant.

"Mom!" The usual bangs and crashes.

"I'd better run." Angie ducked into the hall.

Paul walked Joanna to the door. He let his eyes give her a kiss and whispered, "I'm sure Jesus had a very good time."

❄

"You'll be the queen of the Christmas Tea." Paul whistled.

"You look wonderful yourself." He wasn't tall, but Paul certainly looked dark and handsome in his black sports coat. She wanted to touch his hair, but didn't want to mess with his quality haircut.

He handed her a wrist corsage of crimson roses that matched her cranberry outfit. She displayed them to the Christmas cactus that refused to bloom. "See. *This* is how you do it."

"Doesn't look interested." Paul grinned. "It will bloom someday."

"Yes, it will." She had special plans for it.

The Heart's Harbor Inn resembled a Christmas fairy tale. Joanna backed away from the massive front door. Paul hadn't attended the Christmas Tea since Suzanne's death.

"Oh no, you don't." Paul rang the bell and gave her a gentle push. "No second-guessing."

He already knew her too well. Joanna decided to enjoy every minute of this dream come true. Exquisite Christmas trees in every room. The air full of glad tidings and cinnamon fragrance. Candlelight reflected in tinsel, satin, and Paul's deep, dark eyes.

They greeted Lola, her son, Jordan, and their lovely helper, Amanda, who had planned the tea when Lola found herself sequestered on jury duty.

"Thanks for your concern and prayers." Joanna clasped the innkeeper's hands. How she wished she could tell Lola the cactus had bloomed.

They sampled the Door County delicacies, far more tasty than any Christmas sugar plums. Sadie and their church friends warmed the evening with laughter and fun.

Where were Angie and Doug? Joanna had to admit she'd enjoyed their evening as a solo couple, but she saw Paul scan the room, looking for them.

"Hope they make it." He frowned. "Angie deserves a nice evening out."

At that moment, they entered. The sleek red velvet tunic showed off Angie's full, lovely figure, and Doug looked almost movie-star handsome. But they appeared a little strained.

Paul looked relieved. "Let's give them a little space, then wander over."

Talking to their pastor, Joanna couldn't help but glance at Angie and her husband. She heard Doug and his buddies discussing basketball across the room. But Angie wilted like a flower, sitting alone.

"Let's go talk to her." Dad to the rescue.

Joanna stopped him. "Paul, I want to go alone."

His eyes widened. "You think that's a good idea?"

"Maybe God's idea."

"All right." He squeezed her hand. "I'm praying."

"Give me five minutes. And don't stare." She smiled. "I'll take her something. Eggnog or hot chocolate?"

"Hot chocolate, lots of whipped cream, and a peppermint stirrer. She's loved it since she was a kid."

Joanna brought her a steaming mug. "Hi. Want something to drink?"

Angie's tired face lit up. "Thanks." She took a long sip and sighed. "The boys didn't want to go to bed."

"When they're little, going out hardly seems worth it." Joanna sat across from her.

"Here, at least, I can sit more than sixty seconds."

"In a room with people who don't need their faces washed."

Angie actually smiled. "Even Dad looks classy tonight."

Paul had joined Doug's group. Joanna watched him. She loved, loved his hair. She paused, then asked Angie in a low voice, "Did you talk your dad into a haircut?"

Angie gave a sudden giggle. "Yes. I told him he couldn't come to the Tea looking like a redneck."

"Thank you," Joanna said fervently. "Do you think you could keep him going?"

"Maybe." Angie hesitated. "Maybe between the two of us, we can manage it."

Her eyes dawned with sudden hope. "Maybe we'll even get him to leave my kids' hair alone."

They giggled. Paul paused in his conversation. Unbelief, then suspicion filled his eyes. He wandered over. "Just what were you lovely ladies talking about?"

"Nothing, Dad." Angie looked too innocent.

Joanna smiled and thanked God for hair miracles.

A gaggle of Paul's relatives spotted them. Paul helped Joanna with their names. But occasionally, Angie filled in the gaps.

❄

Should she have called first?

No. Better to catch an adversary off guard. But she didn't see Angie as an adversary now. . . .

Her temples throbbed, announcing an imminent headache. She rang the neat white bungalow's doorbell and dropped her chin.

She should have called first.

"Hello?" Questions crowded Angie's face. Behind her, Joanna saw the boys hypnotized by a Wii game.

"Merry Christmas, Angie." Through Paul, Joanna already had given the family go-cart gift certificates. But now she offered Lola's Christmas cactus, tied with a big red ribbon.

Angie's eyebrows rose. She opened the door a little wider.

"After my husband died, a wise woman gave me this plant and told me hope would bloom again. She prayed for me." Joanna touched a leaf one last time. "So now, I'm praying for you. Angie, this plant didn't bloom for me, but I hope it blooms for you. May the Lord bless you with hope and joy after deep sadness."

Angie accepted the cactus, her eyes moist. Joanna patted her arm twice. Lightly. Then returned to her car, praying as if her life depended on it.

❄

Why did Angie dress the boys up for Christmas Eve service? They looked cute in green pants and vests, but at supper, Daniel and Elijah dipped their Christmas ties in ketchup. Now, before worship, P.J. tossed his into the restroom wastebasket. Paul held a similar opinion of ties. But he knew better than to cultivate it in his grandson.

Paul and P.J. rejoined Angie and the older boys in the foyer, only a few minutes late for service. He was glad to help his daughter, as Doug was clearing roads tonight. Angie was talking to an elderly new usher who led their family parade into the candlelit, almost-full sanctuary. Paul provided rear guard.

A child's wonder stirred him. *Thank You, Jesus, for coming to this earth. Happy birthday.*

Angie, halfway down the center aisle, turned with a deer-in-the-headlights look. Why hadn't she told the guy they wanted to sit in back? A realization hit Paul between the eyes. She didn't know the usher was hard of hearing.

Soon he saw the other reason for Angie's nervousness. The usher was seating them directly beside Joanna and her family.

Pastor Morton rose to read the Christmas story. The organ music faded. Angie slipped into the pew beside Joanna. Paul, not daring to look at the women or Andrew, held P.J. on his lap.

Pastor Morton read the ancient words in a reverent tone. "In those days Caesar Augustus issued a decree that a census should be taken of the entire Roman world. . . ."

Lord, You came to a difficult world. Things haven't changed. How many people in these pews were trying to cope with life's pressures and their own weaknesses?

But nothing is impossible with God. The words rang so clear, he thought Pastor Morton had read them. Assurance blanketed him like a forest snowfall.

He sang with his family, with the woman he loved, and with Christian friends he cherished. *"Glo-o-o-o-o-o-o-ria in excelsis Deo. . . ."*

The boys loved singing the *o*'s in "Angels We Have Heard on High." He had to stop Elijah from singing them in every carol. Still, Paul's serenity seemed to flow into the children, as if they were connected by pipes. Few fidgets and no fussing. He prayed the Holy Spirit would help the grown-ups in the pew as well.

More blessed scripture that fed him like a Christmas feast. A quavery but lovely rendition of "O Holy Night" by a teenager.

"Let's sing 'Joy to the World' as we welcome Christ into our lives." Pastor Morton lit the last candle in the Advent ring, then those of people along the aisles.

Paul watched the tiny flames spread from person to person. Surely Christ's love could do that, too.

"Want one! Want one!" His quiet reverie—and those of nearby worshipers—was broken by P.J.'s cry.

"Share Grandpa's." Paul lit his candle from the pastor's and grasped his grandson's hands, holding them around the candle with an iron grip.

P.J.'s contentment lasted twenty seconds. He blew out Paul's candle, yelled, "Happy birthday," then loudly demanded Daniel's candle. And Elijah's.

As Paul hauled his howling grandson out of the service, he dared glance back at Angie and Joanna.

They were exchanging small mother smiles.

❄

"Grandma, she's got a Christmas dress like mine. And yours." Michaela's big smile exceeded her doll's. She gave her a hug.

Joanna's eyes filled. Sometimes Christmas dreams did come true.

"Can we all put on our Christmas dresses today?"

"You'll look like princesses." Andrew gallantly followed this female Christmas script. He inspected the doll's face and glanced at Joanna in wonder. "She really looks like you, Michaela."

"And she's got hair like mine." The little girl giggled. "We're twins."

"What are you going to name her?" Andrew continued the girly conversation. "Merry Christmas? Then you can be Michaela and Merry."

His daughter shook her head. "No. I'm gonna name her Myrtle. Myrtle Melita."

"Myrtle Melita it is." Joanna giggled at Andrew's expression.

"As always, I bow to your wishes, my princess." He made an elegant bow.

"You're a funny prince, Daddy. Your hair's sticking up."

Andrew took beautiful photos of Joanna, Michaela, and Myrtle Melita, resplendent in their dresses. Later they played new board and computer games, built a snowman as tall as Andrew, and watched *It's a Wonderful Life* before tucking Michaela and Myrtle Melita in.

Joanna dropped onto the sofa, ready to relax. A magical day.

"Paul wants to talk to me. About you and him." Andrew stoked the woodstove as if he were heating the whole block.

Joanna sat up. "Yes. And I plan to join in the conversation.

But do we have to discuss this tonight?"

"Yes, we do," he said grimly.

So much for Christmas magic.

"Putting it off isn't going to help." He fumbled with the stove door and stood. "You need to hear this, ASAP."

She stared as a smile broke out on his face.

"I've been praying about you and Paul for months. The more I pray, the more I realize my attitude has not been helpful." Andrew shook his head. "I haven't yet found the person God has chosen for me and Michaela. But maybe you have.

"I'll be glad to talk with you and Paul. But what God says to you is your business."

Joanna blinked. Twice. Was she dreaming?

"This," Andrew kissed her on the cheek, "is my Christmas gift to you." He grinned boyishly. "Sorry I acted like such a kid. But I couldn't help it. You're my mom!"

Joanna laughed and hugged him. Hugged him again.

The phone rang.

"Young lady, it's past nine thirty." Andrew growled in a "dad" voice. "Far too late to accept phone calls from gentlemen."

"Oh, really? Doesn't this fall under the heading 'my business'?"

"Just practicing for the future." He tried to look menacing. "I'm good, don't you think?"

"You're good." She headed for her bedroom to talk.

But it wasn't a gentleman. "H–hi, Joanna."

She couldn't believe it. "Angie?"

"It's been a crazy day. I couldn't call until now." Angie paused. "The cactus—"

"Yes?" She'd thought her heart so full of joy, she couldn't find room for more. But she was wrong.

"The cactus has a bud. A big one. I found it this afternoon."

Thank You, Lord. "That's wonderful, Angie."

"I thought I'd let you know," she repeated, sounding almost as happy as Joanna. "See you!"

"Good-bye. And merry Christmas." Joanna barely said it before Angie hung up.

She hit the speed dial before she even realized she was calling Paul. Could he handle this much good news in one day?

"Thank the Lord." He echoed her joy, his voice soft. "I miss you, Joanna. Don't we deserve a little Christmas together time tomorrow?"

"Absolutely." Maybe a candlelit dinner at the White Gull? Or the Whistling Swan?

"Can you meet me at Eagle Tower, about three thirty?"

"The Tower? Why?" She tried not to sound disappointed. Or nauseated.

"You'll see. Bring your snowmobile gear. And a Christmas ribbon."

"Huh?"

"A skinny Christmas ribbon. About a foot long." He laughed.

"Any special color?" Joanna couldn't believe this conversation.

"No. Just bring one." He laughed and hung up.

He'd called her a scary woman. Maybe Paul wasn't so tame, either?

❄

"Will you climb the tower with me again?" Paul looked at her with his heart in his eyes.

In the dead of winter? Still, he had scaled it with her. "All right. I will." *Help us, Lord. And thank You the steps aren't icy.*

"My turn to go first." He smiled and began to climb. She grasped the rail and followed. In better shape this time, she didn't breathe so hard. The first platform appeared much faster this second time around. During the next few flights, she heard Paul whisper scriptures. She added her own.

Joanna felt a snowflake's chilly kiss. Another. Another. Still, they stepped up, up, never looking down.

Both hesitated on the last platform. Soft white flakes brushed their faces like angel fingertips. Three more flights to the top.

"We prayed here last time." Joanna stopped. "Can we pray again?"

Paul put an arm around her. "Father, I believe You brought us here this evening. We know we can climb higher with Your help."

"Jesus, climb with us." She leaned against him.

Paul quoted the Psalms, " 'He will not let your foot slip.' "

"Of course, the psalmist knew we'd be climbing Eagle Tower." She tried to grin.

"God knew." Paul touched her face and turned to the final stairs.

Foot in front of foot. Flight above flight above flight. The top. At last.

Trembling, they held each other and looked up. Thousands of white flakes, like winter manna, poured from the heavens. Thousands of black trees gathered it below. She and Paul drank in the dark blue water shimmering peach, rose, and gold, reflecting the sun's imminent grand farewell. And God's greatness.

"I couldn't have done it without you." He drew her closer.

"Nor I without you."

He raised her chin. "Joanna, will you walk to the edge with me?"

"I think I already have." She laughed. "But, yes. Last time we agreed to do that."

"Then let's go. One. Two. Three."

Like children, they marched the few steps together to the edge of the highest platform. The town of Ephraim glimmered across the frozen bay like her lighted Christmas village, complete with church steeple.

"It's perfect," she whispered.

"The perfect place to give you your special Christmas present." He handed her a skinny satin red ribbon.

She'd already given him a new brown flannel shirt, and he'd given her a darling little navy hat. What was this "special" gift? She looked at the plain ribbon. He'd hauled her clear up to the edge of the tower for this?

"I'm not finished." Paul's eyes glowed like a fire's embers. He removed his left glove and held his hand out. "Joanna, will you tie the ribbon on my ring finger?"

She held her breath and tied it.

"Will you take my hand?"

Dizzy now, she didn't dare look out at Ephraim. She grasped his big, rough hand with the ribbon bow.

"Joanna, I love you. I want to marry you. I would have bought you the biggest diamond in Door County this Christmas if I could."

Rainbows danced around her. Climb? She could fly.

"But we both know it's not time. Still, I wanted to commit myself to you." He paused. "If you want me."

She almost knocked him over with her hug. They swayed and squeaked in terror.

"We both want to go to glory." Paul's voice shook with laughter and fear. "But this soon?"

"Sorry." She giggled. "I'm just so happy!"

"Did. . .did you bring a ribbon?"

"Yes." She pulled the silver ribbon from her pocket, took off her left glove, and held out her hand.

He tied it on her finger. And kissed it.

"I commit myself to you, too, Paul." She suddenly felt shy. "If you want me."

"Oh, Joanna." He held her, and she felt his tear on her cheek. "You are God's precious gift to me."

She wanted to share their joy with the One who gave it. "Let's pray again."

"Absolutely." He paused and looked down. "But I don't think God will mind if we do it on the ground."

❊

Gliding, sliding across frozen Fish Creek Bay together on a snowmobile, flying as if on a magic carpet, Joanna hugged Paul's waist and laid her cheek against his back. The night sky couldn't hold all the stars, so they'd spilled onto Door County's shores, covering towns with their twinkling, glowing lights.

Back on the park trails, they sailed over rises. Leaning together, they whipped through the sleepy, blanketed trees. They squiggled across broad white meadows like children decorating a giant frosted cupcake, circling and circling.

The past year, Joanna had cried until she thought she could weep no more. She knew Paul had shed tears, too.

But now, they laughed without limits.

What a Christmas. What a year.

What a ride.

Erma Bombeck Global winner Rachael Phillips and Steve, her high school sweetheart and husband of thirty-five years, have never crashed on their tandem bicycle—so far. *Ride with Me into Christmas* is Rachael's first published fiction. She also authored four biographies: *Frederick Douglass, Billy Sunday, St. Augustine,* and *Well with My Soul.* Rachael has written four hundred columns, articles, and devotions for newspapers and magazines such as *Today's Christian Woman,* as well as *Pearl Girls, Guideposts,* and other collections. Visit her at www.rachaelwrites.com.

MY HEART STILL BEATS

by Eileen Key

Acknowledgments

Thank you, Rebecca Germany and Tamela Hancock Murray, for believing in my work. And to my novella partners for taking me to experience Door County, Wisconsin: such a beautiful place. Kim, Margie, Connie, Donna, and Crystal, I appreciate how you improve my writing.

Any love demonstrated in this short work is a direct result of love showered on me, much by Hesta (Sissy) Williams. Trevor and Eliana, Nana loves you!

Trust God from the bottom of your heart; don't try to figure out everything on your own. Listen for God's voice in everything you do, everywhere you go; he's the one who will keep you on track.

PROVERBS 3:5–6 MSG

Chapter 1

The house at the end of the driveway took Madison Tanner's breath away. She pulled the sedan closer, peered beneath the visor, then glanced in the rearview mirror. "You two tricksters. Some cabin. I thought we'd be roughing it."

Eighty-four-year-old Vestal Grissom cackled from the backseat. "Told you we'd be on a Door County adventure, never said exactly where."

"I never get tired of seeing the Beacon." His wife, Hilde, sighed. "Isn't it gorgeous? Built in 1920 by my papa."

The one-and-a-half-story home on the Green Bay side of the peninsula sat in the middle of a lawn dotted with leaves and patches of snow. Well-maintained flower beds outlined with large rocks awaited spring planting. The head of a concrete L-shaped pier was barely visible from Maddy's vantage point, but the end extended into the water. She imagined the Grissoms watching sailboats and sunsets with their feet dipped into the cold water.

Hilde patted Maddy's headrest, a whiff of White

Shoulders perfume wafting from her hand. "Park, so we might take a walk."

Maddy pulled up to the main entrance, the large weathered door welcoming in the wintry light. She'd barely stopped before a back car door flew open, and the octogenarians spilled out, laughing like children on a holiday.

Vestal grabbed Hilde's arm and helped her from the car. "Birdie, don't you break one of those skinny legs tromping across the backyard."

She straightened her green velour pants around her ample hips, tugged on a jacket, and swatted at his hand, then clasped it. "Oh you. I'm perfectly capable of taking a walk in my new tennis shoes, Grumps." She pulled out mittens and slung a scarf about her head.

Vestal coughed out a laugh, wrinkles forming parentheses around his mouth. Wisps of white hair stuck up in every direction. He fumbled with a cap. Hilde beamed at her husband. Celebrating their sixty-second anniversary, the two still acted like young lovers.

Maddy chuckled and slid from the car. Wind from the lake lifted her hair and tossed it across her face. "I'll unload and you two bundle up for a short stroll." Her breath puffed from her lips. She looped a headband around her hair and ears. "Emphasis on short. It's cold."

Vestal handed Maddy the house keys and grabbed Hilde's arm, a twinkle in his eyes. "Come on, Birdie-girl, let's head to the water." He wrapped a bright blue muffler around his neck. Hand-in-hand the couple made their way toward the concrete pier.

Tiny waves frothed across the bay, tossed about by the strong breeze. Maddy shivered and wrestled the suitcases from the car. She pulled off a glove and unlocked the front door. Stomping her feet against the chill, Maddy slid the suit-cases against the stairs and turned around.

A great room greeted her, a stone fireplace in the center. Adjacent was the dining room with a long Shaker-style table. Highly polished maple wood floors sparkled when she flipped on a light. Vestal had said the log walls and beams had been recently refurbished. They shone.

Maddy pursed her lips. "Naomi must be hoping for a buyer, pretty quick." She frowned at the thought of the Grissoms' only relative. "Papers aren't even signed and she's trying to push them out of the way."

Maddy peered out the glass doors and watched the couple meander back to the house, arm in arm, leaning into each other, Birdie chattering. Sixty-two years. Vestal and Hilde's last Christmas at the cabin. A shaft of sadness pierced her peacefulness.

She shook off the gloom and eyed the fireplace. Kindling, newspaper, and logs sat on one side of the hearth. Maddy opened the damper and placed some crumpled newspaper and small kindling in a pile in the center of the fireplace. She lit a match and soon the fire took hold. She added larger kindling and held a medium-sized log, watching as the flames spurted up the wood. She slid the log onto the iron cradle. Tiny flames licked the log, smoke stinging her nose. It quickly built into a soothing fire, a rich, musty smell filling the room. She held out her hands and felt the cold leave her bones.

The door flew open, and Vestal stomped his shoes against the welcome mat. "Birdie-girl, maybe you'll get that white Christmas." He motioned Maddy to the door and pointed out the roiling clouds, silvery gray on the undersides, and shivered. "Could be snow by nightfall."

Hilde grinned. "Honeybunch, that would be fine with me. I love snow." She slid out of her jacket and handed it to her husband. She beamed when she spotted the flickering flames. "Vestal, our Maddy started a fire." She clasped her hands, turned to Maddy, and chuckled. "I think you're spoiling us rotten. We need to adopt you. Do you think knowing you six months would give us an advantage?" She turned her back to the fire.

Maddy placed another small log in the fireplace, embers scattering. "I bet it would. I can check with my mom. She might be ready to relinquish rights." Her mouth turned down.

A tiny frown creased Hilde's forehead. "Now, Maddy, your mom will come around one of these days. She loves you." She shoved gray hair from her forehead. "Did you get your packages shipped?"

Maddy nodded. "Yes, ma'am. Mom's gifts are winging their way to Austin as we speak."

Hilde reached out a hand. "And you're sure you don't need to wing with them? Christmas at home this year?"

A sigh escaped Maddy's lips. "One of these days, just not this year." She used the brass-handled poker to stir the fire. "Besides, I'm hired out this Christmas to some pretty special people."

"Special people? You leaving us today?" Vestal snorted. "Girl tells us she'll be around for a week and now she's leaving town."

Maddy laughed. "Mr. G., you know you're stuck with me. Santa's already gotten my list and he knows where to find me." She replaced the poker in the stand. "How about some cocoa?"

Vestal waved a hand in their direction. "You girls settle in,

I'll stir up cocoa. Lola called and said she'd been to the grocery. Let me see what she brought."

Maddy sank onto the settee and watched the tiny flames flicker. Hilde scooted beside her and patted her knee. "I'm awfully glad you're here, darling."

"Me, too." Maddy blinked back tears. The concert season was over and the few friends she had from the School of Music had gone home. Minneapolis would've been a lonely place.

"We're so grateful God brought you into our lives. Ever since we met you, you've been so thoughtful." Hilde gave a soft chuckle. "Most people don't spoil their next-door neighbors like you've done." She shoved her shoulder gently against Maddy. "What would we do without you?"

Maddy leaned against the proffered shoulder and inhaled Hilde's sweet fragrance. "What would I do without you two?"

"If God hadn't brought you along when Vestal was so sick—" Hilde heaved a sigh.

"I'm glad He did." Maddy closed her eyes. Six months earlier, her limo service had been hired by Hilde to carry Vestal back and forth to doctor's appointments, and she'd been their chosen driver. The couple's tenderness with each other and kindness to her had chipped away at the wall she'd built around her heart with her escape to Minneapolis. She snuggled a bit closer to Hilde. "Without you watching over me, I might get into some serious trouble."

Hilde wrapped an arm about Maddy's shoulders. "Trouble? Now I can't imagine what kind of trouble you could get into."

"Don't ask Mama. She's got a different story." Maddy stared into the flames.

Vestal tromped into the living room. "We've got a few groceries, compliments of our good friend Lola. And look what else she left us." He bore a Christmas cactus in one hand and a card in the other. "An anniversary gift."

A bright red ribbon encircled the gold foil-covered pot. Vestal held the card at arm's length. "Welcome home," he read. His eyes brightened with tears. He looked at them, surveyed the room, then smiled at his wife. "Welcome home, Birdie."

❄

Maddy walked from the kitchen, balancing a tray loaded with two mugs of steaming cocoa and grilled cheese sandwiches. While Vestal showed off the Christmas cactus, Maddy stirred up lunch for the couple. "Here you go." She placed the tray on a small table.

"Lunch for two?" Vestal's mouth quirked. "Where's a bit of food for the hired help?"

Maddy waved her hand. "I nibbled on cheese and crackers. Think I'm going to stretch my legs. Enjoy the fire."

Hilde reached for a mug and beamed. "Thank you, dear. Again, your thoughtfulness shines through." She took a sip and tilted her head. "Watch the weather. Don't go far. Storms can build in a hurry, and we don't want you wet or chilled."

Maddy shrugged into her maroon parka and tugged gloves from her pocket. "Yes, ma'am. This Texas girl's learning." She grinned and stepped outside.

The cold air brought tears to her eyes and made her nose burn. She sniffed and slid her fingers inside the lined leather gloves, a birthday gift from the Grissoms, and pulled her headband over her ears. "Need to move these legs. Exercise. Good for the soul." She laughed and began to walk. One lap around the house on the gentle incline pulled at sore muscles—her legs had grown stiff on the long drive to the cabin. How grateful she was there had been no snow on the highway. The mild winter in Minneapolis hadn't tested her driving expertise yet.

Maddy stretched and walked the length of the driveway, then circled back for a jog. She sprinted toward the road in an easy stride. Gravel and leaves crunched in rhythm with her feet. She neared the road and decided to swing out around the birch tree and enter the drive from the other end to complete a full circle. Three or four laps would give her a good workout.

She slowed and swiveled around the tree at the end of the lane. Her tennis shoe bit into slick ground and stuck. Maddy's knee gave way and she lurched toward the road, arms flailing in vain to catch her balance. She glanced up then clenched her eyes shut. A silver Jaguar perched on a hood was about to greet her, head-on.

❄

Grant Sterling slammed on the brakes, his arm flung wide to protect his daughter in the passenger seat, and swerved to miss the runner. He gripped the steering wheel and maneuvered to the side of the road, then thrust the car into Park. He shoved open the car door and scrambled out, headed toward the runner.

"Are you crazy, lady? I could've killed you!" His heart beat double time in his heaving chest. He ran his hands through his hair then flapped them like an orchestra conductor. "Do you know how lucky you are?" He glared at her.

She slid to a sitting position close to the passenger side of the car, rubbed her ankle, and groaned.

Grant stepped closer. "Are you hurt?" Would rental car insurance cover an injury sustained when he almost ran over someone? He fingered the hood ornament.

The woman looked up, tears sparkling in hazel eyes. "I'm okay." She sniffled and swiped hair from her face. "So is your car." Struggling to stand, she winced. Grant reached out to offer a hand, but she shook her head. "I'll be just fine. Thank you for your concern."

The sarcasm wasn't lost on Grant. He gave her a sheepish grin. "Sorry. You just scared the liver out of me." He placed a hand on his chest. "Heart attack, too."

A small smile played at the edge of her lips. "Didn't do much for my heart, either. All I saw was your hood ornament, and I thought I was a goner." A flush crept up her cheeks and her eyes narrowed. "You were driving like you belong in the Indy 500."

Grant frowned. "I wasn't speeding."

She plopped a hand on her hip. "I believe the speed limit on this narrow road is fifteen." She spit out the words. "You certainly weren't going fifteen." She pointed to the road. "Not with those skid marks."

Grant looked at the pavement then back at her. "I was not speeding, lady." He gritted his teeth and began a count to ten. On three, he snapped, "You shouldn't be running on a road without a shoulder."

"Don't worry. I'll take your advice"—she clapped her hand on her chest—"to heart." She turned and began to limp up the driveway.

"Hey." She continued walking. He noted her slim figure and the tumble of blond hair cascading down her back. "Do you need a ride—to the house?"

She glanced over her shoulder. "No, thank you. I'm quite capable of making my way home." She tugged the pink headband over one ear. "Good-bye. Have a safe journey."

"Daddy." Lizzy's head protruded from the window. "Do

we need to help her?"

"No, sweetie." Grant sighed and eyed his ten-year-old daughter. "She'll make it fine on her own." He walked back to the car and slid in. "Roll up the window, you're letting warm air escape." He peered through the glass until he could no longer see the woman. He backed up and inched forward slowly. She'd almost reached the crest of the drive. He gripped the steering wheel, adrenaline draining from his body.

"Are you okay, Daddy?" Lizzy's blue eyes bored into his.

"Yep. I'm fine." A dull throb at the base of his head signaled a headache approaching. He lifted a yellow slip of paper from the console and handed it to his daughter. "Read the numbers again."

"Fifteen thirty-three." Lizzy tucked a leg beneath her. "We are really close." She gasped. "Daddy, look." She pointed to a marker near the tree where the woman had appeared. "It's her house you're going to sell."

Chapter 2

Maddy leaned against a boulder at the end of the frostbitten flower bed and stretched her leg. Strained muscles throbbed and took her breath away. She rubbed her ankle. Last time she'd wrenched it, it had brought crutches for several days. This pull didn't seem as bad, though she might need to ice it. She took a couple of steps.

The driver had been more concerned with his car than her condition. *Mr. Big Shot.* His broad shoulders had filled his cranberry Ralph Lauren Windbreaker, and dark hair swept across his forehead to almost cover chocolate brown eyes. Fancy clothes and an expensive car—that spelled trouble in a man. At least it had in Tim.

Hilde caught her attention with a whistle. "Hurry in by the fire. It'll take the chill off that rosy red nose."

Maddy straightened. She didn't want the Grissoms fretting over her injury. They needed to enjoy this last Christmas here, not be her nursemaid. She waved a hand. "Be there shortly." Placing her weight on her foot, she bit her lip and tried to walk it off.

She meandered down to the pier, ignoring the small pinch in her ankle, and stared at the gray water, the city of Ephraim sparkling white across the bay. Two church steeples punctuated the skyline. Docks empty of patrons stretched into the waterway. No sailboats out in the cold wind.

It would be fun to ski across this bay. Her lips tugged up in a half smile recalling her dad's encouraging words. "You can do it, punkin', I know you can." And she had. She'd eased up on the skis and flown across Lake Travis time and again. She toed a rock into the water and watched the concentric circles spread. Her father's funeral had started concentric circles of loss in her life: Dad, Tim, her mom's affection.

A gust of wind caught a spray of water and splattered Maddy. She shivered and turned around, staring at the silvery clouds. Snow? She longed to see deep drifts, sculptured ice on trees, not the wintry slush of the city. She clapped her hands, the gloves muffling the sound. "Maybe this year." She lifted her foot and rotated it in slow circles. "Better." Just bruised. Like her heart.

Maddy shoved her headband back and headed to the house. She scooted inside and tugged off her coat, cheeks burning. "Brrr, that wind's cold."

Vestal snorted and lifted a poker from the stand. "Different kind of weather here. Good for the soul."

Maddy jerked a look in his direction, her mouth half-open. Vestal poked at the fire. She shook her head, hung up her jacket, and backed up to the fireplace. "The waterway is beautiful. Reminds me of home."

"You don't mention Austin much, dear." Hilde fingered a loose thread on her shirt. "Do you miss it?"

Tears stung the back of Maddy's nose. She swallowed,

lowered her head, and bit her lip. Emotions under control, she answered, "Not much. I'm becoming a Minnesota girl now."

Hilde said softly, "I think this week we're going to make you a Door County gal."

"It's beautiful." Her throat tightened. Careful of her ankle, she faced the fire, hands held out. "Have you celebrated every Christmas here?" She glanced over her shoulder at Hilde.

Vestal laughed. "Not every one, but many." He handed her the poker with a nod. "Something about stirring those flames is calming."

Hilde plopped on the sofa. "I can't believe this will be our last." She slid an afghan from the back of the couch and pulled it around her legs.

"Doesn't have to be." Vestal folded his arms and looked at his wife, his lips in a straight line. "Not too late to change our minds."

Maddy glanced toward Hilde.

Hilde straightened. "We decided it's best. Naomi said we'd make a tidy profit if we sell now."

"Naomi." Vestal snorted. "I told that Realtor man who called we weren't available today."

"Grumpy, we need to think—"

Vestal raised his wrinkled hand, knobby arthritic fingers forming a duck's bill. "Squawk, squawk. That's all those guys do." He sat beside Hilde. "Today we are enjoying the Beacon. We can discuss business another time." He pressed Hilde's hand to his lips, his eyes sparkling. "Anniversary right now."

Maddy poked at a log, sending sparks flying. She mashed her lips together. Naomi Long, the business suit–clad niece. She stood to inherit everything from the Grissoms. And she made sure anyone close to Hilde and Vestal knew it.

"Don't think you can weasel into my family and steal my

aunt and uncle from me." She'd fired a parting shot at Maddy the last time they'd been together in the hospital waiting room.

"Steal your relatives?" Maddy raised her eyebrows.

Naomi frowned. "They've told me how kind you are—" Her acerbic tone angered Maddy, but she kept her peace. "But blood runs thicker than kindness, just you remember that." Naomi flounced from the room leaving Maddy speechless.

Hilde's voice broke into her reverie. "Why don't you take a rest in your bedroom, dear?" She smiled. "We gave you the rose room, second on the left."

Maddy slid the poker into the stand and nodded. "Thank you, ma'am. I'll do just that. Think I'll grab a glass of water first." She bit her lip and minimized a limp as she walked to the kitchen. She filled a tumbler with ice, grabbed her suitcase, and hobbled up the stairs, her ankle pulsating with each step.

Roses in every shade of pink dotted the wallpaper. A rose-patterned quilt covered an iron bedstead. The colors were soothing to the eye. She sighed as she sat in a maple rocking chair. She tugged her shoe and sock off and dumped ice into the sock. She propped her foot on the end of the bed and gingerly placed the ice pack on the side of her foot, the cold biting into her skin.

Maddy leaned back and closed her eyes, visions of a cranberry-clad man darting through her mind. Her shoulders slumped. She was tired—very tired. And she certainly didn't need man complications.

❄

Grant parked the rental car in front of the shabby cabin. His family usually stayed at a beautiful bed-and-breakfast, but it wasn't open this time of year. However, the owners were in town. Mrs. McKenzie assured him she'd be available to babysit. At the moment, she was not around. Grant sighed. With his sister sick with the flu, he'd had no choice but to bring his daughter to Ephraim.

He might have to put his visit to the Grissoms on hold until Mrs. Mac returned. The phone call to Mr. Grissom had not been positive; he'd need a face-to-face appointment. He shoved the address into his pocket and slid the key from the ignition.

Lizzy bounced on the front seat. "It's so pretty here." She gestured toward the water. "Can we come back in the summer?"

Grant grunted. "We'll see. Right now I need an aspirin and a nap."

"Daddy," Lizzy dragged out the last syllable. "I want to explore." She slipped out of the car and bounded to his open car door. "Can't we go for a walk or something? I've been in that car forever."

"Lizzy, it wasn't forever. And, no, not right now," Grant snapped. Her crestfallen face stabbed him with guilt. "I'm sorry." He reached into the backseat for their luggage. "Here, take your bag."

His daughter jerked it from his hand and stomped toward the cabin doorway. The throbbing in his temples accelerated. He had an anxious client and a drama-queen daughter; his nerves were shot. "Caron, you'd better have the flu," he muttered through clenched teeth.

The drab rooms smelled musty. He followed Lizzy into the bedroom where she'd flopped on a bed, her iPod buds inserted, already tuning him out. If he made a recording of "You Are My Sunshine," would she remember snuggling in the rocking chair when she was little? His lips tipped up.

But not now. No, he had to settle in, relax, and plan. He massaged his temples.

Naomi Long had railed about her relatives. "They're ancient. Uncle Vestal can be stubborn. He just doesn't realize the property values. My father died some ten years ago"—her tone held no sorrow—"and Aunt Hilde is the only surviving member of that generation." She huffed. "Proceeds from the property should stay in the family." She'd leveled a steely glare at him. "You found nothing wrong with the house last month, correct?"

"The inspection I did was thorough, Miss Long, but are you sure your aunt is ready to sell the house?" Grant waved a hand at the papers in front of him. "I'd hate for you to pay my expenses for another trip—"

"Mr. Sterling, I have no doubt my aunt is ready to dispose of the property. She's aging and knows what's best. I've made your reservations and will reimburse all expenses." Her toothy grin seemed insincere. "I'm even paying for your child." The grin faded. "I have two prospects lined up. Show the house and get a signature." She had spun on her heel and left his office.

Grant sank onto the other bed and propped a lumpy pillow under his head. A water stain marred the ceiling. "Miss Long, thank you for the five-star accommodations. Work begins tomorrow." He closed his eyes. *Fifteen minutes, Lord, give me fifteen minutes of peace.*

A blond-haired jogger flitted through his brain and he smiled. Her hazel eyes had blazed when she accused him of speeding. He frowned—he had not been speeding. He rubbed his forehead. Had he? He rolled to his side and punched the pillow, a niggle of worry rippling through his chest. Was the girl hurt? He should've checked more thoroughly. "Ha. Right," he whispered into the pillow. She probably would've bitten him. Grant rubbed a temple, the muscles in his jaw working. "She's not their granddaughter; Naomi said they never had kids. Another niece?" He sighed. Would she interfere with negotiations? They certainly hadn't parted on friendly terms. He groaned. More drama, that's just what he needed. No, what he needed was this paycheck to cover tuition for a full year at Lizzy's private school.

Grant opened his eyes and peered at his child. She'd drawn up her knees and fallen asleep. A flood of love swelled up in his chest, and a smile spread across his face. Maybe he'd get his fifteen minutes after all.

❄

Maddy's eyelids fluttered open. She glanced at the clock and jolted from the rocker. She'd dozed for almost two hours. She shuffled into the bathroom and freshened up. Vestal and Hilde might be ready for dinner, and she didn't have a clue what their plans might be.

Gingerly she took the stairs one at a time. The ice had done its trick and her ankle barely gave a twinge. Listening for voices, she neared the living room. No one sat before the dying fire. Strains of music and tantalizing smells came from the kitchen.

Maddy stepped to the entrance. The couple waltzed to a tune floating from a radio, flour-coated hands about each other's shoulders. Cookie cutters, cookie sheets, and batter mix sat on the center island.

Maddy smiled and tucked back around the corner, not wishing to disturb their moment. She stepped to the sofa. A scrapbook lay open on one end. She pulled it closer. Black-and-white photos were glued on black pages—scenes from yesteryear. A young Vestal tugging a canoe into the water. In the next photo Hilde waved a paddle, her mouth quirked. Across the page, Hilde emerging from under the tipped canoe, bent at the waist, laughing. Maddy chuckled. The two were cutups even then.

She stepped to the fireplace and stirred the embers. "How did they ever keep a love alive for sixty-two years?" She shoved a small log closer to the center and a flame spurted up.

"Lots of patience and bites of the tongue," Hilde said. She wiped her hands on a checkered towel. "Did our music disturb your rest?" A residue of flour coated one cheek.

"Not at all." Maddy brushed a finger across Hilde's cheek. "Cookies for dinner?"

"Soup's thawing, we'll have it soon." Vestal tossed a dish towel over one shoulder. "We ran out of sugar."

"I'll go get some." Maddy turned toward the door.

Hilde held up one hand in protest, but Vestal shook his head. "We wanted cookies to send to Lola and some for ourselves. Let the young'un go. It's just up the road."

Maddy laughed. "Be back in a flash." She shrugged into her parka and grabbed her headband. The cold wind bit into her cheeks and she shivered.

The evening sky glittered with diamond stars. Her daddy enjoyed lying on a blanket in their backyard trying to point out constellations to Maddy. She never got more than the Big Dipper. Tonight the glistening array tugged at her heart. "Oh Daddy, how I miss you." Tears welled up. Grief caught her so often in unexpected moments. "If only Mom had insisted on those treatments—"

Maddy bit her lip. No use going down the *if only* route. She'd beaten it to death. She climbed into the car. Her lips turned up and she searched for the Dipper through the dirt-speckled windshield. "Daddy, I miss you." She turned the key in the ignition and circled out the driveway.

Everything in Ephraim was shut up tight, darkness cloaking the stretch of road. She continued on the highway. When she reached Sister Bay, the grocery store's red neon light flashed a welcome against the inky sky.

Maddy parked and walked inside. She strolled the short aisles and found a bag of sugar. Her sweet tooth jerked her toward the candy aisle, and she fingered three types of chocolate. What would satisfy her craving?

"Glad to see you up and about."

Maddy swung around and faced the man who almost ran over her. She gave a curt nod and turned back to the candy boxes.

"Did you sustain any injuries?" The man leaned toward her.

"No, I'm fine."

"Listen"—he stepped into her line of vision—"we got off on a bad foot." He glanced down at her tennis shoes. "No pun intended. Let me introduce myself." He tugged a business card from his wallet and handed it to her. "I'm Grant Sterling."

Maddy fingered the card. "The Realtor."

"Yes." Grant's eyes searched her face. "You're a relative of the Grissoms?"

"No." More information than she wanted to give. "Excuse me, I have to go."

Grant's hand shot out toward her elbow, and she jerked back. The bag of sugar toppled to the floor and split open, spewing sugar crystals in every direction. Maddy bit her tongue to keep from lashing out at the man.

"Oh, I'm sorry." He danced backward, his black loafers twinkling with sugar. "I'll pay for the damage."

Maddy balled her fists at her side. "Yes, you will. Seems like you cause damage wherever you go."

Grant flashed a look at her. "That's uncalled for. It was an—"

"Accident. I know," Maddy said. "Do accidents always follow you, Mr. . .Mr."—she glanced at the card—"Sterling?"

The clerk stepped into the aisle with a broom and dustpan. "If you'll excuse me." He motioned at the two and they stepped aside. Maddy reached behind her and scooped up the last bag of sugar. "I'm glad there was another bag, or you'd be driving to the next store." She glared at Grant.

"Look, lady, I came over to see how you were doing. The spill *was* an accident." In the harsh fluorescent lights, he scrutinized Maddy's face. "I might add, you seem to be prone to accidents as well."

Maddy spun on her heel, sugar crunching under her tennis shoes, and sped to the cash register. She tapped her fingernails on the counter waiting for the clerk. Grant lined up behind her, a bottle of soda under one arm. Neither spoke. The clerk took Maddy's money and gave her the change. She swiped up the sugar and whirled out the door.

Behind the wheel of the sedan, she glowered at the low-slung Jag next to her. If she flipped her door open really wide, she could probably put a dent in the side of the silver car. She bit her lip and flipped the key in the ignition. "Not worth the hassle. Rich men hunt their prey." And he would profit from the sale of the Grissoms' beautiful home. Seemed terribly unfair.

As she backed from the parking space, she sensed the car tug and felt the clunk of a tire. "No, can't be." She climbed out and circled to the back passenger side. "A flat tire?" She groaned. She glanced at her mittened fingers. How would she ever maneuver a tire iron without freezing? She punched a button on the key fob and opened the trunk, shoving aside a collection of magazines and removing a bag of Hilde's yarn to reach the trapdoor that hid the spare tire.

"What are you doing?" Mr. Sterling said. "Ahh, flat tire." He stepped back as Maddy lifted the lug wrench.

She glared at him. "Yes, flat tire."

"Can you change it?"

Maddy bit her lower lip then spit out the words, "Do I have a choice?"

Mr. Sterling gave a reassuring smile, small crinkles in the corner of his eyes. "I believe you do. I have some Fix-A-Flat. It'll get you to a service station"—he peered into the darkness—"in the morning. It will hold enough to get you back to the cottage, can't drive much farther than that." He walked to the rear of his car and opened the trunk. He returned with a yellow can.

"What do I—"

"You want to use it? I promise, the tire can be repaired later." His brown eyes peered into Maddy's.

A flush crept up her face. She reached for the can and his fingers brushed hers. Despite herself a tingle ran up her arm.

Mr. Sterling jerked the can back and stared at her. He was close—close enough for her to smell cinnamon-laced breath. She glanced into the trunk and sighed.

"Okay, you're probably right." She slid the lug wrench back into place and tossed the bag of yarn inside. "We'll try things your way."

A grin spread across his face. "I've found my way often works best."

Maddy gave a halfhearted laugh. "We'll see, Mr. Sterling. We'll see."

Realtor-man knelt beside the tire and unscrewed the can's top. He inserted the needle into the tire's air valve. Within minutes, the tire was repaired. "There you go." He tossed the empty can into the garbage. "You can make it to the house, slowly." He frowned. "Do you need me to follow you?"

"No, I'll be fine," Maddy snapped.

The man raised a hand. "Fine, just checking."

Heat rushed into her cheeks. "Sorry. . .I mean. . ." She looked at the ground, face burning. He must think she was an ingrate. She glanced up. "Thank you for your help."

"Always glad to help a lady in distress." His brown eyes twinkled as though he were enjoying himself.

She stared at him, his dark hair framed with the red neon light, a self-assured smile on his face. "Thank you again. I'll be glad to repay you."

"Not a problem. I'm glad I was around. Could've been bad had you been on that dark stretch of highway." His glance took in the surroundings. "Beautiful up here, isn't it?" He sighed, his breath forming a cloud. "Guess I need to go." He saluted. "Nice seeing you again. Glad to know I fixed one limp."

Maddy laughed. "Yeah, one ankle down, one tire inflated." She slid into the front seat and he pushed her door closed. She started the car and headed for the highway. A warmth flooded her as she watched the gentleman in her rearview mirror. "Maybe I had you pegged all wrong, Mr. Realtor-man."

❄

Grant let his eyes linger as the woman left the parking lot. For once, he was grateful he'd taken his dad's advice and carried an emergency kit. Even in a jazzed-up rental he could be a Boy Scout. He jingled his keys and tucked under the steering wheel. He watched the taillights fade into the distance. "Will she be around when I show the house?" A smile started, then he shook his head. No, he didn't need a woman in his life. Lizzy was enough. For now, his focus was strictly on her. Bringing in a lady friend would cause havoc; he could feel it in his bones. He turned and drove the mile back to the cabin where Lizzy and pizza waited.

Chapter 3

Maddy woke to the mouthwatering smells of breakfast. She dressed, then padded down the stairs and into the kitchen. Hilde was plopping biscuits on a pan.

"You need any help?"

Hilde pointed to a pitcher and a can of orange juice. "Stir up some?"

"Sure."

Vestal smiled at Maddy, then dipped his head toward his wife, a frown creasing his brow. "We don't have to go through with this, darling. You know that."

Hilde's lips pursed, and she whistled a few bars of "You Are My Sunshine" while sliding the tray into the oven. She lifted the lid on a pot of gravy that simmered on the stove and sniffed. Pungent, tangy sausage smell filled the kitchen.

Vestal sighed and sat at the table. Maddy stirred the orange juice and poured him a glass. He sipped and stared out the window.

The backside of the cottage faced the empty marina at

Eagle Bay Harbor. The church steeple and village buildings dusted with snow created a picture postcard. Maddy could see why Vestal would hate leaving this place.

He toyed with a saltshaker on the table. "Birdie-girl, I don't want to sell. Period."

Maddy cleared her throat. "I'll wait in the—"

"No, don't leave." Vestal clutched her wrist, his forehead furrowed. "Nothing I have to say needs to be hidden from you. Ain't that private." He straightened his sweater vest and continued, "I want us to be able to visit the shore whenever we've a mind to, Hilde. And if we let go of our place, no telling where we'd have to camp out." He waved a hand toward Ephraim. "There's some amazing sleeping rooms over there, but I surely do like my bed here better." He frowned at his wife. "Tell me you don't feel the same way."

Hilde brushed crumbs from the counter into her hand. "I do feel the same way, Grumpy." She tossed the crumbs into the garbage and settled her hands on her hips. "But if the money is that good—"

Vestal snorted and tipped his face toward Maddy. "Reckon you can carry a bag of gold with you through the Pearly Gates?"

Maddy grinned. "Not from what I hear."

He swiveled in his seat and glared at Hilde. "So we sell the Beacon. The place your daddy built. What are we going to do with all the money? Give it to the sourpuss?"

"Now, Vestal." Hilde stepped beside him and kneaded one shoulder with her hand. "We are getting up there in age, and we might need that extra money."

"True." Vestal clasped her hand and intertwined his fingers with hers. "But we've got a good-sized amount of income right now. And we could sell next year if we need to." He gazed into her eyes. "Please, not this year." His voice sounded childlike as he pled his case. "I don't want to give the house up."

Hilde sighed and pulled her hand free. "I thought we had an agreement." She slid into a chair. "With you getting sick last year, we decided this was best. Remember?"

"I remember." Vestal glanced at Maddy. "You remember, too. Doctor said I was fit as a fiddle now, didn't he?"

Maddy nodded.

"See there. Fit as a fiddle." Vestal laughed. "I might last another twenty years, and I want to spend my free time here in the Door."

The stove timer dinged, and Hilde jerked the biscuits from the oven. She slid them on a plate and set them on the table beside a gravy boat then sat down. "Eat up. Biscuits and gravy will stick to your ribs, my mama used to say."

"She said it here in this house." Vestal chuckled. He reached a hand toward Maddy. "Let's pray."

Maddy squeezed his fingers during the blessing. Door County had captivated her, too.

"Eat." Hilde's eyes sparkled as she watched her husband.

The steamy aroma of fresh-baked biscuits and gravy made Maddy's mouth water. She filled her plate and took a bite, savoring each flavor. Sipping her orange juice, she smiled at her hosts. "Thank you for bringing me to this amazing place."

Vestal pointed to her with his butter knife. "Maddy's not been here twenty-four hours and she knows it's amazing." He slathered butter across a biscuit. "Think about it, Birdie-girl, one day Maddy could haul her kiddos to our beach."

Hilde laughed. "You don't give up easily, Grumpy. Let's pray about this decision again. I must admit, I'd miss the

Door, too. No place like it, year 'round."

Vestal's mouth turned up, the parenthesis appearing. "Praying is just what we'll do." He looked at Maddy and winked. "I know God is on my side."

The phone rang. Vestal stood and grabbed the brown receiver. He nodded a time or two and said, "Three o'clock. That's fine." He replaced the receiver and faced his wife. "So we've got to decide, Hilde. He's a'comin' at three."

Hilde's eyes filled with tears. She shoved from the table and left the room, Vestal following. A lump filled Maddy's throat. Breakfast held no more appeal. Grabbing her plate, she stood and cleared the table. She filled a plastic pan with warm, soapy water and rinsed the dishes. It had been quite awhile since she'd been without a dishwasher. Staring at the lake, the soothing activity of dish washing relaxed her shoulders.

Vestal's comments made her smile: her children. What would they look like? A chuckle made its way up her throat. Her eyes roved the water and she imagined the Realtor on the rocky shore, one arm about her waist. No doubt about it, he was one good-looking man. His broad shoulders, tapered waist, just the right height to tuck her under his arm. And kind. Despite her bark, he'd helped with the tire. She sighed. "Stop dreaming, Madison. Look what it got you last time." She popped a soap bubble. "Ended just like that."

❄

Grant bit his lower lip and counted to ten, his daughter set in his sights. "Elizabeth." He puffed out his cheeks and tried again. "Punkin, I have to go." His hand itched to tug her blond ponytail.

"You care more about selling a house than making Christmas cookies or singing carols or anything else." Lizzy clamped her hands on her hips, her lower lip trembling.

"Look, honey, we'll cookie bake and celebrate when we return home, promise."

She cruised around the Formica table and put her hand on his shoulder. "Daddy, please don't go. I don't want to be stuck here by myself." She batted her eyelashes. "Please."

His gut tightened as he thought of his girl alone in the cabin. Grant closed his eyes. Since his wife's death four years ago, his daughter had practiced her manipulating with her singsong tone and sugar-sweet smile nearly every day. He twisted his lips and cleared his throat. "Elizabeth"—he rubbed her arm, his tone softening—"try to understand. Daddy needs to meet with some people for just a bit about selling their house. It's important to see them face-to-face."

"Don't they celebrate Christmas?" Lizzy's lower lip stuck out farther.

"I'm not sure. I haven't met them yet." Grant fingered the contract on the table. Naomi Long had offered a bonus should he get the contracts signed by year's end. Demanding, the dour-faced woman had bought and flipped several houses through his company. He didn't want to lose this client. But he did feel uneasy about leaving Lizzy alone. He scanned her face. "Grab your coat. You can wait for me in the car."

"Sweet." She bounded to the closet and pulled out her jacket. "Then we'll go for ice cream?"

"Ice cream? After the breakfast we had?" Grant smiled. He'd taken her to one of his favorite restaurants. The White Gull Inn served some of the finest French toast he'd ever eaten.

His daughter grinned. "We'll shop and then have ice cream. Breakfast is a long time from three o'clock."

Grant's heart swelled. The smile across his child's face made up for any problems encountered so far. They'd cruise by the Grissoms' house, schedule appointments, and be on their way in a hurry.

❄

Hilde plopped Christmas cookies on a tray and turned the slow cooker on low. The scent of apple cider and cinnamon filled the air. Maddy placed holly berry napkins on the counter. "Anything else I might do to get ready?"

Vestal laughed. "We're as ready to say no as we've ever been." He clapped his hands. He'd grabbed Hilde and danced across the room when she decided they'd keep the Beacon, and ended with a verse from "How Great Thou Art."

Maddy's eyes watered. The difference of opinion that had seemed to rise at breakfast had dissipated after their prayers. She wished her parents had experienced such a sweet prayer time as the Grissoms had.

"We're ready to say no after we promised Naomi." Hilde sighed. "I hope she'll understand."

Vestal frowned. "She won't. Be prepared for that. She's about the money, Birdie-girl."

A rap at the front door startled the three.

"Showtime." Vestal hitched his pants and straightened his sweater vest. "Let's put on our happy faces."

Hilde and Maddy laughed. Maddy faded into the kitchen doorway. She'd mentioned going upstairs, and Hilde had nixed the idea. Maddy had to admit, she was quite curious to see the Realtor again.

"Mr. Grissom?" The deep voice in the foyer made Maddy's pulse race. She could barely hear the ensuing introductions and waited for more.

Mr. Sterling walked into the living room and shook hands with Hilde. Vestal glanced toward the kitchen, and Maddy shrank against the wall.

"Maddy, come meet our guest."

She ran her fingers through her hair, yanked her T-shirt over her jeans, and stepped into the room. She smiled. "We've met briefly. Hello, Mr. Sterling."

Hilde's eyebrows shot up. "Really?"

"He was the gallant knight who helped with the tire last night." Her ears burned under his stare. She leaned against the wall.

Vestal said, "Well, fellow, we thank you for rescuing our girl."

Grant's wide smile showed even white teeth, and his deep brown eyes crinkled at the corners. "I don't believe I got your name."

"Madison Tanner."

He stepped toward her with an outstretched hand. "Grant Sterling." He looked toward her foot. "I do hope your injury—"

Maddy waved a hand to stop him and glanced sideways at her friends. "Everything's fine. Nice to see you again."

Hilde sat on the sofa and patted a cushion. "Sit here, Maddy." Once Maddy sank into the plush cushion, Hilde grasped her hand with shaking fingers. Maddy looked at her friend's face. Hilde had flushed a deep red.

"Mrs. G., you okay?" Maddy whispered.

"Right as rain." Hilde's lips twisted in a small smile, but the worry didn't leave her eyes. "Just you being here is a help." She squeezed Maddy's fingers.

The Realtor cleared his throat. "Well, now. Your niece sent me here to make things easier for you—"

"More'n likely easier for her." Vestal snorted. He motioned for Grant to sit on the settee. "We've got some things to say about those papers." He pointed to a folder in Grant's hand.

"They've been perused by your family lawyer." Grant smiled.

"Hmph," Vestal said. "Naomi's team of lawyers, maybe. Not ours."

A frown crossed Grant's brow. "I don't understand. I was instructed to get your signature and show the house while I'm here." He smiled. "Two prospects arrived yesterday."

"Prospects? Oh my." Hilde sagged against the couch. "Show the house?"

Vestal's face was grim. "To strangers."

"Yes. Our contract states we will show the house—"

"We don't want to sell." Vestal's eyebrows formed a V.

Maddy watched Grant grow pale. "Not sell? But I have contractual obligations—"

Hilde stood. "We can show them the house. But not today." She motioned toward the door. "I believe I'm tired and need a nap."

Grant stuffed papers into the folder and stood. "I'm not certain I understand, Mrs. Grissom. Naomi was positive—"

"Another time," Vestal said.

Maddy watched a splotch of red grow on the man's cheeks.

"But, Mr. Grissom, I need to do a walk-through on the property." Grant dragged along behind the couple toward the front door. He draped his coat over his arm and pulled a scarf around his neck.

"My wife needs her rest." Vestal propped a hand on his hip.

Hilde pulled the front door open. "My stars and garters. There's a child out here." She waved Maddy closer.

Grant groaned and walked through the door. A young girl stood in the yard, watching a flock of geese on the shoreline. "That's my daughter."

Hilde's eyes flashed. "You left a child outside in this cold weather?" She motioned for Lizzy to come closer. "Child, are you frozen?"

"No, ma'am. I'm just fine." Lizzy smiled at Hilde, Vestal, and Maddy. "I'm Lizzy." She stuck out a blue mitten.

Hilde grasped it and tugged the child indoors. "Let's get you to the fireplace and ward off any chill."

Grant raised a hand. "It's fine, Mrs. Grissom, we'll be on our way." A muscle worked in his jaw. "I'm sure you need your rest."

"Nonsense." Vestal huffed, his hand reaching for Lizzy's jacket. "This child needs some hot apple cider and—" He raised an eyebrow. "Maybe a sugar cookie?"

Lizzy beamed. "Sweet." She swung around to her dad. "Okay, Daddy?"

Confusion was written across Grant's face. "But I thought—"

Maddy laughed. "Just give in, Mr. Sterling. It's a whole lot easier." She reached for his coat. "We'll allow you some cider and a cookie, too." She leaned forward, taking in his musky smell.

Vestal tilted his head and said, "Might be a good time to view the property, Mr. Sterling." He reached for Maddy's arm. "Why don't you grab a jacket and walk through the work-shop?"

Maddy scrutinized Vestal's serious face. What could he be up to? "Sure, be glad to." She grabbed her jacket and headband from the hall closet and readied herself to meet the cold.

They walked along the cobblestone path to the small log cabin with its brick chimney. Grant shoved the door open. Something squealed and rattled along the wall. Maddy drew her arms against her chest. "I'll wait out here, thank you."

Grant grinned and stepped inside the darkened room. He withdrew in seconds. "I inspected this before, so I don't really need to again." He rubbed his hands together and shoved them in his coat pockets.

Maddy tilted her head. "The boathouse?"

He nodded. They trekked by the bay side of the house. A small shed sat on the corner of the property. Hilde said it held anything needed to make a day on the beach fun. Grant peeked inside. "Good shape."

Maddy walked around the corner of the building, closer to the water. A small bench sat on an outcrop of rock. She propped her foot on the bench and leaned against the railing. Through a few silvery birch trees, she could see the marina and town. A tucked-away spot, perfect for solitude.

"Beautiful sight." Grant leaned against the outer railing and watched the water. "I don't think the Grissoms will have any trouble unloading this place."

"Unloading it?" Maddy's cheeks flushed. "Do you think this is easy for them?" She straightened and waved a hand toward the house. "Been in Hilde's family since 1920 and you think she wants to *unload* the place?" Her ears burned. She bit her lower lip to stop the trembling.

A flash of uncertainty crossed Grant's face. "I thought that was the purpose of my visit."

Maddy leveled a stare at him. A muscle worked in his jaw. She could see he'd nicked himself while shaving. A breeze stirred; his musky aftershave wafted across her nose. His gaze scanned her face. Heat crept up her neck. She'd be splotchy by now. She turned toward the water. "The purpose? I suppose it is," she whispered.

Chapter 4

Chilled by the bitter wind, Grant followed Maddy inside. He smiled at Lizzy, perched on the sofa with a cookie in her hand. She waved it in his direction. "Want a bite, Daddy?"

"I'm fine, thanks." Pride swelled in his chest at her good manners. He headed for Vestal. "I'd like to make a pass through the house, if you don't mind."

Vestal nodded. Grant removed a pen and a small spiral notebook from his coat pocket and walked into the kitchen. He opened two drawers and tested the pantry door, his shoes squeaking on the hardwood floor. He progressed through the dining room, glancing at the ceiling, and moved into the living room.

"It's remarkable what a fresh coat of varnish will do." He ran a finger across a chink in a log. "Well done."

"Fine craftsmanship." Hilde folded her hands in front of her. "Feel free to go upstairs. I suppose our guest made her bed." She chuckled.

Maddy blushed. "I'll check."

Grant trailed up the stairs behind her. He scanned the hallway, made a notation, and began to inspect a bedroom. She scooted into another room. He opened and shut the closet door, then glanced out the window. Cedar trees hid the view of the road.

He walked into Maddy's room just as she stuffed black undergarments in her bag. Her cheeks burned bright red. He hid a smile and pointed at the rose wallpaper. "Don't see this pattern often."

"You're a connoisseur of wallpaper?" Maddy raised a brow, shuffling to close her suitcase.

"In my business, you recognize patterns." He patted the wall. "And this is vintage."

She straightened. "I think this room is lovely." She looked out the paned windows. "Such a terrific view." She swiped a curl behind her ear.

Grant looked at the blond curly mane tumbling down her back. What an attractive woman. He shook off the thought and joined her by the window. "God created a beautiful spot in this peninsula." He stared at the rocky shore below, waves lapping at the beach. What fun Lizzy would have romping in the water, sailing... Grant sighed. This house wouldn't belong to anyone he and Lizzy would visit. Just another sale. He inhaled Maddy's faint floral fragrance and tried to keep his mind in real estate mode. Grant studied the window frame as he'd done before. Excellent craftsmanship, indeed.

Maddy shifted, her arm brushing his sleeve. She jerked away. "I'll head downstairs." She rushed out the door.

Grant returned his gaze outside. Madison Tanner would be at home on the water, he'd bet. He tapped his notebook against his leg, then proceeded to the master suite. Its charm would woo any buyer. Reassurance seeped into him, then bubbled into a warm pool of optimism. A sale could definitely be his before long.

Tempted by the smell of spicy apple cider, Grant walked downstairs, a smile on his lips and in his heart.

❄

Grant settled on the settee beside his daughter and sipped the warm cider. Maddy watched the little girl's eyes dance when she talked about their drive to Door County. "Coolest of all, my dad got this uber-deal on renting a sports car. I've always wanted to ride in a sports car."

So the fancy car wasn't his. Maddy tucked this information away.

"Daddy promised we'd get ice cream after a while. In this town is a store called Wilson's where my dad went when he was a kid, but it's closed for the winter." Lizzy heaved a sigh. "I really wanted to go there, because he said it was awesome."

Maddy hid a smile at the dramatic rendition.

Vestal said, "Wilson's is awesome." He leaned forward. "Did you know every ice cream cone has a jelly bean in the bottom?"

Lizzy's eyes lit up. "Sweet." Her brows drew together. "Why?"

"Keeps ice cream off your knees." Vestal cackled.

Maddy laughed. "Smart idea."

Lizzy set her cup on the end table and smiled at Hilde. "Thank you for the cider, ma'am." Her brown eyes crinkled like her dad's.

"You're welcome, Lizzy." Hilde's lips turned up. "I'm glad you enjoyed it." She coughed lightly. "So your mom didn't make the trip?"

Lizzy's eyes clouded over, and she reached for her dad's hand. "She died when I was six."

Hilde sat forward, one hand on the little girl's knee. "I'm so sorry. You must miss her a great deal."

Lizzy nodded, tears welling in her eyes. "It's just me and my dad." She brushed at them with her sleeve.

Maddy's throat tightened, and she blinked furiously to keep a tear from spilling over. Poor child. Her admiration for Grant rose. A single dad.

Grant broke the silence. "I think we'd better be going. I wanted to show Lizzy some of the peninsula before it gets dark." He folded his napkin and handed a cup to Vestal. "Thank you for your hospitality." He clapped his hands on his knees. "Will it be permissible to show your house tomorrow morning?" He tipped his brown eyes in Vestal's direction.

Vestal started to protest, but Hilde raised a hand. "Ten o'clock will be fine, Mr. Sterling." She smiled into Grant's face. "And please feel free to bring Lizzy with you."

"I wouldn't want to impose." Grant and Lizzy stood. He ran a hand across her shoulders. "I think I have a sitter."

"No imposition," Hilde said. "We can tuck ourselves away while you show off the Beacon." She gazed at Lizzy. "No imposition at all."

Grant's eyes moved from Hilde to his child. "Well, then, we'll be here tomorrow morning. I believe the Craddicks will be pleased with your home. I'm sure we'll arrive at a fair price."

Vestal snorted. "Fair price, indeed."

"Hush, dear." Hilde beamed at Grant. "I'm sure our Realtor knows best."

Chapter 5

Grant stood on the steps of a beautiful white building at the back of the Eagle Harbor Inn listening to the petite Mrs. Craddick chatter. "Being a regular in Door County has been my dream since I was a child." She fluttered her hand in front of her face. "I can hardly believe we're here. My cousins had a place on the quiet side of the peninsula, in Bailey's Harbor." A whisper of a smile crossed her face, and her voice dropped an octave. "They were quite wealthy." She shot a glance at her husband. "Now I'm about to own property here."

Mr. Craddick cleared his throat. "Susan, enough. He doesn't care if you keep up with your cousins." He leaned forward. "We like the brochure you sent us and are ready to look at the house. I assume it's in tip-top shape."

Grant smiled. He had inspected the property thoroughly when it was first listed, and yesterday's walk-through had eased his mind. "It's in fine shape." He glanced at his daughter sitting in the car. Mrs. Mac still hadn't returned to Ephraim, and he blessed Mrs. Grissom for her willingness to watch Lizzy.

The Jag didn't provide room for the large-framed Mr. Craddick, so the couple followed in their car down the highway to the turnoff. Grant felt his stomach tighten when they swung onto the narrow lane. Would Madison greet them? He shook off the thought and tucked a cinnamon candy in his mouth.

"Daddy?" Lizzy looked out the window. "May I walk on the pier and see the water?"

"We'll see." Grant spoke through taut lips.

Lizzy sighed.

At Grant's first knock, Mr. Grissom opened the front door. Grant held the hood of Lizzy's coat, locking her in place, while he introduced the Craddicks. Mr. Grissom motioned them inside. The older man beamed at Lizzy.

"How's this cute young'un this morning?" Vestal chucked her under the chin.

"I'm fine, sir." She grinned. "I'd like to see if the ducks are on the water."

Grant tensed. He hoped Lizzy's stubbornness wouldn't pop up. This sale meant so much. "She'll be fine at the kitchen table." He pointed to a backpack Lizzy carried. "She has things to keep her occupied."

"Nonsense," Hilde piped up. "Keep your coat on, honey. I'll grab mine, and we'll go look for geese."

Grant looked down at Lizzy, a protest forming in his throat, but her big brown eyes begged for permission. "Be nice," he whispered. Lizzy shot out the door with the older woman.

"Mr. Craddick"—Mr. Grissom hitched his pants and ushered them into the living room—"welcome to the Beacon. Been in Hilde's family since 1920. Fine place here. Fine place."

Mrs. Craddick peered into his face, her beak-shaped nose pointed up. "Why are you selling it?"

"Retiring, I guess you'd say." Vestal heaved a sigh. "Yep. Maintenance around here can suck the life. . ." He paused and watched Grant. "Well, I suppose you will want to have a look around." Vestal perched on the arm of a sofa. "Don't mind me." He pointed toward the kitchen. "And our help. Maddy's doing dishes right about now."

Grant inched around the corner until he caught sight of Maddy. She wore navy sweatpants and a white sweatshirt, her hair cinched in a ponytail.

She seemed to sense his presence. "Good morning, Mr. Sterling." She smiled.

"Miss Tanner." Grant felt the tips of his ears burn. "Nice to see you."

Mr. Craddick stomped across the living room floor toward the roaring fire. "Sound-looking structure." He whapped the mantel and pictures wobbled. "Good craftsmanship."

Vestal nodded, his lips mashed together.

"I want to see the bedrooms." Mrs. Craddick headed up the staircase.

Grant trailed behind the couple. In the master suite, the windows faced Eagle Harbor. He sucked in a breath as he took in the view. Again, he imagined the waterway in summer, sailboats skimming the water's surface.

Mrs. Craddick stepped around three large boxes and murmured something about lack of space. Grant couldn't see her point. The bedroom seemed sumptuous compared to the one in the small apartment he and Lizzy shared. Mr. Craddick reached for the closet door. It stuck. He jerked the knob until it opened. The four-panel door hung crazily from one hinge. The man stared at Grant.

Grant's cheeks burned, the smell of mothballs stinging his nose. He shrugged a shoulder. "An easy fix."

Mrs. Craddick continued down the hall to the last bedroom. "This would be fine for your office, Harvey." She took hold of a drawer in the built-in desk. The handle dangled uselessly in her hand. She flashed a look at Grant.

"Here, let me." Grant slid his fingers alongside the drawer and opened it. He fastened the handle on loosely and gave the woman a warm smile. "Easy fix."

She raised an eyebrow. "Again, not much space." A stack of suitcases sat alongside the wall. "Does the cottage lack storage?"

Where had *those* come from? "Oh no, there's plenty. The attic affords space as well."

Mrs. Craddick glanced at her high heels. "I doubt we'll maneuver that today."

Four stuck closet doors later, Mr. Craddick's mouth was in a grim line. Grant's assurances about *easy fix* fell on deaf ears.

Downstairs, Mrs. Craddick stepped into the kitchen. Grant shot across the living room and listened to her talk with Maddy.

"It's cool in the rose room. Drafty." Maddy sighed. "I'm sure you'll be able to find any leaks and easily fix them." Dishes clinked. "Excuse me, I need to get these washed up."

Mrs. Craddick's shrill voice rang out. "No dishwasher?" She moaned.

Her husband charged into the kitchen, Grant on his heels. "Not acceptable." Craddick pounded the counter with a fist. "Not even enough cabinet space to add one." He jerked a drawer handle. The front gave way, and it slid out of the hole, crashing to the floor, silverware bouncing. "Easy fix, Sterling?"

He glared at Grant.

Grant gave a jerky nod and a knot formed in his belly. He and Naomi had specified this house to be fine-tuned. He shook off his worry. He was right; most of the issues could easily be fixed, but how to convince Mr. Craddick?

❄

Maddy watched Grant out of the corner of her eye. She'd spoken the truth to Mrs. Craddick about the draft. She noticed it when she returned to her room after her bath. She'd noted, too, Vestal scurrying down the hallway with a small toolbox in hand.

"Shall we view the grounds?" Grant touched Mrs. Craddick's elbow gently.

Her husband reached for her hand. "I believe we've seen enough, thank you." He stepped over knives and forks and tugged the lady's wrist. "Let's go, dear."

Mrs. Craddick's lower lip trembled. "Harvey, this is the location—"

"I said, let's go." Mr. Craddick's tone indicated he'd brook no interference.

His wife toddled behind, her hand in his clutches. "Thank you." She waved over one shoulder. "We'll be in touch."

Grant hustled out the door behind them, his business card in hand. Maddy studied the drawer front, then scooped up the silverware and dumped it in the dishpan. Had Hilde opened the drawer earlier in a special manner to prevent a disaster?

When Grant returned, he stuffed the card in his pocket, his cheeks a mottled red.

Maddy tossed a dish towel on the counter and faced him. He squinted in the direction of his customers. "Would you like some coffee?"

"I. . .uh, no." A muscle worked in his jaw. "I need to find my daughter." He spun toward the window, his gaze searching.

"She's with Hilde; she's fine." Maddy poured a cup of coffee and held it toward him. "Are you sure?"

Grant grasped the cup, then set it on the counter. His eyes searched her face. "What just happened?" His eyes narrowed, and he toyed with the cup. "My inspection yesterday. . ." He rubbed the back of his neck and tilted his head toward Maddy. "Did Mr. Grissom. . ." He sighed. "Never mind." Grant took a sip of coffee and frowned. He motioned toward the sugar bowl.

Maddy slid the bowl closer. His fingertips grazed hers and she jerked back. The bowl tipped. Sugar spilled on the countertop, sparkling in the morning sun.

Grant looked at her and released a laugh. "Seems like sugar is not our strong suit."

Maddy tucked a strand of hair behind her ear and reached for a sponge to wipe the counter. "Not a problem. Consider it payment for fixing the tire."

Grant spooned sugar in his cup and stirred. "You have it fixed, or do you need me to take you to a garage?"

"Mr. G. called someone. They took care of it." She leaned against the counter and watched Hilde and Lizzy wander through the empty flower beds. Hilde pointed to tiny signs that indicated what flowers would bloom. "The Grissoms have quite a network of friends in Door County. There's an inn nearby and the innkeeper is a longtime friend. She's having a Christmas Tea Hilde keeps talking about."

"Lola."

Maddy nodded. "You know her?"

Grant shrugged. "If you've spent any time in Door County, you know Lola and her Christmas Tea."

"So you've been up this way before?"

A flash of pain flitted through Grant's eyes. "I spent several summers here with my grandparents." He sipped coffee. "And two Christmases."

"So you're staying with them now?"

Grant shook his head. "I lost them a few years ago." He set the cup on the counter. "I should corral my daughter. She's probably run Mrs. Grissom ragged." He started toward the back door. "Are you spending Christmas here?"

"Yes, I am."

"You're a niece? A cousin?" Grant's eyes peered into hers, and Maddy felt a red flush crawl up her face.

"No. Not related." Maddy pressed her lips together, not sure how to explain she was merely their driver, spending Christmas without family.

He stepped to the back door and called Lizzy. She spun around and raced toward him, excitement lighting her face.

"Daddy, you should've seen the flock of geese on the rocks. I think I saw the same one from yesterday." Her eyes sparkled and her blond hair flew about her face, unleashed from the ponytail. "Mrs. Grissom said I could come back and see them again." She reached her dad's side and grasped his arm. "Please, can I come back?"

Grant pulled her close. "Let's not wear out our welcome, punkin."

Maddy gasped. *Punkin?* Her dad's nickname sent a tremor through her. A flood of love welled up. She'd hung on her daddy and begged more than once, just like Lizzy.

Hilde entered the kitchen and stomped her feet on the welcome mat. "Oh my, Lizzy-girl, I think I need a sugar cookie and some cocoa. How about you?" Her ruddy-red face peeked from her jacket hood. "Dad, want some? Maddy will fix us up, I imagine."

Grant pointed to his coffee cup. "Thanks, Mrs. Grissom, I'm fine." He tugged Lizzy's coat sleeve. "We really should get on our way."

"Daddy." Lizzy's last syllable whine echoed in the kitchen.

Hilde laughed. "Daddy," she singsonged. She tipped her head to one side. "If you're not in a hurry, Mr. Sterling, I'd love for Lizzy to visit." She reached for the child and hugged her close. "We've got Christmas secrets to discuss, and we could bake more cookies."

Maddy's eyes watered. How Hilde loved children.

A puzzled look crossed Grant's face. "I suppose. . ."

Lizzy slid out of her coat. "Thanks, Dad." She tossed it on a chair and helped Hilde from hers. "Want me to get the stuff out for the cookies?"

Hilde caught Lizzy's hand and swung it. "Let's wash up first." The two angled for the downstairs bathroom.

Grant chuckled, his face relaxing. "Well, guess we're visiting for a while." He picked up his coffee cup. "Mind if I refresh my drink?"

Maddy nodded. "Just be careful of the sugar bowl. It has a mind of its own."

Grant stepped closer and Maddy caught a hint of cinnamon. A shiver ran up her spine. *Cool it, Madison. No romance for you. Focus. School.* But standing beside Grant Sterling made focusing difficult.

❄

The afternoon sun warmed the kitchen, and Maddy dashed upstairs to shrug out of her sweatshirt. While she, Hilde, and Lizzy had baked three dozen sugar cookies, Grant and Vestal had disappeared from view.

Maddy slipped on a T-shirt. She smoothed out wrinkles

and noticed a stain at the bottom. She'd packed for a more rustic trip. Rummaging through her suitcase, she came upon a lightweight maroon pullover sweater decorated with tucks across the bodice. Fancier than she needed for baking. She held it up at arm's length. Lovely enough to attract attention. A flush tingled her cheeks, and she tossed the shirt into the suitcase. She wasn't out to attract attention.

She closed her eyes. Two years before, she'd been the center of attention in Tim's life. His green eyes danced before her. "Marry me and you'll lack for nothing." How true that would've proved and how happy it would've made her mother.

No, she didn't need to attract attention. The stained T-shirt would work just fine for baking. She hurried back to the kitchen, cinnamon filling the air. The next batch of cookies should be done.

Hilde stood beside Lizzy at the kitchen table, confectioner's sugar spilled over the tabletop in a swirl, and each baker had a dab of frosting on her face.

"Here's our expert," Hilde said. "What do you think, Maddy-girl? Red and green only, or should we make other colors for the frosting?"

Lizzy held a box of food coloring. "I think we need all the colors."

Maddy laughed. "I think you're exactly right, Lizzy. We just need five bowls of icing and we dab color in each bowl."

Hilde reached into a bottom cabinet and extracted the bowls. "Mix away, mad scientist. Let's experiment."

Lizzy giggled. She dribbled a tiny dot of blue food coloring on a mound of frosting and whirled a spoon through it. "Sky blue." She tasted a bit. "And yummy."

"Whatever will we paint sky blue?" Hilde's gray eyebrows rose.

"A bell?"

Maddy reached for a misshapen sugar cookie. "I think this looks like a mitten. Don't we know someone with blue mittens?"

Lizzy grinned. "Me." She reached for the cookie blob and slathered it blue. "Could be a mitten."

"Or could be a taste test for Mr. G." Maddy placed the cookie on a paper plate. "I say we feed our guests our errors."

With the two occupied decorating the baked goods, Maddy mixed up another batch of dough. Maybe she'd run out of sugar and need a trip to the store in a Jag. She smiled and watched Lizzy. The youngster shoved a strand of hair from her face with a shoulder, but it drooped down again. Maddy reached over and tucked the baby fine hair behind Lizzy's ear and was rewarded with a red frosted grin.

What would it be like to have this child in her life? A knot twisted in Maddy's middle. *Focus, Madison, focus.*

❋

Maddy cleaned the kitchen and waited for the Grissoms to finish their conversation in the living room. She glanced around the corner to see Vestal prodding a log in the fireplace. Flames jumped up, lighting his face. His mouth was twisted in a crooked grin. He caught sight of her. "Come here, girlie. Got something to talk about."

Maddy settled on the sofa beside Hilde, who wore a shy smile. Her sweet perfume drifted about the room. Maddy frowned. "What are you two up to?"

Vestal pointed to himself. "Me? Why, Maddy, you sound suspicious."

Hilde's chuckle gave them away.

"Suspicious? I probably have reason to be suspicious. A draft in my bedroom? A drawer disaster?" Maddy tapped her foot. "I repeat, what are you up to?"

"Well, we figure if the buyers don't like the Beacon, they won't want to purchase it, right?" Hilde's faded blue eyes danced. "So we just have to be sure they don't like the place."

"I've got a trick or two up my sleeve to make sure they don't," Vestal said.

Maddy's brows drew together. "Mr. G., you can't be devious, that's not. . . legal?" She flashed a look at Hilde.

"Not going to swindle anyone. But if there's a problem or two around the place, might steer 'em from setting down money, right?" He cackled. "Just have to stir up some itty-bitty problems."

Hilde pushed from the sofa. "Vestal's right, dear. We have to stir up some problems. We might have to show this house to please Naomi and fulfill her contract, but we don't have to sign the dotted line." She plopped her fists on her hips. "And I don't aim to."

Maddy tucked one foot under her and watched the dancing flames. "Dare I ask what problems will pop up besides a draft and a wave of silverware on the floor?" She peeked at Vestal. "Or am I supposed to be in the know?"

"You'll be in the know, honey child," he said. "You might even be an accessory." He slapped his hands on his thighs, and bent over with laughter. He raised watery eyes to Maddy. "Can't wait to see the look on that boy's face."

Maddy ran her fingers through her hair. What in the world was she getting herself into? A momentary pang of guilt surfaced. The handsome Realtor had no idea he would battle a fearsome twosome. She almost felt sorry for him.

Almost.

Chapter 6

Lizzy curled up on her bed, tugging the red blanket over her head and talking nonstop. "She plays the piano, did you know that?" Her muffled voice rose from under the covers. "Maddy's a sweetheart, Hilde said." A dramatic sigh ruffled the pillowcase. "I think so, too." Lizzy peeked at her dad. "I wish the Grissoms were my grandparents."

Grant's throat tightened. He hadn't realized how much his child had missed out on grandparents. After the death of his parents, the loving care of his grandparents molded him. Marie's mother and father lived on the West Coast and seldom interacted with their granddaughter. Lizzy certainly had never received the attention the Grissoms had showered on her.

"Get to sleep, punkin. We'll be over there in a couple of days."

Lizzy sat up. "Days? Why days? Why can't we go tomorrow?"

Grant rose from her bed. "Because we're not showing

their house until then, that's why." He kissed her cheek and turned toward the cabin's living room. "Get to sleep. I love you."

He shut the door but heard her whine, "Days? That's too long."

Grant agreed. Days until he saw Maddy? He groaned. A few chance encounters with this hazel-eyed blond and he'd become entranced. How could that happen?

He paced the tiny living room and then leaned against the windowsill, staring into the inky night. "Madison Tanner, spending her days with old folks and a little girl, now that's special." Grant's shoulders drooped, loneliness enveloping him. He closed his eyes. "Lord, You've got to get me through this rough patch. You know how hard holidays are for me." He glanced at the closed bedroom door. "Keep me from gloom for her sake. Give me Your joy." A smile crept up his cheek. "Bless the Grissoms, Father, for their attentiveness to Elizabeth. She needs extra love." His heart sped up. "Bless Maddy." His smile deepened. "The sweetheart." He settled into a chair at the rickety table and opened his laptop.

"Sterling, you've got a job to do." He clicked open an e-mail and read it twice. A Facebook notice? From. . . Did he want to be friends with Madison Tanner? He tapped the link and accepted the invitation. You bet he did.

Grant opened his Facebook account and posted a picture of Lizzy on the front steps of Wilson's Ice Cream Parlor and another with the silvery sky and gray water behind her. He made a few comments on other posts, then chewed his lower lip.

Did he dare contact Maddy? He shifted in his chair. She had befriended him first. He sighed. What did he have to lose? He pinched the bridge of his nose. What did he expect of this trip? "To sell the Grissom house. That's it." The unexpected pleasure of meeting Madison Tanner had blindsided him. He hadn't dated or been interested in. . . "Dating? Sterling, where's your brain going?" He slapped the laptop shut, shot to his feet, and stomped to the window. Black as pitch outside. Empty. Lonely. "Like me."

Grant pulled a soda from the refrigerator and settled at the table to work. He opened the computer, the brightness of the screen causing him to blink. "Light trumps dark." Maddy had reached out to him through cyberspace; he could be polite and reply with the private compose feature. But what to say?

He sipped and stinging cold bubbles washed down his throat. After a few seconds, he smiled, rubbed one hand over his face, and typed.

❄

Maddy's e-mail inbox held a note from Grant. She swallowed hard.

> *Lizzy enjoyed her day at the cabin. Ephraim's a lovely town.*
> *We're going to lunch at the Chef's Hat tomorrow at noon.*
> *If you are free, join us.*
>
> *Grant*

Ephraim sat just across the marina, an easy reach. The Chef's Hat? Hilde had mentioned how good the café was. Maddy ran her fingers through her hair. A date with a pint-sized chaperone? Her mind raced. She closed the lid on the computer, placed it on the nightstand, and slid under the covers. She flipped off the light. Tomorrow she'd see the dark-haired stranger with chocolate brown eyes. She drew the quilt over her shoulders, anticipation keeping sleep at bay.

❄

The morning dragged. Maddy lounged in an armchair and read the same five pages of her novel over again, and still didn't know what they said. She glanced at the clock.

"Maddy, what's going on?" Hilde stood by the chair. "You're as nervous as a long-tailed cat in a room full of rockers."

"Nervous?" Maddy squeaked and sat upright, her finger stuck inside the book. "What makes you think that?"

Vestal snickered. "You've plumb wore out the hands on that mantel clock for one thing. And you haven't listened to a word we've said."

Maddy smiled. "Sorry, guess I'm gathering wool, as Mom would say." She frowned. "According to her, I'm an expert at wasting time."

Hilde shook her head. "Don't believe that for one minute. It's not a waste of time to gather your thoughts, and I believe that's what you were doing." She flapped a piece of paper in her hand. "But if you don't mind, I'd like for you to go to the store for a few things."

"I don't mind one bit." Maddy's heart thumped against her ribs. The clock read eleven forty-five. She jumped from the chair, tossed her novel aside, grabbed her coat, tugged the headband around her ears, and jangled the keys.

"Record time," Vestal laughed. "I called the store in Sister Bay, and they've gathered up what we need. Won't need to push a cart around."

Hilde handed her two twenties. "If you want to sightsee a bit, darling, we're not in a hurry for this. You might enjoy a ride down the peninsula. The snowplow's been through, so the roads are clear. Don't rush." Her smile warmed Maddy down to her toes. "Have fun."

"Thanks, I will." Maddy moved toward the front door then paused. "You'll be all right?"

"Right as rain," Hilde said. "You go on. You've been cooped up with the old folks for too long."

Maddy smiled and dashed across snow-covered grass to the car, wind biting her cheeks. With a shiver, she turned the key in the ignition and read the clock. "To go or not to go. That is the question." One minute. Two. . .

Maddy made her decision and turned left onto the highway. A half mile down the road, she pulled into the small complex of historic Ephraim buildings and circled the parking lot. The Jag sat in front of the Chef's Hat Café. Grant leaned against the passenger door, his coat collar turned up against the cold, his dark hair ruffled by the wind.

She parked beside him and rolled down the window. "Wouldn't it be warmer inside the café?"

"It would, but they're closed. One of my favorite places to eat, too." He smiled through the window at his daughter then looked at Maddy. "She's lobbying for pizza, and I know Jo Jo's is open." His brows rose. "Have time for pepperoni?"

Maddy laughed. "Always time for pepperoni. I'll follow you."

A short time later, they shared a table and a large, thin-crusted delicacy. Maddy took a second bite and closed her eyes. The tangy sauce and blend of cheeses was heavenly. "Haven't had pizza this good in. . ." She wiped her lips. "Maybe ever."

Grant's mouth twisted and pulled a strand of mozzarella between his lips. "I know. It's habit forming. This is our second visit in three days." He chewed and looked at Lizzy, his brown eyes twinkling. " 'Course, she could live on pizza." He nudged the child with his shoulder.

"Who couldn't?" Lizzy licked tomato sauce from her fingers. Grant frowned and handed her a napkin.

"I still haven't found a favorite pizza place in my new hometown."

"Where's that?" Grant bit into another slice.

"Minneapolis." Maddy sipped soda.

Lizzy bounced on her seat. "We live across the river. In St. Paul."

"Practically neighbors." Grant smiled. "We know an amazing pizza parlor." His eyes twinkled. "Maybe we could introduce you to the place."

"That would be nice," she murmured. Maddy looked into his eyes. Flecks of gold tipped the irises. Heat rose in her cheeks.

Lizzy leaned forward. "Maddy, do you think I could go see Grampy after this?"

"Elizabeth Sterling." Grant's eyebrows rose. "You know better than to invite yourself to someone's home."

"Daddy." The last syllable strung out.

Maddy grinned, happy memories floating to the surface. She'd worked her dad in the same manner. "Well, ma'am, it's up to your father." She glanced at Grant, then propped her elbows on the table. "But if you want my opinion, a visit to Grumpy would brighten his day."

The young girl's eyebrows drew together. "Grampy."

Maddy lifted her brow.

"Mrs. G. calls him Grumpy because she says he's grumpy. But to me, he's Grampy. Like a grampa."

Maddy swallowed a lump in her throat. "Then I think visiting him would make his day."

"Sweet." Lizzy tilted her head in Grant's direction. "Can I?"

"May I," Grant immediately corrected.

Lizzy rolled her eyes. "May I?" She held up a hand and looked at Maddy. "He's going to say, we'll see." She eyed her dad. "Right?"

Grant grinned. "You're right. We'll see." He folded his napkin and tossed it on the table. "Now go wash your hands and dab at your chin."

Sliding out of the booth, Lizzy angled for the restroom.

"She's a squirt." Grant watched her walk away, his voice filled with pride.

Maddy smiled. "A smart squirt. I did my dad the exact same way. Knew how to mold him around my little finger."

"Really?" Grant fingered the napkin. "Is this a trait taught in the girls' section of newborn baby nurseries?"

"Exactly right." Maddy sipped from her soda.

" 'We'll see.' I think I mutter those words more than any other." He watched Lizzy approach. "We'll see how long it takes before she asks again."

"Daddy—?"

Maddy and Grant burst out laughing. Lizzy's lips turned down. "It's okay, punkin." Grant swept her into the crook of his arm. "If Miss Tanner thinks a Grampy visit would be good, then we can manage one."

"Sweet," Maddy said and grinned at Lizzy.

Lizzy interlaced her fingers with Maddy's and tugged her toward the door. "Sweet is right. Let's go."

❄

A twinge of pain raced through Grant's chest as he watched Lizzy and Maddy. His daughter hadn't been that animated in quite some time. It was the sweetheart-blond influence. He paid for their dinner and followed the girls outside. Cold air snatched his breath. He glanced at Lizzy and saw Maddy arranging the child's muffler inside her coat. She tapped Lizzy's nose with one finger and spun to face him. "Grant, I've got one errand to run. I'll meet you at the house."

Grant nodded, his face stinging from the wind. What a sweet sound. *I'll meet you at the house.* His cheeks burned. He lifted one hand and followed Lizzy to the car.

"She's the nicest, Dad." Lizzy giggled.

"The very nicest." He stared at Maddy's car in the rearview mirror until his squirming daughter demanded his attention.

Chapter 7

Maddy plopped the groceries on the kitchen counter and turned as Lizzy rushed into the room. She threw herself at Maddy with a hug, her hand extended. Maddy squeezed her shoulders. "Whoa, girl. What'cha got?"

Lizzy placed a bit of soap in Maddy's hand. The stringent smell burned Maddy's nose. "It's a carving. Grampy makes a lot of birdhouses and stuff, and he decorates them with pretty carvings. But he practices on soap in case he makes a mistake." She gently ran her fingers around the design. "Isn't it beautiful?" She sighed. "I wish I could carve something pretty like this, but Grampy says I can't use his sharp knife yet."

Yet. The word hung before Maddy. A promise of future time spent together.

Hilde entered the kitchen, folded dish towels in her arms. "So he's carving again, eh?" A hint of a smile played across her face. "He loves that workshop. Always smells like smoke and sawdust when he comes in." She slid the towels in a drawer.

Lizzy tilted her head in Maddy's direction. "Does

my hair smell smoky?"

Maddy hugged the child's shoulders and took a whiff. "Smells like oranges and a hint of tomato sauce." She inhaled again. *Might be a trace of Grant's cologne.*

Lizzy laughed and faced Hilde. "We ate really good pizza, but we didn't have dessert."

Hilde placed one hand over her heart. "Oh what a shame. It's too bad all my cookies are gone."

"Really?" A shadow crossed Lizzy's face.

"Of course not. She's teasing." Maddy smiled. "We can rustle up one, I think."

Hilde pulled the cookie jar from a shelf, and the three sat at the table. Hilde tipped the jar forward and Lizzy withdrew two sugar cookies. "Here, Grammy."

"Grammy?" The older woman paused.

"Umm-hmm." Lizzy wiped her mouth. "Grampy and Grammy." She licked her fingers.

Hilde batted tears from her eyes then grasped the child's hand. "That's about the nicest thing I've ever heard."

Maddy swallowed hard. This little girl spread her love like frosting on the cookies.

"I brought this downstairs to read." Hilde pulled an envelope from her pocket and tapped it on the tabletop. "It's the invitation."

Maddy raised a brow.

"*The* invitation." Hilde's lips tipped up.

The young girl's eyes danced between the two women. "What invitation?"

Hilde swallowed her bite of cookie. "To Lola's Christmas Tea. A special Door County event." She dusted her hands and opened the envelope. "I wanted to see what time it starts tomorrow." She scanned the page then glanced at Lizzy and

Maddy. "And I wanted to see if you two would join me."

"Me?" Maddy reared back in her chair. "I have nothing fancy to wear to a tea."

"I'm sure we can find something upstairs. My stars, I've got enough clothes in differing sizes. . ." Hilde's eyes crinkled, and her hands shot out to grasp Maddy's wrist and Lizzy's fingers. "It would be such a pleasure to take my two sweethearts."

"I'll ask Daddy." Lizzy rose then stopped. "He'll say 'we'll see,' but I'll ask anyway." She darted out the door.

Maddy watched emotions play across Hilde's face. "You sure you're okay?"

"Right as rain." She stood and picked up the cookie jar. "You will go with me, won't you?"

Maddy took in Hilde's face: age spots dotting her wrinkled cheeks, thinning lips painted rose pink, and gleaming blue eyes that noticed everything. "I'd love to go."

Hilde stood, reached over, and hugged Maddy. Maddy inhaled White Shoulders perfume and Coty face powder. "If I had a daughter, I'd want her to be just like you." Hilde sniffed and patted Maddy's shoulder. "We'll examine our wardrobes and see what's available."

A pang of loneliness shot through Maddy's heart. Her mother had hugged like that once—now it seemed Eloise Tanner was surrounded by sharp barbwire. Maddy leaned her elbows on the table and placed her face in her hands. What she wouldn't give to have a Hilde-hug from her mom.

❊

Lizzy entered the workshop, her eyes aglow. "Daddy, tomorrow's *the* Christmas Tea, at Lola's. Can I—may I go?"

Grant held out one arm, and his daughter slid into his embrace. He kissed the top of her head, citrus shampoo-smell making him smile. "We didn't get an invitation."

"I did." She leaned back and smiled at him. "Grammy asked."

"Grammy?" Grant's eyebrows shot up.

Lizzy nodded and faced Vestal. "If you're Grampy, then Mrs. G. will be Grammy."

Vestal ran a hand over his face, his mouth quivering. He cleared his throat. "Think that's right nice of you." He held out a hand. "Come here, punkin, got something to show you."

Grant shoved up from the stool he sat on and opened the door. "I'll be back in a second." He stepped into the cold winter air, his chest tight. Lizzy had just adopted a family she might never see again. He looked toward the house. And he'd become fascinated with a woman—

He bent his head against the wind, tugged his coat collar up, and shoved his hands in his pockets. He angled around the house toward the boathouse and the hidden bench.

Stepping onto the small pier, Grant stopped. Maddy sat on the bench, her maroon parka and bright pink headband a startling contrast to the pewter-colored water.

"Hey there." She smiled at him, her hazel eyes watery in the wind, and patted the bench. "Room for two, if you'd like to sit."

Grant sat. He found leather gloves in his coat pockets and pulled them on. "Beautiful spot."

"Um-hmm." Maddy pointed toward the marina. "Can you imagine that dock full of boats? Colorful sails?" She laughed. "What an amazing place to experience."

Grant watched her. "I think that's what you do with this area."

Maddy faced him.

Grant smiled and waved his hand in an arc. "You experience it. Door County's not just a place to visit, it's an experience." He shoved his hand back in his pocket before he reached out and guided a blond strand of hair into place. He cleared his throat. "Have you been anywhere along this peninsula that wasn't fabulous?"

Maddy chuckled. "I've eaten pizza and gone to the store. 'Bout the limit of my experiences."

"Oh." Grant leaned against the back of the bench. "I hear you're going to the Christmas Tea tomorrow." At her nod, he said, "Maddy, that's a real experience. Door County flavor ala Lola." He smiled. "She's like no other."

"Will you and Lizzy go?"

He shook his head. "I have to show the house tomorrow. And Lizzy shouldn't intrude."

Maddy cocked her head. "Intrude? I don't think Hilde would think that."

"Hilde's Grammy now."

"That's right." She smiled. "So fits Hilde." She sighed. "It's a shame those two didn't have kids." She glanced at the water. "I think this place cries out for children"—she looked at him—"to experience."

Grant's heart rapped double time. Her reddened cheeks and rosy nose created a canvas for her hazel eyes. He slid a hand from his pocket and pulled a leaf from her hair, the desire to hold her welling within.

Maddy dipped her head and stood. She lifted her cell phone. "Not much good without charging it."

Grant fumbled in his pocket and lifted his BlackBerry. "Want to use mine?"

"If you don't mind."

He held out the cell. Her fingers overlapped his. For several seconds they stood, unmoving, looking into each other's eyes. Grant cleared his throat. "I'll take a look in the boathouse." He ducked around the corner.

❄

Maddy stared at her gloved hand. A shiver ran up her spine, not induced by cold but by chocolate eyes. She leaned back. Grant's love for his daughter, his kindness to Vestal and Hilde, had captured her heart. "Impossible, Madison. You've known him how many hours?" She bit her lip.

Time didn't seem to matter. Maddy wished she could gather Grant and Lizzy in her arms and have a family. Rearing a teen wouldn't be easy, but she could do it. Grant was a wonderful father—like her dad had been. Caring, thoughtful. And those qualities would create a wonderful husband.

"Whoa, Tanner. You've gone off the deep end, daydreaming again."

Since spending time with the Grissoms, her heart had softened, and she longed to talk with her mom. She lifted the phone and punched in the Austin number. The call went straight to voice mail, her mother's crisp tone insisting she leave a message. Maddy chewed her lip. The Christmas greeting she'd decided to send fizzled.

Shrugging off disappointment, she searched for Grant. He stood at the end of the shoreline, near the water's edge, a brisk wind flapping his coat and hair. She trekked across the yard and held out a hand. "Thanks for your phone."

He spun on his heel and grinned. "Want to skip a rock?"

"Uh-uh." Maddy laughed. "Too cold out here."

Grant climbed the slope and grabbed for his phone. "Chicken."

She grasped his hand and pulled him up the incline. "Frozen chicken, more like it. We need to get inside by the fire."

He leaned forward, his face nearly touching hers. "Sounds

good to me." He crammed the phone in his pocket and swiveled around. "Race you." With those words, he jogged toward the cottage.

Maddy watched him enter the back door then spin around as though looking for her. She grinned and hollered. "You win."

Hilde approached and waved to Maddy then disappeared. Maddy faced the water. "What a lovely day. Thank You, Lord." Tears sprang to her eyes. "Lord, we've not been talking much lately." She straightened. "But I surely don't want to walk the path of stupid once again." She shut her eyes, a picture of Tim forming. "Please direct my path." A verse from Psalm 9 found its way to her lips. " 'Those who know your name will trust in you, for you, Lord, have never forsaken those who seek you.'" She smiled and turned toward the house, her heart lighter.

Chapter 8

Maddy smoothed the back of a long black skirt and eyed herself in the mirror. Coupled with the maroon sweater and black boots, the outfit worked. Hilde's skirt had just been promoted to vintage.

She fluffed her curls. "Lorena, I need you today." Her Texas-based hairdresser and good friend would know how to tame her hair and calm her heart. Lorena was quick with advice and prayer. But with no charger, Maddy's dead cell phone kept her from seeking counsel on a heart racing toward the unknown. She sighed and spun on her heel. "Pray and see where God leads. I know, Lorena. I know."

"You ready, Maddy?" Hilde paused at the bedroom door. "Ohh, you look scrumptious." She smiled. "I'm so glad I'll get to show you and Lizzy off."

Maddy linked her arm in Hilde's, inhaling a puff of White Shoulders. "Ready and excited to go." She guided Hilde to the staircase as the front door swung open wide. "And I think the third member of our party has arrived."

Lizzy burst in the cabin, her blond ponytail flapping

across her face as she swiveled her head. "Where are—?" Lizzy looked up the stairwell and her face lit. "There you are." She clapped a hand to her thigh and stuck out a foot. "Look at my boots. Sweet, huh? Dad bought them for me for Christmas only he wanted me to look good today so he let me open them, and they fit—"

"Hey, kiddo, take a breath." Grant walked in behind his daughter, a laugh filling his voice. His eyes brushed across Hilde and landed on Maddy. Crimson worked its way up his cheeks. "You ladies look beautiful."

Maddy ducked her head and hid a smile, the compliment warming her heart.

Hilde patted Grant's arm. "Thank you, kind sir. I'll take all the compliments I can get at my age." She squeezed his elbow and walked into the living room.

Lizzy grasped Maddy's fingers. "Can we go now?"

"May we—" Grant said.

"May we—" Maddy said.

Vestal laughed. "Lizzy, you don't stand a chance around these folks." He grabbed the hood of her coat. "You bundle up. Snow's starting again."

Hilde bustled around the sofa and into the dining room. "Where's that thank-you card for Lola?" She raised a hand. "Give me a minute."

Grant reached for Maddy's elbow. "Why don't I start your car, warm it up?"

"Awesome, Daddy." Lizzy dashed to the fireplace. "Let me know when it's toasty."

Maddy grinned, then turned to Grant, passing him the keys. "Would you mind if I used your cell phone again?" She wrinkled her nose, shooting for a pitiful demeanor. "My charger is at home."

"Sure." He chuckled and pulled it from his pocket. "Be right back."

Maddy stepped into the foyer and punched in her mother's phone number. After three rings, Eloise Tanner answered. Maddy's tongue felt heavy. "Hey there, Mom."

"Hello, Madison."

"Just called to see if your packages arrived."

"They did." Her mother cleared her throat. "Thank you for your thoughtfulness."

"You're welcome." Maddy fished for other words. She toyed with a stray curl. "Look, Mom, about our last conversation. . ."

Her mother sighed. "Maddy, I love you. You're my daughter. I only want what's best for you."

Tears formed in Maddy's eyes. "I know. I love you, too." Her chest tightened. Hilde's sweet ways made her long for the "old" mom. "Thought maybe on spring break I might come to Austin."

"Really? That would be—" A sob sounded in Maddy's ear. "Oh Maddy, I've been foolish." She sniffled. "I thought if you had Tim, you wouldn't need to work so many long hours at the conservatory."

"I love teaching piano, Mom. I love what I do."

"I know that now. Professor Goshen and I had a long discussion after you left. I'm extremely proud of you. Getting the scholarship—" Mrs. Tanner halted.

Maddy drew in a sharp breath. When was the last time her mother had given out a compliment?

"Would you give me the chance to make it up to you, Madison?"

Maddy turned and grabbed a tissue from a table. "We'll make it up to each other, I promise." Her words strangled.

"Merry Christmas, Mom. I love you."

"Merry Christmas, darling. Call again soon."

Maddy tapped the screen and ended the call, her heart full, blessed. She startled as the phone vibrated in her hand. A text message? She glanced at the phone. The words *Harvey Craddick* caught her eye.

Harvey Craddick closing deal. Good job. Expect bonus. Naomi

Maddy's heart beat double time. Craddick? The man who first looked at the Beacon was closing the deal? Anger tightened her chest. She gritted her teeth. Grant Sterling *knew* how the Grissoms felt about this place. She thought after he'd spent time in Vestal's workshop and Hilde's kitchen he understood they didn't want to sell. The conversation near the water—experiencing Door County. He was experiencing it all right. Experiencing a profit.

She could feel her face flame. Of all the nerve. She punched DELETE. He could discover his sale tomorrow.

Hilde stepped into her line of vision. "Maddy, what's wrong?"

What's wrong? This is your last Christmas in Door County, that's what's wrong. She held her tongue and turned toward the mirror in the hallway. "Not a thing. Right as rain." She smiled at Hilde and spun around when Grant entered the house.

"Lizzy, let's go."

Lizzy jumped, turning an apprehensive look in Maddy's direction.

Realizing her tone was sharp, she held out a hand and softened her words. "Your dad has the car ready."

Vestal met them in the hallway and caught Lizzy by the arm. "Eat plenty of Lola's cookies. Think you can manage that?"

The youngster giggled and hugged the old man. His face softened as he squeezed her shoulders. "Get along now." Misty-eyed, he looked at the women. "All of you. Get along. This fella and I'll be there in a bit."

"Be careful," Grant urged.

"Yes, sir." Maddy resisted the urge to blast him. Now was not the time. She spoke through tight lips. "We'll be fine." She held out the cell phone.

Grant nodded. "I've got a couple coming to see the house in a bit."

Maddy bit her tongue. She wasn't sharing the news.

A shadow crossed Hilde's face, and she glanced at her husband. Vestal raised a hand. "Things are as right as rain, sweetheart. Go on, relax, and have a good time. Give my regards to Lola."

Hilde nodded and the threesome trooped out the doorway. Maddy glanced over her shoulder, and her eyes caught a longing look on Grant's face. *Traitor.* She bit her lip and marched to the car.

✳

Grant watched Maddy back out of the drive. He hadn't missed her chilly exit. What changed? He shoved the phone in his pocket. Vestal made his way to the kitchen, mumbling about coffee. Grant slid out of his coat and warmed his hands in front of the fire. Had he said something wrong? Had Lizzy? She was prone to blurt out whatever entered her brain.

He rubbed his hands together. The last look Maddy shot him made his ears burn. The signal read: *This woman is ticked off.* His shoulders slumped. How in the world had he messed up this new friendship already?

A burning log collapsed, spraying embers. Just like his hopes. His desire to get Maddy's phone number and see her when they returned to the Twin Cities were dashed. He closed his eyes. He wanted to hold her in his arms. And now—

A car crunched down the drive. Grant looked out the window, and his stomach tightened. Couple number two trekked up the walkway, ready to inspect a house he knew the Grissoms didn't want to sell. He shook off the concerns and walked outside.

"Morning, Sterling." Chris Malcomb stuck out a hand.

Grant kept his grip light lest he crush the man's fine-boned hand. Malcomb's grimace at their first handshake last week made Grant feel like a heavyweight champion. "Mr. Malcomb, Mrs. Malcomb." The large, dark-haired woman stomped past him without a glance. Grant was hard-pressed not to laugh at the disparities in the couple. Wasn't there an old nursery rhyme—"Jack Sprat would eat no fat, his wife would eat no lean. . ."

"You gonna knock, Sterling?" Mrs. Malcomb glared at him under bushy brows. "Or are we gonna freeze out here?" A brisk wind caught a flurry of snowflakes to prove her point. "Ridiculous coming here in this weather. How you gonna know if you like the lake if you can't stick a toe in the water?" She glowered at both men.

Vestal swung the door open. "Come in, come in." He bowed at the waist. "Step over to the fire. It's mighty cold outside."

The Malcombs obeyed. Grant stood in the foyer, scratching his chin. Vestal seemed mighty chipper in front of these people. He knew the old man's heart wasn't in the sale.

"I'm Vestal Grissom. You folks warm up a bit then shed your coats." Vestal glanced at Grant. "I'll be in the kitchen. Just take a tour when you're ready." He smiled at Mrs. Malcomb.

Grant nodded. "Thanks. We won't take too much of your time."

"Not to worry." The faded blue eyes sparkled. "Not to worry at all."

Grant chewed his lower lip, worried. What would greet them on this visit?

Mrs. Malcomb flung her coat and scarf over the sofa and followed Vestal. "Don't plan on spendin' a great deal of time cookin' while I'm on vacation." Grant caught up to the woman. She jerked out the silverware drawer. It slid in and out with ease. He let out a pent-up breath and stepped back to watch Mr. Malcomb examine the log walls in the living room.

"Just refurbished." Grant smiled.

Malcomb nodded, his thin lips tipped up.

Grant looked back at Mrs. Malcomb, her lips turned down, deep furrows across her brow. Vestal had a broom in his hand.

"A problem?" Grant's heart thudded.

Vestal brushed under the refrigerator with the bristles. "Nope. Took care of it." He swiped again. "I think." His fierce concentration extended beneath all the counters. "Pretty sure."

Grant stepped closer. "What is it?"

Mrs. Malcomb shuddered and barked, "I want to go upstairs." She turned on her heel and stomped away, her husband following behind.

Grant watched Vestal. He leaned on the broom at the kitchen's entrance and smiled, then flicked his hand. "Go on, son. Folks want to see the rest of the house."

Shrugging, Grant slowly climbed the stairs.

"In here, too?" Mr. Malcomb said.

"Didn't I just tell you that, Chris? Do I have to repeat myself?"

Grant winced. Mrs. Malcomb's raised voice reminded him of his tenth-grade English teacher: always angry. "Is there a problem, Mrs. Malcomb?"

The large woman smacked into him.

"Outta my way, Realtor-man. Outta my way." She pushed past Grant and down the steps, her hand clamped over her husband's wrist as though he were a toddler.

Grant pounded behind them. "Mr. Malcomb?"

The woman swept up their coats and thrust one to her husband. "Can't abide cold, can't abide pesky—" The rest of her words were muffled beneath a coat and knitted scarf. "Chris, get me outta here."

Mr. Malcomb shot Grant a wan smile. "Thank you. We'll be in touch."

Mrs. Malcomb scooted out the door. "No, we won't." The door slammed to punctuate her words.

Vestal chortled and slapped his thigh. "She's a dilly, that one."

Grant shoved his hands in his pockets. "Want to explain?"

"Explain?" Vestal cocked one eyebrow. "I didn't do a thing." He waved a hand. "Just swept the kitchen floor."

Grant sidled past Vestal into the kitchen. The floor was clean. He angled toward the pantry. The door opened and closed securely. "What made Mrs.—"

A huge red and yellow box was wedged between the counter and refrigerator. He bent and tugged it out, then read aloud. "D-Con. Kills rats and mice." He eyed Vestal. "Must be nice to have such a load of this stuff."

"Box upstairs isn't as big as that one." Vestal sat at the kitchen table, his lips quivering until he let out a full-blown belly laugh. Wiping his eyes, he said, "Didn't take but a nudge of the box with my foot to get rid of that lady."

Grant sat beside him. "Okay, Vestal. You've made it clear you want to keep the house." He sighed, visions of a bonus disappearing. He'd dip into savings for tuition. Keep from unsettling the Grissoms. Maybe that attitude would chip away at the wall Maddy had put up. "I promised Naomi at least two showings." He held out his hands. "Obligations met." He poised his hand for a high five. "Duty done?"

Vestal's knobby fingers grasped Grant's hand. "Duty done well, my boy." Leaning back in his chair, their gazes collided. Another round of laughter shook the checkered kitchen curtains.

Chapter 9

Beautifully decorated Christmas wreaths festooned the doors of Lola's Victorian inn. Maddy straightened her maroon jacket and stamped one boot on the doormat to shed melting snow.

Lizzy mirrored her movements. "Mushy outside, isn't it?" She grinned. "Daddy and I might make a snowman."

The thought of the handsome dad playing in the snow picked up Maddy's heart rate; then she considered his actions—his self-centered, greedy actions. Her tight smile belied her thoughts. "Hmmm, sounds nice." Maybe she could bury him in the snow, neck deep.

"Can't wait for you to meet Lola." Hilde grasped each of their hands. "She's the sweetest lady." She tugged them past the entryway. "And I'm anxious to meet her Amanda."

Maddy followed. Her hope to relax and enjoy the tea had been dashed when she read the text message on Grant's phone. Despite the Grissoms' desire to keep the Beacon, Grant went behind their backs to assure the sale. Deception. She'd pictured the handsome stranger all wrong. He'd painted himself pretty, and she'd fallen for it. She mentally nudged sadness away and dug inside for another smile.

Lizzy giggled at something Hilde said. Maddy trudged behind the happy child, wishing she could join in the joy. Woodenly, she acknowledged introductions and shook hands.

Buffet tables lined one wall. Maddy followed Lizzy, piling a plate with cookies and other Door County specialties, listening to the chatter.

How could she have been so off the mark once again? Anger puffed her cheeks, and she blew out a breath. Hilde wanted them to enjoy the tea; she needed to crumple up her thoughts about Grant like a piece of paper and toss them away. Sadness arrowed through her heart, and a tear welled up. She dashed it with a napkin and swiveled, searching for a place to sit. There—in the corner. She'd nestle in the corner and make nice. A practice her mom had taught her well. She sighed. At least she'd begun mending Austin fences.

A swirl of men and women came in and out, tasting, complimenting Lola and Amanda. The young woman seemed as uptight as Maddy felt. *Poor woman.* "I'd be a nervous wreck planning *this* event."

Lizzy and Hilde mingled as Maddy settled back to watch the crowd. Lizzy had left her half-eaten plate and crumpled napkin on the edge of the table. Maddy fished for the leftover cherry tart, soothing her frayed nerves with sugar.

Sugar. The chance encounter with Grant at the grocery store, a tipped sugar bowl in the kitchen. Both events led her down a path she'd hoped would be. . .

"Sweet." Lizzy scooted beside Maddy. "Did you know Lola's husband drives an old ambulance?" Lizzy lifted her napkin. "Hey." Her bright eyes turned toward Maddy. "Someone's been eating my porridge."

The sprite's glee proved contagious. Despite herself, Maddy laughed. "Okay, Goldilocks, go find yourself another treat." Maddy reached for Lizzy's sleeve. "One, okay? Don't want your father—"

Lizzy shot off toward the table. Maddy rested her hand on her chin and watched the child wrinkle her nose and peer at the arrangement of goodies. So like Grant. "Oh Lord, how I wish for her innocence." She shredded the napkin in her hand. "I'd hoped—"

"Mom. . .uh. . ." Lizzy's bright eyes dimmed and her face flushed. "Maddy, I mean." She slid into her chair and tossed her ponytail over her shoulder. "Wonder when Dad will get here? He's missing the fun."

Tears stung the back of Maddy's nose. *Mom.* She struggled to speak. "I'm sure he'll be here soon." With a trembling hand she gave Lizzy a napkin. "Cherry juice. Wipe your chin." A sinking feeling tugged at her stomach.

❊

Grant slammed through the door of the inn, his chest so tight he thought it might explode. Three ladies in the foyer stood behind a tall counter. He rushed toward them and gripped the counter, his knuckles white. "Hilde Grissom." His raw whisper interrupted the conversation. "I need to find Mrs. Grissom immediately."

An auburn-haired lady raised a brow and pointed. "She and her guests are in there. How might I help—"

Grant whirled and charged toward the dining room, his mouth pulled in a grim line. It had taken him close to twenty minutes to get here. Every second counted. Where was Hilde? He spotted Lizzy and Maddy at a table in the corner. Grant angled their way.

Maddy stood when she spotted him, color leaching from her face. "What's wrong?"

Grant grasped her hand and tugged her to his chest. Lizzy clamped on his hip. "Daddy, what's wrong? Is Grampy—"

"He's sick, punkin." He didn't have to meet her eyes to know the word *dead* played through her mind.

His eyes searched Maddy's face. "Vestal complained of chest pains, so I called the paramedics. They insisted he go to the hospital in Sturgeon Bay."

Maddy shoved from his grip, a frown firmly in place. "I'll find Hilde. Lizzy, meet me in the foyer with our coats."

Grant followed Lizzy, his eyes roving the group of guests. Several stared. He shot a tight smile at the lady who might be the hostess and hustled behind his daughter. In a moment, Maddy and Hilde joined them. He swiftly explained Vestal's condition.

Hilde nodded as she tugged on her coat and swept her muffler about her neck. "I'm ready." Her steely-eyed gaze fixed on Grant's face then dropped away. "Get me to my husband, Madison."

Lizzy leaned against Grant. "Let's go, Daddy."

Grant stared at Hilde's stiff form. Something was wrong. And it wasn't just Vestal's heart.

❄

"Your husband's stabilized, Mrs. Grissom." The doctor clutched a chart. "His blood pressure is down after a nitro-glycerin tablet." He glanced at the bed. "We've run a few tests. However, I don't think an overnight stay would be out of the question." With a brisk nod, he exited the room.

Maddy placed a hand on the older woman's shoulder. "I'll stay with you." The hospital smells brought back memories of the bedside vigil with her father, but her friend didn't need to be alone.

Hilde shook her head. "No, darling. You go back to the house. I'll stay with Grumpy." Tears shimmered in her eyes.

Maddy sighed. "I'm not leaving yet."

Hilde slumped into the bedside chair, her eyes never leaving Vestal's face. "Tell me again, Maddy, what you know."

Maddy glanced at Vestal's sleeping form, sat down, and leaned close. "A text from Naomi on Grant's phone stated *Craddick* was happy." She picked at a towel flapped over the arm of the chair. "It seems our Mr. Sterling sold the cabin."

"Guess that's it then." Tears spilled down Hilde's cheeks. "We never out-and-out told him we didn't want to sell. Got what we deserved for fooling around." She jerked a tissue from the box on the bedside table and wiped her eyes. "I'll miss the Beacon." Her eyes scanned Vestal's face. "But none of that matters now."

Vestal groaned and twisted in bed. His eyes fluttered open, and one corner of his mouth tipped up. Hilde grasped his hand. "Hey. How you feeling?"

He nodded and pushed against the mattress in an effort to sit up.

"Be still, darling. The doctors don't need you shifting about."

Maddy watched them. Sixty-two years. *Lord, don't take Vestal from us just yet. We love him so.*

Vestal cleared his throat and motioned toward a pink plastic jug.

"A drink?" Hilde filled a matching cup and tucked a straw inside. "Sip slowly."

A few swallows later, Vestal croaked, "Wasn't 'bout the Beacon."

Hilde said, "Shhh," and kissed his cheek. "Hush now. We

don't need to be talking."

"We?" The wide parenthesis formed around Vestal's mouth, inching the oxygen nose tube up. "I'm the one blabbing." His voice sounded raspy. He motioned toward Maddy.

"Mr. G., you'd better listen to Hilde. You know she's—"

Vestal shook his head. "Got some celebrating to do."

"Celebrating you being alive," Hilde said.

"More'n that." He closed his eyes. "Need us a Christmas tree with company coming." Vestal tugged the sheet higher onto his chest. "Can't rightly take care of it myself. . ." He coughed. "But you could manage with a little help, Maddy."

Hilde reared back. "What company?"

He reached out and swiped a strand of Hilde's hair from her face. "Grammy and Grampy got to get us some presents for a special girl, too."

Maddy felt her face flush. She didn't want Vestal to know about Grant. "I'm sure I can manage a tree." She stood and patted the old man's knee.

Vestal clutched Maddy's fingers. "Don't know what you think you know, young lady"—he cleared his throat—"but Grant Sterling didn't sell our house." A grin crept up his grizzled cheek.

She frowned. "He's planning to."

"No, I'm not."

Maddy swirled. Grant and Lizzy stood in the doorway. The youngster leaned against her dad's leg, her cheeks tearstained. She waved toward Vestal. "Is Grampy going to be okay?"

Hilde said, "Come here, punkin." Lizzy darted around Maddy toward the bed.

Maddy lifted her chin and poked her hands in her pockets, the desire to hug Lizzy so strong she thought she'd choke. She fixed Grant with a level stare and watched a muscle work in his jaw. "I saw the text."

"What text?"

"Harvey Craddick is closing the deal." She narrowed her eyes.

Grant raised a brow. An amused smile played at his lips. "I see."

Anger surged through her chest. She moved toward him, a finger jabbing the air. "Making *Naomi* happy means selling the Beacon."

"No, it doesn't." Grant shrugged. "It means selling the redbrick storefront in Minneapolis."

A flush tingled in Maddy's cheeks. "Minneapolis?" she squeaked and backed up.

He stepped closer. "It means finding a buyer, even the week before Christmas."

Maddy studied the pattern of the linoleum. Three green, one pale yellow.

Grant took another step. She could see the tips of his brown loafers.

"It means explaining to her some things aren't available at any price."

Maddy raised her head and stared at Grant. "She wanted Hilde and Vestal—"

He latched on to the knitted scarf dangling from her neck. "The Grissoms didn't want the same thing."

Captured, Maddy stared into Grant's eyes. "But—"

"It means staying a few more days so we can celebrate Christmas. . .with you."

Lizzy piped up, "We're staying with Grampy and Grammy and you, Maddy. For Christmas." She giggled. "Dad said we can celebrate with family."

"Celebrate Christmas? With family?" Maddy willed her tongue to form other words rather than parrot what she heard. "You're staying with us?"

Grant nodded, eyes crinkling. "Yep. Staying. Celebrating." He tugged the scarf taut.

"Oh," Maddy whispered.

"Staying so I can do this." Grant tilted his head and stared into her eyes.

Maddy's heart rat-a-tatted against her ribs. She inhaled his cinnamon breath. Grant pulled her closer, and she closed her eyes. He kissed her.

Maddy leaned into the kiss, his lips firm and sure against hers. She heard Lizzy giggle and Hilde and Vestal laugh, but she didn't back away. She slid her arms around Grant's neck.

Like polarized magnets, their lips held. And she knew she wanted them to stay that way. Forever.

You've never forsaken me, Lord. Thank You for this Christmas gift.

Eileen Key, freelance writer and editor, resides in San Antonio, Texas, near her grown children and two wonderful grandchildren. She's published nine anthology stories and numerous articles and devotionals. Her first mystery novel, *Dog Gone*, from Barbour released in 2008.

CHRISTMAS CRAZY

by Becky Melby

Dedication

To the blessings who make Melby Christmases joyfully crazy:
Scott, Kristen, Reagan, Sawyer, Sage,
Jeff, Holly, Keira, Caden,
Aaron, Adrianne, Ethan, Peter, Cole, Lilly,
Mark, Brittany, and Oliver.
To baby Finn, who hasn't yet experienced the craziness.
And to Bill—once upon a time there were only two stockings.
Look what we started!

Thank you to—
Jon Jarosh, Door County Visitor Bureau Director of
Communications & Public Relations, for so many beautiful
lighthouse pictures to choose from. Todd Frisoni, owner of the
Door County Ice Cream Factory & Sandwich Shoppe. Jan Glas,
as always, for reading this with a sharp eye. Lee Carver, for
Portuguese expertise. And a special thank-you to the Door County
Gals who were a blast to write with and a joy to pray with when
the lights went out. Hold those glow sticks high, ladies, and let the
Light shine!

And thank You to God for a Reason to celebrate.

Be joyful in hope, patient in affliction, faithful in prayer.
ROMANS 12:12

Chapter 1

"C an you say va—ca—tion? Can you say *paid* vacation?"

Through the cracked windshield of her red Hyundai, Jillian Galloway drank in the rich tapestry of flaming maples, bronzed oaks, and peeling white birch trees. As she rounded a curve and glimpsed Sister Bay's dark teal water glittering in the sunlight, a near-extinct smile snuck up on her. "Door County therapy. That's all I need." She followed a soaring seagull down the hill and into town.

Canada geese congregated around the park gazebo. Three goats grazed on the grass-covered roof of Al Johnson's Swedish Restaurant. White masts stood like sentinels guarding the tranquility of the marina. The familiar sights welcomed Jillian like a grandmother's hug.

And then, at a spot where first-time tourists thought they'd left Sister Bay behind, she reached her favorite part of town. The shingled, octagonal steeple of the Tannenbaum Holiday Shop directed her gaze and her sagging spirits to a dazzlingly blue sky. Her imagination scampered through the store, sniffing cinnamon-scented candles and bayberry potpourri. A week of twinkling lights and ornament shopping in this oasis of never-ending Christmas would do wonders for her battered heart.

She parked in front of Doorbuster's Comedy Theater and wiggled a plump leaf on the barren Christmas cactus that had patiently absorbed her carbon dioxide on the eight-hour drive from Davenport, Iowa. "Thanks for letting me vent, Jolly." She shoved open the dented car door, and Jolly nodded in a blast of October air.

"Let's go interrupt rehearsal and surprise the suspenders off Uncle Buster." She unfastened Jolly's seat belt. The car door whined as it closed, the noise an irritating reminder of the last date she would ever have.

Walking up the steps to the old plank door, she looked up at the marquis. One letter hung upside down, swaying in the breeze. The unlit sign now advertised FROST ON THE UMPKINS.

Every synapse in her advertising brain sizzled. The Friday night dinner show would begin in just over an hour. "How does he expect to attract business like this?" Her right boot skidded in a drift of wet gold leaves. "If Buster doesn't clear this off he's going to have a lawsuit on his—"

"*Para!* Stop! Don't open that. . .doooor!"

The command filtered through the hood of Jillian's coat as the brass lever gave way beneath her thumb. The latch clicked. The hinge groaned.

"Look out!" From the shadows beneath the steps, a dark form lunged, tackled, and shoved her into the iron railing. Terra-cotta hit the step with a sickening crack. Air rushed from Jillian's lungs in a sharp, burning *whoosh* as a tsunami of warm, inside air engulfed her.

A crash. A scream.

And silence.

Stars spangled the darkness. But it wasn't night and she wasn't facing the sky. Her face was pressed into buttons and flannel that smelled of cedar and wood smoke, held there by arms of steel. She ordered her lungs to expand.

"Help!" The sound that should have come from her lips came from somewhere near her ankles.

Strong arms released their hold. The man who had either rescued or attacked her dropped to his knees.

One lung filled. Jillian was sure the other had collapsed. But the stars faded and equilibrium returned. She looked down. . .at a woman lying prone on a plywood shepherd as if it were a surfboard. "Wilma!" Jillian folded beside the man in the flannel shirt.

"Don't move. We need to make sure you are all right." His accent hinted of a country where summer didn't end.

Wilma Riley sat up, blew a wayward white corkscrew curl from her forehead, and peered through cockeyed trifocals. Flannel Man put his hands on her shoulders. "Does anything hurt?"

"My pride is killing me. Take your hands off me, or I'll be forced to give you a purple eye." From the folds of her denim skirt, Wilma produced a paintbrush and brandished it like a saber. The man dropped his hands. Reaching to the side, Wilma picked up a pottery chunk. "Jilli! Jolly!"

Eyebrows tented over dark eyes, the man tapped his finger on the wavy black hair at his temple. "She must have hit her head."

"Don't talk about me like I'm deaf or daft, Ricky Jimmy. I've got way more screws in the attic than you do." Wilma turned away and her countenance transformed. She kissed Jillian's hand. "Buster said you weren't coming when the roof caved in. But you're here. We're saved." Blue-framed glasses slipped to the end of her nose. "I'm freezing my bunions. Jilli, Jolly's catching pneumonia. Ricky, help the poor girl."

"Gladly." The man with two first names held out his hand. "Enrique Jimenez. You can call me Ricky."

Jillian's hand slid nicely into his. "Jillian Galloway. You—"

"*Can't* call her Jilli." Wilma lifted the naked cactus and set it in his free hand. "That's reserved for people she can trust."

"Wilma! Let's get you inside." Jillian stood, eased Wilma to her Birkenstocks, and moved her toward the door as she shrugged an apology at the insanely handsome stranger still kneeling at her feet. "Don't step on your shepherd, Wilma. Why in the world is our famous actress painting the nativity scene in October? And why in the lob. . .by?" Her jaw unhinged.

No tiny orange lights glittered on artificial maples, no resin pumpkins sat amid cornstalks. The glass candy case under the snack counter gaped like a hungry, waiting mouth. The only smell of popcorn hung in the air like the faintest of memories.

Jillian scanned the desolation and stopped when she came to her uncle. Like a huge hulking statue, he stood mute and motionless, a grimace chiseled on his double-chinned face.

"Jilli-girl!" From behind a cutout pine tree popped a man who looked like he ought to be wearing an elf suit. "You changed your mind! You're here!" Mort Riley's wire-rims slid down his knobby-potato nose. "Buster said you weren't coming, but you're here. Now we'll get things sorted out."

Wilma shivered, bringing Jillian out of her trance. "Find Wilma a place to sit, Mort. I think she's okay, but keep a close eye on her. Uncle Buster, go fix her a cup of tea."

Behind her, the man who had swept her off her feet shut

the door. "Now I see why they wanted you in charge."

"Funny." She stared at the suspenders crossing her uncle's wide back as he opened the doors to the theater. "What's going on here, Uncle Buster? You can't get this cleaned up by—" Once again, her lungs emptied in a gust.

Buckets and bath towels littered the stage in the center of the room. Instead of crisp white linen, sheets of plywood covered the round tables surrounding the stage. Arms hanging limply at his sides, Buster walked to a banquet table and pulled a cup from a jumble of coffeepots and pizza boxes.

Murmuring over Wilma, Mort dusted off a chair and settled her in it then hugged Jillian. "Put me to work, boss. I'm not afraid to get my hands dirty. With you at the helm we'll get this place whipped into—"

"What are you talking about? I'm here to make up fliers for you and relax and go to the Fall Festival, and—"

"Be our new manager."

"*What?*"

Bushy white brows converged. "When the roof collapsed and Cecil left with Darcy and the money, Buster said you'd move back and take over and—"

"Bus*ter!*"

❄

Ricky needed to find a place to put the drooping mass of roots and dirt and cactus limbs, but he didn't want to miss a single scene of the drama playing out in the theater-in-the-round.

Buster Galloway lumbered down the aisle toward the stage, where his niece stood beneath a sagging blue tarp. The stage was lit by the only fixture that hadn't shorted in the leak—a single six-inch Fresnel light. The red gel over the lens gave the girl in the red-framed glasses a rosy glow. Her long leather coat opened in front, and she tugged at the tails of a white blouse that stuck out beneath a black sweater.

Looking down at his feet, Buster spread his hands in supplication. "Jilli. . .I didn't expect you until tomorrow. I was going to call and tell you not to come."

"When? I got a week away from my desk to come up here and work on your publicity." Flipped-up dark hair bounced on her shoulders. "I'm on company time and there's nothing here to publicize. What happened?"

As she waited for an answer, her shoulders lowered. The anger seemed to melt from her trim frame. "What happened?" she repeated. "Darcy left with Cecil?" The tone of her voice said she understood how the real-life Doorbuster drama had hurt Buster.

Buster sank to the edge of the stage. "I guess I was the only one who didn't know my director and my head chef were an item."

"And the money? What money?"

"Cecil emptied the safe—our take from four performances. He helped himself to my cook and my money and disappeared. Last night he came back for more. His key broke off in the lock."

Jillian sat next to Buster and rested her head on his shoulder.

"I'm no manager, Jilli. I'm the funny emcee. I've been doing a lousy job these past two years, and now. . .we're through."

"Why didn't you tell me? Do Mom and Dad know?" She spoke in hushed tones, but even with the hole in the ceiling, the acoustics were perfect.

Buster shook his head. "They've worried over me enough since Viv died. I was going to call you. But I had this crazy thought that maybe, since you love this place and you're not happy with your job. . ."

"That I'd swoop in and fix everything?"

"Yeah. You've got your Aunt Viv's instincts, Jilli." He sighed. "Maybe we could have kept going without Cecil and Darcy, but a tree fell on the roof and the light board shorted. My insurance only covers the replacement cost. That's not enough. Maybe I could have gotten a loan, but. . .I gave up. I let everyone go." He folded his hands.

After a long silence, Jillian smacked both palms on her knees and stood. "Take out that loan. Fix the roof and get the lights working. The fall season is shot, so let's put all our energy into Christmas. We'll cut corners, streamline, but make it the best Christmas performance ever. I'll promote like no one's ever promoted. You'll be sold out, I guarantee." Shoving long bangs off her forehead, she manufactured a smile. Ricky wasn't fooled, but he was definitely in awe. "Well, everybody, what are we waiting for?"

Now I see why he wanted you in charge, Jillian Galloway.

Her coat fell to the stage. She rolled up her sleeves. "I'll get a few more days off work. We'll start with lists. Mort and Wilma, you guys are all pros—you can pull off the show without a director."

"Um. . ." Mort's moustache dipped at the corners. "Huey and Ardis flew south."

"Call them and tell them the show can't go on without them. If they won't come, we'll figure out something. We'll rewrite the script for only two actors. It'll be fine."

Wilma's eyes widened. "We can't—not without Ardis and Huey. They're the straight guys. It wouldn't be funny with-out—"

"Then it's your job to convince them."

"But it's my job to fix the manger scene. Gaspar and Balthasar have water damage and Baby Jesus is warped and the sheep turned yellow and—"

"We'll get to the sheep, I promise. But we won't need a manger scene if the bank forecloses on the theater. Call them."

"You're staying at the farm, aren't you? We got the port-hole room ready."

"Thank you. Yes, I'll be at the farm. Now I want you to get ahold. . ."

Ricky watched the resilient girl from the shadows and wished he could stave off the death of her optimism.

If only a sagging roof, no employees, and two actors on the lam were her only problems.

Red-framed glasses flashed his way. "Ricky—right? Can you help? Can you cut boards, nail stuff? Anything?"

Tell her what you can do.

"He can bust locks. . ." Wilma's sigh carried across the room.

"Wilma!" Mort pushed his wife's teacup to her lips. "Ricky's been doing sound and lighting. . .and *fixing* locks."

Step up to the plate, Jimenez. Ricky stood in the shadows, wondering if the prompting came from pride or the Holy Spirit. It had to be pride. "I can. . .nail stuff."

Chapter 2

Don't give her water!"

Jillian leapfrogged three buckets, dove off the stage, and grabbed the plastic pitcher out of Ricky's hand. Water splashed, beading on the front of his charcoal gray sweater.

"Her who?"

"That's Jolly."

"What's jolly?"

"She is." Jillian pointed toward the stage where Jolly sat in a plastic coffee can.

Ricky set the pitcher back on the table and took a step back. Mahogany-colored eyes narrowed. "There's no one there."

"The plant."

"It's a jolly plant?"

"No. It's a Christmas cactus. Her name is Jolly."

"It's a she?" Ricky walked closer. "I just repotted it. . . *her*. . .and I didn't notice. . .how can you tell?"

His feigned perplexity reacted in her tired brain like a

whiff of nitrous oxide. She giggled—something she hadn't done in months. "She has girly phylloclades."

"Phyllowhats?" Tanned fingers splayed across his face. "Never mind. I'm blushing already."

"Leaves. Her leaves are called phylloclades." Her shoulders shook; tears sprang to her eyes. "I'm s–sorry."

"No, no. Go right ahead. There is something amusing about determining the gender of a Christmas cactus."

Jillian wiped her eyes on her sleeve. "I guess I'm cracking under the stress."

"Understandable."

"Thanks for taking care of her."

"Huh? Oh *her*. I've never met a nicer plant. I have a prickly pear cactus. We're not on a first-name basis yet."

"It takes time. You have to establish trust. I've had Jolly for almost a year."

"Oh. . .so you brought it. . .*her* from home? Does she always travel with you?" He spoke in the slow cadence people use on those with fragile minds.

Did it really matter if he thought her a crazy cactus lady? *Yes.* "I couldn't leave her behind. My roommate drowns her, and the OCD cleaning lady at work polishes her with Pledge." Jillian stared at the plant that should be gearing up to bloom. "Christmas cacti are sensitive. She's going to hate me for a long time after today."

"It takes a while to recover after getting dumped."

The asthma Jillian hadn't dealt with since leaving the dog lover suddenly returned. Her next breath sounded like an ailing vacuum cleaner. What had he heard about her breakup with Dennis? "It takes"—she wheezed out a cough that cleared her lungs—"a while to recover after dumping someone, too." No way was she going to let him see her as a victim.

She'd been the dump*er*, not the dump*ee*.

"She'll forgive you."

"*She?*" Oh. . .her.

"She knows it was really my fault."

"You gave her a new, not-root-bound home. She'll love you. And you saved me. Thank you for that."

"How many ribs did I crack?"

"Only a couple. And the punctured lung should refill in a few months. What were you doing under the steps?" *He can bust locks. . .* What had Wilma meant by that?

"I was guarding it in case Buster's niece showed up unexpectedly and opened it while Wilma was leaning on it."

"Always in the right place at the right time, huh?"

"I wish." His eyes took on a momentary shadow. "Buster had the locks changed after Cecil and Darcy left. Like he said, someone broke in again last night. Apparently they found a way in through a window, but we haven't found anything missing. Anyway, just before you drove up I was getting ready to install a dead bolt. The same thing almost happened to me when I tried opening the door. My hammer fell under the steps as I was yelling at Wilma to move her shepherd. When I heard you on the step. . .I dove."

It seemed plausible. "Well, I'm glad you were there."

"So am I."

They stood staring at a spindly, bruised plant in a green coffee can. Jillian closed her eyes, feeling the insulated silence of the theater like a familiar embrace. This was her sanctuary—the happy place her thoughts escaped to while she sat in an unproductive meeting. Or the last date she would ever have.

Opening her eyes, she glanced at the man beside her. Who was he? Where did he come from and why hadn't he ebbed out of Sister Bay on the summer tourist tide? Why would a man with an accent like that choose to be in a land of impending snow? "Where are you from?"

The faintest of smiles lifted the curve of high, angular cheekbones. "New York City."

"Right. I thought you had a Bronxy kind of twang."

He leaned against a table, crossed his arms over his chest, and smiled. A rim of white T-shirt peeked out at the neck of his sweater. "I was born in Brazil."

"Bra*sil*?" She copied the way he'd said it. "What are you doing here? Why aren't you sunning and surfing?" She turned away, wishing she could un-imagine him hanging ten on a perfect wave.

"Youch." The white smile became bared teeth. "Got any more stereotypes up your sleeve?"

"Um. . .do you play soccer?"

Ricky laughed. "I do, actually."

"Okay, seriously. How did you get here from there?"

"How much time do you have?"

Jillian raised her gaze to the tarp-covered hole. "Not to be rude, but. . .none. How about if you give me your story in small pieces while I start making sense of this mess?"

"I have a better idea. How about if we take a notebook and head over to the Ice Cream Factory for sustenance?"

Her thoughts slowed like maple sap in winter. "Um. . ." She hadn't thought it necessary to plan ahead for a scenario like this. The odds of any girl, let alone someone with her pathetic dating record, running into a tall, wavy-haired, midnight-eyed foreign soccer player in Sister Bay, Wisconsin, in the off season had to be about a Brazilian to one. "Um. . . you see. . .I don't do that anymore."

"Do what? Eat ice cream? Are you lactose intolerant? Or

do you just not eat anymore?"

"No. . ." *Rrrr.* She couldn't say "date" because maybe it wasn't. Maybe it was just ice cream—fuel to sustain them for the work. But if she went with him and he did think it was a date, then how would she get out of the second one without looking like—

Ricky uncrossed his arms. His left hand emerged from beneath his right arm. On his ring finger was a band of gold.

A wedding band of gold.

❄

Relief crested and curled over her, leaving her precariously giddy. Ricky was married. With the UNAVAILABLE sign flashing, she would be immune to all charms and ice cream would simply be ice cream. "That sounds wonderful. They have the best paninis. And I've been craving an Almond Joy sundae." She skipped over to the stage and picked up her coat. "I'll go tell Uncle Buster and grab a notebook." She waved, suppressed a giggle, and exited through a door in a dark corner of the room.

Buster sat at his overflowing desk, an empty coffee cup dangling from one finger. He stared vacantly. "We can't do this, can we, Jilli?" A sad smile lifted his sagging face. "But I'm glad you're here anyway. It seems right that you'll help me lock up for the last time. You were here on opening night, remember?"

"Of course. It was my first job."

"The customers loved you. I can still see you twirling through the kitchen like a ballerina when you got your first ten-spot tip."

Jillian winced. "I twirled into Darcy and her apple clafouti landed in the minestrone."

"And created a house special. . .spinach apple soup."

Jillian took the cup from his finger and set it on a stack of invoices. "This is going to be just like that. What looks like a disaster is going to end up as a raging success, so don't you give up. All things work together for good."

Buster's jowls shimmied. "That's not the end of the verse, Jilli. 'For those who love God and are called according to His purpose.' What about those who can't believe? No promises for us."

"There's no such thing as people who can't believe. You're a *won't* believe-er. But it's just a matter of time."

"You think, huh? If there's a God then why did He let—"

"We'll talk through all this tomorrow." *Again.* She kissed his cheek. She'd seen his sad eyes arc toward the picture on the wall and knew if he started reminiscing she'd never break away. As always, an oldies song drifted through her mind—"The Tears of a Clown." "I'm going over to the Ice Cream Factory with Ricky." She sifted through a stack of papers and folders until she found a notebook. "By the time I get back, I'll have an action plan and we'll hit the ground running in the morning."

"You think, huh?"

"I think."

❄

"So you think you. . .*we* can pull this off?" Ricky opened the door of the Door County Ice Cream Factory. The sweet smell of handmade waffle cones made his stomach grumble loud enough to make Jillian grin.

"I have to try." Jillian walked through the door. "I can't stand that hopeless look on my uncle's face."

As they perused the menu board, Jillian sighed. "Do you believe in God?"

Ricky's tongue pushed out his cheek. The guy behind

the counter looked up.

"Ready to order?"

Jillian nodded, little red maple leaves jiggling from her earlobes. "I'll have the Cana Island Panini and a glass of water."

Ricky ordered an eight-inch Factory Special pizza and a root beer float. When he asked for two straws a cute little wheezy sound came from the girl beside him. She turned away before he could read her expression. He paid for their food, waited for their drinks, and followed her to a high-backed booth. Aiming one bent straw at her, he offered her a taste. She shook her head. Maple leaves buffeted her jawline.

"Beyond belief." He redirected the straw.

"Huh?" The skin between her eyes scrunched. Confusion looked good on her.

"You asked me a question. I believe in God and then some." He took a long slurp from both straws.

Jillian froze with one arm out of her jacket. "So you're a . . .polytheist."

Ricky took a sharp and poorly planned breath. Ice cream-laced root beer sprayed the back of his throat like a fire hose. "N—no!" He held up his index finger until the spasm stopped. "One God. Only one. I meant I believe. . .lots. Like living out what I believe."

"Oh. . .*oh!* Good." Pink cheeks rose in an amazing smile. "Good. God put you in my uncle's life for a reason."

And what about yours? He banished the thought as soon as it surfaced. Two weeks to go until he could entertain a far-fetched idea like that. "Buster's been good for me, too."

"I didn't mean to sound like I was begging when I asked if you could help. I *was* begging, I just didn't want to sound like it. I'm sure you have better things to do than pound nails."

"Not really." *You sound like a bum, Jimenez.* "I have things to do, of course, but I don't mind helping out in my free time."

"What do you do? For a living, I mean."

Ricky stared through the eighteen-pane windows at the edge of a blue awning. It wasn't as welcoming in the cold mist as it had been in May when he'd rolled through Sister Bay after seventeen hours on a Suzuki CSX. "I'm. . .kind of a handyman. And you're in advertising, right? In Iowa?"

She opened the notebook, tore out several sheets for him, and clicked her pen. "Not happily, but I'm in it. It's not the field I'm dissatisfied with, it's the place I work. I interned at an amazing company where we brainstormed together and laughed all the time. Amazing things got done there. Where I work now—Identity Incorporated in Davenport—we're all like lab rats locked away in little square cubicles. But don't get me started on that. We have work to do. Let's get things down on paper and then we can prioritize. We need waitresses, kitchen help, ush—"

"Jillian." Ricky touched the hand that held the pen.

She jumped. What was that all about? "Yes?"

"There's something else."

"Write it down." She clicked a red-coated nail on the paper she'd given him.

"There's another problem. A big one."

She laid the pen down.

"About the script. . ."

"Yes?"

"There isn't one."

Chapter 3

I think I can. I think I can. I think I can. The little blue engine chugged up the hill pulling a boxcar of faded shepherds and yellow sheep—

And Jillian woke up. In a third-floor loft with slanted maple walls and sunlight streaming through a four-foot-wide porthole.

"Mmmm." Her bare feet slid on satin sheets. Plumping one of seven pillows, she sat up. "Can you say vacation?" She grinned at Jolly, perched on a glass pedestal table, underdressed in her Folgers can. "Can you say ex*tennn*ded vacation?" Not that she'd made the call to her boss yet, but, as unreasonable as Franklin Hiram could be, he couldn't deny her a few extra days, could he? She'd worked for thirteen months without a vacation. Or a raise. . .or a compliment.

Stretching her hand out like the queen awaiting a ring kiss, she picked up a remote, pushed the black button, and sighed royally as drapes parted, revealing tall French doors overlooking the bay. *Lord, what have I done to deserve this?*

The answer, of course, was nothing. The grace of God and

the generosity of Ardis Bourbonnais-Stanford had landed her in temporary luxury. Ardis's grandfather made his fortune building ships in the early 1900s and built "the farm" for his family. His granddaughter, now in her seventies, had turned his Ellison Bay estate, complete with silo, into an artsy retreat for art lovers of all breeds.

And their nieces.

"We'll make this fun, Jolly. We'll get Buster up and running and still get lots of relaxation ti—" Her phone vibrated on the glass table, inching past Jolly as it jiggled on the slick surface. Jillian crawled across the span of ivory sheets and down-filled pillows and grabbed the phone in midair. "Hello?"

"You okay, kiddo? You sound a little congested." Her father, a pediatrician who hadn't yet accepted that his daughter no longer matched the parameters of his practice, *tsk*ed from St. Louis.

"I'm fine, Dad. How could I not be stupendous in this place? The colors are amazing."

"Feels good to get away from the little tyrant, I'll bet."

"Don't fuel the fire." She laughed. Her father had met her boss only once and had nothing flattering to say about him.

"Faster, Miss Galloway. I want it on my desk yesterday if not before!" His imitation was flawless. "What do you mean you can't be productive in this environment? You will feel creative when I say you will feel creative!"

It felt good to laugh. "Stop."

"Okay, enough. How was the show?"

Jillian wrinkled her nose at Jolly. "Well. . ." How much should she tell a man who'd had his second open-heart surgery less than a month ago? "Buster had to close up shop for. . .a bit. A tree limb fell on the roof during a storm and caused some water damage."

"Ah. Too bad. Thank the Lord for insurance, huh?"

Um. . . About that. . .

"Okay, sweet cakes, gotta run. Love you."

"Love you more. Bye."

Swinging her legs over the side of the king-sized bed, she leaned down and grabbed headphones from her computer bag. Her toes disappeared in one of the deep ivory rugs decorating the hardwood floor. After brushing her teeth in a sea green vessel sink in a cedar bathroom complete with sauna, she stood, feet apart and hands raised, in front of the windows. The view itself was a worship experience, an acknowledgment of God's spectacular handiwork. Next to a stone walkway leading to the edge of the water sat two bright blue Adirondack chairs. Orange maple leaves glowed between two white birches. Lazy clouds dotted the azure sky. As she listened to the fifteenth chapter of First Corinthians on her MP3 player, she stretched away yesterday's stress.

Therefore, my dear brothers, stand firm. Let nothing move you. Always give yourselves fully to the work of the Lord, because you know that your labor in the Lord is not in vain.

"Thank You, Lord. I needed that today."

"Jilli! I heard the toilet flush. Are you awake?" Wilma's morning voice grated up the spiral staircase.

Clicking off Corinthians, Jillian leaned over the corkscrew stairs, thrilling at the dizzying jolt of the optical illusion. She imagined her voice echoing off each solid maple step. "I'm up."

Up. . .up. . .up. . .

"I made French toast. It's a little on the done side, but I saved two slices for you."

Jillian bared her teeth. Wilma was a wonder on stage, a disaster in the kitchen. French toast "a little on the done side" probably resembled ceramic tile. Squaring her shoulders with false bravado, she called down, "I'll throw on some clothes and be right there."

"It's just girls this morning, so feel free to come down in your jammies. We're still in ours."

We?

Jillian stepped in front of a massive round mirror and reshaped her ponytail. Her Scotch plaid flannel pants and black pajama shirt with the embroidered Scottie dog looked juvenile but presentable. She padded halfway down the stairs. Life was too short not to slide the rest of the way on the curled banister. She eased her backside onto the railing and lifted her feet off the step. "Weeeeeeee—*ah!*" The man approaching the all-glass front door made her legs forget to stiffen when they neared the floor.

Thunk.

❄

It was a beautiful sight. Well, part of it was beautiful. The girl on the alpaca rug was breathtaking. The little lady hunched over her in pink sweats and flowered nightcap. . .not so much. And who was the woman with bluish-black hair in the fur-collared white robe? Was she for real or on her way to audition for *101 Dalmations*? Cruella De Vil opened the door for him.

He nodded to the woman and looked past her. "Jillian? Are you all right?"

"She's fine." Wilma straightened to her full five feet and stepped in front of Jillian arms out to her sides, palms facing back, she created a human shield. "What are you doing here?"

"I came to talk to Jillian about the theater."

"Anything you want to know, you can ask Bu—"

"It's okay, Wilma." Jillian peeked from behind a baggy pink leg, her face very nearly the same color as the sweatpants.

"I'll handle this."

"You're in your pajamas."

"It's okay." Jillian stood, wincing as she smiled at him. "I like to make a grand entrance."

"It was magnificent. Maybe we should be looking for a script with *five* parts."

Wilma narrowed her eyes. "Who's looking for a script?"

"He's just being funny." Jillian winked over the flowered cap. "The last time I was on stage I threw up on a daisy. I was a watering can, so it was actually quite a stunning effect, but the daisy wouldn't talk to me until second grade. That was the end of my stage career."

Cruella De Vil laughed, apparently startling Jillian as much as Ricky. If he ever needed a foghorn sound effect, he'd keep her in mind. He held out his hand. "Enrique Jimenez. They call me Ricky."

"I know." Her voice rumbled through barn-red lips.

Jillian offered her hand over Wilma's ear. "I'm Jillian."

"Clarissa Bourbonnais—Ardis's second cousin twice removed."

"Nice to meet you."

Wilma pointed a finger at Ricky. "What do you want?"

"Actually, I came to ask if I could call a cast meeting in a couple of hours. And"—he attempted nonchalance—"to see if Jillian could join me for breakfast. I thought we could write an ad for a director to post at the Clearing."

"Director? Why didn't you say something?" Penciled brows huddled over shockingly pale blue eyes as Ardis's second cousin twice removed opened her hands as if testing for rain. "Look no further, people. Give me a copy of the script and let's get started."

The pupils of Jillian's dark eyes suddenly constricted as her lids parted like flapping window shades. "I'd love to go with you. Wilma, save the French toast." With a definite limp, she ascended the stairs—leaving him alone with Cruella De Vil and a little pink woman snarling like a mama tiger.

"Lovely day, isn't it?"

❄

"Jilli? Are you decent?" Wilma's whisper climbed the winding stairs.

Buttoning her new white peplum-front blouse, Jillian leaned over the railing—and flinched in pain. "I'll be down in a sec." This time, the man waiting at the bottom would see her descend gracefully.

"I'm coming up." Wilma spoke with the determination of a climber about to scale Mount Everest without an oxygen tank.

Jillian had time to apply mascara and lip gloss before Wilma reached the summit. "Sit down." She directed her to a brick red mushroom chair that looked exactly like its name.

Tapping her hand against her chest, Wilma complied. "You. . .can't. . .go with him." Her shoulders rose to her ears in a shuddery breath. "I know he's got Antonio Banderas's face and a bod that'll make any girl swoon—"

"Wilma!"

"Fishfeathers." She waved fluttering fingers. "Don't stand there and act all shocked. I'm old, not dead. The point is, Enrique Jimenez is a fake. He'll try telling you he's some kind of handyman—he's handy all right. Handy enough to break into the theater and sneak around in the middle of the ni—"

"Wilma? I'm home! You up there?" Mort's voice echoed up the stairs. "Got your denture cream."

"My sweet little man." Wilma shook her head and stood. "Thank you!" Her stage voice projected across the room. She put an age-spotted hand on Jillian's arm. "The point is, don't fall for the package. You won't like what's inside."

"It really doesn't matter. He's already taken."

"Huh?" Wilma slid her glasses back in place.

"Isn't that a wedding ring he wears?"

"Oh, that. One date with you and he'll forget that silly vow."

"I don't date anymore, and I certainly wouldn't go out with a mar—"

"Wilma?" Mort knocked on the railing below. "You going with me to the park? Last day for tours."

"That man and his lighthouses," Wilma whispered. "He could be the tour guide for the Eagle Bluff Lighthouse. That brings up another point. . .it's good to appreciate history, but we can't let ourselves get stuck in the past."

Jillian smiled. "Well said."

Wilma took hold of the railing then turned and planted a kiss on Jillian's cheek. "You won't be stuck in yours forever, you know. You'll get over Dennis and"—she pointed at Jolly—"that cactus will bloom someday. Just don't get sidetracked by sweet talk." She turned and stepped down into the optical illusion of endless spirals.

Jillian pulled a black sweater with Oreo-sized buttons out of her suitcase. Slipping into it, she stared at Jolly. "Is she right? Was Lola right?" She pictured the smile lines on the innkeeper's face as she'd held out the tissue-wrapped Christmas cactus eleven and a half months ago. The card read, *God bless you on your birthday, Jilli. With proper care, this, and love, will bloom at the right time.*

She'd thought Christmas was the right time. She'd thought Dennis was the right love.

She'd been wrong on both counts.

Chapter 4

Jillian stabbed her last forkful of Swedish pancake at Al Johnson's as she waited for Ricky to finish a phone call. Their waitress, wearing a white apron over a traditional red and blue print skirt and white peasant blouse, refilled Ricky's coffee cup while he nodded and said "mm-hm...yes... right." Jillian had no clue what the conversation was about. Finally, he hung up, looked at her with a distinctly uncomfortable expression, and said, "Think we've covered it all?"

She glanced at the gold band. *All but where your wife is.* "All we do now is pray for a script to miraculously appear before...yesterday." She took a deep breath. "With God all things are possible."

His hand slid over hers then pulled quickly away like the brush of butterfly wings. He picked up their bill. "Think you can handle a spin around the gift shop with that limp?"

"I was hoping you hadn't noticed."

He helped her on with her coat. "That was some fall."

"My very former boyfriend told people I wore banana peel shoes."

"Wow. No wonder he's past tense." Ricky walked behind her to the checkout then followed her into Al Johnson's *Butik*.

Wool sweaters, pewter dishes, Swedish flags, imported chocolate, and T-shirts printed with "Where is that place with goats on the roof?" filled the rooms. A group of Japanese men loaded down with shopping bags and cameras examined a display of Scandinavian neckties. Ricky had just picked up a statue of an adorably ugly troll playing an accordion when "Go Tell It on the Mountain" blasted from Jillian's purse.

"Sorry." She pulled it out. "It's Buster." She said hello.

"Jilli, I need you to talk to Wilma. She locked herself in the green room and won't come out."

"Why?"

"She and Ardis had a fight. Try to talk some sense into her. I'll put you on speakerphone. There. Talk loud."

"But. . ." Jillian shrugged her shoulders at Ricky and walked over to the racks and shelves of sweaters, hoping they'd deaden her voice. "Wilma? Can you hear me?"

Silence. "Wilma?" She upped the volume. "What did Ardis say?" The tourists tittered.

"She. . .she. . ." A weak voice echoed through her phone. "She said I'm a d–diva."

"You're not a diva, Wilma!" Jillian yelled. The tourists turned in unison. Ricky peered at her from behind a rack, amusement dancing on his face.

"And a prima donna. And she said I'm as graceful as a Mac truck and I sing like a turkey vulture."

"You know you don't sing like a turkey vulture!"

A sound like a rupturing water main burst out of Ricky.

"Wilma. . .calm down. You're not as graceful as a Mac truck."

The gawkers snickered.

"What's this all about? What started your fight with Ardis?"

A loud sniff was followed by the sound of a door unlatching. "She's j–jealous. J–just plain jealous." Wilma's voice suddenly became high def. "Eleven years of working together and now she decides to count lines."

"Count lines? What do you mean?"

"She's not coming back unless you change the script so she has more lines than me."

"That's ridiculous. Okay, tell her she'll have more lines."

"She won't get on a plane until you fax her the script."

Jillian nodded numbly and said good-bye. *I think I can. I think I can. I think I can. . .'t.*

❉

"No *script*?"

Buster's voice turned soprano on the last syllable. A tomato slice cartwheeled out of his submarine sandwich and pasted itself to the dry erase board. Hands in choir director position, he stopped pacing. "Cecil told me weeks ago he was ready to. . ." Jowls shook, one finger waggled. "No. He didn't say the script was finished. . .he told me he had everything under control." A rueful laugh echoed off the movie-poster-covered walls of the green room. Eyes that sagged like a lonely hound's looked around the table—from Jillian, to Mort and Wilma—and landed on Ricky. "Well, if this isn't a sign from God, I don't know what is. We're done. It's over." He laid his sub on the table. "Go home, everyone." In two heavy steps, he reached the door.

Ricky jumped out of his chair. His pulse banged out a nervous beat, as if something of more eternal significance than theater were at stake. After struggling for hours to ignore the nudge in his spirit that had awakened him at four this morning, he'd called this meeting. At first he'd been merely surrendered to the idea, but the more he thought about it, the more right it seemed. He turned to Jillian. "I may have a solution."

"You found a script?"

"No. But I think I know where to get one."

Hope shimmered in the dark eyes that today were framed with polka-dot glasses. "Where?"

"Right here." He pointed to her, then swung his index finger back to land on his chest. "You and I can write it."

"Ha!" The tiny laugh popped from her throat like a bottle cork.

A gasp slipped from Wilma's wrinkled lips. Mort's cheeks drew back, displaying gritted teeth. Buster huffed and yanked the door handle.

Ricky blocked it with his foot. "Sit down. Please. Hear me out."

Buster turned slowly. He stared at his chair as if wondering if he had the energy to cross the yard of worn gray carpet. With a breath that hefted his belly above his belt, he took the step and slumped into the chair.

Ricky cleared his throat. "Jillian. . .you're a writer. Buster has your ads tacked up all over his office and I've"—he gulped and hoped it wasn't loud enough to be heard—"I worked at the drama camp all summer."

Buster's jaw grew slack. His thumb and forefinger ran along the wide "O" formed by his open mouth. "That's very. . . nice, Ricky. I appreciate you trying to help, but. . .no offense . . .this is a professional troupe. You taught mime to eight-year-olds all summer." His mouth closed. His eyes followed suit. A whisper of a smile rippled his cheeks. "And I've seen my niece's attempt at a Christmas story. Not that I didn't love *Rudolph and the Angry Candy Cane*, but—"

A Ripple potato chip, launched from Jillian's fingertips, hit his chest. "I was eight when I wrote that." She raised an eyebrow at Ricky. "Not that I'm defending my abilities. It's a nice gesture, but I could probably sprout wings easier than I could write a play."

"Stage drama is a whole different animal." Buster pinched the bridge of his nose. "Cecil may be lower than a snake's belly, but he's a skilled playwright. Doorbuster's has never claimed to offer the same caliber productions as the American Folklore Theater or Peninsula Players, but Door County is known for the arts. An amateur production would be worse than. . . Thank you anyway."

Jillian nodded. "It was a very sweet thought."

Her patronizing smile hit like a miniscule dagger. *Lord, what should I say?* They had no idea what he was actually offering. And telling them would ruin everything.

For him.

"Creative writing is your thing, Jillian. It's what you do. With my experi—" His voice faded out. "Experience, we can come up with something workable. At least we can try."

Jillian's bangs brushed back and forth across her forehead. "I don't know. . .I guess we could talk about—"

"Thata girl! Give us two days, Buster." Ricky stared at the whiteboard behind the giant of a man. The tomato slid in slow motion and hit the floor with a wet slap. "You worry about the roof and let us see what we can come up with. If you don't like the first couple of pages, we'll hang it up. Okay?"

Jillian shrugged and lifted her hands, palms up. A gesture of surrender. "We might surprise you. No mad candy canes, I promise."

Wilma smacked the table with an open hand. Her gaze

drilled into Ricky. A moon-shaped piece of pickle jiggled on her chin. "What are you trying to do to us?"

Involuntarily, Ricky's head jerked back. "What do you mean?" When he'd first volunteered at the theater, she'd treated him like her long-lost grandson. Ricky softened his approach. "I just want to do what I can to make this place a success."

"I'd sure like to see some evidence of that. All I've seen so far is a busted lock and you sneaking around here in the middle of the night. Before you came, everything was perfect."

Mort's face blanched. "Wilma, you make it sound like Ricky's responsible for the thunderstorm."

The pickle slice vibrated. "And the missing money and probably Cecil and—"

A giant pumpkin-shaped cookie crash-landed on her lips. "Try this, dear. Jillian got them from Grandma's Bakery." Mort's fake smile created rosy, apple-shaped bumps on his cheeks.

Wilma sputtered but quickly diverted her gaze to the orange-frosted cookie. Mort's cheeks returned to normal. "I'm touched that you would even consider such an endeavor, Ricky. And Jilli, you're a true sport to agree to it. It's the thought that counts."

"That's right." Buster patted Jillian's hand. "Just the fact that you wanted to try means more to me than you'll ever know. I'll pay your company for your time, and you just enjoy yourself this week. Rent a moped, enjoy the fall colors. No sense beating a dead horse. It's time we all move on."

Through polka-dot glasses, one long-lashed lid winked at Ricky, sparking a fire beneath his breastbone. The girl was on board. She was willing to try.

And, deep down, that's probably just what her uncle was hoping for.

Chapter 5

I've been studying old scripts."

Ricky's leather boots echoed on the boardwalk as he walked out of the Silly Goose General Store. "The Hoopers and Maxwells are just blown-out-of-reality caricatures of the Rileys and Stanfords." He pulled a slice of caramel apple out of a waxed paper bag and handed it to Jillian. "Can you think of real-life situations that could help us build a skeleton?"

Jillian took a bite. "Lash yer mrt shined rup fer—"

"Stop! Chew. . .swallow. . .now talk."

She gulped and hoped her smile wasn't tinted caramel. When they got in the car, she continued. "Last year about this time, Mort made out a budget that would get them debt-free in a year. It allowed them only a hundred dollars for Christmas. . .gifts, food, decorations, everything. I've never seen Wilma so mad. So she decided to make her own money. She started writing for a greeting card company. . .for their 'love notes' line."

"Wonderful." Ricky pressed his lips together. The action

softened his perfectly chiseled profile.

"During rehearsals, she'd scribble her ideas on scraps of paper."

"And Mort found them."

"Yep. He found a stack of them in an envelope."

"Perfect." Ricky slapped the steering wheel as he headed south. "What did he do?"

"He simply asked her to stop seeing the other man. It was when he found out she was cheating on him with a job that he went ballistic."

"Ah. . .good plot twist." Ricky rubbed his smooth-shaven chin. "Let's take that and add some 'what ifs.' Like what if Mort had a different reaction to the notes?"

Jillian turned to face him and instantly regretted it. The relief of finding out the gorgeous Brazilian was married had faded after the first hour, replaced by questions she didn't know him well enough to ask—and other questions she should have asked by now. "Um, where are we headed?"

"Someplace inspirational."

All of Door County, Wisconsin's thumb, was inspirational. Wave-smoothed rocks on the shoreline, sailboats bobbing in the bay, tree-lined hiking paths splashed with the colors of autumn. . .every scenario painted a picture of hand-holding walks. She ordered her meandering thoughts back to "what ifs," but it only lengthened her tangent. *What if I'm falling for a married man? What if I spend my whole life going from mistake to mistake and the right one never comes along?* She yanked on her earlobe to change the channel in her head. "What if he hired a private investigator?"

"And what if both Mort and Huey are doing the budget thing?"

"And both women get jobs. What could Ardis do that

would make Huey suspicious?" Adrenaline coursed along the nerve pathways to her fingertips. If she had this kind of teamwork at work, she'd love her job.

Ideas layered the crisp air until Ricky drove into the parking lot behind Doorbuster's Theater. Jillian swallowed her disappointment. It wasn't the inspiration she'd imagined.

Ricky reached her door and opened it before she'd zipped her jacket. She swung her feet out. And stared at his outstretched hand. *Not good.* Pretending not to see it, she got out and turned toward Doorbuster's.

"Not there. *There.*"

Jillian followed the line of one muscular arm to the tip of his finger—which pointed toward forest green double doors. The Tannenbaum Shop. "You don't know what you're doing. If I go in there I won't come out 'til they close. I'm a little bit Christmas crazy."

Ricky laughed. "This'll be fun."

Naive man. He had no idea what he was in for. She led him into the building and straight to a display of Fontanini nativities. "Feel free to wander around. If you stick by me, you'll get bored."

The look that answered her sprouted goose bumps rivaled only by the "Hallelujah Chorus." "I can't imagine being bored with you."

"Jillian Galloway!" A middle-aged woman behind a counter waved. "Our favorite customer."

"Uh-oh." Ricky grimaced. "Maybe I spoke too soon."

"You were warned." Jillian waved back.

"Did the kings' accessories arrive okay?" The woman took money from another customer, but her eyes were on Jillian.

"Yes. I love it. What's new in the last week?"

"Last *week*?" Ricky whispered.

"We got the new Willow Tree angel."

"Put it on my tab."

"Tab?" Ricky sounded like a feeble old man.

"You were warned." She led him to a Dickens' Village display. Tiny buildings nestled on a snow blanket scattered with iridescent flakes. "I have this at home."

"All of it?" Ricky seemed in danger of losing his eyeballs.

Jillian raised her right hand. "My name is Jillian Galloway and I am a Christmasaholic." She turned toward an eight-foot decorated blue spruce. "I'm pretty much always in a Christmas mood. Maybe we need to be here for you to get inspired."

Ricky fingered a crystal icicle. "Maybe." His gaze rose to a spot a foot below the angel at the treetop. He took something off the tree and held it out to her—a glass Scottie dog with a red bow on its head. Other than the wreath around the neck, it was exactly like the one on her pajama top.

Heat prickles rose from the collar of her blouse.

" 'Christmas crazy,' huh?" His fingertip touched the tip of her nose. "What a perfect name for our production."

❄

Silence reigned in the green room for two sweeps of the second hand. Jillian nibbled on the end of a pen. Too edgy to sit, Ricky stood across the table from her. In spite of his obvious tension, he covered a yawn. He'd spent most of the night putting the beginning of their story in script format. Act One Scene One lay in three neat stacks in front of Doorbuster's skeleton cast and reluctant manager.

Another minute passed. And then a high-pitched hiccuppy sound accompanied a rattle of papers.

Wilma was giggling. "It's us! You captured us!" Mort's guffaw soon followed. But the valleys between Uncle Buster's eyes deepened. One hand covered his mouth as he read.

Four worried gazes crisscrossed the table. The second hand circled the clock again. Ricky paced until he stood behind her.

Buster blinked. A tear leaped over his bottom lid. "It's"— his lips pressed together, smacked apart—"amazing. A great setup. I'm. . .shocked."

Tipping over his chair, Mort rose to his feet, Wilma stood next to him. As if on cue, the two began to clap. Buster joined in.

Ricky's arm slid around Jillian's shoulders. And a kiss skimmed the top of her head, starting a shock wave that threatened to melt the polish off her toenails. But her attention on the married man was diverted by a steady *tap. . .tap . . .tap*. With her glasses threatening to leap to their death, Wilma bent over the first scene, tapping her pencil all along the margin. Suddenly her head popped up and her glasses dove to the table. Squinting in Jillian's direction, she commanded, "Call Ardis. Fax this to her. Right now."

"Are you two on speaking terms again?"

"Oh. . .fishfeathers. We've been fighting for three decades. Never stopped the show from going on. She has four more lines than I do in this. Tell her if she and Huey don't get here ASAP you'll put on one of her wigs and take her part."

A frightful vision flashed before Jillian's eyes—standing in the middle of the stage in one of Ardis Maxwell's lace-and-pearl-laden dresses and a brassy blond wig, arms and legs paralyzed by stage fright. Would the Brazilian come to her rescue? Toss her over his shoulder and carry her motionless body off into the night? *Stop!* "I'll fax it. Right away." She needed to remove herself from the vicinity of Ricky Jimmy.

Wilma took her husband by the hand. "And we'll get the ambience."

"Ambience?"

"For our brainstorming session."

Our? Jillian locked eyes with Ricky. Smile lines fanned into shiny black hair. "I'll go get food," he said.

When Jillian returned from a victorious fight with a cantankerous fax machine and an equally stubborn Ardis, the "ambience" that greeted Jillian reminded her of a scene from the movie *Elf.*

The Trans-Siberian Orchestra thundered "God Rest Ye Merry Gentlemen." A ceramic Christmas tree with tiny colored lights glowed from the counter. Mort stood on a chair, hanging a string of red icicle lights while Wilma perched in the center of the table, attaching an enormous, shimmery green snowflake to the light fixture. She jiggled the snowflake. "How's this for *Christmas Crazy?*"

Days of tension morphed into giggles of relief. When Ricky walked in with pizza from Moretti's, the look of shock on his face sent Jillian into a new spasm of laughter. Wiping her eyes, she opened a cupboard. Ricky stepped beside her. He reached out as if to take the stack of paper plates she held, but his hands slid over hers. Mesmerizing Brazilian eyes caressed her face. "I like being the other half of your team."

Pulse pounding, Jillian pulled the plates. . .and her hands . . .out of his grasp then tore her gaze from his.

This can't happen.

Maybe it was just his Latin way. Maybe it meant nothing to him.

But it didn't mean nothing to her, and she couldn't keep working with a man who didn't respect her, his wife, or boundaries.

Tomorrow they were going to the Clearing. Tomorrow they would talk.

❄

Ricky paced the length of one wall in the miniscule shed-turned-apartment. He stared out his only window at the sun rising over the orchard. The morning rays glistened on the grass between rows of Montmorency cherry trees shedding their leaves for winter.

The view never got old. He'd moved in when the blossoms were at their peak—a riot of pink reminding him of Coney Island cotton candy. In the middle of the summer, between drama camp sessions, he'd helped pick the bright red cherries and manned one of the roadside stands owned by his pastor's in-laws, doing his part to sell some of the thirteen million pounds of cherries produced in Door County each year.

Who would have thought, a year ago, that Enrique Jimenez, aka J. K. Henry, would be living in a toolshed, carrying only singles in his money clip, and going by the name Ricky Jimmy?

Opening his laptop, he began writing Act One, Scene Two. But his thoughts strayed to the girl who'd inspired the title. Christmas Crazy Jillian Galloway. The girl who wore only red and black, who had glasses frames to match every outfit, who could giggle like a little girl but run a theater like a tenderhearted drill sergeant.

Lord, is it time?

Chapter 6

S orry you had to follow me out here for nothing." Ricky opened his two-door teal hatchback. "I was sure they'd know of someone."

"This isn't for nothing." Leaning on her Hyundai, Jillian swept her arm toward the building they'd just exited. "Your friends in there said they'd put the word out that we're looking for a director—that's not nothing."

So far, she'd only seen the visitor center of the folk school, but everything about the setting and the stone building beckoned creativity. "And I'm finally getting to see this place." She waved a campus map. "All these years I've heard people talk about the Clearing, but I'm not the artsy type."

"You have an artsy-colored car."

"It's called Apple Red Pearl." *And please don't ask what happened to the door.*

"Sweet."

"I call her Lucy. Redhead—get it?"

"Got it." Ricky's laugh blended with the earthiness of the place. "Do you name everything?"

"Just cars and plants. I'm not on a first-name basis with my vacuum cleaner or anything. Oh, wait. . .my laptop. . . he's Sam."

"He? I'm not even going to ask."

"His last name's Sung."

Eyes that matched the shingles on the stone building behind him rolled toward the heavens. "Got it." He pointed to his car. "You can ride with me."

"Uh. . ." *Think*. She'd turned down a ride to the school, claiming she had errands to run afterward. If the talk she had in mind didn't go well, she wanted an easy escape. "I was thinking I might stay around awhile and. . ." And what? Walk? He could walk with her. Draw? She'd already said she wasn't the artsy type. The answer popped like an old-fashioned flashbulb. "Take some pictures."

"Oh." He didn't seem convinced. "Okay. Follow me."

She did. Along a rustic dirt lane where gold leaves fell lazily and crimson bushes hid among still-green cypresses. *Lord, You used every crayon in the box when You made this place.* She rolled down the window. Geese honked above the trees; tires crunched in the gravel.

Ricky stopped and was out of his car by the time she parked hers. He pointed toward the painful scar below her open window. "Accident?"

I wish. Well, the guy who caused it had been a huge accident. Turning away from the concern in Ricky's eyes, she slipped her camera strap over her wrist, closed the window, and got out. "Actually. . .it was parking lot rage." Hot fingers of humiliation scampered up her neck.

"Seriously? Somebody rammed you because you took their spot?"

Jillian sucked a strained breath through a narrowing

windpipe and instinctively searched her jacket pocket for the inhaler she no longer needed. *Relax.* "No." She walked away from Ricky, kept walking until she stood in front of a two-story stone building with a weathered shake roof.

"That's the lodge." Ricky came up behind her. So close she could hear his breeze-blocking presence. "You know," he whispered, "I have a master's degree in listening."

She stepped away from his woodsy scent. Her pulse tripped.

So did her feet.

"Whoa!" Ricky grabbed her right bicep with one hand, her camera with the other.

Her momentum halted mid-fall. She hung from his hand at a forty-five-degree angle, her left arm doing windmills, her feet fighting for traction. "Let me. . .down."

He did. Right onto her bruised hip. She gasped. He crouched. "Are you okay?"

Eyes stinging, she nodded. The movement shook tears over the dam. Hot rivers coursed to her jaw and dripped on the ground.

Ricky's arms slid around her. His hand stroked the top of her head. . .and brushed away self-control. The dam broke. Collapsing against him, she conceded defeat to the tears she'd sworn she'd never shed. Suddenly she was back in the parking lot of For Pets' Sake Veterinary Hospital. *And if you think for one second that I'm going to lose an ounce of sleep or cry one measly tear over somebody as sel*— "I opened the car door"—she swiped a hand across her slick face—"on a p–poodle." Fresh sobs consumed her.

"I'm so sorry. That must have been awful. Was it. . . did it. . .die?"

Her tears stopped. Like a tight crank on a spigot, Ricky's

last word shut off the water. . .and took her to an emotional expression only beats away from tears. She covered her face with her hands as laughter quaked her entire body. She shook her head against his jacket. "It was a statue. A cement poodle. It wrecked my door and cracked my window. But it was Dennis's fault. If he wasn't such a selfish jerk, I wouldn't have smashed my door on a poodle."

Ricky's chest convulsed as he laughed with her. She liked the feeling. And pulled away. "We broke up because he loves dogs more than me."

He was silent through several breaths. "But you don't actually *hate* dogs, right?"

"No. Of course not."

"Then couldn't you come up with a compromise? Like, if he wants two dogs you compromise on one really small dog? It doesn't seem—"

"No!" A fresh phase of giggles shook her shoulders. "He loves dogs more than he loves *me*! I'm allergic to cats and dogs, and I can't even be around people who've been around them without swelling up and wheezing. But what does my so-called boyfriend go and do? He gets a job working for a vet and then he announces he's not going to be a plain old normal dentist after all. . .he's going be an *animal* dentist. So I told him we were through, and I shoved my door into a big pink poodle and gave up dating forever."

❄

Dennis the dentist was a dope. What kind of man would take basset hounds and Siamese cats over this amazing woman? Ricky ran his hand over chestnut hair. "It's good you can laugh about it. But it had to hurt."

She pulled away again, but not too far. Just enough for him to look down at her face, which was turning sober. "It did. But

I'm glad I found out his priorities when I did. I mean, if he really cared about me he'd put my lungs above dog teeth."

Her expression was dead serious. The time for laughter had passed. Ricky tried desperately not to picture Jillian's lungs dangling over open jaws. "You're right." *Breathe. Slower.* He pulled her tear-spattered glasses off. With his fingertips, he swept away her tears. "How serious was your relationship?"

A pause sign formed on her forehead. The corners of her mouth lifted. "It was serious. . .ly boring." Her face took on a rain-washed glow. "I haven't really missed him. I've just been mad."

"At Dennis or the poodle?"

A full-fledged smile crinkled her cheeks. "Both."

"You have a fascinating smile."

"Mm." Her hand slid over her mouth. "I know. It's huge." Her gaze dropped to the ground. "Dennis used to tell me to tone it down."

"*Nao me diga.* You're not serious." He tugged at her wrist. "It's a Julia Roberts smile."

She let her hand fall away. Into his. Her smile blazed. For a moment. And then her eyes seemed to follow the line of his arm to her hand in his. She retracted it, picked up her camera, and stood.

He couldn't decipher the change in her expression. Whatever it meant, it wasn't good. By the time he got to his feet, she was climbing the lodge steps. He followed at what he hoped was a safe distance.

She stood in front of an oval plaque declaring the Clearing was on the National Register of Historic Places. Hands slid to trim hips, her elbows stuck out. "1935."

"Yes. It was built—"

"Where's your wife?"

❋

Ricky Jimmy wriggled like the bright green tomato worms she'd trapped in canning jars as a child. His right hand slid over his left. Fingers twisted the gold band.

"I'm not married."

Right.

He held up his hand. "This is. . .protection."

Okay, so he was make-your-heart-stop-forget-to-breathe gorgeous. But there was nothing uglier than a cute guy who flaunted it. "Keeps the girls at bay, huh?" She hated sarcasm. But some occasions required it.

"Yes. *No.*" A coal black hank of hair slid across his forehead. "I mean. . .it works that way, too. Not that anyone's looking, but. . ." The worm squirmed. "It's for me. A reminder. A symbol. I made a promise to God that I'd spend a year focusing on Him and on serving and not on. . .other things."

Oh. *Oh.* "Like a monk?"

"Kind of. I just needed to get my focus back where it belonged, back to only worrying about pleasing God, not men. I'd gotten full of myself. I had to stop doing everything that enabled my self-absorption. Cold turkey."

Jillian grabbed the railing. Brain gears squealed and jammed. It was too much to process. The man in front of her looked like he should have nothing on his mind but lobbing a ball over a net on a sand court. And yet here he stood— sincerely professing his devotion to God. And utterly single. "Oh."

Ricky studied his shoes. "Do you want to see the rest of the place?"

"Yes." She needed the change of subject as much as he seemed to.

Leaves crunched under their feet as they walked beside a foot-high, moss-covered rock wall. On either side of them stood low, rough-hewn log and stone cabins. Red geraniums still bloomed in window boxes. Set against a backdrop of fiery maples and copper-leafed oaks, the cabins were at one with the nature surrounding them. Jillian breathed in the musky scent. "Don't you love the smell of fall?"

"I never get tired of it. I was eighteen the first time I smelled it, or saw snow."

"Is that when you moved from Brazil?"

He shook his head. "My father's a pastor. We came to Florida when I was ten so he could train missionaries. I didn't see snow until I moved to"—his phone rang—"New York. Excuse me."

Again, he gave only cryptic answers. When he hung up, he pointed toward one of the larger buildings. "I taught a class on dramatic reading here in July."

"You're a teacher?"

"Not officially."

"So what are you...officially?" The question came out a bit sharper than she'd planned.

"That's a hard question to answer. At the moment I guess I'm a gypsy."

A stiff breeze whipped the end of her scarf against Ricky's cheek. Gypsy? Her fantasy Brazilian fell off his surfboard and tied a red silk scarf around his head. A gold earring caught the sun from his right earlobe. Swarthy, dark, mysterious. She blinked, sweeping the vision from her mental screen.

"I'm renting a dinky place from my pastor's in-laws, and I take odd jobs when I can find them. Like fixing broken locks."

"And writing scripts and working at a drama camp and

teaching at the Clearing. Who are you, Ricky Jimmy, and what are you doing in Sister Bay?" The question that had danced on her tongue jumped out unbidden on a voice that was part curious, part confrontational. The knowledge that he was single put everything in a different light. He knew what he was doing to her. But she didn't know the first thing about him.

"First of all, it's Jimenez. Wilma came up with Ricky Jimmy." His laugh seemed forced. He pointed toward an old black metal pump in front of a split-log cabin. "Let's go up there."

Beyond the pump sat a semicircle of Adirondack chairs faded to the color of the logs. Jillian led the way and chose a single, rather than a double-seated chair. Instead of sitting beside her, Ricky struggled to drag a chair in front of hers. He sat down, knees only two inches away from hers. "I got my master's degree in drama therapy, but I wasn't using my training and, like I said, I was getting full of myself and caught up in the New York social scene. When God opened my eyes and I saw what I'd become, I knew I had to get away. So when I heard about a drama camp in Wisconsin for Al-Anon kids, I volunteered."

He worked with children. Though his explanation didn't dispel the air of mystery, the fact made him even more endearing.

"I met people at the Clearing and they connected me with Buster and I started helping him with sound and lighting and when summer was over. . .I stayed."

"You plan on going back eventually, don't you?"

He shrugged. "I love it here. It's like no place I've ever been. . .fish boils, orchards, bike trails, cherries, fudge. . .cherry fudge." A wistful smile graced his features. "I love the way the personality of the peninsula changes with the seasons, and I can't wait to experience snow. I've only been here six months, but it feels like where I belong."

"But with all your training. . ."

He waved away her unfinished comment. "I used my training at drama camp. Helping those kids express repressed emotions and turn them into something constructive felt better than any paycheck ever could. And I'm assured of a position at the camp next summer."

"But. . ." She let her objection drop to the leaf-cluttered ground. What could she possibly find wrong with a man who loved Door County, fudge, and children?

Chapter 7

"J illian." Her boss sounded almost pleased to hear her voice.

Good. She needed him happy for what she was about to ask. "I wanted to—"

"I need you back here by morning."

What? "Tomorrow's only Thursday!"

"Marcie broke her leg. Gotta have you finish the Malcomb ad."

"Can't"—she rasped like Darth Vader with laryngitis—"I do it from here?"

"Need some on-site pictures. Weather's going to be perfect tomorrow, so get an early start."

Jillian shut her phone and kicked the stage. *Rrrrrrrrr!!* "What am I supposed to do in one day?" Her mental list went into overdrive. Contact restaurants, design and distribute fliers, brainstorm the next scene with Ricky. . .

Ricky. A hammer rapped overhead. She looked up.

"Hey, Christmas crazy girl." The Brazilian accent cascaded down on her like tropical rainfall.

Ricky stood on a dark catwalk ten feet over her head.

"What are you doing up there?"

"The tarp ripped." He held up a roll of duct tape and leaned over a one-by-four rail, short dark waves spilling over his forehead. "Jilli?"

A mini shiver scooted up her neck. "What?"

"Can I call you that yet?"

She stared up at the shadowy face of the man who seemed suspended in the darkness. "Yes."

"What are you doing tomorrow night, Jilli?" His hushed words fell as soft as the rose-red glow from the single canister light. "Let's do a fish boil. I know you don't date, so think of something else to call it."

Tragic. That's what she'd call it. There was nothing else to call a not-date that wasn't going to happen. She looked down at the dusty stage. "I have to go home in the morning."

"What?"

"My boss wants me back tomorrow."

"I thought you were going to stay another—" *Crack!* The sickening sound of splintering wood reverberated off the stage floor.

"Ricky!" He hung from the railing by his hands, feet swinging wildly two yards above her head. A jagged board swayed beside him. "Hang on!" She darted toward a black curtain, slung it out of her way, and shot up the narrow, unlit stairs. *Please, God. Hold him.* "Don't let go!"

"Hurry, Jilli! *Apresse!*"

She could see the stage between the parallel boards that shook under her feet. "I'm here. Hold tight!" Slamming to her knees, she grabbed the waist of his jeans. If he lost his grip, if the board she kneeled on broke, too. . . "One. . .two. . . *three!*" She pulled with everything in her. His biceps bulged, elbows and knees bent. He swung toward her, and she scrambled to make room.

His chest shook as he exhaled. He held out his hand. It quaked like an oak leaf rattling in the wind. Jillian's shaking matched his. "You saved me," he breathed.

After a long, dizzying moment, Jillian's breathing slowed enough to squeeze out a few words. "That makes us even."

"No." He sat up, shifting away from her, and crossed his legs. "I'm still indebted to you."

"For what?"

His trembling hand touched her face. "For giving me the gift of possibilities. I have a history of running from my problems, but watching you tackle things head-on has given me a whole new perspective. I can't explain it all just yet. . ." His fingertips slid under her chin, lifting it ever so slightly. "Just trust me, Jilli."

Slowly, she nodded. "M—maybe we should get off this thing."

❄

"Any word from the bank?"

Uncle Buster looked up from the disaster he called a desk. "There was a message on the machine. I haven't gotten around to returning it."

"Haven't gotten around to it?" Jillian planted her knuckles on two dusty paper stacks. "If you can't fix the roof, you can't open."

"I'll call." He looked away. "I'm picking up Huey and Ardis in Green Bay at two. Want to go along?"

Jillian brushed crumbs off a stack of envelopes. "I have to work on promotion." Her gaze landed on a huge wall calendar. "I have to go back home tomorrow."

"*Tomorrow?*" Buster's face sagged. "Why?"

"My boss needs me."

"*I* need you!"

Tears stung. "We'll talk and e-mail every day. I don't have to be here to get things done."

"Jilli, I can't pay you for a while, but I just feel in my gut that if you stay we'll get back in the black and. . ." His chin rested on his chest. "There I go again."

Leaning across the desk, she laid her hand over his. "If I didn't have school loans. . ."

"I know." His thick right hand covered hers. "Do you think God's trying to get my attention, Jilli?"

"Do *you* think He is?"

"It sure feels like it."

"Can I make a suggestion?"

A closed-lip smile lifted his cheeks and turned his eyes to slits. "I think I know your suggestion."

"All you need is enough courage to say, 'Jesus, if You're out there, I'm willing to listen.'"

His gaze traveled over her left shoulder. She knew exactly where it stopped. On the picture of her aunt and uncle cutting the ribbon at their grand opening.

"You've always joked about me being the eternal optimist who'd dig for a pony in a pile of manure, but what I've got isn't optimism, it's faith—and not blind faith. Aunt Viv's death ripped me apart. But I looked for God's hand in the middle of the pain. I saw His provision for you in the life insurance policy you'd forgotten about, in the friends who brought you meals. I saw His hand in the timing—Dad was off work after his surgery, but well enough to come and stay with you, and I was free to spend the summer right here in this office. It was a horrible time, but God was there in the middle of it." Her voice lowered. "And He's here in the midst of this. You just have to be willing to see Him."

"I can't get past the 'whys.'"

"Can I make a suggestion?"

He blinked hard and nodded.

"Try asking 'what now?' instead."

A long moment passed before he nodded. "I'll try."

Two little words, but a giant step. She walked around the end of the desk and put her arms around her uncle.

❊

Where is he? Jillian turned from the lengthening shadows below her balcony and stared at the circle of raised black numbers on her loft wall. The minute hand confirmed what the changing sunlight over the bay had already told her. Ricky was half an hour late.

Trust me. The track his fingers had burned on her cheek still tingled. *I'm trying to.*

She strode to the monster mirror. She'd taken the time to flat iron her hair. It gave her a sassy look. . .like a woman who knew what she was all about. If she could look the part, maybe she'd regain the feeling. Turning sideways, she stared at her silhouette. Her long red sweater was formfitting. Not that she had a form to fit—like Jolly, she was still waiting to blossom. With a shrug, she pulled her shoulders back to make the most of what God had given her. When she tucked her black pants into knee-high boots, the overall effect would be about right for a not-date progressive business dinner.

Her aching hip took away the urge to slide down the stairs. She descended slowly and normally and headed for the kitchen.

"Boy's late." Clarissa Bourbonnais sat in a steel-framed rocking chair next to the freestanding cherry red fireplace. She didn't look up from a book on her lap that rivaled *War and Peace* in size.

"I'm sure he has a good reason." Jillian had no sooner finished defending Ricky to a woman she'd only met once than the sound of a stammering motor met her ears.

"Boy's loud." Clarissa peered over jeweled cat's-eye glasses. "Wilma's taking a bath. She told me to tell you not to go out with him alone at night."

Jillian slipped one foot into a boot. "Thank you." She tugged on the other boot. "Tell her I appreciate her concern."

"Like fun you do." Clarissa gestured toward the glass door. "If I were still smooth-skinned and sylphlike, I'd thumb my nose at an old lady's advice."

Sylphlike? If not for the slam of a car door, she'd hunt down a dictionary. "Wilma is just a little overprotective."

"Wilma's a little overparanoid. Go. Live. Enjoy. Someday you'll be stuck home with sagging skin and a six-hundred-page book."

Biting back a smile, Jillian opened the door. Ricky stepped in. "Sorry I'm late. Something came up."

Something?

"Don't stand there waiting for him to make excuses, girl." Clarissa flicked silver-nailed fingers as if she were shooing a flock of pigeons. "Get out of here while you still have, collagen."

Answering Ricky's unspoken confusion with a double eye-roll, Jillian walked under his arm and into the growing darkness.

When they got in the car, she pulled out the brochure she'd worked on all afternoon and read the ad copy she'd written for *Christmas Crazy*. Ricky nodded his approval.

"This is what I'm saying about the food—'A Tantalizing Tour of Door County Christmas Cuisine.' Too tongue-twisterish?"

"It's perfect. Makes me hungry."

"Thank you. I work best under pressure. Unless the pressure comes from my boss, that is. Sorry, I digress."

"I like your smorgasbord idea."

"This way we only need a couple of people to supervise the serving table and pour coffee, but no kitchen staff. The restaurants I've talked to so far had only positive responses. We have a catered dinner, they get tons of exposure."

"A win-win. Where are we going first?"

"Mission Grill. We'll be sampling their lobster bisque."

Ricky's stomach growled loud enough for Jillian to hear. She laughed. "That's not good. If you're starving you'll scarf. I need you to be a critical eater."

"Then take me to Fred & Fuzzy's Grill for a basket of fried potato chips before the gourmet fare."

"Sorry. We're on a schedule. We have eight restaurants to hit before—"

"A moonlit walk." He pointed toward Jillian's window. A giant orange harvest moon rested on the horizon.

"Before"—she smiled across the front seat—"a moonlit walk."

❄

Ricky groaned as he opened the car door for Jillian. It was just after ten. They'd sampled Montrachet and tomato tartlets at the Inn at Kristofer's, walleye cakes at the Harbor Fish and Grill, peanut butter cream pie at the Gibraltar Grill, and a few other delicacies he couldn't remember. A year ago he'd eaten at places like Le Cirque and the Oak Room at the Plaza Hotel in New York City. None of those experiences compared to the fun he'd had tonight sharing brown bread and cheese with Jillian at the Bridge Café in Egg Harbor.

The moon was now high above Sister Bay, casting eerie

shadows across the grass. He offered her a hand. "*Bela*. You look very chic tonight."

"Thank you. You're very gallant tonight." She took his hand and stood.

"Can I ask you a question?"

"I think you can."

"Do you wear other colors at home? Black and red suits you, but. . ."

"When I get rich I'll wear pink." She smiled. "I was a starving student who wanted a sense of style. This way, everything's interchangeable." As they walked toward the water, she held up one finger. "I do, however, have ten different colors of frames for my glasses and the world's largest collection of ugly Christmas sweaters. I'll bring a few when I come back."

"And when will that be?"

"I'll be here for dress rehearsal."

That was more than six weeks away. *Lord, I guess I misunderstood. I was so sure. . .* "Buster said he asked you to stay."

She nodded. "I have obligations." She turned her face and spoke to the night. "I have a job."

"Which you don't like."

"But it's a stepping-stone to something better. If I quit without notice, it—"

"Would make you very free."

A small, very attractive moan came from the girl whose hand nestled in his. They stopped in an open-sided octagon gazebo, looking out at the moon-licked ripples on the water.

"I have a favor to ask." Her voice was so low he had to lean closer to hear.

"Anything."

"Will you watch Jolly for me? It would be a long commitment—she can't go outside when the weather turns cold."

He smiled, but didn't allow himself to laugh. "What's the story with that—I mean her? Why the emotional connection with a Christmas cactus?"

"She was a gift. Have you met Lola Peterson? She owns the Heart's Harbor Inn in Egg Harbor."

"No, I haven't."

"She's an amazing lady. She reads between people's lines, if that makes any sense. She gave me Jolly last December and assured me that love and Jolly would bloom for me. Neither of them did."

Her melancholy sigh twisted something in his gut. He turned, put his hands on her arms. "Is it possible"—he bent and brushed his lips across her forehead—"that she was being prophetic? Looking ahead to *this* Christmas?"

Chapter 8

The clock hands kissed on twelve as Jillian zipped her suitcase. With a loud yawn, she slid between the satin sheets without bothering to wash her face. The alarm was set for five a.m.

She'd just drifted into an alpha state where moonlight gilded the shore along the bay and warm lips touched her forehead when a thought hit like an electric shock. Her eyes shot open. *Camera!*

She'd set it on a pile of papers on her uncle's desk while she printed copies of the brochure. Her memory card was still stuck in Buster's computer. She couldn't work without it. If she left it until morning she'd have to set the alarm for four-thirty. A moan started in the bottom of her lungs and grew until her cranium vibrated. She punched the pillow. "It's all Hiram's fault!"

After shoving feet into slippers and arms into jacket, she tiptoed down the steps and drove back to Sister Bay in her pajamas.

The moon was straight above her when she got out of the

car at Doorbuster's. The sky was peppered with bits of crystal. Silence engulfed her. Alone in the dark parking lot, she raised her hands to heaven and whispered, "Creator God, what a gift this is. Thank You." She smiled into the starry night. A little over an hour ago, she'd lifted her face to the same sky but hadn't seen it. Rich brown eyes and a shy dimple had blocked her view. *And thank You for the gift of possibility.*

She unlocked the front door and walked into the lobby lit only by the crimson glow of the EXIT sign. She opened one of the double doors and walked across the theater without turning on lights. In here, too, the red letters lit the way for eyes now accustomed to the dark. She soaked in the enshrouding peace, the palpable quiet in which she could hear her own breathing and nothing else. If only she could record the sound of this nothingness and play it through her headphones at work.

"Be still, and know that I am God."

The words from Psalm 46 padded softly through her thoughts. "Thank You for waking me up, Lord." *I needed this more than I need my camera.*

She walked into Buster's office. The insulated door swung quietly shut on its spring hinge. Turning on a gooseneck lamp, she stared at the piles that had shifted since this afternoon. If her camera was still here, it was buried in a lower strata. She popped her memory card out of the computer and began sifting through debris. Two unopened telephone bills hid under an empty, flattened tortilla chip bag. Sticking her hand bravely under a bridge made by two coffee cups and a stack of nine-by-twelve envelopes, she felt for her camera. Her fingertips touched something cold, metal, and familiar. Wrapping her hand around the camera, she pulled it out. The bridge collapsed. Envelopes surged onto her hand.

And out of one spilled hundred dollar bills.

❆

Her gasp echoed in the soundproof room. Hardly daring to breathe, she counted. *One. . .two. . .three. . .* She stacked the bills. *Forty-eight. . .forty-nine. . .* And there were more envelopes just like this one. She hadn't counted half of it when she found a typed note in the pile.

Buster—it's not all here, but I will do everything I can to get it back to you, if it takes the rest of my life to do it. I could not, in a million years, tell you how sorry I am.

"What in the world. . .?" Had Cecil snuck back in and returned it? Why hadn't Buster told her about this? Why was it here and not in the bank or the safe?

There was only one logical answer. In all the mess, he'd never seen it.

She walked over to the safe in the corner. If Buster was smart, he'd changed the combination since she'd worked here. She dialed Viv's birthdate. It opened. She stashed the envelopes inside. *Lord, thank You.* She snapped off the light and opened the office door, still praying. *Maybe now he'll see Your hand in—*

She froze.

The door to the lobby was open. Beneath the glowing red letters, a familiar silhouette exited.

Ricky.

❆

Curled on the couch in her too-quiet Iowa apartment, Jillian stared at her e-mail.

From: Enrique Jimenez
To: Jillian Galloway
Sent: Tuesday, October 26
Subject: Guess what?
I hired Clarissa to direct. She's fantastic! First rehearsals went well. Wish the script was as funny as real life with this crew. Kept thinking something was missing, though. . .you. The Web site looks fantastic. Just promise you won't use my picture on it. I'm serious about that. Everything okay? I've left two messages on your phone. Jolly says hi.

Ricky

"Everything okay?" he'd asked. *Other than all the evidence pointing to you stealing my uncle's money and sneaking around to return it, everything's peachy.* How many midnight trips had Ricky made? One to steal the money and make it look like Cecil and Darcy took it, at least two to return it, breaking a key in the lock on one trip. *Lord, what should I do?*

Buster had been elated when she called him about the envelopes. "Thank God," he'd said. Had he ever used those two words together before? He'd report it. Would the police watch the theater to catch Cecil delivering the rest of it? And catch Ricky instead?

That's what he deserved. Wasn't it? *There have to be logical consequences to our actions.* But if he was repentant and making restitution. . . Maybe she should tell Buster, let him confront Ricky face-to-face before the police caught him.

But it would kill Buster. First Cecil and Darcy desert, then this. The man would collapse. The Christmas show would never open. Doorbuster's door would close for good. And the ripples went even further. Ricky had gotten the men in his church together to start working on the roof—a guilt-ridden move most likely. If they found out what he'd done. . .

She had to keep silent. At least until after Christmas.

❄

Facts and figures.

He'd heard people say that's all e-mail should be used for. Nothing personal, nothing that needs tone of voice to be clear.

Was Jilli one of those? She'd been gone eighteen days. In that time they'd exchanged dozens of e-mails—all about the show. He stared at his computer screen and reread the last few.

> *From:* Enrique Jimenez
> *To:* Jillian Galloway
> *Sent:* Saturday, November 6
> *Subject:* The PI
> Your greeting card sayings are perfect—we make a pretty good team. I'm thinking the PI needs to be a real character. Any thoughts? He (or she!) wouldn't have to have a lot of lines. I could ask one of the drama camp kids. Hope all is well. There were a few snowflakes in the air this morning.
>
> R

> *From:* Jillian Galloway
> *To:* Enrique Jimenez
> *Sent:* Sunday, November 7
> *Subject:* Re: The PI
> *Make the private investigator unique. . .not a Columbo in a wrinkled trench coat. What's his cover? He should have a job that's specific to Door County—a*

fisherman or cherry-grower.

J

> **From**: *Enrique Jimenez*
> **To**: *Jillian Galloway*
> **Sent**: *Sunday, November 7*
> **Subject**: *Re: The PI*
> *Or artist? He could pretend to be an eccentric French painter (with an awful accent) in DC for inspiration. That would allow him to pop up anywhere. Hey, it's almost time to break out those ugly sweaters. We're planning the staff Christmas party for the night of dress rehearsal. Jolly's missing you.*

R

> **From**: *Jillian Galloway*
> **To**: *Enrique Jimenez*
> **Sent**: *Monday, November 8*
> **Subject**: *Re: The PI*
> *The painter idea is good. I think you should play the part.*

J

Every question about how or what she was doing went unanswered. He'd called several times, but she hadn't returned a single one.

Buster talked to her every day and thought Ricky must be imagining things. She was fine, just busy. *Right.* Too busy for *him*. He knew he hadn't done anything to upset her. Their moonlit walk had ended within an inch of a kiss. And he'd been the one to hold back. Only one explanation seemed plausible.

Dennis the dentist.

Ricky closed his computer, grabbed his flannel shirt, and left his homey toolshed on foot, the last scene rolled in his hand. He walked the mile and a half to Doorbuster's not by choice, but because his car sounded like it had swallowed a giant pumpkin and was digesting it whole. He needed to replace it. Which meant he needed a real job. Which meant maybe it was time to go back to New York, do what God had gifted him to do, and actually get paid for it. And try not to get sucked back in.

The walk would be good for him. He spent too many hours cross-legged on his little iron-framed bed, hunched over his laptop. Maybe Jilli's silent absence was just God's way of giving him time to finish the script. But it wasn't easy writing comedy when he felt like he'd lost his best-friend-to-be.

So much for possibilities.

Chapter 9

Jillian stared at the ad layout on the screen in front of her, but her mind was eight hours north. She'd awakened in the middle of the night and opened her computer, only to find Ricky's final scene. She'd laughed until she cried. And then she'd simply cried.

"Daydreaming?" Mr. Hiram leaned on a partition at the opening to her cubicle, arms crossed over his ample stomach.

"No! Just. . .meditating on this."

"It's soup, Jillian. Meat, vegetables. . .not a spiritual experience. We've been a bit distracted this past month, haven't we? Your work is excellent, Jillian. Your attitude is above reproach. You just don't produce at an acceptable rate. I know you'd like things run differently, but I can't have people coffee klatching on my clock, and you need to adjust if you're going to remain at Double I."

"I—"

"What have you got so far?"

Not a thing. "I think we should really push the 'all natural' idea."

Her desk phone rang. Uncle Buster. Not good. She brightened her smile and ignored it. "If we hope to reach a younger—"

"Answer it."

"I can return it."

"Answer it." Thick brows pushed the skin on his forehead like two bushy push brooms.

"Identity Incorporated." She infused her voice with added professionalism. Buster had better play along. "Jillian speaking."

"Jilli! You won't believe this—Darcy was just here." His voice cracked. "She's the one who returned the money. When she found out Cecil stole it, she grabbed what she could and left him. She was scared to go to the police, but she finally did and. . ."

Jillian turned away from her boss's glare and tried to concentrate on Buster's words, but only one thing registered. Cecil took the money.

Ricky was innocent.

Wiping her eyes with her sleeve, she laughed. "That's wonderful. I'm so happy for you." *And me.*

"You were right, Jilli."

"About what?"

"I just needed enough courage to say, 'I'll listen.'"

Jillian closed her eyes. "God is so good."

"I'm beginning to believe that, Jilli-girl. Now get back to work."

"I will. Love you." She shut off the phone and turned around. Mr. Hiram was gone.

With a sigh of relief, she turned back to the screen. The steaming bowl of soup turned into two. She blinked away the tears and tried to think of cream of broccoli instead of the phone call. . .and apology. . .she'd have to make tonight.

"*Eh-hem.*" Mr. Hiram filled the opening. "Jillian, we need to talk."

Eyes still swimming, she stared at the melon-shaped man in front of her desk and listened to the muffled sound of nine computer keyboards. An occasional phone voice added to the mix. *I just needed enough courage to say, "I'll listen."*

Jillian pushed back her chair and stood. "Mr. Hiram, you have my word. I will never again ask for extra time on a project or suggest teamwork or disagree with your suggestions."

A shocked and triumphant smile creased the doughy face. "Now that's what I—"

"Because I quit!"

Maybe she wouldn't make that phone call after all.

❄

Wilma walked to her mark at center stage, stuffing scraps of paper in her purse. She looked both ways. A man in a black beret approached her.

"Excuse me, mah-dahmmm. But you have dropped ze pay-*purrr.*" He held up an index card and moved it close to his eyes and then away, like a trombone player. "Ahhh. Eet eez a love note, no?"

Jillian stood near the doors, mouthing the words with the actors, goose bumps chasing each other on her arms.

"No." Wilma grabbed the paper, flipped it over. "Eet eez a grocery list. See? Bran Flakes, denture cream, BENGAY, prune juice, Metamucil. . ."

"Ahh. But on ze back it sezzz, 'When I zink of you'"—he turned away from Wilma—"'my heart sezzz. . .pitter. . .pat. . .'" The Frenchman's mouth opened. His moustache dropped to the stage.

And Jillian snapped a picture.

"Jilli!" Ricky jumped off the stage, took half a dozen huge strides, and stopped, raking his gaze over her face.

He was searching for clues. She gave him a Julia Roberts smile.

"Jilli-girl!" In seconds she was engulfed in a group hug.

When the frenzy settled, she turned to Buster, planted a loud kiss on his cheek, and said, "Put me on the payroll, Mr. Galloway."

"You lost your job?"

"I left my job. . .for a better one."

Wilma jumped up like a schoolgirl. Her wig didn't land with her. Holding it in her hands, gray hair pin-curled to her head, she clapped. "Now everything will be okay."

Jillian put one arm around Huey and the other around Ardis. "I'm so glad to be back with—*Buster!* You fixed the lights! And got new ones. . ." She walked toward the brightly lit stage, eyes on the ceiling.

"Wait here." Buster ran toward the control booth. In moments, the theater filled with music. The sound was richer than anything she'd ever heard in this place. Suddenly, a blue laser light arrowed toward the stage and was joined by a red one. Spotlights, floodlights, can lights, and a mirrored ball. . . the room swam with color.

"How. . . ?"

Ardis pulled a lace hankie from her pocket. "Ricky did it!"

Ricky shrugged. "I. . .talked to some people I know in New York. Philanthropists."

Philanthropists? "They *gave* all this?"

He nodded and shoved his hands in his back pockets.

"I. . .oh. . ." Tears rolled, dripped from her chin, but she didn't care. "Thank you. How can—"

An eardrum-puncturing whistle split the air. Clarissa stood on the stage, thumb and forefinger between her lips. She wore black heels and leggings and a short purple dress, cinched at the waist with a wide red belt. "The lights are marvelous and it's dandy you're here, Jillian, but the show must go on. Act One, Scene Three. Take your positions."

Everyone scurried but Ricky. Hands stuck in back pockets, he stared at her.

She opened her mouth, but words abandoned her tongue.

"You didn't answer my calls."

Studying the toes of her boots, she shook her head. "Can you get away for a few minutes?"

"Yes."

She led the way to the green room. When she walked in, a torrent of fresh tears began. The overhead lights were off. A fully decorated Christmas tree glimmering with blue lights took up one corner. An electric fire glowed in a faux-brick fireplace. Eight red felt stockings hung from hooks under the cupboards. She swallowed hard and mopped her face. "Ambience," she whispered. "Let's sit by the fire."

They pulled chrome-legged chairs away from the table and sat down. Orange points of fake flame leaped around plastic logs. Jillian swiveled on her chair to face Ricky. "I was here. . .the night before I left. A little after midnight."

"So was I."

She nodded. "I saw you."

"Why didn't you say something?"

"Because I thought. . .I found the money and I thought. . ."

"That *I'd* taken it? Jilli. . ." His forehead pleated in pain.

"I didn't want to believe it, but after the things Wilma had been telling me and the phone calls. . . All this time you were arranging things for the new light system, weren't you?"

The right corner of his mouth tipped up. "I was."

"Is this the 'possibilities' you were talking about?"

"One of them. I'd started working on the lighting system—at night—before you came. I wanted to surprise Buster by fixing it myself. But when I listened to you paint a vision for this place, I knew I could find a way to do something more."

"You asked me to trust you."

"I did." The shallow impression in his cheek turned into a full-fledged dimple. "And you didn't." With both hands, he picked up the beret and repositioned it on his head. "I zink you will have to pay ze penance."

"Anything."

One eyebrow rose, disappearing under unruly waves. "Anything? So you'll take a part in the play?"

Her heart stopped then smacked her ribs. "Anything. . . else. Make me learn Portuguese or something."

"Hmm. I just might, *minha amor*. But I was thinking of something much. . .much. . .less difficult."

"What?" She mouthed the word. Her voice no longer worked.

"This." He lifted her to her feet. His hands bracketed her face and he kissed her. Warm, lingering. "Just this."

❄

Ricky woke before dawn on the first day of December with a sense that something was different. The world seemed somehow hushed. An ethereal, silver glow filled the room.

As he pulled the covers back, his phone rang. He opened it. "*Bom dia*, Christmas Crazy."

"Get up. If we hurry we can see the sun come up at Newport State Park. Can you be here in ten minutes?"

"Nine." He pulled back the curtain. Every branch and twig

shimmered with a coat of white frost. Swirls of glitter floated around the cherry trees, and gray clouds held the promise of more to come.

He picked her up in eight minutes. When they stepped out of the car at Newport Park, snowflake clusters the size of cotton balls drifted down on them. Wave-smoothed rocks clattered beneath their boots as they walked to the edge of the water just in time to see an orange orb lift out of Lake Michigan. He put his arm around Jillian. "Wow."

"Amen." She looked up at him through glasses with red plaid frames. "That promise you made. . .that you'd spend a year focusing on God alone. When did you make it?"

His pulse thumped out a few extra beats. "Twelve months and twenty-one days ago."

Her smile spread like the line of the horizon. "Then I have a favor to ask."

"Anything."

"Will you go with me to the Christmas Tea at the Heart's Harbor Inn?"

"Anything. . .but wear lace gloves and eat watercress sandwiches."

She poked his ribs. "It's not that kind of Tea. They serve man food, too."

"Then I'd love to go. But wouldn't that be considered a date?"

"I think"—she rested her head on his chest—"I might make an exception to my rule."

Chapter 10

B uster banged a spoon on a copper-bottomed pot. "Ladies and gentlemen, may I have your attention?" he yelled over the clamor of seven people scurrying around Doorbuster's kitchen. When the din lessened, he cleared his throat and lifted a glass of cherry cider. "I would just like to take a moment to thank every one of you for pulling this together. Tonight these walls witnessed the smoothest dress rehearsal in the history of theater. We are sold out for every show this weekend, and I'm confident no one will walk away disappointed. . .or hungry. So, to our actors. . ." He bowed from his nonexistent waist. "I thank you with all my heart for your faithfulness. To our amazing director. . .you run a tight ship and we are all indebted. To the most gifted amateur playwright and his beautiful assistant. . .there are no words to express the depth of my gratitude. Ricky, I'm sure we'll lose you to Broadway someday. Jilli. . ." He ran his fingertips across his eyelashes. "You have restored my hope. . .and my faith. Thank you. . .and thank God."

Quiet blanketed the kitchen. Then Mort began to clap

and, one by one, everyone joined in. When the clapping stopped, the bustle began again. Serving dishes filled the island in the center of the kitchen. Over the noise, Huey made a loud gagging sound.

"What in the name of desecrating tradition is *that*?" With the mouthpiece of a meerschaum pipe he hadn't smoked in decades, he gestured toward a platter. On a bed of red cabbage leaves lay a two-inch thick dark brown, black-around-the-edges turkey-with-feathers-shaped object.

"It's tofurkey, silly man." Clarissa fingered an enormous cameo tied about her neck with a black ribbon. "Ginger-garlic tofu turkey. The other kind"—she wrinkled her nose—"is in the oven."

Jillian laughed as she spooned lingonberries into a glass dish. Ricky leaned toward her. His lips touched her ear. "Have I mentioned how nice it is to have you back?"

She took a bacon-wrapped water chestnut off a plate on the counter and held it in front of his lips. He opened his mouth and playfully bit her fingers as he closed it.

"I believe you have once or—"

"Ricky! Phone call for you in my office."

Eyes narrowing, Ricky stared at Buster. "For me? Who is it?"

"Didn't say. Some woman." He glanced at Jillian and winked. "Not a young one."

The color left Ricky's face. He nodded and walked out of the green room. Pulse accelerating, Jillian busied herself dishing up sweet potatoes. Buster called everyone together and Mort prayed. They were halfway through the meal when Ricky returned. Without looking at her, he filled a plate and sat in the empty chair beside her.

"Anything wrong?"

He shook his head, stabbed a piece of turkey, and laid his fork down again. His hand closed into a fist. "You put a picture of me on the Internet."

"No, I didn't. You asked me not—oh. . .there was one goofy picture of you and Ardis and Clarissa on stage that I put on the blog, not the Web site. You can't even tell it's you."

Ricky inhaled and pushed his chair away from the table. "You can tell." He stood, threw his napkin on the table, and left the room.

❋

Jillian closed her laptop and rested her head on the desk in the loft. She'd blogged, Facebooked, and updated Doorbuster's Web site. She'd delivered flyers and posters to every tourist spot in Door County. She should be ecstatic. But she hadn't heard a word from Ricky since he'd walked out last night. Clicking the switch that turned the Dickens' Village black, she walked down the steps.

"Jilli! Just in time!" Mort called from the kitchen. Beside him, Wilma grinned while singing "I saw Elvis dressed as Santa Claus. . ."

"How 'bout a Mistletoe Malt?"

Jillian's lips puckered. "Isn't mistletoe toxic?"

Mort laughed. "What's toxic is living without mistletoe."

". . .I saw his whiskers slip, when he curled his lip. . ." Wilma danced a two-step.

"It's made with peppermint candy ice cream. Want to try it?"

"No, thank you." Then again, it might be the closest she'd get to another kiss this season. "Sure. I'll—"

The doorbell rang.

"It's the boy!" Clarissa yelled from the living room.

Mort smiled. "I'll make two and serve you in the den."

He pinched Jillian's cheek.

Opening the door, she stared into grim brown eyes. "Let's go in the den." She led the way down a hallway walled with stained-glass windows and into the first floor of the silo. Two burnt-orange barrel chairs faced a round brass-and-glass table in front of a cobalt blue tiled fireplace. They walked across champagne-colored shag carpeting and sat down. Jillian twirled a sequin snowman eye on her sweater and waited.

"Jilli. I'm sorry I got mad at you. I was upset. There's something—" Mort walked in, set two frosted glasses on the table, and left. Ricky took a deep breath. "I have never lied to you. . .but there are things I haven't told you." He rubbed his empty ring finger. "I told you the reason I came here. I need to tell you the rest of it."

"You don't—"

He held up his hand to stop her. "I'm not what. . .who. . . I've let you all believe. I'm not an amateur playwright."

"What do you mean?"

"Two plays I wrote were produced on Broadway."

Jilli's lips parted. She couldn't think of what to say.

"They did well. Very well. I went from being Ricky Jimenez, an unknown grad student, to being J. K. Henry, the playwright, the focus of a lot of attention and a lot of money."

Jillian tried to swallow, but couldn't remember how.

"I let myself get swept into a materialistic, superficial whirlwind. Every stereotype of New York City social life. . . that was my life for two years. The right parties, the right people, doing whatever it took to enhance my image and my future. I lost sight of God. My wake-up call came when I overheard my agent talking about me on the phone like I was a commodity. I might as well have been a Porsche or a Ferrari.

So I left. I gave everything I owned to a homeless shelter and I ran. I ran here. . .and back to God."

"So you're. . .famous."

"No. But I was told I was on my way."

"And you didn't want anyone to find you."

He nodded. "That was an agent on the phone last night. She offered me a contract."

The muscles over Jillian's ribs tightened. He was going back to New York. "Congratulations."

Ricky's eyes widened. His lips formed a straight line then tipped upward. "I said no, Jilli. I don't want anything to do with that life. That's why I didn't want anyone to know where I was. I don't want publicity, or attention, or any of it." He leaned forward, resting his elbows on his knees. "Everything I want is right here."

She held his gaze as relief washed over her. A smile tugged at her mouth. Without breaking eye contact, she picked up his glass. "Mistletoe Malt?"

One eyebrow rose. Deep brown eyes sparkled. "Isn't mistletoe poisonous?"

Jilli laughed, kissed the tip of her finger, and touched his cheek. "What's toxic is living without it."

❄

Opening night. It looked like the snowstorm slamming the Midwest wouldn't hit until after midnight. The roads were clear. The house would be packed.

Jillian walked into the theater half an hour before show-time. Round banquet tables covered in white linen sparkled with mirrors, candles, and hurricane lamps filled with blue and green glass balls. Silver chafing dishes lined long tables, ready to be filled with the delectable dishes that had been arriving at the back door all afternoon. The stage was set for the first scene. She closed her eyes and listened to the stillness. *Lord, thank You for all You have accomplished. All the glory goes to You. I ask for Your blessing upon this place and the people who will fill it. Give us peace and the kind of confidence that can only come from You.*

"Jilli."

She opened her eyes. Uncle Buster walked across the room, dressed in a black tux with a red cummerbund. "Wow. You look. . ." The expression on his face didn't go with the outfit. "What's wrong?"

"Sit down." He guided her to a chair.

"What? What's wrong?"

"Ricky just called."

"Where is he? What happened?"

"He couldn't tell me. But. . ." He looked down at his patent leather shoes. "He's going to be late."

"Late? How late?"

"He hopes. . .he'll get here before the end of the first act."

"But. . ." She rubbed her temple, where a tiny hammer had started to pound. "He's *in* the first act! Did you tell Clarissa? What can we do? Can we rearrange the—"

Her uncle's hand slid around hers. "I talked to Clarissa. She agreed with Ricky's solution." His hand tightened. "You need to take his part."

"Wha. . . ? No!" She jumped out of her chair. "No! Absolutely not." The room began to twirl around her. "I can't. I. . . Remember the watering can? I'll throw up. I'll freeze. I'll faint. I'll—"

"Do it. I know you'll do it because you're our only hope, Jilli. God's gotten us this far because you opened your eyes and ears to Him. You listened when the rest of us didn't." He lifted his hand to her face. "I need to do for you what you did for me. It's my turn to push you and to not let you live scared." He pressed a kiss to her forehead and walked away.

❄

Jillian Galloway, aka Jean-Pierre Marseilles the painter, aka Jack Jones, Private Investigator, paced the floor of the green room, smoothing his. . .*her*. . .moustache and clutching a paintbrush as if it were life support. "I'll kill him," she whispered. "If that man dares show his face here tonight, I'll smash that Brazilian nose into a Brazilian pieces! I'll—"

"Forty seconds, Jillian." Clarissa motioned with a red-nailed finger.

God. . .oh God. . .please, please, please don't let me forget the lines. Please don't let me throw up. Please—

"Now."

Black ballet slippers somehow transported her through the curtain and onto the dark stage. The lights came up. She looked out on the crowd but couldn't see a thing beyond the spotlights. She turned, slowly, stealthily.

Wilma sat on a park bench, shivering, pen suspended over a notebook. "When I am cold," she wrote, "you make me warm."

Jillian tiptoed around the bench with wide, exaggerated, slow-motion steps. Wilma turned toward her. Instantly, Jean-Pierre froze then began painting the air. The crowd laughed.

"When I am. . .cold. . .bold. . .gold. . .mold. . . When I am old, you'll make me—I know you're there."

Jillian put her foot down to freeze in place again. But the ballet slipper slipped. Her right foot went forward. The paintbrush flew. Her arms arced windmills in the air. Time stood still. And the audience laughed. Her backside thudded to the stage. And the audience laughed.

"You oaf. What are you doing?" Wilma ad-libbed, panic somewhat concealed by a scowl.

Jillian stood, brushed off Ricky's pants, and bowed. *The show must go on.* "Jean-Pierre Marseilles at your service, madam. I am painter of all zings beautiful in Door County. I paint ze lighthouse and ze sunset and now, *mon cheri*, I paint ze beautiful you writing ze poem to your sweetheart. . ." She faked her way back to the lines she'd helped the soon-to-be-dead Brazilian write.

❊

At the end of the first act, Jillian ran to the bathroom and left behind her sampling of "A Tantalizing Tour of Door County Christmas Cuisine." Wiping her mouth, she walked out.

Ricky stood in front of her, looking squirmier than a tomato worm. "Jilli. I can't explain right now, but. . ."

He held out his hand for the beret. She ripped it off her head and whipped it at his.

He ducked. "I know you're mad, but everyone says you did an amazing job and the crowd loves you and—" A moustache hit him in the eye. "Jilli, *confie em mim.* Trust me on this. You'll know—"

"Trust." She spat it at him. "Never. Never, ever, ever again." She grabbed her clothes from a hook, stomped into the bathroom, and threw his clothes out, one piece at a time.

He was gone when she got out. She found a place in the shadows along the wall to watch the rest of the show. A place where no one would notice her tears. But try as she did, she couldn't maintain the anger. Scene after scene had the audience alternating between laughter and empathy. She lost all sense of time until the end.

The lights came up on a plywood manger scene. The shepherds were no longer faded, the sheep no longer yellow. The four actors, dressed in coats and scarves, faced the crowd.

Mort reached toward the audience. "Christmas is for giving."

Wilma walked toward him and held out her hand. "And for forgiving."

"It's not about the tree or the gifts." Huey set a wrapped package next to the manger.

"Or the turkey or the goodies." Ardis laid a tray of cookies next to the package.

Wilma walked to the manger, bent over, and picked up a wrapped bundle. "It's about Jesus."

"Si–i–lent night. . ." Huey's rich baritone rose. Music poured, softly at first, from the new speakers. The others added their voices. "Ho–o–ly night. . ." The audience joined in, the sound swelling.

And it started to snow.

White flakes floated onto the stage, slowly at first, then increasing, blowing out into the audience as if the blizzard forecast for midnight had hit early—inside the theater.

This wasn't in the script. Jillian looked up to the dark maze of catwalks. If she squinted she could just barely make out a familiar silhouette.

The ballet slippers that had carried her onto the stage let her pad like a kitten around the curtain, up the unlit staircase, and onto the narrow walkway above the stage as "Silent Night" floated through the snow.

Ricky looked up, his smile wide in the faint light of the snow machine. "I had to pick it up at the airport in Green Bay. The flight was delayed because of the storm." His hand cupped her chin. "*Sinto muito*," he whispered. "I'm so sorry."

Her hand slid over his. "Christmas is for forgiving."

"But I still owe you."

"This." She touched her lips to his. "Just this."

❋

"Jilli? You decent?" Wilma's voice wound up toward the loft. "Package for you."

"Come on up."

Wilma chugged toward her, something silver and shimmery under her arm. "Found this," she huffed, "on the doorstep." She handed her the flat box. There was a card tucked under the red ribbon.

Jillian sank to the edge of the bed and opened the card.

You once said that when you were rich you would wear pink. Jilli, you are rich in so many ways. If you don't want to wear an ugly Christmas sweater to the tea, here's an option.

She opened the box and pulled out a cable-knit raspberry sweater. Wilma walked over and touched it. "That'll be perfect on a day like this." She patted Jillian's hand. "That boy's a keeper. I'll let you get dressed."

Jillian stood in front of the mirror. As she slipped into the feathery-soft sweater, "White Christmas" sang from the bed. She lunged for the phone. "I love the sweater!"

"I'm glad. I have a surprise to tell you about."

"No more surprises."

"This is a good one. The agent I told you about was in the audience last night. She wants to market *Christmas Crazy* and she wants me to keep writing—right here—from home."

"Seriously? Ricky, that's wonderful."

"It is, isn't it? Hey, I was wondering. . .could you come pick me up for the tea? My car's acting up again." His voice had a mysterious edge, as if there was something he wasn't saying.

Lord, I can't take any more surprises. "O. . .kay. I'll be there in a few minutes."

"Great. Thanks. Come on in when you get here."

What was he up to?

She got there in seven minutes. He met her at the door, left hand behind his back.

"What are you hiding?"

His smile widened. "Jilli. . .Jolly." From behind his back he produced a green coffee can bursting with a multitude of pink blossoms.

Jillian gasped. "Wha. . . How. . . ?"

"Where do you think these things originated?"

"I don't. . .oh. . .*Brasil*?"

"*Sim, meu amor.*" He lifted her chin and leaned toward her. "*Brasil.*"

She lifted her lips and whispered against his ear. "When are you going to teach me to speak Portuguese?"

"How about now? You can start with '*Te amo*.' Do I need to translate?"

"No." She slid into his arms. Jolly's phylloclades patted her back. "I love you, too."

A Wisconsin resident, Becky Melby has four married sons and eleven grandchildren. When not writing or spending time with family, Becky enjoys motorcycle rides with her husband and reading. Becky has coauthored nine Heartsong Presents titles and a novella for Barbour Publishing.

A Letter to Our Readers

Dear Readers:

In order that we might better contribute to your reading enjoyment, we would appreciate you taking a few minutes to respond to the following questions. When completed, please return to the following: Fiction Editor, Barbour Publishing, Inc., P.O. Box 719, Uhrichsville, OH 44683.

1. Did you enjoy reading *A Door County Christmas* by Eileen Key, Becky Melby, Rachael Phillips, and Cynthia Ruchti?
   ❑ Very much. I would like to see more books like this.
   ❑ Moderately—I would have enjoyed it more if _____
   _____
   _____

2. What influenced your decision to purchase this book?
   (Check those that apply.)
   ❑ Cover   ❑ Back cover copy   ❑ Title   ❑ Price
   ❑ Friends   ❑ Publicity   ❑ Other

3. Which story was your favorite?
   ❑ *The Heart's Harbor*   ❑ *My Heart Still Beats*
   ❑ *Ride with Me into Christmas*   ❑ *Christmas Crazy*

4. Please check your age range:
   ❑ Under 18   ❑ 18–24   ❑ 25–34
   ❑ 35–45   ❑ 46–55   ❑ Over 55

5. How many hours per week do you read? _____

Name _____

Occupation _____

Address _____

City _____ State _____ Zip _____

E-mail _____

CHRISTMAS
MAIL-ORDER BRIDES

Four-In-One-Collection

When marriage arrives by mail-order—and just in time for Christmas—the results are unpredictable. Can true love grow after an awkward start?

Historic, paperback, 352 pages, 5⅜" x 8"

HEARTSONG
PRESENTS

If you love Christian romance…

$10.99

You'll love Heartsong Presents' inspiring and faith-filled romances by today's very best Christian authors. . .Wanda E. Brunstetter, Mary Connealy, Susan Page Davis, Cathy Marie Hake, and Joyce Livingston, to mention a few!

When you join Heartsong Presents, you'll enjoy four brand-new, mass-market, 176-page books—two contemporary and two historical—that will build you up in your faith when you discover God's role in every relationship you read about!

Imagine. . .four new romances every four weeks—with men and women like you who long to meet the one God has chosen as the love of their lives—all for the low price of $10.99 postpaid.

To join, simply visit www.heartsongpresents.com or complete the coupon below and mail it to the address provided.

Mass Market, 176 Pages

- -

YES! Sign me up for Heartsong!

NEW MEMBERSHIPS WILL BE SHIPPED IMMEDIATELY!

Send no money now. We'll bill you only $10.99 postpaid with your first shipment of four books. Or for faster action, call 1-740-922-7280.

NAME _____

ADDRESS_____

CITY_____ STATE _____ ZIP _____

MAIL TO: HEARTSONG PRESENTS, P.O. Box 721, Uhrichsville, Ohio 44683 or sign up at WWW.HEARTSONGPRESENTS.COM